PUKI HORPOCKET PRESENTS

FIVE LEGENDARY TALES
FROM BEYOND THE BLACK

EARTH EDITION BY
ZACHRY WHEELER

eBook ISBN: 978-1-954153-21-9
Paperback ISBN: 978-1-954153-24-0
Hardcover ISBN: 978-1-954153-37-0
Edited by Jennifer Amon
Published by Mayhematic Press

This collection contains five titles:
Roy: The Most Chaotic Midlife Crisis in Cosmic History (novel) *
Nimi: When First Contact Becomes Last Call (short story)
Phil: A Maddening Chat with the Smartest Being in the Universe (short story)
Boo: The Greatest Bounty Hunter Ever to Sail the Black (novella)
Max: Public Enemy Number One of the Fourth Dimension (novella)

* B.R.A.G. Medallion Honoree
* Readers' Favorite® 5-Star Selection

PARENT SERIES

Puki Horpocket Presents is a spin-off series from *Max and the Multiverse*, in that it takes place on the massive Durangoni Space Station. The stories are intertwined, share many characters and settings, and can be read in any order you please.

EARTH EDITION

Greetings, Earthling!

My name is Zachry Wheeler and I'm a science fiction author based on Earth. I was chosen to serve as translator for all terrestrial editions of *Puki Horpocket Presents*, a literary series beloved throughout the universe.

It's been a great honor.

It's also been super stressful.

Decoding an alien tongue is daunting at a baseline, let alone through the prestigious lens of Puki Horpocket. He is renowned for his unique blend of commentary, interviews, and dramatic depictions. My job is to stick the landing for human readers. I sincerely hope that I do his words justice, but admittedly, I sometimes feel like a toddler translating Orwell.

The Durangoni Space Station is home to countless species and cultures, and thus, countless lexicons. Some things are universal, like beer. Other things are regional, like atmo barriers on artificial oceans. Some things are truly horrifying and do not warrant translation, regardless of their pop culture equivalents.

I did my best, but aliens be weird, y'all.

Puki Horpocket tales are chock-full of excitement, debauchery, and blatant disregard for delicate sensibilities. Fair warning: the language is lewd and the characters are crude, so keep your wits inside the vehicle and enjoy the ride.

One lonely plumber.
One bad decision.
One trillion lives upended.

This is the story of Roy, the architect of an epic crisis that paralyzed the largest space station in the universe. The aftermath created a legend, but the lunacy behind it remained a mystery. That is, until now. With the aid of footage and eyewitness accounts, this book reveals the outrageous truth behind the greatest pandemonium ever recorded.

ROY

The Most Chaotic Midlife Crisis in Cosmic History

CHAPTER 1

It is a well-known fact that every being in the universe is biologically compelled to talk smack. If three beings exist on a planet, it is inevitable that two of them will gossip about the third. In addition, most beings are convinced that their tiny corner of the cosmos is much more important than it actually is. But every so often, one of those beings will rise from the muck to stamp their mark on history.

This is the tale of one such being.

But before we begin, I must introduce myself. My name is Puki Horpocket. I am an editor at large for the Definitive Directory of Durangoni, the panoptic mega-wiki for life aboard the largest space station in the universe. Durangoni is a planet-sized colossus. It houses a trillion active residents, all of whom access the directory for their daily needs. And to ensure those needs are met, the station employs a massive staff of writers, reporters, editors, and baristas, all wholly dedicated to keeping the directory au courant.

Tenants consult the directory for a variety of reasons. Perhaps they need a ship mechanic, or a warm meal at a mid-level restaurant. Perhaps they would like to fist a dominurb while wearing a tutu inside a womp-brothel. The directory is an indiscriminate depot that treats all inquiries alike. No tracking, no history, no snarky comments or unearned ratings, just a freely accessible index of current and relevant data. Under a veil of complete anonymity, anyone in the midst of a titanic midlife crisis can easily search for a hot enema of sinful delight.

Enter Roy.

As strange as it may sound, nobody knows his last name. I devoted countless hours to this mystery, all of which uncovered bupkis. Not a single employer knew his full name, nor is Roy short for anything more distinguished. In fact, he is listed as "Roy" in the civilian archives. Astoundingly, in the grand totality of station operation, not a single Roy resident thought to register as just Roy.

That is, until Roy.

He is, for all intents and purposes, just Roy.

I never met Roy, but I came to know him through his friends, enemies, and confidants. I interviewed several along the way, many of whom are featured in this very book. Most will be new to your eyes, but some carry infamous reputations that you will undoubtedly recognize. After all, one does not attain a legendary status without crossing some of the universe's most notorious inhabitants.

Roy's tale was thrust upon me during a jaunt to the outer rings. I was working on a field piece about district taverns, which involved a dreadful amount of sensory-hostile interviews. However, what began as a vapid chore would blossom into a full-blown obsession. It became abundantly clear that every gutter rat, every bar slag, and every spittoon-filling whoremonger upheld Roy as some sort of folk hero.

I wanted to know more, so I went digging.

What I found was a treasure trove of lunacy.

The story of Roy is so burdened by stupidity, so marred by absurdity, that it bewitched me from the start. It is a tale wrought with love, loss, danger, and a healthy dose of folly. In other words, it ticks all the right boxes for a whimsical train wreck.

I must preface anything further with an important disclaimer. To tell the story of Roy is to tell the story of "The Incident."

Every citizen of Durangoni knows about The Incident, but few are aware that Roy was the instigator. To be fair, the term "instigator" may be a tad generous. Roy was many things, but a cunning mastermind he was not. I am forced to use "was" in reference to Roy because no one has seen or heard from him since. The Incident is capitalized because it managed to affect the entire population, thus earning its definite article and prominent lettering. But to be honest, the event was so jarring and disruptive that I firmly believe it should be referenced in all caps.

Yes, even as an editor.

So without further ado, let us begin to unravel this tale of intrigue. As with any good story, it starts with a kerfuffle.

* * *

The charred impacts of plasma bolts stained the interior of a popular brewpub. A firefight had erupted a few days earlier, an exceedingly rare occurrence inside Durangoni. The station was a neutral harbor to an extreme degree, even housing a private security force that rivaled the best militaries in the quadrant. Firearms of any kind were strictly forbidden. A zero-tolerance policy included flash flogging for violators, so residents moseyed through the corridors without much regard for safety. Therefore, staring at the blackened remains of plasma fire conjured the same confusion as an abstract painting.

Toppled chairs and tables cluttered the interior, the remnants of patrons making their hasty exits. Broken glass and shattered plates littered the floor, creating a labyrinth of foot-stabbing fun. The stench of rotting food floated around the pub like a wandering fart that refused to dissipate. The dark wood and rustic metal hid some of the filth, but the exploded terrace was difficult to ignore. Security had completed its investigation, leaving a swarm of maintenance crews to tend to repairs. The constant roar of saws, drills, and laser cutters infected the space with a rumble of restoration.

The commotion created quite the nuisance for anyone within earshot. The terrace overlooked an open-air garden that spanned several stories. Balconies surrounded the space, which served as a hub for numerous galleries and restaurants. A prime location for any pro-

prietor, should they afford the rent. The pub was an old establishment and one of the first to claim the area. As such, it enjoyed lower
rent and grandfathered perks. It rested along the third tier and protruded like an unsightly pimple, given its ritzy neighbors. This rang
especially true as spectators gazed upon the splintered shards that
used to be its terrace.

Its neighbor across the way was impacted the most, in a very literal sense. On top of having a front-row seat to the battle, it had endured a barrage of wayward blasts. It also emitted the growls of restoration, complete with yellow tape to underscore the inconvenience.

A handful of flowering vines dangled from an overhead lattice.
Before the assault, a thick assortment of foliage had hung inside the
hollow as a waterfall of greenery, the handiwork of a famous artist.
The plasma fire had ripped through the display like a flock of ma-
chetes, dropping most of it to the floor. A mess of leaves and vines
clogged the sidewalks and fountains, creating an aggravating cleanup
for plumbers and gardeners.

One such plumber stood ankle-deep inside a small fountain
while staring at the shattered terrace. A pair of soiled overalls hung
from his meager shoulders and tucked into a set of knee-high waders.
He was an average creature with an average height and an average
build. His hybrid-like body resembled a salamander that decided to
become human, but lost interest halfway through. He carried some
extra belly weight, not that he minded, as impressing the opposite sex
had been abandoned long ago. His balding head and blotchy green
skin amplified a midlife persona. To say this chap was forgettable
would be to undermine the very notion of memory.

He sighed and dropped his gaze to the fountain water, once
clean and crystal clear, but now dark with soot and debris. The filter-
ing unit beneath the surface belched and gurgled as it tried and failed
to sift through the sludge. Roy cringed and turned for his toolbox,
only to meet the bulging eyes of a sentient man-pear.

"Shit fuck!" Roy said and sloshed backwards.

Duncan laughed, causing his plump belly to poke out from beneath a plaid work shirt. Thick gray skin, stumpy limbs, and a bulb-

ous torso created the portrait of a land-tromping manatee. His species enjoyed a lush homeworld with low gravity, so life aboard the station was challenging at a baseline. He never complained, though. Duncan rolled with the punches better than anyone. A pair of work slacks started to slide off his waist, cueing a well-practiced grip-n-tug. His laughter slowed to a hearty exhale. "Heya, Roy," he said with a core-cocked accent (the local equivalent of a Midwestern car salesman).

"You really need to wear a bell, man."

"And give up my ninja-like stealthitude?"

Roy rolled his eyes. "Dunc, you're a ninja like a ... um, like ..."

Duncan nodded and motioned to continue.

"Dammit," Roy said, adding a heavy sigh.

"Wow. Not like you to miss a good rib poke."

Roy frowned and glanced at the terrace. "Just not feeling like myself today."

"You depressed again?"

"I'm always depressed, you know that."

"No, I mean, like, uber depressed. Long weekend at the Kink Rinks depressed."

Roy raised an eyebrow. "There's an idea."

"You can always return to group."

Roy huffed. "No thanks. If I wanted to listen to someone drone on about their feelings, I'd phone your mother."

Duncan chuckled, then leaned forward to rummage through Roy's toolbox. He grunted and wheezed on the way down, like a sumo wrestler trying to touch his toes. Dropping to a knee, he paused for a breather before reaching inside and withdrawing a pair of scissors. The struggle back to his feet was equally cumbersome. He tested the scissors for their scissoring scissorness, then nodded with approval. "Yes, these will do nicely."

Roy had studied the effort with little emotion, content to watch his friend struggle through the simple tasks of living. If anything, it made him feel better about his own miseries. "You're a fucking gardener, Duncan."

"True fact," he said with a wide smile.

"How is it possible that you didn't bring any shears?"

"Oh I did, but they're way over there." Duncan pointed to his satchel, which rested on the sidewalk a few meters away.

"Get back to work, assholes," the foreman said as he strolled by.

Roy and Duncan turned to the hairy beast.

"Piss off, Clancy," Roy said as a canned retort.

The beast stopped in its tracks and whipped an angered gaze to Roy, revealing knobby tusks, puffy lips, and lemon-yellow eyes. An orange vest hung from its sturdy shoulders, which fanned through the air when he spun towards the insubordinate plumber. The beast stepped forward and loomed over the fountain like a lion claiming a waterhole. His eyes narrowed as bull-like nostrils expelled puffs of heated breath. "What did you say to me?"

Roy maintained his apathetic stare. "Sorry, I misspoke. What I meant to say was, lick my salty nether sack."

Duncan snorted.

The beast's eyes widened. "You insolent little shit nugget."

"Like the ones on your hairy asshole?"

"I can fire you right now."

"But you won't."

The fountain gurgled and spat a dollop of mud onto Roy's leg.

Clancy glanced at Duncan, who smiled back through his always-cheerful demeanor. The beast sighed, mumbled some curses, then softened his tone. "We still on for The Pipes tonight?"

"That's the plan," Duncan said.

"Assuming we can clean this up in time," Roy said as he glanced around the filth.

"Ain't no way," Clancy said. "We have a bunch of new regulations to satisfy, so plan on being here all week. On the upside, the budget has ballooned with the schedule. You got a full green light on overtime, so milk it all you like."

"Nice," Duncan said.

Roy groaned, as per usual.

Clancy huffed and shook his head. "Jeez, Roy. Would it kill you to fake some gratitude? I could hand you a sack of money and you'd bitch about having to carry it."

Roy grimaced. "Says the salaried employee who makes more than the two of us combined."

"You say that like I didn't earn it."

"You didn't. Sandra just wanted some eye-candy in the main office."

"It's not like that at all."

"It's a little like that," Duncan said, adding a finger pinch.

"Pretty boy gets the cookie," Roy said with a hint of disdain.

Clancy sighed and glanced away.

"So what happened up there?" Duncan said, eyeing the splintered terrace.

"Yeah," Roy said. "They haven't told us shit. All we got is hearsay and rumors."

Clancy shrugged. "You know as much as I do. Some mystery goon snuck in with a plasma pistol and shot up the place. They've been pretty tight-lipped about the encounter. Oh, I did learn that some Mulgawat ladies were involved."

Roy dropped his jaw. "Are you fucking kidding me?"

"What?" Duncan said.

"My one chance to meet a Mulgawat and I missed it."

Clancy snort-chuckled. "Like you would ever be in this area for any reason. Hell, the fountain you're standing in probably costs more than you'll ever make."

Roy narrowed his eyes.

"I never knew you had a thing for Mulgawats," Duncan said.

"Not a *thing* per se. They're just so ..." Roy stammered a bit, then grinned like a creepy uncle. "Exotic."

"Oookay," Clancy said, raising his mitts. "The last thing I need is another one of your Kink Rinks recaps. Save it for The Pipes."

"You're getting the first round, salary boy."

"If I say yes, will you shut up and get back to work?"

The fountain belched a ribbon of muck onto Roy's cheek. "My work fulfills me," he said without flinching.

7

Clancy snickered, then resumed his trek down the sidewalk. "See you guys at eight."

Duncan hook-yanked his pants and turned to Roy. "Why do you always have to be such a sourpuss?"

Roy glowered at Duncan as a wad of mud fell from his chin and plunked into the fountain.

"Ner'mind," Duncan said. "Just get through the day as best you can and we'll toss back a few frosties later."

"As if you needed to tell me."

Duncan huffed. "Tim almighty, this pity party got an end?"

Roy cracked a smile. "Fine, I yield to the court. Now piss off and trim something."

Duncan nodded and returned the smile. He tested the scissors on some imaginary vines, then waddled towards a mess of foliage.

Roy glanced down at the gurgling muck, then over to his sad little toolbox, then up to the exploded terrace. His feigned grin inverted itself as he battled a wave of dejection. He couldn't help but imagine the ruckus, the destruction, the excitement, and most importantly, the fact that he wasn't there and never would have been. Roy had slogged through the swamp of mediocrity, bound by doubt and slave to resentment. But as he stared up at the wreckage, a strange new itch infected his psyche. An itch that he had no idea how to scratch.

* * *

That was the moment.

I have watched the story of Roy from its curious start to chaotic finale. I have studied his every action, from the tiniest intonations to the galloping insanity. But that moment, that brief and beautiful moment etched into the security footage of history, ignited the flames of destiny that would entangle a trillion souls. It gives me chills to this day, watching the avatar of apathy stare into the great unknown without qualm or trepidation. That was the moment when Roy the plumber became Roy the would-be legend.

CHAPTER 2

I reviewed The Pipes for the Definitive Directory of Durangoni, which remains one of my shortest entries to date. In its entirety: "The establishment seems to exist solely to exacerbate a throbbing headache. Avoid at all costs."

In retrospect, the review may have been a tad harsh. However, this is not to say that it was in any way inaccurate, because it wasn't. The Pipes is a cauldron of noise, an audible assault from every direction. But as I delved into the story of Roy, I discovered a strange new affinity for the hideous little pub.

The Pipes is a junction room about the size of a large garage. The place gets its name from the countless pipes and conduits that cover the walls and ceiling. It's a hellish maze of metal that includes water lines, atmo ducts, everything a healthy station needs. Most junctions are properly zoned and automated, but this one had suffered from a critical design flaw. The resulting morass was so convoluted that it required a constant stream of upkeep.

Fixing the mess was deemed too disruptive, so a dedicated technician was assigned to the junction. Two weeks later, he quit. Another technician was assigned and quit the following day. A droid was assigned, but the chaotic nature of the room quickly drove it insane.

The junction became notorious for its endless cycle of hire-quit-repeat. In fact, only one technician managed to stay for longer than a month, and she was legally deaf.

But as with most bizarre conundrums, the eventual solution was equally bizarre.

Fiona was a talented mechanic who lived near the junction. One day, she met some friends at a nearby pub and proceeded to drink herself silly. As she stumbled home, she decided to swing by the junction room to see what all the fuss was about. She ducked inside and marveled at the clattering labyrinth before passing out. When she awoke, she came to a sobering realization. To quote her business proposal, "It's not that bad when you're drunk."

Her solution was simple: convert the room into a workman's pub and offer free drinks in exchange for maintenance. The station agreed and The Pipes was born. It quickly became a haven for working stiffs with limited booze budgets. Whenever a gauge popped or a fitting leaked, the most sober and qualified guest would make the repair. The strategy proved wildly successful, transforming the space from a hole of despair into a model of efficiency. (It's still a hole of despair, just a very efficient one.)

Fiona has worked there as the owner-manager since day one and also serves as a frequent bartender. The Pipes celebrated its 30th anniversary as I was compiling this book. Fiona has amassed a large and dedicated customer base, solidifying her status as a barfly matriarch. Her patrons are fiercely loyal, granting her a cult-like following. Roy was a proud member of that sect, and Fiona knew him better than most.

I remember meeting Fiona on my first visit to The Pipes. She greeted me kindly as I was stuffing wads of tissue into my ears. Her stout frame is an impressive ratio of width and height. Not overweight so much as overly brawn, complete with a pair of sumptuous bosoms that could double as deadly weapons. She embodies the role of a gruff marm, one who can toss you over a table and then soothe your ego with a mug of hot chocolate. As one of the few Earthling females living in the station, she is largely hairless, apart from a thick mane of curly locks.

Fiona was kind enough to agree to an interview for this book (and grant my request that it take place outside of the brain-battering pub). We met at a small cafe near her home, one of the countless caffeine stops inside the station. I spoke with her about Roy and his relationship with The Pipes. The following is an excerpt of that conversation.

* * *

First and foremost, I would like to thank you for agreeing to speak with me, and at the same time, apologize for my brazen review of The Pipes.

Oh sweetie, you don't need to apologize for nothin'. In fact, your review boosted my bottom line, so I should be the one to thank you.

Really? That's surprising to hear. How so?

It shouldn't be surprising at all. Your words are only heeded by a certain class of citizen. When you say "avoid at all costs," my clientele hears "a distinct lack of proper folk." That's a five-star rating for my establishment.

Be that as it may, even the uncultured have ears. How does anyone stand it inside that head-splitting horror pit?

(laughs) You get used to it. But even so, the sub-core folk have a built-in tolerance for racket, and they make up most of my patronage.

Ah, yes. Most of my readers will be unfamiliar with the sub-core, the shanty-like area that surrounds the cylindrical hub of the station. Can you give us a sympathetic insight into the citizens that call the area home?

Happy to. And thank you for asking, because these folks deserve more than a passing glance.

(I smile, nod, and swallow the not-so-veiled dig on my charac-

ter.)

As you know, Durangoni is a giant disc system, like a stack of barbell plates with the biggest in the center and the smallest at the poles. Hundreds of these discs rotate around the core, a giant cylinder that acts like a spindle.

That's actually a very effective visual. Mind if I steal it?

Please do. Anything to curb the zarpobblement (a word unique to the station, denoting a potent mixture of shock, awe, vertigo, and a sudden desire to contemplate the meaning of life).

Thank you. Apologies for the interruption, please continue.

So in order to answer your question, we must first understand how wealth is distributed inside Durangoni. As with most stations, money is traced from top to bottom. The posh live near the surface and the dregs inhabit the core, kinda like a cruise ship on a planetary scale.

Well, Durangoni is a bit different in that the core is the most expensive place to live. The sheer scale of the station requires a genius-level of engineering to keep it afloat, and the nerds that do so are held in the highest celebrity status.

But, being nerds, they ain't the type to bask on surface beaches. They just stay locked inside the core like neckbeards in a basement. As a result, the wealthy come to them. They purchase plots around the labs and build luxury abodes. For the super rich, proximity to the super nerds is seen as a status symbol. It's kinda like squatting in Bill Gates's pool house.

Bill who?

Oh, sorry. He was King of the Nerds back home, the Earth equivalent of Loomba Varvar. (King of the Nerds on Durangoni, if that wasn't obvious.)

Ah.

So tell me, what typically surrounds the wealthiest parts of a city?

The poorest ghettos.

That's right. The rich insulate themselves and wall off everything adjacent, which strips the area of business potential. But, when you apply this rule to a station the size of Durangoni, you create one of the starkest inequalities in the galaxy. We're talking a matter of meters between the richest and poorest residents. Ten meters of pure titanium to be exact, the outer casing of the inner core.

Proles will typically live near the core because that's where the work is, but that's not true on this station. The work here is near the surface because everything is automated. Durangoni represents the biggest service economy in the universe. The AI handles all the important stuff, so plumbers here ain't maintaining the water supply. They're unclogging public toilets. And the great irony is, they'll make more doing that than working respected jobs on their home planets.

And Roy was one such plumber.

Yup. And like so many, he came here to support his family.

Can you tell me more about his family and backstory?

Sure. And for the record, Roy was a good man. I understand that The Incident was a colossal shitshow. But knowing him the way I do, ain't no way he did anything out of malice. He did everything with his family in mind, despite the pain of circumstance.

Can you elaborate?

Well, Roy came here as a divorcee. He needed some extra income to support his three million children. When he—

Wait. Did you say three *million*?

Yes sir. Roy's species is a cannibalistic amphibious breed that lays millions of eggs all at once. When they hatch, they start eating each other down to about two or three. Those are the keepers that you send to college and whatnot, but until that time, the parents are liable for the lot. Roy's wife had birthed about a dozen million and the brood was down to about four million when they divorced. Their legal system favors the mother, so Roy was left broke and destitute. His child support and alimony forced him to Durangoni for better-paying work.

This is all from his side of the story, by the way. I never saw a picture of his wife or learned much about his homeworld. He was very guarded about those details. But, I do know bullshit when I hear it and he gave me no reason to doubt him. He just seemed like a bro-ken-hearted critter who fell on bad times.

Did you ever press him for details about the divorce?

Lordy no, that would've been rude. But if I had to wager a guess, I would peg her as a gold-diggin' floozy. Roy was making a decent wage as a general plumber on the station, but he still lived in the worst part of the sub-core. Even if most of your credits are going home, there's a certain level of livin' you don't want to slip beneath. Roy was always stressed about his footing, which told me that his pockets were lighter than intended.

What is life like down there?

It's noisy as hell, for one thing. Lots of engines, pumps, drones, standard rumble of upkeep. But, the Durangoni sub-core is its own special hell.

Why's that?

When the uppers started to relocate, they got all butt-hurt about the constant racket. And what happens when the rich get inconven-ienced?

Shit changes.

(nods) But rarely for the betterment of others. And so, the station decided to insulate the core to appease the bucks. Unfortunately, that included a lot of venting into the sub-core. Now it's like everyone lives on the tarmac of a busy spaceport.

I had no idea it was that bad down there.

The uppers seldom do. A ghetto is a ghetto to them. But, some are measurably worse than others. Roy endured the worst of it.

So he viewed The Pipes as a peaceful retreat.

Very much so. The Pipes are sandwiched between the ghetto and merchant lines, not quite derelict but not quite proper. It's largely ignored by the locals, but serves as a refuge for the sub-core folk. Several of my regulars travel a long way to get there.

Including Roy?

Nah. Roy lived in the same disc, so his trek was reasonable. Good thing too, because he was a handy bloke to have around. I funneled a lot of work to him, assuming he wasn't blackout drunk. He was more than happy to do it because it felt like a friendly favor. The free booze was a bonus, but not the primary reason he came. He just wanted to feel appreciated.

* * *

Fiona and I chatted for several hours before parting ways. I offered to amend my review, given her kindness and fresh perspective. She refused, noting that a first impression is where honesty lives. Fiona was a fount of insight, a fruitful springboard into a frantic investigation. While the morsels were plenty, it was the last line that stuck out the most.

Roy was an underappreciated nobody.

Hardly a groundbreaking revelation, but it provided a necessary foundation. Of course Roy was capable of sparking The Incident. He was starving for gratitude.

CHAPTER 3

After a full day of cleanup, the garden floor rested under a normal layer of filth. A notable improvement, given the original mayhem. Robotic dumpsters carried off the debris while brooms and mops tended to the remainder. Most workers had called it a day, but some were content to milk the overtime.

Fountain filters were busy returning their pools to a crystal clear persuasion. An open porthole belched steam as a socket wrench echoed from the depths. Soon after, the cranking stopped and the wrench flew out of the shaft, clank-landing near its toolbox home. A greasy Roy poked his head out the port. He inhaled a lungful of garden air, then grunted with exhaustion as he climbed out of the hole.

Roy stood up straight, arched his back, and rolled his shoulders. Every joint pop and bone crackle drew a cringe and pucker. He capped it off with a few neck rolls, one of which caught a view of a hologram wall clock.

"Shit," he said with a stymied tone, like a father forgetting to pick up his son from soccer practice. Roy double-checked his comdev, just in case the wall clock was lying out of spite. He could greet his chums in time, but the trip would be hurried and his personal hygiene would be less than ideal. Not that he had much choice, so he gathered his wayward tools and stuffed them into the box without much care for order. A grimy rag served as a mobile shower. He dunked it into the fountain and wiped his face, transforming his filthy complexion into a mildly dirty one. The rag dropped to the floor as he unhooked his jacket from a nearby lamppost. A no-look grab lifted the toolbox and he was off to meet his social obligations.

The hasty exit resulted in some stumbles and curses as he weaved through the garden maze. A standard day in the world of Roy, but no less irritating. Locals gave him a wide berth when he slipped into the corridors, likely due to the one-two punch of aromas and grumbles. The stench forced many into the walls, like a school of fish avoiding a passing shark.

A short jaunt later, he arrived at the nearest pod train station. Durangoni, being a planetary behemoth, needed a massive transport system to shuttle its trillion inhabitants from port to port. The solution was a spaghetti-like network of maglev tubes that shot pods around the station like a pinball machine. Each pod was an independent vessel that held a max capacity of two dozen lifeforms, assuming average heights and weights. The pods managed their own routes, but could also form trains for added efficiency. They could even pass through the open space between each ring, using specialized ports and tracks. In addition, their gyroscopic design kept them upright in relation to the core, no matter what direction they traveled. This allowed the tube system to snake anywhere it damn well pleased.

Roy stood to one side of a crowded pod with every other passenger crammed to the opposite wall and trying not to vomit. They all stared at Roy with cringing faces while Roy maintained a lazy-eyed stare right back at them. He killed time by making awkward eye contact with the most revolted expressions.

The ping of an approaching stop cued Roy to release his grip on an overhead strap, much to the relief of everyone on board. The pod slowed to a halt and the doors slid open, releasing a puff of odor that turned some unsuspecting heads nearby. Roy moseyed out into a small station, little more than a drab gray box that connected service tunnels. In fact, one could discern the depth of any train depot based solely on the bore factor of its interior. Unpainted panels and a sad lack of decor marked the transition from merch to maint districts. Paneling disappeared entirely when pods dropped into the sub-core. Station management deemed them unnecessary, as dregs would simply rip them from the walls and sell them for scrap.

Roy strolled through the mouth of a service corridor, a large semicircle with laser-etched letters. No holograms or fancy names at that level, just cold coordinates that reminded tenants how little the uppers cared about them. Roy's toolbox clattered with every lumbering step. The crowd maintained its forward stare as a parade of tired feet clanked along the walkway. Lighting strips bathed the passage under the harsh glow of a gas station restroom. Roy switched the box to his other hand and rolled away some soreness. A burly brute shoulder-checked him from behind, causing Roy to lose his grip. The box hit the floor, popped its lid, and coughed some tools into the tunnel. The beast smirked over his shoulder and kept walking.

"The hell is your problem?" Roy said.

The beast ignored him.

"Yo! I'm talking to you, shit nugget!"

The beast stopped in its tracks, as did most of the crowd.

"That's right, the tubby fuck with the tiny cock!"

The crowd went silent.

The beast turned to Roy, revealing its scaly skin and decidedly un-tubby frame. Radically muscled, more like it, the kind of brute that lurked in the dark corners of gyms where mortals dare not tread. Everyone else pushed to the walls, forming an arena of conflict. The beast lifted its chin and stared at Roy over a wide and blocky jaw, as if the jaw itself had also hit the gym. He snorted through a pair of gaping nostrils and flexed a pair of pecs that could double as manhole covers.

The monster was two Roys tall and a full Roy wide, creating a showdown that would make most Roys crap their pants. But not this Roy. This Roy was excited, eager even, because he had two distinct advantages. One, Durangoni Security would never allow such an event to transpire, so confrontations were little more than vanity struts. Should a fight come to actual blows, stun rods along the ceiling would knock them both out. And two, Roy's species wielded a peculiar form of natural defense, one that he could summon at will. It provided no boons to strength or dexterity, but the psychological effects were devastating.

"Say that again," the beast said with a deep and graveled tone. He took a step forward, expecting Roy to recoil.

Roy did no such thing. Instead, his bulging eyes frosted over, as if suddenly possessed. A gurgling sound erupted from his throat, the result of boiling stomach acid. The vile concoction climbed his esophagus and foamed through his mouth, spilling onto the floor like a fountain of dry ice. Croaks and neck twitches created the image of a demonic gremlin. His voice completed the transformation, dropping into a raspy seethe.

"I said." Roy took a step forward. "You're a tubby fuck." Another step. "With a tiny cock." Another step.

The brute hesitated, much to the surprise of everyone watching. His eyes widened as a confused brain fought through a loop of fear and emasculation.

A tense silence fell between them.

"Um ..." the beast said, which Roy heard as *Come at me bro!*

Roy hissed and gave charge.

The beast yelped, then spun around and sprinted down the corridor.

Roy scuffed to a stop and smirked as the brute disappeared around a corner. "Yeah, that's what I thought."

The hum of a maintenance droid broke the tension as it fluttered in to mop the floor. Roy moseyed back to his toolbox, careful to step around his own gunk. He wiped his mouth with a sleeve as his eyes slowly defogged. The gathered mass watched his every move, trying to make sense of what just happened. Roy ignored them. He gathered the spilled tools and continued on his way. The crowd lost interest soon after and the arena closed. The roars of conversation filled the tunnel as foot traffic resumed its normal pace.

Roy grinned as he sauntered down the corridor. The confronta-

tion had added a few minutes to his arrival time, but it was a worth-
while inconvenience. A public scuffle was a rare treat and he never
backed down from a fight. They seldom ended with shocks and the
risk was worth the stress relief, especially given Roy's uniquely revolt-
ing talent. At the very least, random tussles served as great pub fod-
der.

Roy emerged into an open bazaar teeming with merchants. It
carried the same chaos of a crowded mall, but the hucksters there
were offering tools and fittings instead of clothes and jewelry. Industrial lights hung from the ceiling, punching through clouds of dust.
Roy scanned for deals as he hiked through the clutter. He made it to
the other side without breaking stride and continued down the next
corridor.

Several rights and a few lefts later, Roy ducked into a residential
shaft. The roar of traffic quieted, leaving the whine of the sub-core.
At this level, the station emitted a constant thrum, everything from
air reclaimers to fuel processors. Even so, Roy much preferred the
racket of machines to the racket of people. His own steps found his
ears again, drawing a brief smile. He passed a numbered door every
few meters, the tiny apartment homes of anyone needing to save
some credits. The passage ended at a small foyer where a few alien
blokes were in mid-chat. A single gray door was attached to the
space, featuring *The Pipes* etched into a nondescript plaque. To the
average passerby, it may as well have been a janitor closet.

"Eric, Geoff," Roy said as he stepped into the foyer.

"Heya Roy," Geoff said.

"Hmph," Eric said, his version of a cordial greeting.

"How's it hanging?"

"Low and knobbly," Geoff said.

"Hmph," Eric said, conveying that the nature of his dangling
member was neither relevant nor interesting.

Roy chuckled in solidarity, then hooked the door handle and
yanked it open. Clanks and clatters flooded the foyer, along with a
fart of machinery steam. Roy slipped inside and the door closed behind him.

The lights softened to a dusky hue, like a swamp cave with an ambient glow. Roy trudged through a short hallway full of blinking lights and pressure gauges. Numerous breaker panels hummed behind panes of clouded glass. Thick bundles of wires drooped overhead. Towards the end, a large red button stuck out from the wall like an infected zit.

Roy smacked the button as he entered the main room.

Everyone pressed the big red button. It was an oddball tradition, like tapping the feet of a campus statue. When The Pipes first opened, nobody pressed the big red button because nobody knew what it did. But then a wobbly drunk accidentally pressed the button. A panic ensued, but nothing happened. From that day on, everyone pressed the big red button.

It served some unknown purpose back in the early days of construction, but the nature of its function had faded over time. Strangely enough, a connection was bridged when the button was pushed. It did *something*, but affected nothing in the immediate area, so that something remained a mystery.

"Roooy," said a chorus of barflies.

"Hey guys," Roy said as he dropped his toolbox along the wall. He hooked his jacket on a valve handle and approached the central bar.

The entire room radiated a workman vibe. Countless pipes and conduits stretched vertically along the walls. Steel, copper, plastic, every feasible housing carried something from somewhere to elsewhere. Valves and wheels of all shapes and sizes peppered the assembly, serving as a giant control hub. The hums and clatters of moving material filled the room with a constant racket. A potent stench of moldy fuel lingered inside like an unwashed vagrant who refused to leave. The chamber seemed to go out of its way to assault every sense with reckless abandon.

Many pipes forked at the ceiling and slithered across the room, creating a zigzagged mosaic overhead. Fiona used them as anchors for decor and lighting. Pub flags and Edison bulbs dangled at random intervals. The bar itself rested at the center and resembled a welded heap plucked from a scrapyard. This was intentional, as anything residing in the pub needed enough resilience to tolerate a vigorous power wash. Thus, a fresh coat of paint was regarded as a needless luxury. Mismatched panels decorated the rectangular frame, and that was good enough. It was a sturdy structure, and as ugly as the patrons surrounding it.

Standard bar fittings littered the rest of the room. A handful of waist-high tables, stools of various sizes, all of it welded for strength. Fiona never lost sight of the place from a practical standpoint. Yes, it was a pub. But it also served a vital purpose. Fiona commanded that purpose from behind the bar, instructing able-bodied patrons to address repairs as needed. That was the price of admission. She ruled with an iron fist and a dirty apron.

Roy plopped onto his favorite stool along the bar, a Norm-like position that he claimed years ago. As one of the primary regulars, the seat vacated as soon as he walked into the room, not that there was ever much clamoring. Duncan and Clancy had already claimed their seats beside him, as per usual. A pair of half-empty mugs rested on the counter.

"Evening, gents," Roy said.

"Howdy," Duncan said with a wide smile.

"About time," Clancy said. "Where the hell you been?"

"Shove it, haircut. I'm like a minute late."

"Yeah, and that's a big deal for you. How many times have you chastised us for not being on time? You say 'eight means eight' like a fucking brain tick."

"Fair enough. Got into another scuffle."

Duncan chuckled. "Did you go all frothy loony?"

"Yup. Fucker turned tail like a frightened child."

"What sparked it?" Clancy said and took another sip.

"Stupid shit. Got checked by a meathead and I checked him back."

Clancy smirked and nodded. "Few things sweeter than owning a bully."

"Says the asshole foreman."

"Hey, I get paid to be a bully. Difference."

A frosty mug of beer clunked in front of Roy, compliments of a smiling Fiona. "There you go, sweetie."

"Ah, thank you, Fifi." He snatched the grog and raised it to his chums.

They raised their own in response.

"To the horses," Roy said with confidence.

The toast paused in mid-air.

"Huh?" Duncan said.

"What, like cowboy horses?" Fiona said.

"The fuck is a cowboy?" Clancy said.

"I don't get the context," Duncan said through a vexed expression.

Roy sighed. "Jeez, nevermind. I heard it somewhere and thought it sounded cool. Fuckin' cheers, you uncultured pricks."

"Cheers," they said in unison and clinked glasses.

Roy took a long swig, then nodded and smacked his lips. "Not bad."

"Got it in this morning," Fiona said while leaning on the counter. "Small batch, strong and malty. It's been quite popular, so get your fill while you can. Third tap from the left."

"Noted," Roy said as he eyed the unlabeled tapline.

Fiona click-winked and turned her attention to a waving patron.

Part of the *free beer for free work* deal involved a stipulation on quality. The inherent nature of such a deal attracted a certain breed of clientele, the kind unburdened by flavors and nuance. Therefore, Durangoni decreed that any beers delivered must adhere to a certain character, or lack thereof. Countless breweries called the station home, everything from tiny brewpubs to massive corporate outfits. The Pipes usually received a steady supply of macro overstock. But every now and then, an "off" batch from a brewpub got added to the mix. A rare treat for the peasants, and one that didn't last long.

Roy palmed his mug and sank into his seat. He released a heavy sigh as Duncan blathered on about something he believed to be interesting, which was rarely interesting. Roy just stared at his mug and nodded along, like a tired parent suffering through a teenage rant. He kept nodding long after Duncan had finished.

"You okay there, Roy?" Clancy said.

Roy kept nodding.

Duncan nudged his shoulder.

Roy flinched and cleared his throat. "Oh, um ... sorry."

Clancy angled himself towards Roy and rested an elbow on the counter. "What's wrong with you today?"

"Nothing."

"Malarkey," Duncan said. "You've been a Negative Nelly all day."

"More than usual," Clancy said. "Seriously, what's wrong?"

Roy sighed and tapped his mug. "It's just, the whole thing is one giant reminder of how stupid and dull and worthless my life is. Everything I do is a cleanup. Everything I am is an afterthought of something else."

"That's not true," Duncan said, then turned to Clancy for support.

Clancy stammered for some positivity, but eventually threw in the towel. "He ain't wrong."

Duncan gasped and whipped his gaze between the two, cycling through *how dare you* and *don't listen to him.*

"It's okay, Duncan." Roy grimaced and shook his head. "My ex-wife hates me, my children don't know me, and I live in the bowels of a mechanized mega-station in order to support them. I was a goddamn architect back home. Respected. Comfortable. But nooo, that wasn't enough for Greedy McBitcherson. So here I am, a divorced slave to someone else's betterment." He tossed back the remainder of his beer as the other two looked on with concern.

"Well, um ..." Duncan searched for the words, but couldn't find any.

"Could be worse," Clancy said.

Roy narrowed his eyes and turned to Clancy. "Do tell, foreman to the stars."

"What's that supposed to mean?"

"I will never understand why you come here. You are hot enough and rich enough to never set foot in this place. For fuck's sake, you live a thousand levels above the merchant line. Why slum it down in this shithole?"

Clancy shrugged, refusing to take the bait.

Roy grunted and bowed his head. "Sorry."

"No offense taken," Clancy said and finished his brew.

Duncan emptied his lungs, relieved by the diffusion. He downed the rest of his brew and slid the empty mug towards the ledge.

Fiona wandered back and hooked all three mugs with one swoop. She refilled them with a practiced hand and distributed them accordingly, prompting a round of thanks. "Roy, I need a pressure calibration on A113."

"I got it," Clancy said and rose from his stool. He gestured at Fiona, as if to say *Dude needs a break tonight.*

Fiona smiled and nodded back. She patted Roy's hand, then grabbed a rag and moseyed out to wipe some tables.

"How do you do it, Duncan?" Roy said.

"Do what, guy?"

"Be happy. How do you find joy in this pit?"

Duncan thought for a moment while shifting his blubbery jowls. "There's always a worse pit, I suppose."

"Do you not want a better life than this?"

Duncan shrugged. "Never give it much thought, to be honest. I find it's easier to be content where I'm at."

Roy stared at a smiling Duncan. "I can't decide if that's wise or stupid."

"I'm fine either way." He grabbed his mug and took a large gulp.

A half-grin lifted Roy's cheek, then he returned to his own mug. His face went limp as he studied the fading suds. The surrounding racket faded with them, as if sinking into a deep pool. For once, the cold blanket of depression had morphed into something else. Maybe it was the good beer talking, or maybe it was the flink that flarked the plumbo. *

25

(* Some cultural sayings do not translate well into Earth tongues. In this case, the easiest substitute would be "the straw that broke the camel's back," but this visual fails to capture the intended severity. A more apt comparison would be the final handful of dung dropped into a trebuchet that hurls a sheep into a brick wall. But alas, saying "the final shit that slaughters the sheep" elicits more confusion than understanding.)

CHAPTER 4

To understand Roy, one must understand the loyal regulars that call The Pipes home. And to understand them, one must understand the newcomers. First-timers are very easy to spot. Simply look for anyone shouting.

The sheer quantity of noise overwhelming the space rivals most death metal concerts. As such, new visitors will often feel the need to exceed the ambient volume when ordering a tasty beverage. However, screaming a drink order is a needless exercise because the bartenders have developed a keen sense of inference, using a mixture of body language and lip-reading. Most newcomers lose their voice and never return. But for the brave few, the unspoken reward is a new and covert form of communication.

Barflies actually converse at normal volumes inside The Pipes. Granted, they are not discussing the philosophical meanings of Nurmquashi (the local equivalent of Shakespeare, known for stirring productions that involve actual stage death). It does not take a whole lot of brainpower to infer the core meanings behind typical pub chats. Bad day at work, wife got the fleas, the local leader of whatever is a total douchebag. In fact, many regulars can enjoy entire conversations using only grunts and shrugs.

So why does this matter in the slightest?

In a word: cameras.

The vast majority of Durangoni is under constant surveillance. Managing a trillion residents inside a planet-sized space station requires a massive security force and a highly sophisticated AI system. Every square inch of public space is monitored around the clock. Private domiciles are technically exempt, but the sheer scale of dominion means that everyone assumes they're being watched anyway. Thankfully, the station does not give two flurming flarps about how residents spend their me-time. They're much more concerned with keeping the station afloat.

The Pipes are also monitored, but the pub is so obnoxious that even the most advanced cameras record little more than choppy static. Sound is disabled because playback would be pointless. Not that they care much, as any criminal in their right mind would never conduct dealings in such a place.

The great irony is that The Pipes were instrumental in the lead-up to The Incident. Thus, learning about this lead-up is nigh impossible without interviewing those who shared regular interactions with Roy. In conducting my own inquiries, I found no one more important than his best friend, a mild-mannered chap named Duncan.

I sat down with Duncan numerous times. The first thing one notices is his jovial demeanor, which can be utterly infectious and wholly disarming. I never heard him complain once about anything or anyone. This is due in large part to the nature of his species, a plump and leathery lot known for their passive take on pretty much everything. They depart the womb with a mind for leisure, content to wander through life with a one-way ticket to anywhere. They are found all over the cosmos, and none of them arrive with any formal plan. They are, in a very orthodox sense, just winging it.

Duncan was no different. He left his home planet as a single gardener, traveled the galaxy as a single gardener, ended up on Durangoni as a single gardener, and currently maintains his status as a single gardener. He is perfectly content with this backstory and is more than happy to regale it when prompted. He lives in a tiny apartment deep inside the sub-core, which he has maintained for over 30 years. This utter devotion to inertia is how he came to meet Roy.

Every discussion I ever had with Duncan took place inside his spartan home. He was always happy to receive me and treated my visits like a pampering grandmother. I was initially skeptical about conducting an interview down in the turbulent sub-core. I thought for sure that the noise would be too distracting. Or at the very least, the inevitable headache would force me to cut the meeting short. But as always, Duncan managed to surprise me.

The following is an excerpt from our first interview.

* * *

I rounded a final corner on my way to Duncan's home, and not a moment too soon. I had experienced rowdy districts before, but the sub-core put them all to shame. It was a ceaseless assault of hums, drums, clanks, and clatters. How anyone could tolerate this turmoil, let alone live inside it, was beyond my comprehension.

I entered a narrow corridor with dim light, musky air, and tarnished paneling. Countless doors littered the passage, like steerage on a starcruiser. Their close proximities foreshadowed the scale of their interiors. One door stood out among the rest, as it was covered with stickers, posters, flags, and various shades of permanent marker. It wasn't Duncan's place, but I would learn through Duncan what it represented.

The apartment I sought was four doors down, another empty pane with etched numbers that matched the ones on my comdev. I gave it a stout knock, assuming the noise would get drowned out. Duncan opened the door right away, always the vigilant host. He donned a wide smile and extended a plump hand with sausage-like fingers. I gripped it, we exchanged pleasantries, and then he ushered me inside.

When the door closed, the room went dreadfully silent, enough to stop me in my tracks as if something were afoul. Duncan chuckled and explained that a combination of special foliage and noise cancelation rendered the space, well ... audibly normal. And indeed, a tangled forest of leaves and vines crawled up the walls and along the ceiling, all of which was lovingly trimmed and pleasantly arranged. In lieu of knick-knacks, he decorated the interior with a cornucopia of potted plants. His love of greenery was on full display. As a result, the air was as crisp and clean as the station surface.

Calling the place a studio apartment would be a tad generous. It was a box. Specifically, a stumpy rectangle that would get uncomfortably crowded with a handful of visitors. Furnishings amounted to a small table, a few cabinets, shelves stuffed with plants, and a plush lounge chair that filled much of the space. The lonely table was adorned with sweet morsels and a steaming pot of tea, a kind gesture considering the cramped confines.

Duncan retrieved a folding chair from beside the table and offered it to me proudly, as if to brag on his ability to receive guests. I accepted it, unfolded it, and took a much-needed seat. He poured himself a cup of tea and plopped his rotund body into the lounge chair, expelling a grunt as he landed. His chubby jowls, tiny eyes, and stumpy ears gave me the distinct impression of a kindly krombaloom (think hippo with an injection of koala cuteness). He grinned and patted the armrests as I started my recorder and placed it on the table.

To start, I wish to thank you for welcoming me into your home. It was a very kind offer and I must admit that I am pleasantly surprised.

You betcha. First time down in the sub-core?

First extended visit, yes.

It's not as bad as they say. It can be a bit brassy, but one can manage just fine.

That's a healthy way to look at it.

A lot of good people call the sub-core home. Yes, many of them are of modest means, but many choose this life, as I have. There's a certain authenticity to it that you can't find anywhere else on the station.

What kind of authenticity?

Well, the folk you meet down here are honest from the get-go. There's no reason to wear a mask because there's no lesser stature to contend with. (chuckles) I mean, who ya gonna impress with all your diddly-do?

Did Roy understand that?

I think he did, even though his presence was largely financial.

Fiona informed me of his situation. I imagine that's a tough spot for anyone.

He was just trying to be a good dad. No shame in that. A lot of subbers work here to support somewhere else. Here's a fun fact: Durangoni generates more wealth than the next thousand solar systems combined. It's why the station is a thriving plentitude of culture. It's a big shiny beacon for anyone looking for a better deal. I have met migrants from clear-cross the cosmos, wide-eyed folk who spent their life savings just to get here. If I had to wager, I would say that a solid two-thirds of the sub-core is made up of working transients.

And that's not a source of animosity?

Why would it be? We're all here for the same reason, so there's dinky-do to fight about. Don't much care if someone talks different or wears a funny hat.

I guess we're all transients inside Durangoni.

(smiles) In a big fake world, everyone is from somewhere else.

The upper tiers hear stories about scuffles in the sub-core. Are those unfounded?

Well, when you cram a bunch of roustabouts into close quarters, there are bound to be some fisticuffs every now and then. Not saying they don't happen, but I imagine they aren't near as sensational as headlines suggest. Take Roy for instance. He had a way of neutralizing scuffles that would scare the dickens out of the average upper.

How so?

Ghost-eyed acid puke.

(awkward silence)

So how did you meet Roy?

Hmm. If memory serves, he moved into the row about eight years back. You actually passed his unit on your way here.

You mean the one with all the flair?

(nods) Yes sir. Roy is a bit of a folk hero these days. His lease is still active, so it just sits there empty. Fans come and go, leaving doodads and whatnot. Tim bless 'em, I hope he's doing well, wherever he may be.

So you have no idea what happened to him?

No one does, far as I reckon. I was his closest friend, so if he wanted to be noticed, I imagine a pop-up here would have been at the top of his list. (sighs) But I haven't seen him since the, um, thinga-ma-doodle.

The Incident.

That's the one. (grins) Sharp fella, you are.

How did you weather the fallout?

Just sat in my chair and waited for it to pass.

Really? Did you not, um ... *see* things?

(widens eyes and slowly nods) Oh yes, it was scary as a mud-rucker. But what could I do? I just rode the freaky deaky like everyone else.

Fair enough. So let's talk more about your friendship with Roy.

How did it start?

Plodders on the same row tend to work together fairly often. Management likes to hire by block whenever possible, makes it easier to monitor tardiness. We came to know each other through odd jobs and the like. Gardening and plumbing tend to crissy-cross, so I spent a lot of time with Roy. I was one of the first regular faces he encountered after moving to Durangoni. He wasn't peculiar by any means, just another grunt in need of a friend.

Fiona said that he didn't talk much about his past. But being his closest friend, did he ever elaborate to you? Not meaning to pry, just trying to understand the launch point.

Totally understand, no fouls afoot. And to answer your question, yes and no. Roy was candid about many things, mostly pertaining to his life aboard the station. He griped about the work, complained about the boss, you know, standard grunt prattle. He would always tie it back to his home plights, but we never learned where that home was. For whatever reason, he guarded that info like a noozipup with a parpalapple. *

(* This saying has never been recorded anywhere else in the known universe. It's a Duncan original, so let's just say a "squirrel with a nut.")

Any guesses as to why?

No idea, to be honest. For most subbers, those stories are what get them through the day. We drink suds and chat about our home-worlds like you drink fancy wine and chat about frilly shoes and whatnot. (raises hands) Meaning no offense.

None taken.

But Roy was different. He carried a grouse about losing dignity, which he blamed on that harpy of a spouse. But again, none of this was verified because nobody knew where he came from. It could have been a flagrant fib for all we knew.

Did you ever ask him directly?

No, never. That's a subber blunder. There's an unspoken rule when chatting about the past. You can ask for more, but only after the course is served.

That explains a lot, actually. When I started delving into the details that led up to The Incident, I learned early on that Roy had never registered a surname or applied for trusts. He maintained a unit account, but all you need for that is a retinal scan. As such, sleuthing out a backstory became nigh impossible. It often feels like I'm chasing a shadow.

None of us did any better, and we *drank* with him.

* * *

The rest of our chat provided no additional insights. Subsequent chats would uncover bits and pieces, as Duncan was always a willing and forthright interviewee. It is perfectly forgivable to overlook obscure details, so I never minded the return visits.

More on that later.

I returned to the surface with a small dose of clarity, but answers to the major questions still eluded me. I was no closer to sussing out a motivation than when I started. In reality, it felt like a step in the opposite direction after learning how evasive Roy had been with his closest ally. In a strange way, he made more sense as a supervillain.

As a parting observation, I would be remiss not to highlight the incredible plant life growing inside Duncan's humble abode. I learned that many were selected for their medicinal properties, some of which required the care and attention of a hospice patient. Duncan is a rare breed in that he possesses an encyclopedic knowledge of interstellar botany, both from cultural and scientific bookends.

Durangoni is home to the largest biodiversity in the entire supercluster, a fact that attracted Duncan to the station. Locals came to view him as a medicine man of sorts, someone to call upon when the standard pharma failed to treat. He also grew a collection of rare herbs and spices that he used to season meals and brew pots of tea. Having sampled much of the latter, I would rank his tiny sub-core home as the single greatest teahouse aboard the station. I am also fully aware that this would send a shockwave through the Definitive Directory of Durangoni, so it remains a personal opinion.

Of all my interviews with Duncan, I cherish the first above the rest. It left me with a better understanding and a deeper appreciation of the hardworking folk who call the sub-core home.

CHAPTER 5

Roy glanced down at his comdev resting on the bar and cringed at the wee morning hour. A return to the gardens was fast approaching, but the weight of depression kept him glued to his barstool. His foggy gaze slogged over to the stools beside him, long empty since Clancy and Duncan departed. A sigh escaped his chest as he surveyed the remaining barflies around The Pipes. Just a handful. A spotted reptilian with stumpy limbs, a transparent blob that jiggled with the ruckus (perhaps it viewed the pub as a cheap spa), and a long-necked creature with a trio of ring marks around its throat.

Roy narrowed his eyes as Fiona filled a mug with dark beer and plunked it in front of the long-necked patron, who sat a few stools down. It nodded and smiled, which Fiona returned in kind. She dried her hands with a shoddy rag and tossed it under the counter. Roy and his soured face caught her eye, reeling her over for a chat.

"What's the matter?" Fiona said.

"I can't believe you serve those filthy creatures."

The alien met eyes with Roy, then looked away in discomfort.

"The hell you talking about?"

"Those fucking ringnecks."

Fiona cocked an eyebrow. "Wow. I never took you for a Bob-hating bigot."

Roy stopped mid-sip and clunked his mug on the counter. "Bob's awesome, I don't hate Bob. Why do you think I hate Bob?"

"You just ragged on ringnecks."

"No, no, he has *two* rings. *Huge* difference."

"*What?* They're the same fucking species, Roy."

"No, numbers matter. I love Bob like a brother, but three rings is an abomination."

Fiona shook her head. "That's a very specific racism."

"Just saying, the station would be a much better place without so many goddamn ringnecks." He glanced at the creature, who replied with a miffed gaze. Roy stiffened his posture and spread his arms. "You wanna go, boy?"

The creature rolled its eyes and turned away.

Fiona grabbed Roy's forearm. "No, none of that shit in here. You know the rules."

"Not gonna do anything, you know that."

"I don't know that, actually. And since I rarely see this side of you, I do not intend to find out."

"Oh c'mon, I—"

"Finish your drink and head home. You're cut off."

Roy stammered, then bowed his head with embarrassment.

Fiona eyed him like a disappointed mother as she stepped away. She offered an apology to the offended, who shrugged it off as drunken idiocy.

Roy, now berated and dejected, tossed back a final sip and clunk-slid his mug to the edge of the counter. He spun out of the stool and hit the floor with a brief stumble. A vomit-burp teased his throat, prompting a wince and swallow. He eyed the exit, then shuffled towards his toolbox. He plucked his jacket from an overhead valve and slipped his arms inside, careful to avoid eye contact with anyone. The stench of shame was palpable. Even the blob had angled its jelly head for a better view. Roy hooked his toolbox and stumbled into the hallway. A limp slap on the big red button concluded his visit.

The journey home was a slog through predictability. Roy wandered back to the train station, boarded a pod, and descended into the sub-core. His dignity seemed to fade with every stop. By the time he arrived at his destination, the pod featured a who's who of dregs and drifters. A ding overhead signaled the end of the line, the deepest that deep goes, at least for someone like Roy. From there, the train would start its long climb back to the surface.

The doors opened and the pod dumped its unwanted cargo. Roy stepped into a station that resembled the inside of a derelict shack, complete with a tattered sofa that no one dared to use. Bits of trash stirred with each gust of dank air. Numerous dents and scratches adorned the drab walls. The train consumed a few new passengers and hurried away, like a minivan fleeing the ghetto. Roy stood inside the dirty station like a mental patient dumped on Skid Row. He sighed, then straggled towards his homeward tunnel.

Roy moseyed through a small maze of dark alleys and side passages. He ducked a steam vent just before it released, a habitual reaction even when drunk. Rounding a final corner, he entered a narrow tunnel with a grated walkway and numerous doors to either side. A wearied brain tallied the passing units before hooking his own handle and yanking it open. He glanced down the hallway to Duncan's abode and paused for a moment. It was late and he knew it, big workday ahead. Hardly the time for a chat, no matter how much he needed it. Roy sighed, then slipped into his crummy apartment.

Curiously, nobody locked their doors in the sub-core. The unspoken assumption was that nobody had anything worth stealing. All currency was virtual and all activities were recorded. Thus, locking a door had precisely the opposite effect. It showed that you harbored something worth taking. Contrary to popular opinion, robberies were exceedingly rare down in the bowels of Durangoni. Most breaches of privacy amounted to new tenants entering the wrong units by mistake, sometimes during a vexing avocation. Instant regret ensured that the correct unit got memorized in a hurry.

Roy stood inside his modest apartment. His tired fingers released the weight of the toolbox, allowing it to clunk onto the hard metal floor. The funk of his own filth nagged his nostrils, now that it could fester inside a confined area. Roy cringed at the sudden awareness, but was too tired and depressed to do anything about it. He just stood there, silent and alone inside what amounted to a cramped storage locker.

Roy never coveted much. He was fond of saying that all he needed was "a place to piss and grub to gobble." A small cooler satisfied the latter, but the former required a long stroll to the communal wash facilities. Sub-core life was simple to the point of shared misery. Roy had since amended his favorite saying with the suffix "in the same place." Heeding the call of nature in a group setting was awkward enough with the same species, let alone in a bathroom full of aliens with conflicting hygiene standards. There was a better than average chance that cleaning oneself meant foraging through a fog of mental, physical, and sensual horror. It was a battle that Roy just couldn't deal with at the moment.

Instead, he shuffled over to a simple cot along the wall and tossed his wearied body on top. His back thumped against the wall, forcing a grunt of exhaustion. The heartbeat of the sub-core surrounded him, from the rattles in the walls to the distant sounds of grinding gears. Roy could only close his eyes and expel a weighted sigh. His troubled mind took stock of its own reality, as it was prone to do from time to time. A lazy gaze wandered the room, uncovering little more than the artifacts of a meager existence. No decorations, just four blank walls with a few dings and scratches. A small stack of boxes leaned against the corner, containing the basics for continued survival. Three wire hangers clung to notches in the wall, serving as an official closet. A handful of frumpish clothes hung from their warped frames.

Roy reached over to a small red cooler beside the cot, i.e. the kitchen, and retrieved a dented canteen filled with lukewarm water. He popped the top and chugged a large portion, initiating the long march back to soberness. The jug found a home beside his leg as he fished the comdev from his pocket. Roy stared at the black mirror in his hand and caught a glimpse of his own disheveled reflection. His brain recoiled in disgust, resulting in another heavy sigh.

"Directory," Roy said with a flat tone.

The device pinged to life and glowed with a pleasant blue sheen. A white "D" appeared on the screen and spread into three distinct letters, the opening sequence to the Definitive Directory of Durangoni. Roy flicked the screen onto the far wall, then dropped the comdev to his side. The room dimmed as a deep blue consumed the space, like his own personal movie theater, but minus the fun and enjoyment. A short melody signaled a readiness to receive command.

"Kink Rinks," Roy said, as he had so many times before.

The directory pinged in response, then displayed a grid of relevant categories. Bold titles hovered above numerous video clips. An outline of the space station floated in the upper corner with the target rings selected.

Roy shifted his lips. "Brothel District 7."

The directory pinged, the grid filtered, and the station image zoomed.

"Celestial Seraphs."

Ping, filter, zoom. A selection of scantily clad aliens filled the wall.

Roy scanned the options, then grinned. "Elora."

The directory pinged and the grid faded, revealing an erotic creature with cherry-red skin, luscious lips, and striking pink eyes. She swayed her hips and winked with naughty intent. Every so often, she would kiss her palm and blow through her fingers, prompting hearts and ribbons to swirl around her body.

"Schedule."

A calendar popped up beside the image with available dates blinking.

Roy opened his mouth, but paused. A sudden and crippling sadness infected him. He bowed his head as his eyes began to water. Whimpers built inside his chest and clawed their way to the surface. Tears rolled down his cheeks and dripped onto his dirty shirt, turning spots of grime into salty mud. Despite having every reason in the world, he refused to wail. He just sat upon his cot, slumped and alone, weeping in silence.

The directory pinged and suggested a psychiatrist. Or rather, a prostitute dressed like a psychiatrist. (Many customers conflated the two.)

Roy took offense and tossed his canteen at the wall. The impact sprayed some water across the image, giving it a moist sheen that seemed like overkill. The canteen clanked to a rest on the floor. Roy concluded the outburst with a rude gesture.

The directory pinged and suggested a dominatrix. And not just any whip-toting harlot, this vixen wore a full gimp suit with deep red eyes that screamed pain. The upper arms cracked a studded whip while the lower arms thumped a leathery bat. Her firm breasts refused to move inside their skin-tight confines. The thick trunks below her waist seemed well-suited for an Olympic track event.

Roy shuddered as a scheduling calendar popped up. Much to his surprise, the mistress was booked solid, but she was kind enough to offer Roy a cancellation slot. His brain considered it for a split second, then remembered that it frowned on torture.

"Reset! Reset. Please reset."

The directory pinged and returned to its default state.

Roy stared at the three white D's floating on the blue backdrop. His mind descended into a dark yet comfortable place, far away from the cold realities of everyday life. Time lost meaning as the tug of responsibility faded from reality. His breathing slowed, like a plump bear prepping for hibernation. He slumped against the rear wall like a gunshot victim awaiting the sweet release of death. After a spell of intense yet involuntary meditation, Roy filled his lungs with the stale air of poverty and exhaled a sigh of fortitude.

"Monger District, Northern Ring."

The directory pinged, filtered, and zoomed to an area just below the Kink Rinks. A listing of specialty services filled the wall, everything from bootleggers to exotic traders.

Roy squinted as he scanned the options. "Extractions."

Ping, filter, zoom.

Roy cringed at a selection of mercenary outfits and non-network dentists. "Back."

The directory complied.

"Um ... the Underminer Network."

Ping, filter, zoom. Another list of unsettling options.

"Back."

The directory complied.

Roy sighed and rubbed his face with both hands. "Okay, let's try something different. Reset and open a conceptual search."

The directory pinged and wiped clean. A lonely cursor blinked in the upper corner.

Roy bowed his head and thought for a while, allowing a collection of seldom-uttered words to organize themselves. "Excitement."

The word appeared on the search screen.

"Danger."

The directory appended the list.

"Seductive. Thrilling. Provocative. Extreme."

The list appended each term.

Roy grinned as he studied the input. "Search."

After a short churn, the same dominatrix appeared on the screen.

"Dammit." Roy grunted with frustration. "Reset."

The directory complied.

Roy plunked his head against the rear wall and closed his eyes. "All I want is a break. An actual break from the never-ending bullshit. This life, this fucking life. I want to do something, see something, be part of something, anything, anything with actual consequence. Something that matters to somebody else. Not for money, not for fame, not for the greater good, whatever the fuck that means. I just want to feel something other than regret when I wake up. I want to sleep without hating every second of the day. Is that too much to ask?"

He huffed with chagrin, then lifted his eyelids. Much to his surprise, the directory had recorded his every word into the search field. A blinking cursor hung at the end of a woeful monologue. Roy re-read his own words with a steady and deliberate eye. The weight of every letter settled upon his shoulders. His gut twisted with self-pity. While staring at the cursor, he allowed a single word to escape his lips. "Search."

The directory complied.

After a long churn, it returned a single name.

Roy studied the bio of a larger-than-life character, a scoundrel of sorts with a legendary reputation. It seemed fictitious beyond words, like the profile of an *Indiana Jones* villain. But the name rang true, at least to anyone who had ever gossiped inside Durangoni. The entry offered no calendar, no schedule, only a simple message option.

"New message," Roy said with a stomach full of butterflies.

* * *

Roy awoke several hours later, having gotten less than adequate sleep. In fact, the sleep had been downright shitty, partly due to a throbbing hangover, but mostly due to the intense anxiety over sending an unsolicited message to a fearsome thug. Perhaps an unfounded anxiety, as Roy wasn't the most formidable of assets. A damn good plumber, but a warrior he was not.

He grabbed his comdev from atop the cooler and hesitated before powering it on, like a teenager awaiting a reply from a crush. But alas, no messages. He sighed and plunked the device back onto the cooler.

Roy lifted his aching body from the cot and swung his feet to the floor. A pungent aroma began to tease his nostrils, the unfortunate result of forgoing a shower the previous evening. He had slept in his own funk and went so far as to infect the cot. Thus, a deep and thorough cleaning of his tiny abode climbed to the top of his to-do list. He winced at the inescapable odor, but took solace in the fact that he didn't need to dress for work.

Tired joints cracked and popped as he rose from the bed, drawing a grunt and grimace. A quick scan of the interior uncovered the usual dullness, along with a toppled canteen resting in a small puddle of water. He shuffled over to the puddle, plucked the container from the floor, and finished off the remaining water inside. A sudden need to pee captured his attention, cueing the start of a typical day.

The morning routines for sub-core folk were largely similar. After rousing under a blanket of noise, they emerged from their tiny abodes and stumbled towards the communal wash. A chorus of groans filled the space as residents emptied bowels and prepped for a new day. For once, Roy was a major source of nasal discomfort, but at least the visit would be brief.

The facilities were a menagerie of tiled booths, ceiling faucets, floor drains, shitting holes, and pissing troughs. A constant flow of recycled water entered the space through every faucet and exited through every drain. You simply walked inside, did your business, then got the hell out before things got weird. Despite the constant traffic, the washrooms were not social places. They functioned more like assembly lines with a steady flow from start to finish. There was no privacy, nor qualms about its absence. Modesty is a non-issue when everyone has different parts, different habits, and different hang-ups about said parts and habits.

Roy wandered through a doorless portal and searched for a free space along the troughs. He proceeded to empty his bladder while trying to ignore the disgusting sounds of numerous aliens answering the call of nature. A particularly loud plop and moan forced his brain to contemplate a turn and look. Luckily, his brain locked his neck in place and settled for a cringe.

Roy shook once, shook twice, then crashed his forehead into the tile wall. To be fair, the last part wasn't voluntary. After a sharp yelp and a bout of dizziness, Roy turned to find three naked ringnecks staring him down. The horse-like humanoids stood tall with their arms crossed and massive cocks dangling like grandfather clocks. Three rings encircled each of their long necks, guaranteeing an unpleasant experience for Roy. Without missing a beat, his eyes glazed over as stomach acid began to boil. And without missing the next beat, one of the ringnecks bashed him across the cheek, bringing the defensive trick to a sudden halt. Roy stumbled backwards into the trough, splashing piss as he fell. A room full of naked aliens turned to watch, leaving the whine of water pipes to cut the tension.

"So I hear you don't like ringnecks," one of the ringnecks said.

Roy scanned the room for an out, but found a wall of eyes and swinging willies. A beating for sure, so might as well commit. He locked eyes with the obvious leader and spat at his feet. "Only tri-ring fucks like you and your girlfriends."

The ringneck smirked. "This isn't going to end well for you."

Roy shrugged. "Never does."

The brute hooked Roy by the collar and hurled him across the washroom. He sailed through several water jets on his way to the floor, rinsing away some of the piss. The crowd parted as Roy hit the ground and slid into the far wall. The impact forced a grunt from his throat as he settled facedown in the dirty water.

The ringnecks sauntered across the room with their third legs slapping against their thighs. The leader grinned before burying his foot into Roy's flank. Roy yelped as the others followed suit. They kicked the shit out of him, despite already swimming in a sea of actual shit. One of the ringnecks reared back for another blow, but then shrieked with sudden pain. The other two spun around to find Duncan standing behind them with a death grip on the other's cock.

"Howdy fellas," Duncan said with his usual upbeat tone. He waved with one hand and jerked the other, prompting another shriek.

The victim crumpled to his knees and pinched his eyes shut.

Duncan maintained a vise-like grip as he addressed the other two. "So whatcha doing?"

The leader traded glances between Duncan, Roy, and his suffering sidekick. "Teaching this fool a lesson," he said, gesturing to Roy.

"About what?"

"About being a hateful bigot."

Duncan chuckled and squeezed tighter, drawing a high-pitched squeal. "So you beat on 'em to make 'em hate you less?"

The leader started to respond, but huffed instead.

"For Tim's sake, we live in the sub-core. We all irk someone for some reason, but we smile and nod like civil folk." Duncan turned to his trembling victim. "Wouldn't you agree?" he said, then tugged his tether.

The ringneck swallowed a yelp, gritted his teeth, and hastily nodded.

Duncan smiled. "See? We're all friends here."

The other two traded glances, then softened their stances.

"So if you would be so kind," Duncan said, "help him up and make your peace."

The leader sighed and turned to Roy, who was busy spitting and grousing while rising from the floor muck. The ringneck hooked Roy's arm and yanked him to his feet, drawing a groan and grimace.

"Now give 'em a kiss," Duncan said.

The leader whipped a rattled gaze to Duncan, who laughed in response.

"Just messing with you, friend. We all enjoy a good ribbing. You're free to go, and take this whiny doofus with you." He released his grip and the ringneck collapsed onto the floor, cradling his reddened meat sword.

The other two helped him up and they exited the washroom.

With the excitement over, the crowd returned to their morning routines.

Roy limped over to Duncan and palmed his shoulder. "Thanks, bud."

Duncan winced. "Jeez, you smell ripe. And you're welcome. Care to tell me what that was all about?"

"I may have, um, ranted a bit at The Pipes last night."

"About ringnecks? I thought you liked Bob."

"No, um. I mean yes. I love Bob. I just don't, um—" Roy sighed. "Nevermind."

"Anyhoo, I'm gonna wash up and head to the worksite. You on your way?"

"I was, before getting jumped in the shower. Fuck me, as if this place doesn't resemble a prison enough."

"If you want to wait a tick, we can head up together."

Roy battled a burning desire to flee the washroom, to escape his wounded pride. On the flip side, he also heeded a desire to keep his ass unkicked. His gaze wandered an arena oozing with embarrassment, catching a few glances of pity. Shame flooded his mind, but he refused to show it. He turned to his friend and nodded. "Works for me."

"Okie dokie, won't take long. Just gotta scrub the nethers." Duncan waddled beneath the nearest water jet and released a moan of contentment.

Roy grinned, then glanced down to his soggy clothes. "May as well get a proper rinse." He stripped out of his duds, tossed them aside, and joined his naked brethren.

CHAPTER 6

Clancy Monto Von Schlupnick XLII is the kind of man that women crave and every other man wants to be. Anyone who has ever set foot inside Durangoni has seen his family crest (yes, *those* Von Schlupnicks). This illustrious house has maintained seats of power aboard the station for over 20 generations. While they control an array of business interests, their primary claim to fame continues to be their paper empire. To put it bluntly, wiping your bum with a roll of Von Schlupnick is like wiping with a cloud of virgin kisses. Superior would be an understatement. Von Schlupnick *is* paper.

The unrivaled quality of VS products sets the family apart in ways that need no competitive reinforcement. While they maintain a powerful monopoly, they are also one of the most trusted brands within the station. The Von Schlupnick Society fosters more charities than the next 100 factions combined. Greed is not part of their vocabulary. They worry about power and wealth in the same way that ants worry about dirt. They're awash in it, which allows them to concentrate on philanthropy. In fact, they bring so much good to the station that residents regard them more as benevolent deities.

Clancy grew up in a lap of unimaginable luxury, but he never cared much about it. He has the rugged good looks to grace the cover of Glam Goni (the Durangoni equivalent of Haxfrong Zop Zop on Galwock 36 or GQ on Earth). His lemon-yellow eyes and luscious red lips are the envy of anyone with a pulse. A firm and chiseled body rests beneath a layer of silken fur, giving him the presence of a fleecy gladiator. But despite all of his visual and financial advantages, Clancy prefers the grunt life. He likes to work with his hands and have normal conversations that don't involve undertones of privilege. At a baseline, he's just a regular dude.

Be that as it may, the weight of his family name follows him wherever he goes. An aura of celebrity surrounds him at all times, and even if someone doesn't recognize the inherent status, his attractiveness steps up to fill the void. Clancy takes it all in stride. He views it as more of a mild irritation than a significant problem.

This easygoing attitude is what introduced him to Roy.

I sat down with Clancy several times during my research. What struck me immediately was his complete detachment from entitlement. He's a walking enigma, like someone laser-focused on the little things with a winning lottery ticket in his pocket. The following is an excerpt from our first meeting.

*　*　*

Clancy had constructed a small interview niche inside his Von Schlupnick condo, one of the countless units across the station. It was a modest place near the service line, featuring tasteful decor with a distinct lack of ostentation. If I hadn't known any better, I would have assumed the abode was soundly middle-class.

He settled across from me in one of two cozy chairs. A snazzy vest, of which he had a vast collection, hugged his burly chest. While clothing was certainly optional for his species, pockets remained a necessity. He crossed his legs and leaned back into the soft cushion, prepping for a relaxing chinwag. Heeding the cue, I started my recorder and set it on the table beside me. We traded smiles as I battled a sudden wave of resentment.

Goddamn you're handsome.

Well, that's one way to start an interview.

No, seriously. It's comically absurd.

Thanks.

Your life must be haunted by hungry gazes.

(shrugs)

But anyway, we're not here to discuss your stupidly amazing genes. It just needed to be addressed, lest it linger in the air like an elevator fart.

(chuckles) Fair enough.

As a Von Schlupnick, you grew up inside a bubble of immense wealth and prosperity. And yet, for the most part, you choose to reject that lifestyle. Why?

I wouldn't say that I reject it. I often get misrepresented as some sort of "fight the power" guy, but that's not it at all. Some view me as a spoiled rich kid that somehow broke free of the upper crust, as if my family was forcing me to attend fancy parties against my will. I enjoy nice things. I just don't covet them. I am equally happy with grunt grog and expensive brandy. I don't chastise the uppers, or anyone else for that matter. It's just not a life that appeals to me.

So you never viewed yourself as a spoiled kid?

Of course I was a spoiled kid. Every brat with food in their belly is a spoiled kid.

That's a bit harsh, don't you think?

Let me rephrase. Every kid understands the concept of starvation. Being hungry is a terrible thing. But no kid understands the mechanism of class dynamics. My cousin exemplifies this perception. In fact, I can better illustrate it with a story.

My family owns an obscene amount of real estate aboard the station, much of which is rented by other prominent families. My cousin lives in a massive beach estate on a central ocean ring, one of the most expensive properties in the entire quadrant. We're talking thousands of rooms over millions of square feet, which takes a small army of servants and maintenance personnel just to keep it functional. And that's for a family of *six*.

My cousin and I are the same age. I visited that property many times growing up because our parents are close and we often played together. The adults would dine on posh cuisine prepared by personal chefs while drinking bottles of wine that cost more than most people make in their lifetimes. But all my cousin and I cared about was the temperature of the pool. We got more joy out of splashing each other than the adults got from sipping that wine.

But anyway, my parents are more reserved when it comes to matters of opulence. We are still supremely wealthy, but flaunting isn't something they care for. Our primary home is a sub-level condo about a mile below my cousin's surface estate. It's about 50,000 square feet with a small service staff, much easier to maintain.

My cousin loved to visit. Not to gloat or tease, but to revel in the simplicity. This was a kid who griped about having to walk a quarter-mile between the home theater and his bedroom, and that's without ever leaving the property. He loved the fact that he could wander anywhere in our home and never get lost. That's kid thinking. He couldn't give two shits about the paintings or the floor tile. He just liked that he could find the kitchen.

And you carried that attitude into adulthood.

In a way. I understand the pros and cons of class. I just like being close to the kitchen.

The place we're in now is more luxurious than most people could ever hope for.

My parents would consider it a closet. My cousin's parents would consider it a drawer.

I guess it's all about perspective.

(nods)

Speaking of perspective, tell me how you acquired a taste for grunt work.

I wouldn't say that I acquired it, per se. It's always been there, just in different forms. Even as a kid, I was more interested in *doing* things than *having* things. As a teenager, that meant clubbing and partying and traveling and whatnot. But as an adult, it's all about learning new skills.

The family business is more or less automated at this point, so there's not much for me to do there. I have always enjoyed learning how things work. I was the kind of kid who dismantled toys to study the insides, much to the annoyance of my parents. And what bigger toy than the Durangoni Space Station? I know it's strange to say, but I love working in maintenance. And since I don't need the money, I feel like a surgeon fixing guts. It's really cool.

Even though robots do the most important work?

As they should. Have you ever been to the inner core?

No, can't say that I have.

I have. It's one thing to watch a video or listen to stories, but it's a whole other thing to see the heart beating in real-time. Those engineers are gods. Even if I could work on a system like that, I would much rather it be handled by the AI. I could spend my entire life learning how a tiny piece of it works, and still not fully grasp it.

You hit on an important yet seldom seen perspective. The sheer complexity of Durangoni, the core specifically, has been blamed for the unfortunate length of The Incident. The chaos that it generated was harrowing for the general population. But

given the isolated nature of the upper class, how did the afflu-
ent weather the fallout?

(shrugs) Same as everyone else, I suppose. Power and privilege don't
combat something like that. We just had better homes in which to
suffer, not that it mattered much. I was in the general population
when it happened, spent most of The Incident below the merchant
line. I was hunting for a machine part when the first wave hit.

That had to have been ... interesting.

Yeah. Imagine what you experienced, only surrounded by robo-guts
and sub-core ruckus.

Wow.

Exactly.

**Which, somewhat ironically, brings us to the root of this dis-
cussion. How did you meet Roy?**

I worked on a big project with him many years ago. One of those
major development gigs, station-funded, months of hard work with
massive crews. That's actually how I broke into the industry. It took
me a long time to get regular work because the grunts dismissed me
as a tourist. You know, rich boy slumming it for some misplaced al-
truism. However, I assume you've met Duncan at this point.

(I smile and nod.) Yes.

That pudgy sombitch commands more respect than most CEOs. The
companies fear him, the unions fear him, the politicians fear him, and
yet, he's just a gardener. Duncan is regarded as a gatekeeper of sorts.
If you can get his seal of approval, then you are instantly accepted
into that world. I think he understood my intent and took offense at
my ostracization. He befriended me, as he did with Roy.

Were you three close from the start?

Not really. It took a while to build that rapport. Roy and Duncan were friends first. Roy was the guy who always needed emotional support, but would never admit to it. Duncan, being the father figure type, was always happy to provide it. They had a feedback loop that never ended, and they were both okay with it.

I had casual friends and such, basically chat buddies with no real depth. Roy and Duncan were my first real friends down in the sub-core. Roy was fond of saying that I was the most grounded up-fuck on the station. He goaded me like any friend does, but he always showed me a baseline of respect and never asked for material help. I think he just enjoyed being around someone who didn't have to struggle, to provide that flicker of hope he so desperately needed.

Do you think that desperation pushed him to do what he did?

(ponders for a moment) Perhaps.

You don't sound convinced.

Roy was an odd bird. That's undeniable, even from his inner circle. I considered him a brother before The Incident, which holds true to-day. I was as surprised as anyone to hear that he played such a big role. I haven't seen or heard from him since that day he left the worksite.

* * *

Roy stood in the same fountain that he had departed the previous day. One hand clutched a wrench while the other tapped his thigh. The filter hummed beneath his feet as he listened for anything abnormal. After a few minutes of studying the rippling water like a meditating monk, he nodded with approval and sloshed back to the ledge. He tossed the wrench into his toolbox and plopped on the fountain rim to remove his waders. A knock to the access hatch clanked it shut, concluding the fix.

Clancy strolled up to the fountain with a tablet in hand. "What's the count?"

"Fuck off, bossman."

Clancy rolled his eyes. "Just gimme the count, Roy."

Roy glanced around the garden space while running a mental tally. "This was eight, which means I have four to go."

"Damn, dude. You're crushing it. Nice work."

"Well, it finally dawned on me that they're all indie systems governed by a master router, which makes servicing more linear. Kinda like fixing a light switch without having to kill the breakers. Pretty slick, to be honest. My compliments to the chef."

"At this rate, you'll be wrapped up later today."

"Probably."

"You got all week, so why not relax and milk some overtime?"

Roy glanced up to the exploded terrace where a crew had started to rebuild the framing. He sighed and turned back to Clancy. "Thanks, but I'd rather be done with it."

"Suit yourself, but there's plenty more on the docket if you want to keep busy."

Roy nodded, then rose into a shoulder stretch.

"I'll take some more diddles," Duncan said as he waddled up.

Clancy sneered in response. "You haven't even finished the fern gully."

"It's a delicate process. Those nubbins need tender lovin'."

"Then love 'em faster. You've still got the rompum beds to repair."

"Oh fiddle poop. Nothin' a good weed-bleeder and bone saw won't fix."

Clancy narrowed his eyes and wondered if he should be concerned.

Roy grinned as Duncan and Clancy continued their peculiar argument. He twisted his torso from side to side to relieve some soreness, letting the conversation fade into the background. His gaze wandered the room, surveying the rehab. Saws and hammers echoed around the interior as new wood panels replaced their splintered kin. Fresh foliage was returning by the truckload. The space was healing, much to Roy's chagrin.

And then his comdev pinged from atop the toolbox.

Duncan and Clancy kept chatting as Roy scooped the device without thinking. He glanced down to find the notice of a new message. His eyes widened as an immediate dread crawled up his spine. The entire room faded as he gawked at the tiny white envelope. His trembling finger floated across the screen and tapped the icon, opening the message.

"Well that's just silly," Duncan said, then turned to Roy. "Doncha think?"

Roy stood there in silence, staring at his phone.

"You okay there, Roy?"

No response.

Clancy ruffled his brow. "Yo, Roy. What's wrong?"

Roy snapped out of his trance with a sharp flinch. He stammered like a frightened child while trading glances between the two. His widened gaze locked onto Clancy as fluttering breaths fled his chest. "I, um ... I have to go."

"Go where?" Duncan said.

Clancy offered a slow nod as he weighed the situation. He studied Roy with a mixture of pity and understanding. After a tense silence, he smirked and sighed. "Then go."

Roy glanced at Duncan, then hurried away without another word.

"What the doodle—" Duncan whipped his gaze between the two, tossing neck fat from ear to ear. "What in the dickens just happened?"

Clancy watched in silence as Roy disappeared into a service tunnel.

* * *

(staring at the floor) That was the last time I saw him.

Did you ever find out what the message was?

No, but I didn't need to. I've seen that look before. I've been around too many schemers to know when a game-changing opportunity presents itself. That was his shot.

To do what?

To fix whatever was broken, for better or for worse. It's debatable as to whether he understood the consequences, but I doubt he did. Roy was never smug or malicious. At least, no more than the average grunt. I could only assume that he had found an escape hatch.

To where?

(shrugs and smirks) Anywhere.

CHAPTER 7

When an asshole gets an idea, it's rarely a good thing for anyone within shitting distance. More often than not, the asshole gets kicked in the teeth and paints the room with feces, leaving everyone around them with a horrible taste and a hefty cleaning bill. Should it not be obvious at this point, I am comparing Roy to a giant asshole.

As I plowed through my research on The Incident, it became more and more apparent that the general public was less and less informed. Roy was a hero to them, for whatever baffling reason. It's not like he Robin Hooded through the station and filled everyone's credit account. Quite the opposite. The public paid dearly for his deeds through mental and financial hardship. And yet, no one seemed to care.

Puki Horpocket cared.

Puki Horpocket wanted answers.

My quest for said answers took me on quite the tour of the space station. With the help of various locals, I visited several places that I never would have found on my own. Yes, even as a distinguished editor for the Definitive Directory of Durangoni. It would seem that my all-access pass had granted me access to diddly-squat.

Roy had served as a decent tour guide, despite his lack of physical presence. Fiona, Duncan, and Clancy had provided crucial insights into Roy the struggling father. I had loosened the knot, but in order to unravel it, I needed insights into Roy the bumbling crook. The path was apparent, but plunging those depths required more than trunks and a snorkel. I needed gainful access to the station's most notorious trafficker.

As an interesting side note, my research never uncovered the message that Roy received in the garden. Comdev services are technically forbidden from recording chat logs, giving them a wall of deniability. Roy never forwarded the message or backed up his data. He was also careful to guard the message in public, as if watching porn on the subway. Thus, it was never revealed to security footage. I could only study him as he studied the message.

But as with any mystery, digging deeper reveals the truth. At the very least, I would learn *who* sent the message and *why* it was sent.

* * *

Roy tore through the crowded tunnels as if competing in the 100-meter push and shove. He racked up more insults and crude gestures than a brombo shuttle slag (the local equivalent of a New York taxi driver). Not that he cared much, as his brain was laser-focused on a sudden sprint to the Rich Rings. Not the most inspired of labels, but it got right to the point. The Central Rings housed most of the commerce while the adjacent Rich Rings housed most of the wealth. Credits flowed freely between them.

Roy arrived at the nearest pod station as an express connector was loading. He shoved his way aboard and received plenty of curses and sour looks. A hologram map glowed overhead, highlighting the current station and the next several stops. The map zoomed out as the train departed, allowing Roy to plot the necessary connections. His racing mind manifested as rapid mumbles and finger-pointing, like a cult leader speaking in tongues. Several passengers hugged their bags and recoiled. Roy glanced around the pod and offered a sheepish smile to the worried eyes staring back at him.

A ping sounded overhead, signaling that the rear pods were about to break away from the train. Access doors allowed riders to shuffle around as needed. Roy snaked his way to the back and settled inside a unit bound for the sub-chutes. Moments later, the pod split from the train and dove deeper into the station. After several twists and turns, it picked up speed and merged into an express tunnel en route to the next ring.

Lighting panels zipped overhead as the pod melded into a north-bound train. Roy knew the route well as a Kink Rinks regular. But this time around, a nervous apprehension had replaced his usual cloud of depression. He glanced around at his pod mates, a collection of random faces on their way to nowhere. A strange realization drew an unexpected smile. For once, he was the most interesting person in the pod.

The train sliced through a vacuum barrier and into open space. Or rather, the empty space between rings. Time seemed to slow as the colossal walls of the central rings climbed into the atmosphere far above. Massive pipelines snaked from the core like blood vessels, gifting life to Durangoni. Roy lifted his gaze to the heavens where sunlight poured into the breach, painting the drab metal with a bright yellow sheen. Countless ships of all sizes floated through the beams like motes of dust. Roy marveled at the view, one he hadn't seen in months. It always rang as distant and foreign as the people it represented.

But not today.

This time, he sensed an invitation.

And with a blink, it was gone.

The train punched through the next barrier and into the adjacent ring, refilling the pod with pulses of passing light. Roy sighed and lowered his gaze to the floor, content to pass the time in his own headspace.

The remainder of the journey morphed into a restless slog. Roy double-checked his course with every ping, but even so, he almost missed a crucial split. A sudden panic yanked him to an adjacent pod just before the doors closed. He made it, but his heart began to race with the train. As his destination approached, he fidgeted like an excitable toddler. The official ping of arrival forced a cold chill down his spine.

"Am I really doing this?" he said to nobody.

"Huh?" said a voice beside him.

Roy turned to find a stylish teen with long hair and a limp expression. The image caught him off-guard, forcing him to realize that the onboard clientele had drastically changed. Roy glanced around a cabin filled with shopping bags, swank attire, and glittering jewelry. He could sense an air of intrusion, like a redneck at an opera. Several leery eyes stared back at him.

Roy frowned and returned his gaze to the teen. "Nothing."

"Miss your stop?"

Roy opened his mouth to respond in snark, but paused to appreciate the boy's naive honesty. He sighed instead. "Yes."

"That sucks."

"Ah well, misses happen."

"Truth. Safe journeys, bro."

"You too ... bro."

Roy cracked an actual smile. It was the most pleasant conversation he'd had in months, all by way of a random rich kid. Maybe there was hope for the world after all. But not really. The crush of misanthropy quickly returned to invert the errant smile.

The pod train slowed to a stop. As the doors opened, a rush of perfumed air caused Roy to cringe. Not out of disgust, but from pure surprise. He was so used to the sub-core funk that an actual floral scent confused his brain. His legs locked into place as he cycled through memories of what green things smelled like. After a brief loiter, a throat clear from behind jolted him back to attention. He waved an apology and stepped out onto the station platform.

The sight before him flooded his mind with awe. He paused inside a pocket of traffic to admire the sophisticated nature of life in the Rich Rings. Elegant chandeliers hovered along the ceiling, emitting the ethereal tones of heavenly bodies. Sleek kiosks promoted posh doodads and luxury getaways. Sculpted panels covered the walls and ceiling, the life's work of some forgotten master. Ritzy locals wandered by as if it wasn't the most breathtaking artistry they had ever seen. And of course it wasn't. Roy hadn't even left the train depot yet.

He double-checked his comdev and zeroed in on the appropriate tunnel. Hologram signs and directional colors made the task much easier, a notable improvement over the crude etchings he was used to. He merged into the flow of traffic and prepped his brain for an onslaught of visual stimulus. Sure enough, the tunnel ended at a vast bazaar bursting with opulence. Every boutique housed more retail value than his entire sub-core sect combined. It was a staggering amount of wealth in a concentrated area, something his brain couldn't quite process. With mouth agape, he gazed around one bazaar of one sector of one level of one ring.

With his comdev outstretched, he wandered towards a far tunnel and repeated the process through another series of ritz-marts. Soon after, he ducked behind a specific kiosk and slipped into a narrow service tunnel. Dim lights passed overhead as he crept through the corridor. He strolled beneath a final arch to arrive at his destination.

Or rather, the secluded square that housed his destination.

He glanced around a small pocket of modest pubs, serving as a break area for rich shoppers in need of a cheap drink, but without being seen. Hand-painted signs and dark wood exteriors gave him a fleeting sense of comfort.

And there it was, The Craven Compass, a small pub with a plain badge hanging over the entrance. The perfect place for an illicit affair. Roy closed his eyes, argued with his brain for a moment, then gathered his wits and stepped towards the door.

Roy flinched as a sharp ringing sound greeted his entry. He glanced overhead to find a brass bell attached to the wooden frame. Given the nature of the locale, he rather admired the primitive charm. His gaze fell into a hazy interior that radiated passé. Nothing fancy, nothing garish, just simple forms and pleasant patterns. A cramped dining area surrounded the central bar, where a handful of patrons filled a limited number of stools. They all ignored him, content to nurse their suds in silence. Soft jazz played in the background, loud enough to be noticed, but removed from conversation. A single bartender glanced up while drying a mug with a hand towel.

Roy steadied his breath and stepped towards the bar. He gripped the back of a stool, but did not take a seat. The bartender was a slender chap with green skin, thin lips, and a sharply forked nose that doubled as a mustache. He eyed Roy with mild distaste before lifting his brow, asking *Can I help you?* with the least possible effort.

"I would like ..." Roy paused for thought. "A single-malt Matrondin with two cubes."

The bartender looked him up and down without moving his head, then reached beneath the counter and pressed a hidden button. Soon after, a brutish fellow in slick attire emerged from a side door. Without a word, he glared at Roy and motioned to follow. Roy gulped, then tailed the bloke through the rear kitchen. A sole cook with a bloodstained apron paid them no mind. He smoked a cigarette while handling an agitated snoodlecock. The colorful bird squawked as they passed, startling Roy into a hanging pot. He quelled the resulting bong and muttered an apology to the cook, who continued to deny his existence.

The brute exited the kitchen with Roy in tow and proceeded down a dim hallway. He strolled to a stop at an unmarked door, one of many along the passage. He knocked twice, listened for a faint reply, then gripped the knob and turned to Roy. The hinges whined as the door swung open. Roy took a deep breath and stepped inside.

A hairy beast in a gaudy leisure suit sat behind a large wooden desk. It chewed on a plump cigar, needling the air with wet smacks. A pair of stumpy horns poked through a mane of brown fur. Large red eyes gazed over a bovine-like snout. Thick forearms with meaty paws rested atop the desk, a smooth plane with minimal clutter. A reptilian minion with purple scales and slitted yellow eyes stood behind the beast. It wore black slacks with polished shoes and a button shirt, creating the unsettling image of a serpentine accountant.

"You must be Roy," the beast said with a guttural tone.

"Y—yes," Roy said. "It's, um, a privilege to meet you, Mr. Gamon."

"Gamon is fine."

"Yes sir."

"Not sir, just Gamon."

"Yes si—Gamon."

Gamon chuckled. "It's okay, friend. Relax."

Strangely enough, Roy did relax. The command alone from such a lofty mogul was enough to soothe the nerves. He stood in the presence of the mighty Gamon, victorious in his effort to rewrite the playbook, at least for a day. Roy took a measured breath and nodded.

Gamon gestured to a chair in front of the desk. "Have a seat."

Roy stepped forward and complied. He took a moment to admire the chair's sturdiness, a far cry from the rickety stools back in the sub-core. Roy glanced around a small den with very little decor, temporary in every sense of the word. An overhead light with a pull string served as the sole source of illumination.

A tense silence gripped the space as Gamon scrutinized the visitor through a narrowed gaze. He exhaled a puff of smoke through his gaping nostrils and shifted the cigar to the other side of his mouth. "So you're a plumber," he said with a snide tone.

Roy adjusted his posture. "Yes. Been working the station for over a decade."

"Tell me, then. How would you replace a busted T-line with high saline content?"

"Steel connector with greased-up niners."

The reptilian huffed. "*Niners?* Are you serious? Why in the hell would you not use—"

"A grump link?" Roy glared at the minion.

"Y—yeah."

"Because the threads are pre-coated and tend to corrode, especially when moving acidic content. Sure, they'll last a good long while, but niners are die-cast and last forever. Grump links are pretty and easy to install, but I prefer reliability over aesthetics."

Gamon glanced back at the minion and smirked.

The minion sneered in response.

Roy allowed himself a brief grin before Gamon returned his attention.

"So enlighten me, mister plumber. Why are you here?"

Roy scrunched his brow. "Huh?"

"Did I stutter?"

"Um, I sent you a message."

"I'm aware. But *why* did you send it?"

"I, um ..." Roy trailed off and glanced away.

"It's not a trick question, friend. You are aware of my trade, yes?"

Roy hesitated before responding. "You're a trafficker."

"Of what?"

"Of ..." Roy thought for a moment. "Of nothing."

Gamon nodded. "Good. So again, why are you—"

"Because my life is a worthless grind and I don't want it anymore."

Gamon grinned and leaned back in his chair.

"I'm halfway through this failure of existence and I have nothing to point at. Everything I do benefits someone else. I don't care about fame or fortune, or any other status-laden bullshit. All I want is to participate in something with real consequence. Actual repercussion, not just some empty thrill. I have skills. Applicable skills. I'm a first-class architect and a kick-ass engineer." Roy huffed and shrugged. "So why the fuck am I cleaning other people's shit?"

Gamon rapped his fingers on the desk, filling the room with dull taps of contemplation. He glanced over his shoulder to the reptilian minion, who flicked his tongue in response. The cigar shifted as he studied Roy with mysterious intent. He offered a slight nod, then folded his hands on the desktop. "Mister plumber, I need you to unclog a toilet for me."

A painful silence gripped the room.

The minion smirked.

Roy cocked his jaw, then closed his eyes to scream internally. His dignity swirled around the virtual drain and disappeared. He slapped the armrests and started to rise, initiating the long trek back to the shithole from which he came.

Gamon raised a palm, halting Roy's ascent. "Perhaps you didn't hear me, friend. I need you to unclog a toilet ... on the Sunken Isles."

The reveal sucker-punched Roy like a slighted ex-girlfriend. An eyelid twitched as his jaw slacked open. His gobsmacked brain abandoned his forearms, dropping him back into the chair with an awkward plunk.

Gamon grinned. "Do we have an understanding?"

Roy fainted and tumbled to the floor.

* * *

It should come as no surprise that the meeting between Gamon and Roy was not recorded. Gamon was too smart to allow something that stupid. This all comes from a firsthand account, namely the minion over his shoulder, a hatchet man by the name of Zip.

Do not let the cutesy name fool you, Zip earned his nickname through a ruthless efficiency, especially when it came to murder. Zip was an assassin's assassin, someone called into the fray when zealots overplayed their cards. As his many fans put it, he offered "clean whacks to dirty hacks," an event often referred to as "getting zipped."

I should reiterate that Durangoni Security is a force to be reckoned with. They snuff out the vast majority of criminal elements. However, the most clever and nefarious crooks know how to work the system from within. *That* was the pool Zip played in. In fact, Durangoni largely ignored his exploits, regarding him more as an unpaid contractor.

I say that he *was* an assassin because my interviews with Zip came by way of correctional visitation. He now lives as a captive inside the Durangoni prison system where he is serving a two-year sentence for vandalism. Ironic, by definition. Without going into too much detail, let's just say that he got some blood where it didn't belong. The guards know exactly who he is and what he does. He even speaks freely about his unsettling deeds, which are simply dismissed as fanciful fictions. Just some bloke waxing poetic ... about murder.

Much to my surprise, I liked Zip from the very beginning. Our frequent chats revealed an honest and receptive person, considerate even. He paints a worldview that is unemotional and pragmatic, which allows him to do what he does without any sort of undue attachment. In the end, the only thing he covets is a job well done.

Unlike Roy, I actually grew to respect the reptilian reaper known as Zip. Roy had always treated him like rubbish and used him as a convenient punching bag. The fact that Roy retained his head (presumably) is nothing short of a miracle. I can only chalk it up to Zip's dispassionate need to complete his tasks in a clean and timely manner.

I learned a great deal about Roy through the frank and candid lens of Zip. In fact, I would argue with clarity that Zip provided the clearest insights into Roy's perplexing character. Below is an excerpt from one of our many conversations.

I am starting to get the impression that Roy was an unpleasant person.

Roy was a dick. (hard pause)

Well, okay then.

But, considering his lot in life at the time, I would probably be a dick too. He was mad at the universe and everything in it, so it's understandable in a way. He was also very good at what he did, so I never held it against him.

Did he know about your, um, activities?

No, and it was better that way. Roy talked a lot of smack, but he never struck me as someone with an iron stomach. Gamon saw him as a blind but useful gopher. His expertise opened doors that would have otherwise required infiltration.

Speaking of Gamon, how did you two end up working together?

We met through a mutual need. Gamon runs one of the biggest distribution networks on the station, an up-and-up outfit that I greatly respect. He's one of the best getters in the game, so our paths would naturally cross at one point or another.

To make a long story short, he got conned by one of my marks, some headstrong thug with a penchant for backstabbing. Gamon offered a squeeze job and I took it. We split the return after I split the mark in half. We've been working together ever since.

(A ping interrupts the chat, followed by a guard's voice. "Good one, Zippy. You and your stories." The guard laughs nervously, then goes silent. Zip grins.)

You should have seen it. The halves peeled apart like a cheese sandwich and slapped the floor like sacks of wet blankets. The chainsaw was so wrecked, I had to throw it away.

(Ping. "Ha! Such a vivid imagination, this guy." Silence.)

In fact, I left it there in the bloody muck and winked at the nearest camera. I'm sure the footage is out there somewhere if you want to do some digging.

(Ping. "La la la, not listening. La la la." Silence.)

* * *

DISCLAIMER: The Durangoni Office of Corrections does not condone or corroborate the actions described in this work of fiction. Randal P. Throatslitter (a.k.a. "Zip") is serving an appropriate sentence for involuntary vandalism. He is an otherwise upstanding citizen of the Durangoni Space Station and no evidence of additional wrongdoing has been verified by our department. For reasons still unknown, he is often the target of elaborate pranks aimed at tarnishing his respectable image. We cannot stress enough that his depictions in this book are exaggerated for dramatic effect.

CHAPTER 8

There's annoyingly opulent, there's overly extravagant, there's stupidly ostentatious, there's jaw-droppingly exhibitionistic, and then there's the Sunken Isles. The simple act of explaining this locale requires some expositional flair, so I must apologize in advance. However, building the appropriate image is critical to understanding why Roy fainted in Gamon's office.

To set this stage, let's take a giant step back and define what the Durangoni Space Station actually is. This gargantuan structure endures as one of the biggest construction projects in the history of the universe. It took centuries to plan and a millennia to build. It contains more steel than the next thousand systems combined. It orbits a star as an artificial planet because it carries enough gravitational force to rip itself apart. It's large enough to have its own atmosphere and seasons, all of which require careful planning. There are beings living aboard the station right now who earn a decent living forecasting the artificial weather of an artificial world.

Durangoni houses a trillion active residents who populate the station from surface to core. It is not uncommon for beings, workers especially, to live out their entire lives inside the structure without ever setting foot (or tentacle) on the surface. As with most indulgent safaris, a trek to the surface is often regarded as too expensive. It's much easier, and arguably more enjoyable, to visit the nearest sensory deprivation service.

The surface is a realm of riches, and the Sunken Isles take it to an absurd new level.

Dissatisfied with *just* being on the surface, a wealthy pioneer decided to create a *new* surface *below* the surface. How? By enclosing a floating island inside a transparent dome and sinking it beneath an artificial ocean.

I know, right?

Grab a drink and strap in.

Floating islands are a common sight along the Rich Rings. Their surfaces are loaded with luxury resorts, sandy beaches, and numerous harbors for expensive yachts. An artificial ocean stretches around the entire structure, made possible by a miles-deep trench. The walls and base are fortified with aluminum, often a hundred meters thick at the highest pressure points. The combination of strength and lightness puts minimal strain on the station. Apart from the core itself, nothing was planned more meticulously than the ocean rings. After all, a single breach would result in a catastrophic loss of life. A solid decade of stress tests and bomb trials were performed before a single drop of water was poured.

Filling the trenches was its own titanic hurdle. A single ocean ring contains 500 quintillion gallons of water. This far outstripped the local system, so a fleet of ice harvesters was deployed to nearby comets. They dismantled entire worlds and hauled mountains of ice back to the station. The mega-payloads were deposited into the trenches where armies of robots chipped them into meltable chunks. Rocks were pulverized into sediment, allowing treatment plants to filter and repurpose it as sand for beaches.

The massive rings are wide enough to create a horizon, so standing to either side creates the image of a vast and expansive ocean. Filtration systems run around the clock, keeping the water crystal clear and pathogen-free. Their primary purpose is to act as giant aquifers. The immense pressure supplies fresh water to the entire station, rendering circulation pumps all but useless. In fact, the only pump system inside Durangoni does nothing but carry water from core basins back to surface treatment.

Station designers foresaw the appeal of ocean rings, and thus marketed their access to the uber-wealthy. Floating islands were constructed and sold to the highest bidders, often the richest beings in the universe. The custom isles were several miles in diameter and featured an array of trimmings, from palm trees and sandy beaches to volcanic rock and exotic flora. Owners were free to build on them as desired, so long as they continued to pay the ocean access fee, a sum that infused the station with a reliable (and substantial) income. The designers had created a veritable gold mine, but even they did not foresee the advent of the Sunken Isles.

Ocean access fees did exactly what they were designed to do, in that they gave island owners access to the ocean. The only problem was, the agreements never clarified what "ocean" meant, i.e. just the surface. Owners were free to use personal submarines, but nothing explicitly forbade them from turning the entire island into a submarine.

And that's exactly what Mimi Moxarion did.

Mimox, as she was known, decided that owning a floating island on a colossal space station was not exclusive enough. She, like every other island owner, was awash in affluence. Wealth at that level transcends the material world to become a competition in and of itself. It's not enough to raise a virtue flag that only a handful of beings can raise. Your flag needs to be the *only* flag.

And so, she sank her island.

Not in the traditional sense, of course. She hired a superstar team of engineers to tackle the problem, which took several years to solve. But solve it they did, and many island owners were justifiably concerned when a giant glass dome consumed their neighbor and plunged it into the ocean depths.

Mimox had raised her flag.

But it didn't last long.

Excessive wealth tends to short-sight its owners. Mimox had assumed that her neighbors would bow to her grandeur while stewing in surface jealousy. They did no such thing, because she failed to recognize a crucial piece of the equation. Her neighbors may have been filthy rich, but her superstar team of engineers was decidedly *not*. And so, they packaged the dome plans and sold them to her neighbors.

Mimox's reign ended as quickly as it began. Before long, numerous islands sank into the great blue yonder, creating a network of subterranean tropics. The Sunken Isles was born, and remains one of the most exclusive communities in the known universe.

Even so, Mimox decided to sell her island and purchase her own star. Her never-ending quest for ultimate exclusivity came to a fiery end when she constructed a lavish station home in lower orbit, the first and only "sundo" (sun-condo). The views were spectacular, but her wealth proved useless against a coronal mass ejection.

* * *

Roy and Zip strolled down a sleek corridor with no one else in sight. The white walls and seamless panels gave Roy a sense of purpose, as if tromping towards a research ship bound for adventure. And in that sense, he wasn't far off. Zip, on the other hand, maintained a forward stare as his swanky shoes clacked along the floor. His classy garb stood in stark contrast to Roy's workman duds. To the average passerby, one might assume that Zip had caught a pickpocket. But in that particular sector, the very notion of a passerby was a laughable concept.

Near the end of the tunnel, an oval portal came into view. It clung to the wall as the sole feature inside a spacious white foyer. A pair of glass doors split the port in half, leading into a dark tunnel with no markings. It would seem that anyone standing inside that particular room knew exactly where they were and where they were going.

Anyone except for Roy, of course.

Zip strolled to a stop at the center of the foyer, placing him several meters away from the portal. He crossed his arms behind his back and stared at the glass doors. Roy settled beside him and released a muted sigh. Not from annoyance, just happy to rest. Zip had slapped him awake after fainting in Gamon's office. "Follow me and mind your lip" was the command, which Roy heeded while nursing a throbbing headache. The journey up to that point had been a convoluted maze of back channels and ghost pods. The mental fog had started to clear, but Roy had no idea where he was. His gaze bounced between Zip and the portal doors.

"So—"

"Shut the fuck up," Zip said without making eye contact.

Roy swallowed a snarky retort and huffed instead.

Moments later, the dull hum of an approaching pod broke the silence. The stark tunnel slowly filled with light, signaling the arrival of a transport vessel. As it crept into view behind the doors, Roy could tell that it wasn't a normal pod. It was longer, sleeker, and a tad more ostentatious. In other words, it was a private vessel.

The doors slid open, revealing a robed male with tawny skin and prominent jade eyes. He floated into the room with strips of red fabric dangling from his folded arms. Green and gold accents gave him a kingly vibe, or at the very least, an assumption of status. An intricate head wrap matched the robe in weight and color. Roy did not recognize the species, but based on its stout frame and menacing build, it was not one to be trifled with. The creature glided to a stop between the portal and the two visitors.

"Hello, Zip," he said in a pleasant baritone.

Zip nodded. "Good to see you, Werner."

"This the plumber?"

"Seems to be."

Werner grunted, then turned to Roy. "You a plumber?"

"Last time I checked," Roy said.

Werner narrowed his gaze. "Given a flarkian framework with two gromples, three saromarko switches, and a pavrav gauge, how would you reverse a pressure spike of 200 wronks?"

Roy cocked an eyebrow and glanced at Zip.

Zip replied with a nonverbal *Answer the goddamn question.*

Roy returned his gaze to Werner, then shrugged. "Well, given that I was about to die, I would probably rub one out."

"Pardon?"

"You know, flog the cap'n. Spurt the sprite. Visit the knuckle circus."

"Um ..."

"Any pipe jockey worth their salt knows that two gromples on the same line with a pavrav gauge is a recipe for disaster. That's why half of the surrounding quadrants have outlawed the practice. You could, in theory, use a pavrav plus, but that only reduces the knock-fail from 80 to 60. And 200 wronks with *three* saromarkos? That would give you less than two minutes before a catastrophic decoupling, hardly enough time to reverse a damn thing. So again, I would probably rub one out and hope to finish before the end."

Werner eyed Zip, who rolled his eyes.

"What I *think* you are trying to ask," Roy said with a cocksure tone, "is how would I reverse a pressure spike with three saromarko *platinum* switches, a very important distinction. They are designed to negate the swells of outdated regulator tech like gromples. In which case, I would cut power to the first saromarko and spin the pavrav down to 50%. The overall pressure would drop by 25% and stabilize on its own while the other two saromarkos cancel out the gromples. And then I would *still* rub one out all over the console just to stick it to the fuck nugget who botched the configuration."

An awkward silence settled between them.

Werner nodded slowly, then turned to Zip. "I like 'em."

"That makes one of us."

Werner chuckled into a sigh. "Does he know?" he said, basically asking *Does this little twerp know that you are a ruthless murder machine that would happily gut him like a fish and wear his spleen as a hat?*

Zip sneered and shook his head.

"Know what?" Roy said, trading his gaze between the two.

"Forget about it," Werner said, then motioned for the pair to join him in the vessel. "This way, mister plumber."

* * *

Perhaps the most memorable moment from my interviews with Zip came by way of a peripheral encounter. I had asked about the events leading up to the meeting with Werner (an immensely powerful individual who we will examine shortly). Zip pondered the question for a time, as if to choose his words carefully. What I assumed was leery contemplation was anything but. He just wanted to show me the breadth of his reputation.

Zip plucked a cigarette from his pocket and tucked it between his lips, for no other reason than he could. Smoking was banned throughout the station, doubly so in prison, and triply so during visitation. Zip wasn't even a smoker, come to find out. But amazingly, a nearby guard hurried over and promptly lit the cigarette. Zip took two puffs, then snuffed it out in the guard's open palm, all while maintaining eye contact with me. The guard swallowed a whimper, then hurried back to his post and struggled to ignore the pain.

To say I was rattled would be an understatement. For the first time along the journey, the depths began to test my mettle.

Um ...

What was the question again?

That was ... something.

(Ping. "The guard was upholding the station's strict no-smoking policy by extinguishing and removing the contraband.")

(I lift my gaze to the overhead speaker.) With his own flesh?

(Ping. "Standard procedure.")

(My widened eyes return to Zip.)

(smirks) Shall we continue?

Yes, um ...

(I glance around the enclosure, feeling somewhat shaken. Zip tunes into this fact and seems to enjoy the squirming. With my dignity waning, I can do nothing but stiffen my posture and reclaim an air of confidence. And so I do. Or at least I try.)

So, um, Gamon was in cahoots with Werner Xizon Pyrak? *The* Werner Xizon Pyrak?

Everyone is in cahoots with Werner in one way or another. Given the nature of his empire, it's hard not to be. (leans forward) Where do you think your Ruutzo coffee comes from?

(Ping. "Ruutzo coffee is an illegal import and subject to customs inquiry. Should you be caught with this contraband, you will be arrested and prosecuted to the fullest extent of Durangoni law. The minimum sentence is six months in a correctional facility and a fine of 10,000 credits. An enforcement team has been deployed to 623 Bartonian Row, R312, section B4.")

623 Bart—that's my apartment!

(Ping. "Should they find any Ruutzo coffee, you will be immediately detained.")

(Zip responds with a casual wave, as if to reject pepper on his salad.)

(Ping. "I mean ... nevermind.")

(My gaze jumps between the injured guard, the overhead com, and a disturbingly calm Zip.) Um ...

Is that your favorite word?

Um ...

Exactly.

So ...

Um.

(The teasing actually resets the mood, much to my surprise. I crack a smile, despite witnessing the shocking influence of a feared assassin in real-time.)

So how long had Gamon been working with Werner?

(shrugs) Not for me to know.

I only ask from a standpoint of disparity. It seems odd to me that Gamon would let a greenhorn like Roy anywhere near someone like Werner.

You and me both. But at the same time, this was a perfect storm scenario. Werner was in desperate need of assistance, and Gamon was in desperate need to provide that assistance. Anyone below the fold knows that when Werner asks, you deliver.

Or else ...

Or else they call me.

But you were there already.

Which concerned me a bit. You see, for someone like Werner to press someone like Gamon, there had to be something critical on the line.

Like what?

(Zip leans back and crosses his arms. This time, in leery contemplation.)

* * *

As a necessary disclaimer, Puki Horpocket has never and would never consume Ruutzo coffee, despite its delicious and uniquely robust character.

While it remains an illegal substance inside Durangoni, its chemical profile is no different than any other variety. Ruutzo beans contain prototypical amounts of acids and alkaloids. The ban is entirely political in nature.

Ruutzo is a rich volcanic region of Neaz, a lush moon that orbits a desolate planet in the Abell cluster. Its parent system is largely devoid of life, except for Neaz and a hearty form of methane plankton. The Neazan people remained independent for eons, but decided to join the Federation in hopes of expanding their economic reach. Their impact was quick and fruitful, thanks in large part to their delicious produce.

However, the honeymoon period would not last long. Neazans are known for many things, but tact is not one of them. Their ruler at the time, a narcissistic chap with thin skin, insulted the quadrant ruler at the time, also a narcissistic chap with thin skin. They exchanged verbal blows, resulting in a silly battle of wits that ended with a trade embargo.

But as with most prohibitions, it had precisely the opposite effect.

The demand for Neazan goods shot through the roof, creating a thriving tourist economy that generated far more wealth than trade. The moon transformed into a luxury retreat that welcomed deep pockets from every corner of the cosmos.

When the quadrant ruler realized the mistake (read: panicked over the enormous loss of revenue), he offered to lift the embargo, but refused to apologize. The Neazan ruler famously responded with a single word: "Melamook." (Neazi is a complex language that is difficult to translate on a good day. The closest Earth reading would be "Nah, fuck you.")

The embargo has remained in place ever since.

CHAPTER 9

Roy and Zip strolled through the portal and into the sleek vessel. Werner followed them inside and the doors closed behind him. Roy's widened eyes combed the interior of an oval pod without a single sharp corner. A long bench with plush yellow padding encircled the cabin. The upper half was crafted from transparent composite, offering sweeping views of the dank tunnel interior. Obviously not the intended vista, which prodded Roy with nervous anticipation. Grip rails extended from a central hub, like the posh version of a rickety carnival ride. The vessel, it would seem, was designed for speed as well as comfort.

Roy stepped around the hub and settled onto the bench directly across from the doors. Zip and Werner sat near the front, not that the vessel had a front, given its symmetrical build. The front, in this case, was the area pointing down the tunnel. The opposite side faced a solid wall, which clued Roy into a key realization. The port was less of a train stop and more of a launch chute. His eyes traced a dim row of tunnel lights down to a blue barrier in the distance. Instinct compelled him to search for a seat belt, but Werner and Zip had relaxed into their seats without much care for safety. *When in Qwarp*, he thought, then leaned back and draped his arms across the rear cushions.

* * *

Qwarp is widely considered the galactic equivalent of Rome. Its rise
and fall were largely similar, just on a cosmic scale. It even had a
charismatic leader who got murdered by his best friend. But instead
of a tragic "Et tu, Brute?" end to his reign, he mooned his comrades
and shouted profanities before perishing mid-rant. History books
have largely ignored that part.

* * *

"Initiation complete," said a pleasant feminine voice.

"Alpha Tower," Werner said.

A ping responded, followed by a soft hum of initiation.

The vessel began a slow creep through the tunnel. Roy leaned
forward out of habit, but the sensation of motion was almost imperceptible. Tunnel lights whipped overhead as it gathered speed towards the blue barrier. Werner and Zip remained unfazed. They exchanged some casual banter, forcing Roy's headspace to waffle between *everything's fine* and *we're all gonna die.* As the barrier approached,
it finally dawned on him. It wasn't a barrier at all. It was a pressure
gate leading into the ocean.

The vessel punched through the gate and into the blue abyss.
The transition was seamless, like a drop of water joining the whole.
Roy watched the gate fade behind them before lifting his astounded
gaze to the sea. The surface shimmered far above, but something else
had dropped his jaw. A massive braid of cables lifted from the depths
and clutched a suspended platform several miles across. It floated in
the void, encased by a towering dome of glass.

There it was.

An actual Sunken Isle.

The braid anchored the platform to the ocean floor, where it
tapped into various service lines. Titanium tethers prevented the

domes from crashing into one another. Countless conduits snaked around the tethers, feeding the isles with power, plumbing, and a host of other needs. Roy rose to his feet and twisted around the enclosure with mouth agape. A multitude of domes and braids floated in the deep like a school of monstrous jellyfish. Never in his wildest dreams could he have concocted such a vision.

"First time here?" Werner said.

Roy collapsed back into his seat, heeding a pair of weakened knees. His eyes continued to scan the glorious vista above. "First time anywhere. I live near the core and my work keeps me there. When I do break away, it ain't to a place like this."

Werner smirked.

"So ..." Roy's gaze wandered over to Werner. "You need a plumber?"

"Yes," Werner said with a matter-of-fact tone.

Roy responded with a blank stare, clearly expecting some details, but derailed by receiving bupkis. His eyes shifted as he searched for a reasonable follow-up question. None of them were as relevant as the first, so he kept staring like a stoned hippie.

Werner sighed and glared at Zip. "Did Gamon not give him the rundown?"

Zip shrugged and deflected the glare to Roy.

"What's your understanding of the situation?" Werner said to Roy.

"All I heard was 'plumber' and 'Sunken Isles' before I passed out."

Werner groaned and shook his head. After a brief ponder (and another glare at Zip), he crossed his arms and locked eyes with Roy. "Are you familiar with Subatomic Transport?"

Roy snorted-chuckled. "You mean Shrink Ray Shipping?"

Werner narrowed his gaze. "It's a little more complicated than that."

"And illegal as hell. You remember that whole, um ... y'know."

Werner narrowed his gaze further.

"But yes, I'm familiar with it. At least, as much as a peasant can be. Something about sucking atoms dry."

"Well, that's a grossly uneducated way to put it."

Roy sneered in response.

"Atoms are mostly empty space. The physical matter consisting of the nucleus and electrons only occupy a tiny fraction of the whole. The concept behind Subatomic Transport is to remove that space for ease of shipping."

"Like a shrink ray," Roy said with a smarmy grin.

* * *

"Shrink Ray Shipping" was a highly offensive nickname in the industry, of which Werner was the top dog. The methodology received widespread mockery when a giant dildo untethered from its gravity-bind and re-expanded inside a space station, destroying the structure and killing everyone inside. When images emerged of a massive pink cock inside a giant debris cloud, one reporter said, "Well that station got proper-fucked." The clip went viral and Subatomic Transport was swiftly outlawed, deemed far too dangerous for commercial use. "Shrink Ray Shipping," as the media dubbed it, was relegated to powerful sects of organized crime.

* * *

Werner huffed and glared at Zip (again) while reconsidering the arrangement.

Zip sighed and rolled his eyes while reconsidering a double murder.

After some more-than-obvious social cues, Roy sensed the contempt and could feel his appeal slipping away. "Sorry," he said with a sheepish tone. "Bad joke."

"Anyway," Werner said, "my distribution network still uses this tech in a ... somewhat flexible capacity. Do you understand?"

Roy nodded.

"We move great quantities of goods between buyers and sellers.

Simple as that."

"Okay. So why do you need a plumber?"

"Sometimes a shipment gets contaminated. When a corrupted unit expands, it activates the whole and sparks a catastrophic inflation. We can normally deal with this at an extraction facility, but certain cargo types require a little more discretion."

"You didn't answer my question."

Werner smirked, then reached into his breast pocket and withdrew a puck of material. He tossed it at Roy, who caught it with an awkward fumble.

Roy opened his palm and inspected the mysterious puck. It was a few inches wide and forged from a glassy resin. Smooth to the touch, but very hard and heavy. The puck was lighter than an ingot, but dense enough to be dangerous. Roy could tell right away that its rounded edges were more for safety than aesthetics. A clump of dark matter rested in the center, which consumed a third of the overall volume.

"What is this?" Roy said.

"42 billion vials of medication."

"*Billion?*" Roy eyed Werner in disbelief. "How is that possible?"

"Mass retained, space removed. Atoms locked in stasis."

"But it's so light. How do you account for weight?"

"And *that*, mister plumber, is why I'm a very rich man."

Roy grunted, then bounced the puck in his hand. "So what's the drug?"

"Snake Bone."

Roy yelped and dropped the puck, which clanked on the floor and wobbled to a rest.

Werner grinned.

* * *

Roy's fearful reaction was far from unwarranted. Snake Bone is a highly addictive, highly dangerous, and highly illegal drug. It has a complex chemical makeup and a lengthy technical name that willfully neglects vowels. "Snake Bone" is the go-to slang, which was earned during another viral news clip.

A pair of field reporters was filming an info-series about the effects of illegal drugs. One would stay sober and serve as the interviewer. The other would trip on various drugs and serve as the interviewee. It was promoted as a scared-straight campaign, which enjoyed notable success. Some episodes were funnier than intended, but still applauded. Others were steeped in horror and deemed highly effective.

And then there was the Snake Bone episode, the most infamous of the bunch.

The drug was notorious for its strong hallucinogenic effects. It occupied a strange realm in the drug trade because it carried no biological threat. It was largely benign, no more dangerous than a weak cup of coffee. However, the psychedelic effects were second to none. The drug sent the user into a kaleidoscopic dreamscape (or nightmare) that lasted for days.

And therein lay the danger.

The prolonged exposure resulted in countless deaths. There was no such thing as "bring a friend and enjoy the ride." A user could start tripping on their own couch, then wake up a week later in the next quadrant, naked, bloody, and in desperate need of a lawyer.

The drug was developed as a psych med, which worked a little too well. The problem was, the powerful trip was often stronger than the patient's incapacity, rendering them as lethargic as a Goth teen. As they say, when you stare into the void of truth, there's nowhere left to go.

Snake Bone eventually slithered into the public sphere, which created an immediate and voracious demand. The resulting black market basically ran itself. It can be a highly profitable venture for anyone willing to shoulder the risk. Durangoni houses a powerful security force with very little oversight, so the risk can be substantial. "Bone Brokers," as dealers are known, often disappear without a trace.

But anyway, back to the episode.

One reporter took a dose while the other sat and waited. He didn't wait long, because things got weird in a hurry. The imbiber gawked at his own limbs, which had developed minds of their own. The sober reporter commenced the now-infamous short-lived interview. While staring into the great beyond, the drugged reporter uttered the most memorable line of his career: "My bones are snakes, and that's the least of it." The poor fool was carried to the hospital, where he tripped in a padded room for several days.

From that day forward, the drug was forever known as "Snake Bone."

* * *

Roy had scurried to the opposite end of the vessel. He stood atop the bench with his back to the wall, pointing a shaking finger at the puck. "What in Tim's Blue Hell are you doing with 42 billion doses of Snake Bone?!"

"I figured that would be obvious," Werner said.

"That's some wicked fucking voodoo right there!"

Zip pursed his lips and nodded in agreement.

"Oh for fuck's sake." Werner rose from his seat and moseyed over to the puck. He scooped it off the floor and banged it against a grip rail. Sharp clanks echoed around the cabin, causing Roy to flinch with each hit. "This thing can withstand a million plasma blasts. You're in no danger, so get your filthy feet off my leather."

The sting of ridicule pulled Roy down to the floor. He cowered like a scorned puppy and shuffled back to his original seat.

Werner grumbled as he pocketed the puck and returned to his own seat.

Zip had donned a disconcerted expression as he stared off into oblivion, reliving his own wayward adventures with slithering bones.

Moments later, the vessel breached the surface, sending ribbons of water down the hull and showering the cabin with sunlight. However, this was not the actual surface, nor the actual sun. The vessel had breached the atmospheric bubble created by Werner's Sunken

Isle dome. They were now inside a private tropical paradise, complete with sandy shores, lapping waves, and an artificial weather system.

The shuttle hovered above the surface as it pushed towards the nearest shoreline. A mile of water rested between the dome and the island, creating a liquid donut of sorts. The island itself was held at the center by a strong magnetic field. Roy could see dunes and palm trees along the shore as the vessel approached, but strangely enough, no structures. The plot was barren, like a ghostly desert in the middle of nowhere. He stood for a better view, but uncovered nothing. The platform lingered as little more than a blank canvas.

"Well that's disappointing," Roy said.

Werner cocked an eyebrow. "What, an entire island suspended beneath the ocean is not good enough for you?"

"No, I mean, I thought these were supposed to be like, luxury resorts or something."

"This isn't that kind of island."

Moments later, the shuttle transitioned from water to land, churning a cloud of sand in its wake. It floated up the first dune, zipping by palm trees and grassy mounds. Roy watched with cautious interest as the vessel crested the sandy hill. The beach disappeared, snapped away by a sudden transition. The rim of a giant metal valley passed below the vessel, initiating its descent towards the center. The bowl stretched for several miles in every direction, consuming the vast majority of real estate. Its white sheen created the image of a massive satellite dish, primed and ready to receive its digital bounty.

But it wasn't that kind of dish.

The vessel slowed as it approached the center of the dish. Roy glanced around the interior, now awash in reflective light. The rim towered over them like a peakless mountain. A sense of intrusion filled Roy with unease. This was a guarded place, a deep chasm that few knew existed. A place, he presumed, that he could lose his life for seeing.

Werner studied the plumber's reaction without saying a word.

Zip maintained his disinterest. Either he'd seen it before or didn't care in the slightest.

The shuttle pinged, then slowed to a stop and lowered to the ground. The doors slid open, prompting Werner to rise and mosey towards the exit. A gust of tropical air swirled around the cabin. Roy inhaled the briny sweetness, which jostled some distant memories. He could see his homeworld. Bronze beaches, copper sunsets, the same salty air. His cheeks puckered as a smile crept across his face. An actual smile, conjured by a long-neglected muscle memory. And then his ex-wife leaned into the mental frame and killed it all.

"Goddamnit," Roy said. "She even got my memories in the divorce."

"Come again?" Werner said from outside the shuttle.

"Nothing." Roy sighed, then noticed the puck in Werner's hand.

Werner grunted with dismissal, then retrieved a docking device from his pocket. A pair of rounded claws protruded from the handheld base, like a comdev with a handcuff attached. Roy squinted with curiosity as Werner affixed the puck and entered an activation code. The device pinged and a mounting rod rose from the dish. It stopped at chest-height, allowing Werner to connect the device. A drop and twist locked it into place, creating the unsettling portrait of a hostile lollipop. Werner wiped his hands and returned to his seat inside the vessel. The doors closed and the shuttle continued its journey across the dish.

Roy watched the puck assembly fade into the distance as the shuttle climbed its way to the upper rim. He cocked his neck and turned to Werner, clearly confused by the action. Questions were mounting, but a strong apprehension kept his mouth shut.

Werner smirked at the plumber.

Roy was in the game now, and they both knew it.

* * *

Suffice to say, my conversations with Zip provided the most detail into Roy's underworld antics. And given Zip's utter indifference to his captive status, I had no reason to doubt him. It should also be noted that Werner's Sunken Isle dishworld no longer exists. The very nature of The Incident would ensure its destruction.

Roy still had no idea what was happening?

He may have had a clue, but I couldn't say for sure. In any regard, Roy had gleaned enough smarts to roll with the punches. His insolence was hard to wrangle, but even he could see that silence equaled survival.

Just so we're clear, Werner was transporting 42 *billion* doses of *Snake Bone.*

(nods) Yup.

And that didn't concern you?

(shrugs) Why would it?

Well, for starters, that's easily one of the highest capital offenses one could imagine.

You say that like Werner suffers the law.

Doesn't everyone?

(chuckles) *That*, Mr. Horpocket, is adorably naive.

(Ping. "The enforcement power of Durangoni Security is absolute. No individual, citizen or otherwise, is above the law.")

Seems like a reasonable assertion.

(smirks) Garko! Punch yourself in the face!

(The guard behind Zip sighs, then removes his helmet and wallops his own cheek.)

Again!

(Smack.)

Again!

(Smack. His nose begins to bleed.)

Thank you, Garko.

(The guard wipes the blood from his face and puts his helmet back on. Zip softens his smirk and gives me a subtle nod, as if to curtsy after murdering my calm.)

Point taken.

(Ping. "Did something happen? Our feed cut out for a moment.")

CHAPTER 10

Roy turned his attention to the approaching rim, where a lone pillar loomed over the giant basin. The structure stood several stories tall and resembled an airspace control tower, complete with an observation deck. The opaque glass gave it a menacing persona, like an evil eye standing watch over its domain.

The shuttle crested the rim and slowed to a stop beside the tower. The doors slid open with a ping of arrival. Werner and Zip stood from their seats and wandered outside without a word. Roy stayed put, partly out of fear, partly out of confusion. The decorum he knew no longer applied, so he awaited basic instructions like a nerdy kid at summer camp.

Zip moseyed towards an entry door at the base of the tower.

Werner paused and turned back to the shuttle port. "This way, mister plumber."

Roy took a deep breath, then rose to his feet and exited the shuttle. He passed through the oval port and stepped down to a concrete platform that surrounded the tower. Several palm trees lined the perimeter with green fronds rustling in the wind. Roy lifted his gaze to the bright blue sky. Or rather, the dome's projection of a bright blue sky. A handful of white clouds roamed the space, blotting the artificial sun from time to time. Roy could feel the heat on his skin, leaving him to wonder if the dome emitted radiation. *Definitely a question for another time*, he wisely thought to himself.

"Is this actual UV?" Roy said.

Werner cocked an eyebrow. *That's your most burning question?* he conveyed without saying a word. He turned towards the tower and resumed his approach.

Roy swallowed the scorn and followed.

A short trek later, the group reassembled outside the tower entrance. Zip stood in front of a drab gray door with his arms crossed. Werner paused alongside and turned to Roy, who took his final steps.

"Understand, mister plumber. What you are about to do cannot be undone. Your actions from this point on are a pledge of confidence. Should you violate that confidence, your life, as well as the lives you cherish, is forfeit."

Roy gulped. "Understood."

"Good. Then let's unclog this toilet."

Zip grabbed the handle and yanked it upwards. The door clanked like a bank vault, then swung open with a slow whine. Werner floated into the tower base, a drab receiving area that housed an elevator shaft and little else. He summoned the lift as Roy shuffled into the dim room with arms pinned to his side. The trapped air was thick with humidity, no doubt from baking in the sun all day. Zip followed him inside and latched the door shut, turning the dim sauna into a dark coffin. The elevator pinged soon after and a door slid open, revealing a cramped car that two people would find uncomfortable.

Werner stepped inside, spun around, and pressed his back to the rear wall. Roy followed him in and filled much of the remaining area, careful to avoid Werner's personal space. Zip pushed his way inside and crammed Roy into a corner, dropping any pretense of civility. He pressed the only available button and the door slid shut.

An awkward silence filled the space, broken only by the dull hum of ascent. Roy yearned for some cheesy elevator music to break the tension, but he would have to make do with the screams inside his head. Luckily the ride was short, four stories by his estimate. A ping of arrival echoed through the cabin and the door slid open. Zip exit-ed the car, leaving Roy to peel himself off the wall and regain some dignity.

"About time you got here," said a stern feminine voice.

Roy peeked into a control center filled with chirping gauges and blinking lights. He searched for the voice, but was cut short by Wer-ner shoving him in the back.

"Had to fetch the plumber," he said. "You know that."

Roy stumbled to a stop outside the elevator. Werner floated around him and into the control room, a rounded enclosure about ten meters wide. A small observation deck rested at the center, which Werner claimed. It loomed over a large crescent terminal with three distinct stations. The entire console faced a panoramic viewport that overlooked the basin. Various live feeds hovered above the port, eve-rything from dome views to puck zooms.

"And where did you fetch him from? The Kink Rinks?"

Roy turned to the central station, where a chair swiveled towards Werner. An alien female with light blue skin and dark lips revealed herself. Fleshy black dreads were pulled into a ponytail, with single strands dangling above her cheeks. Her build was short and stout, but her attitude towered over the group. Large amber eyes hurled visual daggers at Werner, dismissing Roy's presence altogether.

"We've been waiting here for *hours*," she said.

Werner shrugged. "Gamon had a lead, which took a bit to snag. You know the drill, so feel free to get off my back."

She huffed and turned to Roy. "This the guy?"

"Yup," Werner said. "Sharp fella, too."

Roy allowed his gaze to wander, combing her from head to toe like a creepy pervert. A leather ensemble clung to her frame, giving her a stylish yet practical vibe. The duds looked well-lived and well-loved, a quality that instantly captivated Roy. When his eyes reached her studded boots, she snapped him to attention.

Roy flinched and met her disgusted gaze.

She whipped a finger at the adjacent station. "You're over here, fuckwit."

Roy grinned as if she had asked him out to dinner. He traced her rigid arm to the station on her left, where Zip was prepping the console. Roy sauntered over to the chair as her berating of Werner continued in the background. Zip completed his task and stepped aside, allowing Roy to assume the position. He plopped into the chair, then cracked his knuckles and fanned his fingers as if to work a pipe organ. A hologram grid of bars and gauges glowed beneath his hands, the nerve center for the island's pumps and pressure controls. Each section linked to a map of the isle, creating a handy mental image. A quick scan uncovered nothing abnormal, just standard functions on a massive scale.

"Any questions?" Zip said from over Roy's shoulder.

Roy pictured himself back at The Pipes, adjusting pressure gauges with beer in-hand and a roaring backdrop. "Nope. Piece of cake," Roy said, and actually meant it.

Zip patted his shoulder and stepped away, a rare moment of camaraderie between the two.

Roy smiled, gave the controls another once-over, then spun towards the bewitching beauty that was his console neighbor. She ignored his peripheral gaze, content to trade verbal barbs with Werner. Roy watched her flailing fists and spewing saliva through an amorous glow, but then an insectoid leaned into view from behind her. Roy flinched and kicked backwards, startled by the reveal. The creature occupied the third station, but hadn't said a word since they arrived. Its buggy eyes stared at Roy with an unsettling curiosity, like a praying mantis pining for a snack. A bronze carapace with spikes and nubs rendered clothing unnecessary. Without warning, it lifted a plated hand with needle-like fingers and ... waved politely.

Roy returned the wave after a horrified pause.

The insectoid nodded and went back to its own business.

The background commotion returned to Roy's ears.

"That's quite enough, Vierra," Werner said in retort.

A sudden rush of butterflies invaded Roy's stomach. His gaze jerked over to Zip, who was leaning against the wall next to the elevator shaft. Zip cocked his brow and nodded, as if to say, "Yes, *that*

Vierra."

Vierra Belliosa was a living legend inside Durangoni, a superstar engineer who designed several of the core's modern components. As the story goes, she grew weary of her rock star-like fame and decided to abandon her post. She offloaded most of her wealth and disappeared into the station to work on projects that sparked her interest, everything from perpetual motion machines to helping random kids with their science projects (under a pseudonym of course). However, her core systems were so complex that only she knew how to maintain them. Realizing this, she left a summoning program behind, the Durangoni equivalent of the Bat-Signal. Whenever a critical problem arose, the engineering team launched the signal, prompting her to log into the servers and fix it remotely. She became a literal ghost in the machine.

"Don't you dare patronize me, you wormy little shit," Vierra said to Werner.

Werner signed. "Okay, okay, calm d—"

Vierra cocked her chin and pierced him with a nonverbal *Say it and I'll eat your soul.*

Werner swallowed his words and recoiled, opting to change the subject as quickly as possible. "Alright then, shall we get this show on the road?"

Vierra narrowed her gaze, lobbing a final *fuck you* before spinning back to her station.

Zip slurped a mug of coffee in the background, which diffused the tension a bit. There was something about a well-dressed reptilian enjoying some hot java that felt supremely out of place in the current predicament. Even Werner turned to look, which seemed to reset the entire stage. Zip was surprised by the sudden attention, which he responded to by taking another wet slurp. Werner sighed, then spun to regain control of the room.

"Okay, listen up," he said with a clap.

Roy swiveled to face him.

Vierra ignored him, but kept an open ear.

The insectoid spun to face him, crossing two of its six limbs.

"We have a corrupted puck that needs cleansing. Same dealio, different locale. But for the sake of the new guy and the ... let's say, *problematic* nature of the contents, I'm going to lay this out crystal clear. Capiche?"

They all nodded, albeit in different directions.

"Each of you controls a critical aspect of the island."

Werner pointed at Roy. "Plumbing."

He pointed at the back of Vierra's head. "Systems."

He pointed at the insectoid. "Electrical."

The insectoid chirped in response, which the console automatically translated. "Tight," it said in a metallic voice.

"You're a gem, Orick," Werner said, then turned his attention to the giant dish outside the viewport. "What we have here are 42 billion units of pharma, each housed in their own titan orb container." (Read: super strong, yet oddly light baseball.) "We are going to expand ten million units at a time, all of which will drop into the basin and roll to the reservoir for processing." He tapped an icon on his own control panel. The base around the puck mount detached in sections and lowered from view, exposing a large drop zone beneath the dish. "With me so far?" he said to the group, but eyed Roy.

Roy nodded.

Vierra grunted.

Orick chirped. "Locked and cocked," the console said.

"Each expansion will take a few minutes to process. Ten million into 42 billion is a lot of time sitting on your asses, so get comfortable."

Vierra sighed.

"When the corrupted unit expands, it will cause a chain reaction that expands the rest. We hope to have at least half of the units processed by that time, which will minimize stress on the isle. Please understand that atomic space is *created*, not *consumed*. Therefore, you are going to see spikes in pressure, equilibrium, etc. Your job is to manage those spikes, the worst of which will occur during the chain reaction. Do you understand?" He eyed Roy again.

"Yes sir," Roy said.

Vierra grunted.

Orick chirped. "Indeedily do," the console said.

"Good. Then prepare for the first extraction. Orick, spin up the rod."

Orick chirped. "On it, bossman," the console said as he spun to his station.

Roy heeded the cue and spun to his own station. He tweaked a few settings to get a feel for the hologram controls. Not that there was any feel, per se, but the motions were quite intuitive. The tech used finger positions and eye tracking to gauge response, which it did extremely well. Roy, after all, was used to a more tactile experience. His muscle memory was filled with grips and twists, not taps and swipes. In any regard, he took to the system like a xanpurk to plorpis. (Read: a blind duck to cold soup. An odd translation, but still technically works.)

With prep complete, his gaze lifted to the live feeds overhead. The mounting rod and puck clamp were glowing with a massive energy charge, expelling pops of blue lightning. The puck itself was pulsing with its own current. A deep purple glint flashed and retracted several times per second, giving the impression of a building climax. The entire rig hummed over the drop zone like a star swelling to supernova.

Roy held his breath.

Orick chirped. "Ready to pop pop pop," the console said.

A hush consumed the tower.

Even Zip, the avatar of detachment, craned his neck for a better view.

Werner pulled his gaze across the console, then over the live feeds, then down to the basin. He expelled a weighted sigh, then gestured to Orick. "Release."

Orick tapped a large green icon.

The puck emitted a burst of purple light and belched a hulking mass of titan orbs. They raised high into the air and spread like the petals of a glittering flower. Ten million orbs rained into the bowl like an explosion of popcorn. A sonic boom crashed into the tower, drawing an involuntary gasp from Roy. Windows rattled as the blast bounced around the isle dome. Waves of silver orbs tumbled down the gentle slope and vanished into the drop zone.

The event left Roy wholly dumbstruck. His jaw dangled as he watched the orbs from afar, like a steely ocean disappearing through a massive drain. A handful of icons blinked from green to yellow, signaling a disturbance in the force. He corrected some minor pressure tilts, restoring the island to its baseline. *Easy breezy*, he thought to himself.

"Systems?" Werner said to Vierra.

"Fine," she said like a petulant preteen.

"Electrical?"

Orick chirped. "Smooth 'n groovy," the console said.

"Plumbing?"

"All good," Roy said.

"Excellent. Orick, you have the floor."

Orick chirped. "Cool cool cool," the console said. "Round two incoming."

Another pop, rain, and roll.

Another island reset.

Werner nodded with approval, then joined Zip for a cup of coffee.

Soon after, they did it again.

Orick chirped. "Round three incoming," the console said.

At this point, one might ask, what would be the chances of the entire lot exploding on the third round? Well, that would be a simple computation: 42 billion units, divided by 10 million per round, minus two completed. That's a one in 4,198 chance.

And unfortunately, that's exactly what happened.

A flash of purple light thundered into a gigantic mushroom cloud. The blast consumed the basin and blotted out the sky, shrouding the isle in darkness. A colossal plume of orbs careened off the dome and rained across the island like a monstrous hailstorm, pelting the beaches and splashing into the ocean. The entire structure whined like a wounded whale. The ground quaked as a violent shockwave toppled trees and conjured sand tornadoes. A tidal wave of orbs crashed into the tower and washed over the rim like a raging tsunami.

The control center erupted into chaos. Every feed flashed red with critical alerts. Alarms blared from the console as Werner and Zip watched helplessly from the observation platform. Vierra stood over the central station, swiping and tapping furiously while shouting commands. Orick squawked while playing whack-a-mole at his station. The console barked "Fuck! Fuck! Fuck! Shit! Fuck!" as a reasonable translation.

Roy, on the other hand, remained oddly quiet. The initial explosion had drawn a sharp yelp, but then he fell silent. He digested the problem and leaned back in his chair, having decided that the situation was properly fucked. His console flashed alerts like a red-tinted strobe light, but he didn't seem to mind. Unlike everyone else in the room, Roy had a secret superpower (minus the acidy spit). As a regular at The Pipes, he knew how to relax inside a cauldron of chaos. And so, he stood from his chair and wandered to the rear for a cup of coffee.

The Sunken Isle, on the other hand, was ready to implode.

"What the fuck are you doing?!" Vierra shouted at Roy.

Werner and Zip echoed the sentiment through gobsmacked faces.

"Fuck! Fuck! Shit!" the console continued.

Roy poured himself some coffee, then turned back to the group. He lifted the mug for a sip, but then the tower jostled. He wobbled for balance and was able to save the spill. He smiled and winked at Werner. "That was close."

Zip's dumbfounded gaze whipped between Roy and the empty chair.

Werner shouted questions at Vierra, who shouted back heated retorts.

Orick kept abusing the console translator.

Roy sipped his coffee while studying the live feeds. Data panels whizzed through alerts like hurried movie credits. After a spell of contemplation, he wandered back to his station and stood over the controls. All eyes turned to him, not that he noticed or cared. He took another sip, then tapped a master switch near the bottom of the console. With a calm and steady finger, he swiped across a long row of icons, sending power to them all.

Then it began to rain.

The dome opened all of its shower lines, dousing the island with an artificial rainstorm. Moments later, a few pressure icons blinked from critical to caution. Then they blinked from caution to nominal. The rest of the icons followed suit, slowly returning the island to baseline pressures. Systems restored. Electrical recovered. Alerts and sirens faded away. After several harrowing minutes, the entire network had stabilized. Billions of titan orbs still littered the island, but the implosion had been neutralized.

Roy took another sip while watching the rainfall. A smile puckered his cheeks as droplets pattered the cracked viewport. His gaze fell to the console, where an effects panel snagged his attention. He tapped a lightning icon, which generated some flashes and thunder. "Neat," he said, then took another swig.

He turned to the group, who had retained their wide-eyed stares at the plumber.

Vierra stuttered into a question. "Wha—what just happened?"

Roy shrugged. "Controlled pressure reversal."

Orick chirped. "Huh?" the console said.

"Well," Roy said, "the orbs displaced a shit ton of space, which pushed a lot of water beneath the dome and out into the ocean. The shorelines dropped over 50 feet, but I couldn't just re-flood the beaches. The suction alone would have swamped the island. I couldn't release the valves all at once, because, well, big fucking red flag to station security. We needed a slow re-introduction of loss, preferably from above the shoreline." He leaned onto the console and took a cocky swig. "So I made it rain."

Vierra replied with a slight grin.

Orick chirped. "Fuckin' a," the console said.

Werner stepped down from the platform and over to Roy's station. He slowed to a stop and nodded intently, as if to contemplate his fate. After a tense silence, Werner unraveled his arms and extended an open hand. "Stellar work, mister plumber."

Roy smiled and completed the shake.

* * *

Zip stared at his folded hands atop the table. It was the only time I saw him show a hint of emotion. I will never forget that moment. It felt like unearthing a glittering diamond after toiling in the darkest of mines.

Roy saved your life.

(nods) Saved us all.

And yet, you still hold him in contempt?

(shrugs and resumes his menace) An asshole savior is still an asshole. And besides, his long march to the Jackass Hall of Fame had only just begun.

CHAPTER 11

It should be noted that the Definitive Directory of Durangoni does not report on the private lives of citizens. (Unless they are rampant exhibitionists and request that we do.) Citizens are free to provide personal details, but default profiles are limited to residential addresses. What citizens do inside those residences is known only to them.

This fact rings doubly true for the Sunken Isles. Their owners remain some of the richest and most powerful beings in the universe. As such, they are largely invisible to the prying eyes of the government. In a very real sense, they *are* the government.

This is why the Snake Bone Mushroom Cloud Extravaganza cannot be confirmed. The only thing I know for certain is that Werner Xizon Pyrak had owned the isle in question and no longer does. In fact, there is no evidence to suggest that the expansion basin even existed at all. I can only rely on firsthand accounts, one of which is a murderous psychopath. That alone would be enough for any reasonable reporter to dismiss the event outright. Or at the very least, take it with a giant grain of salt.

But as with every shady tale, there's always a tiny ray of light.

In spite of all the barriers erected between me and the truth, I managed to secure another firsthand account. One that I was honestly shocked to acquire.

Vierra Belliosa.

In the time-honored tradition of full disclosure, Vierra actually reached out to yours truly. Word had reached her ear that I was writing a book on Roy. She spent a great deal of time with the green-skinned folk hero and I was initially skeptical of her intent, but she put my worries to rest shortly into the interview.

Per her invitation, we met at a beach resort on her favorite ocean ring. Below is a faithful transcript from that meeting. Readers be warned, she has a spicy persona and revels in candid language. Delicate ears may find offense.

* * *

There is something you should know about Puki Horpocket. As an esteemed editor for the most widely used periodical on the largest space station in the cosmos, the term "casual" rarely applies to my lifestyle. When I go to work, I wear a suit. When I meet a friend for drinks, I wear a suit. When it's time to shower, I take off a suit. And so, you could probably surmise what I was wearing when I strolled up to a straw hut at a luxurious beach resort. To say I looked out of place would be a gross understatement. I looked like a secret agent, minus the secret.

The sand in my dress shoes was starting to chafe, so I was relieved to park my bum on a barstool. A handful of patrons surrounded the square hut. They sipped on frilly cocktails while eye-humping each other in skimpy beach attire. I selected the corner nearest the water, which afforded me glorious views while cloaked in shade. Lounge chairs and umbrellas littered the sands, most of them occupied by superb specimens of the physical form. The exclusivity of ocean rings meant that perfect bodies abounded. Every time I visit, I always leave a little less confident in my own appeal.

Vierra must have picked up on this insecurity, because she goaded me from the minute she sat down. I didn't even see her coming. As I was gazing across the shimmering ocean waves, a blue-skinned female in an orange bikini plopped onto the barstool next to me. Her fleshy dreads were hanging free, framing her alluring amber eyes. I remember thinking that she looked alien, despite living on a colossal space station filled with a trillion aliens. Her features and proportions were slightly exaggerated, like a cartoon come to life. She oozed confidence from the get-go, despite flaunting an average build among a sea of god-like physiques. I could sense right away that she didn't have to prove a damn thing to anyone. She was a legend, and the gods were lucky to be in her presence.

Vierra Belliosa, I presume.

Whaddup, whore?

It's Horpocket. Puki Horpocket.

I didn't misspeak, jackass.

(We share a brief yet awkward silence. Vierra motions to a bartender, who promptly fills a shot of rum and sets it in front of her. She tosses it down her gullet and cluck-slides the glass back to the bartender.)

In any regard, it is both an honor and privilege to meet you.

Mhmm.

But I must admit, I am very surprised to be here at all. Zip was more amenable, given his incarceration. But you? I would have figured that anonymity was paramount.

Psh. I am the very essence of untouchable. My systems keep this bitch afloat, so an action on me is akin to suicide. They know that, I know that, and they know that I know that.

It's often said that pride goes before the fall.

(chuckles) *Pride?* I suffer many emotions, but pride isn't one of them.

That seems unlikely, given your momentous achievements.

I'm proud of my work, sure. But that's not the same as pride in stature. Think of it like this, someone can take pride in baking the world's greatest meatloaf, which is an entirely subjective ranking. I have no interest in such acclaim. I would rather invent the *oven* that bakes the world's greatest meatloaf. At that point, I control the baker's reputation. Never underestimate the desire to maintain status. People will drain their bank accounts before they part with cool points.

This coming from one of the coolest citizens in all of Durangoni.

(shrugs) Never sought it, don't care if I lose it. I can't help the fact that people think my shit is worth sniffing.

But you have created some of the most sophisticated systems that govern our world. Hell, your relay network alone has assured the purest drinking water throughout the station. If anyone has earned a bask in the spotlight, it's you.

(huffs) Bragging is for broken people. I don't give a fuck about notoriety. And besides, being awesome is like being pretty. If you have to tell people you are, then you're probably not.

So why did you reach out to me then?

Because I care about Roy. I don't want to see his name dragged through the mud.

Well, he *was* the driving force behind The Incident.

(smirks) Was he now?

You disagree?

Didn't say that. But now I'm curious to hear your take.

Fair enough. Let's start with the Sunken Isle episode. According to Zip, Werner Xizon Pyrak solicited the help of three professionals, including Roy and yourself, to cleanse a subatomic transport puck, one that was filled with illegal contraband.

That's right.

As Zip further explains, the extraction went awry and Roy single-handedly saved the island from a catastrophic implosion.

Correct. He "made it rain." (She chuckles and slaps the counter.) Still makes me laugh. You know, despite his foot-in-mouth proclivity, he did have a healthy sense of humor.

What happened to all the Snake Bone orbs?

Cleaned 'em up, I suppose. Our work was done, so we left. I imagine Werner brought in one of his reduction crews. It was a total fucking mess. The entire water rim looked like a kiddie pool stuffed with floatie toys. Probably took weeks to rectify.

Did you and Roy leave together?

No. Zip took him back to Gamon. I didn't see him again until the casino job.

Ah, the casino job, which set the stage for—

Listen, chatterbox. (She leans forward and rests on her elbows.) You may print my words so long as you print them all. Understand?

Yes.

Roy was a good guy. A talented guy. Not just some cocky prick with a few skills to rub together. Sure, he was brash and pettish, but what underappreciated artist isn't?

You make him sound like some sort of genius.

He was, in his own way. I wouldn't trust him to watch my nirfop (read: near-immortal cactus). But, he could stand side-by-side with any core engineer. It still boggles the mind that he was working as a plumber and living in the sub-core. With a little guidance, he could have been a Durangoni superstar. Make sure your readers understand that.

I will. You have my word.

(Vierra motions for two shots of rum, which the bartender promptly supplies. She pushes one over to me, which I hesitantly accept. We clink our glasses and toss them back together. Vierra clunk-slides hers back to the bartender while I cough and hack like a wuss.)

What in the bloody hell was that? Borklum battery acid?

(She chuckles and motions for two more.)

* * *

A small service pod sailed through the open space between two central rings. It was alone inside a void of nothing, whipping along an invisible tube of magnetism. The drab hull served as a stark contrast to the sleek trains passing overhead. Cargo movers were designed to blend into the background. They were the unseen drones that worked around the clock, making them ideal transports for nefarious types.

Zip and Roy sat inside, staring at each other from opposite walls. Waning sunlight peeked through small viewports, not that either of them cared. It was hard to find interest in such things after nearly perishing on a Sunken Isle. The day was effectively shot, so they sat there in silence, staring at each other, but lost inside their own heads.

The crates they sat upon were strapped to the wall, as was everything else. Cargo did not need comfort, so the ride was much bumpier than the shuttles. Sharp turns resulted in stiff arms and sore shoulders. Zip guarded a bag that squished around like a sack of gelatin. It was a large duffle with sturdy straps, one of which wrapped around his scaly hand. Zip had retrieved it from the tower base just before they departed. The constant sloshing had needled Roy's curiosity since the moment they left. He knew not to pry, so he kept his mouth shut.

"What's that?" Roy said and pointed at the bag.

The other plumber, Zip thought. "Laundry," he said after a brief pause.

"Sounds like it needed more time in the drier."

Sounds like you need a knife to the throat. "Perhaps."

Roy nodded, then resumed not saying a damn thing.

The pod punched through a vacuum barrier at the base of the next ring and began its winding approach to the shopping district. Before long, Zip and Roy found themselves strolling through the same bazaars back to Gamon's lair. Luxury surrounded them, from swanky shoppers grazing jewelry counters to the glittering chandeliers hovering along the ceiling. Roy eyed it all through a brand new lens. What had once teased his envy now struck him as oddly tedious. Zip ignored the hubbub by default, content to march forward without distraction. Roy studied his partner's stride, finally realizing that the snazzy duds were little more than a clever disguise.

Zip ducked behind a familiar kiosk and into a dim service tunnel. Roy followed him inside, maintaining a close proximity. The squishing bag caught his attention again. He eyed the duffle and cringed at the unpleasant sound. It wasn't laundry. That he knew. But what he really wanted to know was ... scratch that. He didn't want to know.

A sharp ping echoed inside the tunnel. Roy patted his chest and pants before fishing his comdev from a rear pocket. *Probably Duncan checking in*, he thought. He tapped the screen, read the message, and stopped dead in his tracks.

Zip noticed that he was alone after a few steps, forcing him to stop and turn to a bewildered Roy. The bag sloshed as he sighed and backtracked to his partner. "What's wrong?" he said with a hint of annoyance.

Roy stared at his comdev in disbelief. "I, um ..."

"Spit it out, plumber. We don't have all day."

"I'm ... *rich*."

"Huh?"

"I just received a deposit for 250,000 credits. Look." Roy flipped the screen to Zip.

Zip shrugged. "Yeah, so? That's your payment for the job."

"*Really*? This is more than I earn in a *decade*."

"Sounds like you have a shitty career."

Roy stuttered in response, waffling between shock and offense.

"Listen," Zip said with a more affable tone. "Werner is one of the most powerful beings in the universe. He controls a level of wealth that you and I can only dream of. He could wipe his ass with that payment and never miss it. And besides, you just pulled his ass from the proverbial fire. All of our asses, for that matter. You earned every cent of that bounty. If anything, you were underpaid." Zip turned away and continued his trek down the tunnel.

A wide grin stretched across Roy's face. He glanced at his comdev, huffed with immense satisfaction, then jogged to catch up.

* * *

I watched with fascination as another guard set a fresh cup of tea on the table next to Zip, along with a small assortment of sugars and creamers. This from a corrections officer with a plasma weapon attached to his belt.

I had officially entered Opposite Land.

Review: a strange and perilous place where armored guards serve afternoon tea to serial killers. Intriguing, but not recommended.

"Thank you, Milo," Zip said. "Hellos to the wife and kids."

The guard bowed like a tip-starved waiter and took his leave. Zip dressed the tea, took a sip, then gestured for me to continue. I sat on the opposite side of a security table. He was chained to the floor with titanium shackles, and yet, I sensed that he was in full control of my impunity. But alas, the show (or unfolding hostage situation) must go on.

If you hated Roy so much, then why offer the encouragement?

Like I said, he was very good at what he did. Werner liked him, which meant that Gamon was gonna keep using him. Which *also* meant that I was likely to continue working with him.

Which you did, I presume.

Yes. We returned to The Craven Compass and met with Gamon. As suspected, it was a giant circle jerk of praise and back-patting. Gamon's rep was on the line, so the whole thing ended with a giant sigh of relief. Roy had scored big out of the gate, which inflated his ego a bit. He didn't know how rare of an occurrence that was, so I had to temper his arrogance from time to time. I served as a pseudo mentor on recurring jobs. Granted, they all required my expertise in cold-blooded murder.

(Ping. "Haha, he does love that nickname for graffiti.")

Roy remained blissfully obtuse. Most of my work resided in the background. He'd work a problem while I ducked away to slit a throat.

(Ping. "Spray some paint.")

You know, it's interesting. I spent a great deal of time piecing this all together. I studied hours upon hours of Roy's numerous exploits. I watched you both, along with a host of other characters, wandering in and out of precarious situations throughout the station. And not once did I see any evidence of your ... let's say, special abilities.

I don't think that's interesting at all. Not to point out the obvious, but concealing evidence is kind of a prerequisite for what I do.

No, you misunderstand. I was paying you a compliment. In combing the security footage, I only witnessed a single blunder. And, as a not-so-subtle observation, it was the only event in which you were notably absent.

The casino job.

Yes. Can you tell me more about that?

Well, like you said, I wasn't there. I was in the room when it was issued, but further details are foggy at best. However, I *can* tell you why the evidence is out in the open.

And why's that?

Because Durangoni was the benefactor.

(Ping. "Fake news.")

CHAPTER 12

Gamon lit a fresh cigar from his comfy chair behind a large wooden desk. Puffs of smoke floated through the dim room. It was a different desk inside a different location, but carried the same seedy vibe. Gamon's dealings required a certain amount of mobility, but at the same time, he also valued cohesion. Whenever he held a meeting, one could expect a cloud of cigar smoke and a big damn desk.

Zip stood over his shoulder, as always, maintaining his best "normal guy and definitely not a murderous hitman" persona. Roy sat in one of two chairs in front of the desk, playing a mental game of "spot the difference" from The Craven Compass. Wallpaper darker, floor space bigger, folding chairs needlessly uncomfortable. Annoying squeaks accented his every movement. He thought about complaining, but opted to remain calm and stoic.

"These chairs suck," he said to Gamon.

"What are you, the chair police?"

Zip rolled his eyes.

Moments later, the entry door whipped open and bounced off the wall, drawing flinches from everyone inside. Vierra Belliosa marched into the room and slammed the door behind her. Her dreads were pulled into a tight ponytail. A large pair of sunglasses concealed much of her face. She plucked them off and hooked them to her blouse, a frilly purple bodice that matched her skirt and satchel. In a single fluid motion, she plunked into the vacant chair and crossed one leg over the other.

Roy smiled at her blunt arrival. His chest swelled with adoration, as she was even more enchanting than he remembered.

Vierra dropped her satchel to the floor and noticed Roy sitting beside her. She mirrored his smile and offered a fist-bump. "Eeey, Roy m'boy."

"Great to see you, Vee," he said, completing the bump.

Their attention turned to Gamon, who eyed them both through a haze of impatience.

Gamon released a puff of smoke. "Thank you for finally gracing us with your presence. We've only been sitting here for half an hour."

"Fuck off, hairball. I had a thing."

Roy smirked, which Zip caught from afar. And then Roy caught Zip's resulting scowl, which immediately erased the smirk.

Vierra twirled an arm. "I'm here. Chop chop."

Gamon sighed and swallowed his retort, as Belliosa remained one of the very few who could address him with such brashness. In any other situation, Zip would already be in the process of removing her head. "Okay, so, this job is going to sound a little strange. But before I get into the details, please rest assured that there is no foul play afoot. We are in no danger. We are not being watched, nor are any of us being squeezed in any way."

Vierra narrowed her eyes. "That's not as reassuring as you think it is."

"Given the nature of the assignment, the preface should make sense."

Vierra sighed, then gestured to continue.

Roy shifted a concerned gaze between the two.

"We've been asked to shake down the Zandui Casino."

Vierra burst into laughter, slapped her knees, then leapt to her feet. She shook her head as if to say *you dumb hairy bastard*, then hooked her satchel and drifted towards the exit. "And who, pray tell, is this astoundingly stupid backer?"

"The Durangoni Space Station," Gamon said with a flat tone.

Vierra stopped in her tracks and whipped a stunned gaze to the beast. "Are you fucking kidding me?"

Gamon shook his head.

"Why in the fucking fuck of fuck would you solicit a job from the very entity that you are hiding jobs from?"

"I didn't," Gamon said, adding a shrug. "They approached me."

The statement smacked Vierra across the face, rendering her speechless. She thought for a moment, then about-faced and shuffled back to her seat. Her bum met the rickety chair without breaking eye contact.

"Durangoni caught Zandui funneling massive sums of money to the Varokins."

Vierra huffed and fell back in her chair. "Fuuuck a ferret."

"To who?" Roy said.

"A massive sect of organized crime," Gamon said to Roy. "The Varokin Empire controls the Black Razor fleet and most of the abyssal markets. Normally, Durangoni would purge the casino and install someone else. But, Zandui is the biggest name in the game. They generate more cash than the next dozen combined. And so, Durangoni has found itself in quite the pickle."

"So what's the play?"

"They want us to hack into the Zandui financial block." Gamon nodded at Vierra. "You specifically, and then redirect the Varokin funds to Durangoni charities. The only catch is, they want it done from *inside* the casino."

Vierra cocked an eyebrow. "What the hell for?"

Gamon retrieved a note from a side drawer and placed it face-up on the desk. He pressed a finger to the paper and slid it over to Roy and Vierra. "This is their offer."

They leaned in for a gander.

"Sweet Tim almighty," Roy said. "That's a *lot* of zeroes."

"Not to them," Gamon said.

"He's right," Vierra said, then glanced at Roy. "This isn't about the money. It's about saving face. Corruption at that level under-mines their credibility. They can't shut Zandui down without looking like fools."

"Bingo," Gamon said. "Durangoni *wants* Zandui to see this. They *want* them to see the fix, and they *want* them to know that it was Vier-ra Belliosa. It would send a clear message that they have the eyes and power, but also value stability. The casino would have no choice but to keep the fix in place, lest they suffer a very public scandal."

"Like a penalty tax," Roy said.

"Exactly," Gamon said.

"So why not do it themselves?"

"Same problem," Vierra said. "Durangoni officials shaking down a casino would not go over well in the public eye. The station prides itself on unrestricted commerce. The second they install anything that resembles a tax, the merchants would revolt."

Gamon click-pointed at Vierra.

"And what if I say no?"

"Umm ..." Gamon said, taken aback. "You're ... disinterested?"

"Oh, no, I'm definitely doing it. Sounds like a cracker. However, given that they want *me* specifically, I was wondering what their Plan B was."

Gamon scrunched his brow and rapped his meaty fingers on the desk. The cigar migrated back and forth between his lips. He exam-ined the offer note like a smarmy professor grading a subpar paper. "I believe their Plan B would be to devise a Plan B."

Vierra chuckled. "Sounds about right."

Roy raised his hand and immediately spoke, negating the hand raise. "So where do I fit in with all this?"

"You're her husband," Gamon said, gesturing at Vierra.

"If only," Roy said with a sheepish chuckle. The reply was somewhat involuntary, which infected the group with a twinge of awkwardness.

"No," Gamon said. "You will be playing a married couple in or-der to gain access to the casino. To be fair, Vierra could rock into the place by herself and sling some code, but we want to eliminate as much suspicion as we can. At least, up to the point of hacking. And so, you will both get dressed to impress, visit the casino like any normal couple with money to burn, find a nice cozy table, order a steak, eat the steak, then whip out a tablet and get to work. That should give you enough time to complete the assignment before they wise up."

"And what if we get caught?" Roy said.

Gamon narrowed his gaze. "That's the point, dingus."

Zip rolled his eyes again.

"No," Roy said. "I mean, what if Vierra needs more time?"

"Then *you* provide it. Your job is to run interference, should it be necessary."

"Gotcha." Roy gave Gamon a thumbs-up, then smiled at Vierra.

"I'll do some digging and have everything primed beforehand," Vierra said. "Shouldn't take long once we're inside, just a quick log and load. The only x-factor will be the number of funnels I have to route."

"And what happens when the job is done?" Roy said.

Gamon shrugged. "Get up and walk out."

"Sorry, but, um," Roy said, clearly stumped. "Won't they want to detain us? Question us? Or at the very least, track us once we leave?"

Gamon thought for a moment while chewing on his cigar. "Who is the most famous person you can think of?"

"Kirp Delon." (Read: the quadrant equivalent of Tom Hanks.)

"Okay, so, let's say that you're having breakfast at home. It's a normal day, normal routine, nothing amiss or out of place. Then, Kirp Delon walks into the room. You didn't even know he was in your house. Without a word, he climbs onto the table, drops his pants, shits on your plate, wipes his ass with your napkin, and then smears it on your face before taking his leave. At that moment, would you be worried about tracking him, or would you be utterly paralyzed by what the fuck just happened?"

Roy thought hard about the visual while pulling his gaze around the group. His face cycled between shock, disgust, and total bewilderment. The more he envisioned the act, the more his stomach churned. It all ended with a clumsy dry-heave.

Zip facepalmed himself.

* * *

Vierra watched with great amusement as the bartender poured our fifth shots of rum. At least, that's what they called it. To be perfectly honest, it tasted like the hateful backwash of a demonic enema. As a wandering haze engulfed my field of vision, I was never more thankful for the audio recorder on my comdev.

Puki Horpocket was not a big drinker.

Puki Horpocket was decidedly smashed.

Nevertheless, I persisted.

We toasted to our health (ironically) and tossed back another round of taint juice.

(cough) Sweet mercy.

Way to keep up, wordsmith. Most lightweights would have tapped out by now.

Was that the (cough) intention?

Nah. I just wanted to see how badly you wanted this interview.

Diabolic. But I respect it.

And I respect your tenacity. Please continue, if you can.

So you and Roy (hiccup) inflo ... infur ... infiltrated the Zandui Casino.

Yes, but it was scarcely an infiltration. We just walked through the front doors like every other deep pocket. I will say this, though. Roy was quite the gentleman and walking into Zandui was the closest I ever felt to being a princess.

* * *

When it comes to the Zandui Casino, the word is *extravagance*. While an abundance of swanky haunts is scattered throughout the station, Zandui remains the only public venue that thrills with each visit. I have dined at several of its five-star restaurants in order to revise entries in the Definitive Directory of Durangoni, and those experiences barely scratch the surface. The casino is a veritable theme park for anyone with a swollen bank account.

First of all, Zandui is big. Like, *really* big. It's essentially a giant pleasure cruiser built into the northernmost Rich Ring. It spans 15 floors and covers an area the size of a pomplomo pitch (read: about eight football fields). It houses more hotels, pubs, and restaurants than most actual districts, as well as several premium theaters and playhouses. It even has its own docking portal and full-time valet service. In fact, it's not uncommon for bigwigs to visit the station for months and never leave the casino grounds.

And then there is the casino itself.

Describing the main gaming floor is a somewhat daunting task. It remains one of the few sights aboard the station that drops my jaw. The enormous open space spans ten stories with high-roller tables littering the floor. Countless balconies overlook the action, which remain in near-constant use. This is due to a never-ending holographic spectacle that fills the open space. Sometimes it's a mass of floating orbs set to trippy music. Other times, it's a flock of rainbow dragons pooping fireworks. It's a ceaseless and utterly dazzling light show, one you could stalk for weeks and never see the same thing twice.

Regardless of location, casino sounds are always needling the background. Clinking glasses, clacking chips, the occasional roar of big wins. The entire place is an unremitting churn, always on, never placid. And yet, within this restless arena, Roy and Vierra somehow managed to steal the spotlight. At least, ever so briefly.

* * *

Roy stood inside a restaurant lobby on the third level, adjusting to his tuxedo rental. He had worn one back on his home planet, but the

Durangoni upgrade took some getting used to. It was not uncomfortable, but rather *too* comfortable. Roy was so attuned to poverty rags that his body outright rejected form-fitted clothing.

A reception booth faced a pair of elevator doors. Elegant folk arrived with each ding and were guided into the establishment by one of several uniformed hosts. Roy watched them all through an odd sense of discomfort. Not from the attire, but from a chronic dysphoria. Most of his life aboard the station had been spent in filthy dives. Whenever he met eyes with a host, he braced himself to be shooed away like an unwelcome pest.

Another ding of arrival caught his attention. He turned to the elevator doors, which slid open to reveal an enchanting woman dressed in a shimmering gown. The silky fabric clung to a single shoulder and draped across her chest, giving her the presence of a debutante. Glittering earrings peeked through her black dreads, all carefully teased into a stylish bun. Her heels clacked to a rest in front of Roy, drawing a wide smile across his face.

"My stars, are you a vision to behold," he said.

"Thanks," Vierra said with a playful smirk. "And you're looking quite dapper, mister man. C'mon, give momma a spin."

Roy struck a butler-like pose and twisted in a slow circle.

"Yes, yes, very nice, liking that," she said while nodding.

Roy ended with an outstretched elbow and a toothy grin. "Shall we, m'lady?"

She chuckled and hooked her arm around his, painting the intended portrait.

They moseyed up to the reception booth where a uniformed hostess escorted them into the ritzy restaurant. A faint and pleasant melody welcomed them, serving as a backdrop to cultured conversation. Fine silver rested atop round tables with white coverings. Intricate patterns adorned the walls and ceiling, all illuminated by crystal sconces and chandeliers. Roy smiled as his gaze wandered freely, lost in a sea of opulence.

The hostess presented their table, a private two-seater on its own balcony overlooking the casino. Holographic ribbons twisted around the interior as a muted roar lifted from the gaming floor. Roy and Vierra took their seats, allowing the hostess to bow and take her leave. A suited waiter arrived with a pair of complementary martinis, a tasty house spirit that tempted longer stays. After reciting the specials with pitch-perfect charm, he logged their orders and whisked away like an elvish prince.

Roy and Vierra lifted their glasses and toasted to friendship. They mused on their extralegal adventures, prompting several laughs and sighs. For once, they were able to indulge in personal quirks. Roy learned that Vierra loved tabletop puzzles. Vierra learned that Roy could recite the entire Garlokian Pledge (a statement of loyalty that was widely considered a masterpiece of empty rhetoric). The occasional roar of victory pulled their attention to the gaming floor where boisterous moguls splashed cash around high-stakes tables. The gathered crowds cheered every play like traveling entourages.

"So I have to ask," Roy said. "Why hasn't anyone mobbed you?"

"What do you mean?"

"You are crazy famous throughout Durangoni. If Kirp Delon were to walk in here, he would draw immediate attention from staff and fans. You're arguably more famous than he is, so where are all the groupies?"

"The difference is, Kirp is a famous actor. I'm a famous engineer."

"So?"

"So, you know my work, not my face. When you first met me at the Sunken Isles, did you recognize me?"

"No."

"But you knew my name."

"Yes."

"There you have it."

"But still, you'd think at least someone in-the-know would be fawning over you."

"Ah, that's because I go to great pains to conceal my public identity. Well, not so much conceal. More like overload with false positives."

"How so?"

"See for yourself. Grab your comdev search for my name."

Roy complied. A quick search returned a smorgasbord of non-Vierras. Face after face of random people, all linked to various articles about her exploits. Many claimed to be the "real" Vierra, yet none of them was. It took a solid minute of scrolling before Roy found a matching image, and even that was just a candid picture with no context. "That's astounding."

"True privacy is only found in chaos. I learned early on that it's easier to hide in bad data. Why fight the system when you can turn it against itself?"

"That's damn near poetic."

"Psh. I suck at poetry."

"Somehow I doubt that."

Vierra smiled and added a flirtatious wink.

The waiter returned and lowered two plates to the table, both cragono steaks, another shared interest they had uncovered. Roy followed her lead, selecting the same pieces of silverware that she did. They moaned with culinary pleasure while trading coy glances. Every morsel a delight, every moment a treasure. A strange sensation bubbled inside his stomach. It was wholly foreign, yet oddly fulfilling.

Roy was ... *happy*.

A sudden commotion from the gaming floor caught their attention. Roy craned his neck over the balcony to find a large rectangular pane suspended over a ticketing booth. It was filled with glowing numbers, similar to a bingo board, but bizarrely random. The crowd had moaned with disappointment and began to disperse. Moments later, the board cleared itself for another round. A small bulb in the upper corner started to blink in peculiar intervals. Roy studied it with intense fascination.

"What is that blinking light?" he said.

Vierra glanced at the board. "You mean the Big Sixty counter?"

"What's that?"

"You've never heard of Big Sixty?"

"No. Is it fun?"

"Fun?" she said with a slight chuckle. "It's simultaneously the most unwinnable and irresistible game in all of existence. The cost is huge and the payoff is absurd. It's a sucker's paradise that makes a shit-ton of money for the casino. In fact, I would wager that Big Sixty is their primary source of revenue."

"What are the rules?"

Vierra narrowed her eyes. "You've seriously never heard of this?"

Roy shrugged. "Well, we play it all the time down in the sub-core. Just making sure that *you* understand it."

"Smartass. But point taken."

"C'mon, humor me. How does it work?"

"You're not going to play it." Vierra sipped her martini.

"I'm just curious," Roy said with a glib tone. "I lucked my way out of crippling poverty to relax inside a prestigious casino with the most beautiful woman I have ever known. Trust me, I am not eager to goad my karma."

Vierra smiled and blushed a bit. "Okay, but promise me. Not one ticket."

"Promise." Roy circled his spleen. (Read: crossed his heart. This was a cultural gesture that even Vierra found confusing. She snorted with amusement, then continued.)

"Alright, so, Big Sixty is a simple guessing game. There are sixty squares, each representing a minute of the current hour. The object of the game is to guess the number for each square. Players purchase tickets, log their guesses, and submit them before the hour begins. A random number is revealed each minute, ranging from zero to a hundred. If you guess them all, you win."

Roy pondered the rules for a moment, then tilted his head. "What moron would ever play such a stupid game?"

"Exactly. The odds are astronomical. But then there's the pay-off."

"Must be pretty big to get dumb people to flush money down the toilet."

"Three hundred trillion credits."

Roy flinched into stunned silence. He could only stare at Vierra through a haze of disbelief. His brain inputted the figure, but locked up and sent a critical error to his mouth hole. "*What?!*" he said with a mixture of shock, anger, and a bit of arousal.

Vierra grinned and nodded.

"*What?!*" he said again, adding a table slap.

"Now you get it."

"Sweet Tim almighty."

"I know, right? The game is unwinnable, but the pot is why people play. And here's the kicker. Each ticket costs 10,000 credits."

Roy twitched in response, as his brain had no idea what else to do.

"And even at that price point, there are thousands of tickets played every hour."

Roy leaned back and crossed his arms. "Are you messing with me? You have to be messing with me."

"Ten thousand credits to win three hundred trillion? When you have money to burn, it doesn't seem so reckless, does it?"

"It has to be a scam. No way that game is legit."

"I thought so too, but the algorithm was verified by seven independent bodies. No tricks, no scam, just a near-impossible puzzle. And get this, the casino actually encourages players to try and crack the code. Professional gamblers have been running the numbers for decades. Even the most sophisticated code breakers haven't been able to crack that nut. I've been tempted to give it a go myself, but countless people, intelligent people, have gone broke trying."

"Wait, did you say *decades*?"

"Yup. Big Sixty has been around since I was a kid, and the jackpot has yet to be won. Think about that. Ten thousand credits per ticket, thousands of plays per hour, over *decades*."

Roy leaned forward and rubbed the hurt from his temples.

"That's the kind of monetary flow we're dealing with." Her tone switched from somber to peppy. "And I'm about to hack that shit." She reached into her purse, withdrew a small tablet, and plunked it on the table.

CHAPTER 13

Despite the supervillain level of techno malfeasance occurring at the other side of the table, Roy was oddly relaxed. He munched on his delectable steak, sipped his delicious martini, and watched the colorful light show twist and turn over the balcony. A cheeky grin stretched across his face as he watched a school of hologram fish swim above the casino floor. They glided over the Big Sixty booth, switching his focus to the algorithm counter.

Roy stared at the light for what seemed like an eternity. The pulses teased his conscience, scratching a familiar yet distant itch.

Minute by minute, the blinking light morphed into a beating drum. The little voice inside his head grew louder and louder. He wondered if their digital raid could be viewed as malfeasance if the governing party was the actual government. And then he wondered if the government would protect them should the job go off the rails. And then he wondered who around him was a secret agent waiting to slit his throat after the job was done. What had started as a subtle worry was building into a full-blown conspiracy panic.

"Nervous?" Vierra said without looking up from the tablet.

Roy noticed that he was holding his breath. He released the pent-up air and ended with a shy chuckle. "Is it that obvious?"

"Lil' bit."

"Sorry."

"Don't be," she said while tapping. "If anything, it makes us look like a married couple with unresolved issues."

"How so?"

"Well, we're at a fancy dinner and I'm nose-deep in a tablet. You're acting all weird, like you just confessed to something. I wager that everyone around us thinks you're having an affair."

Roy gasped. "I would never do that to you."

Vierra snorted. "Way to sell it."

"Oh ... yeah." Roy blushed and cleared his throat.

She smirked and tossed him a glance. "Don't worry, I'm almost done here."

"Must be pretty complicated."

"Not really. I finished the hack five minutes ago."

"You fin—*what?*"

"The reroute was super easy. I researched all the funnel points beforehand and had the protocols ready to go. Hacked in, ran the script, *boom.*"

Roy stammered in reply. "So what the hell have you been doing?"

Vierra stopped tapping and gave her full attention to Roy. She took a needed breath as her cavalier demeanor switched to a somber tone. "Once I gained access to the Zandui network, I needed to answer a very important question."

"And what's that?" he said, matching her earnestness.

Vierra nodded, allowing the gravity of the predicament to settle between them. "I needed to know ... " She paused for weight. "Could I hack into the hologram control system and force it to render photo-real pornography?"

Roy responded with a blank stare.

"The answer," she said, switching back to peppy, "is a resounding *yes.*" She waved a finger over the tablet and dropped it onto the screen.

The hologram show crackled and disappeared.

The music stopped.

The roar of conversation faded.

From the depths of oblivion, a smooth and seductive beat filled the empty space. And then the hologram system got down to business, in more ways than one. It created image after image of hardcore alien debauchery. Couples, threesomes, and outright orgies entangled each other in lustful abandon. Their naked bodies towered over the space, plunging every throbbing limb into every gaping hole. Flesh jiggled. Sacks dangled. Juices spilled from moist cavities. Gasps lifted from the gaming floor as shocked patrons sidestepped the rendered fluids.

Every eye inside the casino locked onto the show.

Most jaws dangled in stunned silence.

Roy's was one of them.

Other jaws formed wide smiles of approval.

Vierra's was one of them.

She chuckled at the sultry tableau. "Is it weird to be aroused by this?"

Roy turned his befuddled gaze to Vierra.

"You know what this needs?"

Roy responded by not responding.

"Blongos," she said with excitement, then tapped the screen again.

(Blongos can best be described as highly aggressive, yet oddly adorable goat-like creatures. They are prized as pets due to their superior home-guarding skills, but will often trash the place with their comically large horns, which somewhat negates burglary.)

Out of nowhere, a giant herd of blongos invaded the pornographic wonderland. A chorus of "awww" lifted from the crowd, but was soon quashed when the creatures decided to join the party. Their massive members hunted for any crevice that would accept them. Howls of success married into the moans of pleasure. A few critters preferred to bash each other with their giant horns, accenting the erotic music with violent clunks.

Vierra added claps to her chuckles. "Oh wow, that is balls-out brilliant," she said with several balls swinging overhead. "This might be some of my finest work."

"Ahem," said a nearby voice.

Roy and Vierra turned to find three casino guards blocking the exit from their booth. Not Durangoni Security officers, just three random aliens with blue uniforms and rent-a-badges. The head guard puffed his chest and glowered at Vierra. "You need to come with us, ma'am," he said with a slightly threatening tone.

"Pass," she said.

"E—excuse me?"

"That's a hard no, pal. And for that matter, how the fuck did you even know I was here? I killed the relay trackers, and it's not like there's a ping-trace on the holo—" Her eyes narrowed with realization. "Aaaah, fuck all of you right in the neck."

"Not playing games, ma'am." The guard stepped towards her and motioned to rise. "Please come with us. I will not ask again."

Vierra huffed and turned to Roy. "You're up, partner."

"Uuuh ..." Roy said through his dangling jaw.

"Your job is to run interference. Sooo ..." She gestured to the guards.

Roy looked at the guards, then back to Vierra, then back to the guards, then up to the moist genitals overhead, then back to Vierra.

Vierra sighed with disappointment.

The guard reached for her shoulder, but met a sudden resistance. He looked down to see Roy's hand clamped around his wrist. Anger swelled inside his chest. His gaze crawled up the limb to Roy's face, where a pair of clouded eyes glared back at him. Roy grumbled as noxious spit dribbled from his frothing mouth. The guard yelped and snatched his arm away, stumbling back into one of his cohorts.

Vierra's eyes widened.

"Meet me back at the elevator," Roy said under his breath, then slowly rose from his seat.

The guards braced themselves as a snarling beast in a rented tuxedo stood from the table and turned to face them. Its pupils were lost beneath a milky haze. Acidic slobber pooled on the floor. Roy hunched his back and grunted like a rabid werewolf.

At this point, everyone inside the dining room had given Roy their undivided attention, despite the hologram orgy raging overhead.

One of the guards stammered through his waning authority. "Sir, please put away the ... um, stop doing, uh ... stop being weird, sir."

Roy whipped his clouded gaze to the frightened guard, flinging ribbons of spit across the floor. The guard squeaked and took a wary step back. Roy grumbled with ferocity, prompting nearby diners to abandon their tables.

Roy stepped forward.

The guards stepped back.

Roy stepped forward.

The guards—

Roy shrieked and rushed the guards.

All three yelped, spun around, and sprinted away in different directions. The remaining diners screamed and fled their tables, creating a cauldron of chaos inside the restaurant.

Roy slid to a halt outside the booth and snarled while snapping his gaze between the fleeing guards. Frothy spit poured from his mouth with each whip and grunt. He selected a guard, then raised his arms overhead and gave chase like a hungry goblin.

Vierra snickered as she tucked the tablet into her purse. She rose from the table, straightened her dress, then strolled away as a feast of sexual conquest played in the background.

* * *

The restaurant lobby had cleared out, leaving some lingering staff and a small group of casino guards. Roy entered through a side door, having reset the froth monster and regained some normalcy. Aside from a few lapel stains (which guaranteed the loss of his deposit), his secret identity remained hidden. He twisted around the lobby in search of Vierra, but she was nowhere to be found.

And then he heard her voice.

He struggled to pinpoint the location and eventually settled on the guards. A different lot from the chase, but the same uniforms and lack of authority. They had surrounded someone. A very special someone. Roy caught a glimpse of her gown from within the mass, then readied himself for another frothy attack. But as he started to churn his gut, Vierra's signature cackle erupted from the group. The guards followed suit, matching her laugh in tone and delight. Roy halted the boil and relaxed his stomach, opting to approach with caution. The footsteps caught the attention of the nearest guard, who politely stepped aside to reveal Vierra.

She was signing autographs.

Roy released a heavy sigh.

Vierra met his gaze and replied with a smile. "Okay boys, that's enough." She clapped and shooed the guards away. "Go do whatever you should be doing."

They all groaned and slinked away, albeit with wide grins on their faces. After all, it's not every day that you get to meet a living legend. They ignored Roy altogether and vanished back into the casino.

Roy took his final steps and settled in front of Vierra.

"Well that was an interesting exit," she said with a slight chuckle. "But I gotta hand it to you, it's a very effective strategy."

Roy smiled and shrugged. "Learned it as a child, been using it ever since. Comes in handy from time to time."

"Smells like ass, though."

"Kinda the point, like when animals use musk to deter predators. My species isn't exactly known for their burly frames." Roy offered a meager flex, then waved it away.

"Oh, I get it. Doesn't make it any less funky."

Roy grinned, then retrieved a small bottle of mouthwash from his pocket. He took a swig, then sloshed it around and swallowed. "Never leave home without it."

Vierra smirked. "Roy, m'boy, did you just freshen up for a nightcap?"

Of course he didn't, but she didn't know that. And so began a vicious mental game of *tell the truth, no, lie, no, tell the truth, no, lie.*

She lightly punched his shoulder. "Kidding, dude."

Roy simpered and glanced away.

"Great work today," she said with a coy tone.

"You too. I'm still trying to get those blongos out of my head."

She chuckled softly and ended with a sigh. "I guess this is good-bye, then."

"Guess so."

Vierra patted his chest, then turned for the elevator and pressed the call button. A ping replied and the doors slid open. Roy watched with great affection as she stepped into the car and turned to face him. They traded playful smirks as the doors began to close.

But then she reached out and stopped them.

Roy cocked his brow.

"You coming or not?" she said.

He smiled wide and joined her.

*   *   *

There have been a few low points in my life, the majority of which will remain locked away in the basement of shame. However, in order to complete this tale of intrigue, I must confess to an event that I am none too proud of.

During my interview with Vierra Belliosa, she succeeded in pushing my drinking limit to an embarrassing new level. After an obscene amount of rum shots, we had to cut the interview short because, and these are her words, I was "dancing along the beach like a circus performer caught in a violent hallucination." Apparently, I had to be wrangled several times until I passed out in a lounge chair.

The next morning, I awoke in the same chair.

Vierra had shielded my limp body from the beating sun with a canopy of umbrellas. As my eyes opened, my brain declared its utter displeasure with the situation. My head was pounding, my mouth was parched, and my pants remain missing to this day. There is something unsettling about a man wearing a suit jacket with socks and boxers. Especially on the beach. But that's how the interview resumed, and I owned it for the remainder.

Vierra was lounging in the adjacent chair when I awoke. She had changed into a one-piece swimsuit with a matching sash and hat. The sun reflected off her larger-than-life sunglasses. She looked happy, healthy, and clear-headed, an image that I greatly coveted at that moment. As she explained, "Hangovers are not a thing with me." I still wonder what she meant. Was it a *species* thing or a *supernatural tolerance* thing? I decided not to press, because any further talk of booze would have purged what little remained in my stomach.

Speaking of which, she was kind enough to order breakfast for the both of us. Few things are better for a raging hangover than a hot plate of forfum, shanwap, and a tall glass of gurpoonga. (Read: pass. Some things need a translation. This plate of horrors does not. In fact, learning what this was prompted a two-week hiatus where I almost quit the project.)

We ate our breakfast, exchanged some repartee, and picked up where we left off the night before. Vierra detailed the hack job and took great pleasure in highlighting the most salacious tidbits. I hung on her every word while trying not to vomit.

To be honest, I am surprised that Gamon would sign off on such a plan.

Goodness, no. He had no idea. The whole orgy thing was my own added flair.

Seems a bit cavalier, don't you think?

The casino funded terrorists. I would happily take the lumps for twisting that knife. In fact, I bricked the debug console and tanked the resets. The holo-orgy ran for an entire week before they threw in the towel and wiped the system. That was a mountain of dirty money down the shitter, thanks to yours truly.

What did Gamon say about it?

Tore me a new one, which I richly deserved. Haven't worked with him since. But that's okay, I'm much happier on my own.

And what about Roy?

(slight pause, then shrugs) What about him?

Have you seen or worked with him since?

Roy continued to work for Gamon, as far as I know. I didn't hear much about his whereabouts until the snafu leading up to The Incident. Got a ring-ding out of the blue.

He reached out to you.

Yes.

What about?

He had gotten into a bind and needed some guidance. And *that*, Mr. Horpocket, is as far as I'm willing to take you.

Understood. But if you would be so kind, I do have one last question.

Shoot.

I have studied this event from every angle, from beginning to end, but you and Roy entering the elevator remains the last piece of footage I can find. In fact, I discovered that an entire sequence was missing from the security archives. If I had to wager a guess, I think that Durangoni erased them to conceal your departure.

Seems reasonable, but I'm not hearing a question.

I would like to know where you went.

(smirks) Somewhere private.

Care to elaborate?

Nope.

Fair enough. And, if you will, one final, final question.

(brief chuckle) You're a pushy little prick fuck, you know that?

I've been told, yes.

Okay then. One more. Consider it a hangover gift.

Thank you, dear. I just want to know, for the sake of my own curiosity ... were you surprised when Roy won the Big Sixty jackpot?

No.

Wow. Was not expecting so quick an answer.

(shrugs) It was Roy's to win. He noticed the one thing that nobody else did. And I can think of no one more deserving.

* * *

I departed shortly after breakfast and never saw Vierra again.

It was sad in a way, as her immense persona enters a room long before she does. She's a living legend, a roving apparition that continues to improve our strange and wonderful world. Ironic, given her distaste for the celebrity it bestows.

Vierra provided valuable clues into Roy's final days before The Incident. After our meeting, I realized that I was crafting a story of redemption. Roy was not a villain. He was neither luminary nor enigma. He was a good man, as she insisted.

Roy was a cog.

A cog that wished to be a lever.

And that lever would move the world.

CHAPTER 14

After numerous interviews with Roy's inner circle, I had enough puzzle pieces to begin constructing his meteoric rise into the public conscience. I had examined Roy the grunt and followed his choppy path to Roy the crook, a humble dreg in the throes of a midlife crisis. In another world, on another station, the tale of a working stiff winning an unwinnable fortune would be enough to sell a pile of hardbacks. But life inside Durangoni is a unique brand of vagary. It's filled with special stories about special people doing remarkably special things.

The time has come to reveal Roy the folk hero.

The time has come to address The Incident.

The following is a dramatic reconstruction of the events leading up to Roy's mysterious departure from the station. It is a conjecture based on interviews, security reels, and reams of hearsay. While some details may not be entirely accurate, I stand by the depiction as a faithful and thoughtful retelling.

* * *

Roy sat inside his tiny apartment, trying his best to ignore the funk and racket. Months had passed since he departed, yet there he was, a stranger in his own strange land. The ratty cot was painfully uncomfortable, especially compared to the fluffy beds he enjoyed on assignment. Even the worst outing was vastly superior to his shabby bunk down in the sub-core.

And yet, it felt like home.

He patted the frame like an old friend, then refocused on the opposite wall, the same soiled pane where he composed a message to Gamon. He traced a scratch over to a set of wire hangers clinging to dents in the metal. Dirty clothes hung from their frames, each stain telling a woeful tale. He could smell the grease, taste the brine, hear the clanks of hammers. His gaze fell to his lap, where a pair of fine slacks covered his thighs. A single square inch of that fabric cost more than the entirety of his sub-core belongings.

He had everything he wanted, and yet, nothing at all.

Gamon had released him for several days, as nothing on the docket warranted his skill set. Roy had become a favorite lackey, due to his unique ability to address complex problems while not resembling a complex being. Gamon loved having a forgettable technician at his disposal, which afforded Roy lots of interesting work. And as a result, lots of disposable income.

When Roy received a long-overdue break, he decided to treat himself for the first time since leaving his homeworld. Using Zip's fashionable insight, he purchased a new set of clothes from the same shopping district where he had fixed the clogged fountains. He felt like a million bucks when he left the store. But when he returned home, he felt like a thief.

Roy rolled the fabric between his fingertips and finally understood the dilemma that Clancy faced every day. Rich on paper, poor inside, a bottomless hole to fill. A rush of guilt infected his conscience. Clancy never deserved the abuse, no matter how thick the veneer of envy.

What a shitty friend I've been.

With a heavy sigh, Roy stood from the cot and turned for the door. His somber gaze crept around the tiny abode one last time before taking his leave.

The sights and sounds of a returning shift filled the cramped hallway. Roy sidestepped his former compatriots, who paid him no mind. Not a single grunt recognized him. Their curious eyes stopped at his slacks and dismissed him as a rich wanker who lost his way. Roy sighed into a knowing nod, having replaced his comfort with chagrin. He scanned the mass for his long-time mates, none of whom revealed themselves. His wandering gaze landed on Duncan's apartment, but there was no need to visit. Roy knew exactly where he was.

It was time for a drink.

Roy strolled back to the nearest pod station where a group of grunts awaited the next train. He kept his distance, opting to wait behind them. A few tossed him sour glances, even meeting eyes for a moment, but still failed to recognize him. Roy glanced down at his tidy shirt, which may as well have been a cloak of invisibility.

The ride up to the merchant line was a similar bout of indignation. Roy bit his tongue and bided his time as the group mumbled about the cleaner-than-usual passenger. They poked fun at his shiny shoes, custom belt, and willful use of soap. Roy heard none of this, but understood the mannerisms. After all, he knew them as his own.

The pod train slowed to a stop and released its cargo into the merchant district. Roy made his way through a noisy bazaar of practical shops. He recognized them all and could even name the vendors, but none of them offered anything of interest. His trained eyes could spot deals across the lot, but he ignored them all as beneath regard. Grease was now an obstacle to avoid. Clanks were now curses that abhorred his presence.

Roy proceeded into a far corridor and ducked down a familiar hallway. Several doors later, he arrived at a plain door with a plain plaque. The Pipes, his home away from home. At least, he hoped it still remembered him. His chest released a heavy sigh as he reached for the handle. A sharp and immediate racket assaulted his ears when he pulled the door open. It gave him pause. What once served as a warm and welcoming blanket now felt like a warning. He took a needed breath and slipped into the dark passage.

Conduits and electrical panels framed his field of vision. Recessed lighting painted sinister shadows around the interior. Roy took cautious steps as burly regulars tromped around him. He thought of calling them by name, but they still dismissed his presence.

Bob, the two-ringed ringneck, wandered by without saying hello. Soiled duds clung to his slumped shoulders. A hard day's work radiated from his skin. Roy could feel the tug of respect and friendship, but it was cold and distant. Suddenly, the number of rings along his neck didn't matter in the slightest.

Bob slapped the big red button at the end of the hallway and entered the main bar. A chorus of salutations greeted his arrival. Clancy and Duncan were among them. Roy could see the pair from afar, perched on their usual stools as Fiona tended to their needs. And much to his delight, his own favorite perch was empty and waiting.

Roy smiled, but halted inside the corridor. He settled against the wall and merged with the shadows, content to relive his former life from a distance. Thirsty patrons continued to stroll by without a sliver of curiosity. They punched the big red button and joined their brethren. Reenie, another friend and talented welder, knocked the button with her favorite *ratta-tat-tatta* pattern before receiving her own chorus of welcomes.

Roy smirked and nodded.

And then someone grabbed his shoulder from behind.

Roy flinched into a spin and found Zip looming over him.

The reptilian sneered, then gestured back to the entrance.

Roy sighed and followed him outside.

The door closed behind them, muffling the ruckus. Zip hiked down the hallway a bit, enough to avoid any curious ears. He found a tolerable distance, then turned to face Roy.

"How the fuck do you stand that place?" Zip said, shaking off the experience.

Roy shrugged. "Kinda the charm. Keeps the riffraff out."

Zip narrowed his eyes, unsure of whether the insult was intentional or not. "Anyway, you've been summoned."

"Huh?" Roy checked his comdev. "I didn't receive a message."

"Not that kind of summons." Zip handed him a slip of paper.

"No coms. Power down and report to this location immediately."

Roy unfolded the paper, cocked an eyebrow, then returned his gaze to Zip. "Is this a joke?"

"Does it look like I'm laughing?"

"First of all, I'm not sure you *can* laugh. Second of all, is this a joke?"

"You have one hour. Gamon is waiting." Zip turned away and took his leave.

Roy sighed again, then turned the other way and started back to the pod station. He tossed a mournful glance at The Pipes as he passed.

* * *

Fifty-five minutes later, Roy was speed walking down a colorful corridor. His destination, an obscure education district, was fast approaching. But when he reached the end of the tunnel, his shoes squeaked to a stop. A kaleidoscopic maelstrom assaulted his senses from every direction, forcing his brain into dreamscape mode. There it was, a plenitude of pointlessness, the ultimate haven for the clinically weird and chronically bored.

He had reached the Jester District.

Once again, his pleated slacks and button shirt outed him as a trespasser. The dapper image stuck out among pink tutus, feather hats, rainbow suspenders, and layers of face paint. A small army of eager students crowded inside the junction. They all fought to justify their existence by mastering skills that nobody asked for.

Roy pulled his gaze around the hub.

Omega School of Hack-n-Sack.

Miming Made Easy.

Death Match Juggle Time.

And there, nestled in the center, was his destination: The Yuk Yuk Clown Academy.

Roy sighed, shook his head, checked his comdev, forgot he had turned it off, grunted with annoyance, searched for a wall clock, found one with abstract digits, struggled to understand it, grunted again, asked the nearest mime, realized his mistake, then gave up and leapt into a jog towards the academy.

He ducked some hacky sacks before slowing to a stop at the entrance. The exterior was modest in size, but utterly bonkers in coloration. One could spend an entire day just trying to identify a color they *didn't* use. Sinuous letters and images created a psychedelic portrait that would make a carnival blush.

Roy grabbed a bright pink handle and yanked the door open. A jarring *yuk-yuk* greeted his arrival into a small foyer. Framed images of smiling clowns covered the rainbow-striped walls. They extended onto the ceiling, giving him the distinct impression of an aerial attack. Never in his life had he felt so painfully uncomfortable.

His mortified gaze lowered to a greeting desk along the far wall. Sitting behind it was a smiling receptionist dressed in a frilly outfit. Her bulb-like head and triangular teeth filled Roy with a sense of dread, as if he had stepped into the opening scene of a horror movie. Her three large eyes blinked independently, which didn't help matters.

"Are you down to clown?" the lady said with a nasal voice.

Flee for your life! said Roy's brain. "Uuuh ..." said Roy's mouth.

A side door cracked open.

Roy held his breath and braced for a jolly murder, but then Gamon peeked around the frame. His lungs emptied at the sight, a much-needed and very welcome relief. Gamon plucked an unlit cigar from his lips and motioned for Roy to join him.

Roy maintained a stiffened posture as he shuffled towards the door.

The receptionist maintained a creepy perma-grin as she watched him slip inside.

Roy and Gamon strolled down a vibrant hallway with multi-colored doors, the entrances to small theaters and classrooms. Roy could not help but wonder what horrors were trapped behind them. Gamon stopped at a blue door, surveyed the hallway, then let himself inside. Roy followed him in and the door latched behind them.

Roy glanced around an examination room, the very same that one might find in a hospital. Only in this one, everything was exaggerated to comedic proportions. Giant tongue depressors, giant reflex hammer, funhouse mirror over the sink. A smiling clown adorned the wall, holding its still-beating heart in front of a gaping chest hole. The heart itself had eyes, teeth, and looked to be having a swell time.

The clock on the wall ticked to a new hour.

Gamon grunted. "Good timing." He grabbed a chair, took a seat, and lit his cigar.

Roy, having no idea what to say or where to look, hopped onto the examination table and folded his hands like a would-be patient.

Gamon chuckled. "Relax, my friend."

Roy complied as best he could. He closed his eyes for a quick reset, then fished the slip of paper from his breast pocket. "Got your message."

"My apologies for the abrupt summons. I know you were enjoying some personal time and I regret having to cut it short."

Roy shrugged. "The nature of the biz, right?"

Gamon grinned and nodded. "I should also apologize for the location. Given the nature of the assignment, I needed somewhere inconspicuous."

"So you chose a clown school?" Roy studied the room with a slow pan, as if to track an angry bee. "This is where serial killers are *made*."

"I employ a few gophers here. It's one of the very few places that Durangoni doesn't give a shit about. In fact, I think they have two cameras for the entire district. No sane person wants to monitor clowns all day. At least, no sane person who wants to remain sane."

"Good point. So what's the job?"

Gamon plucked the cigar from his mouth and released a puff of smoke. "Werner needs to make an important delivery. He asked for you specifically."

"Me? Why?"

Gamon reached into his pocket and withdrew a subatomic

transport puck. He tossed it at Roy, who caught it with both hands. A clump of purple matter was encased in clear composite. Same weight, same feel, same rush of panic.

"He said you would be familiar with that particular cargo."

Roy's hands began to tremble, but he managed a slight nod.

"I need you to deliver that puck to a bloat house in the Kink Rinks."

"Bloat house?"

"A processing station. You're going to help them extract the contents for distribution. Werner has placed a high value on your previous experience. He wants you to oversee it."

Roy sighed and bowed his head. "So I'm a drug dealer now."

Gamon huffed and chewed his cigar. "You're in the business, Roy. What you choose to call yourself is irrelevant. The job is the job."

"I know, but—"

"But nothing. This isn't an offer."

Roy thought for a moment, then nodded.

"Good boy. You'll also need this." Gamon retrieved an activation clamp, the same kind that Werner had used on the previous puck. Silver, handheld, touchpad, everything Roy remembered. Gamon set it on the neon pink counter next to him. "The activation code is Pastry Post Deck 8 to 12. Werner said that you were a big enough nerd to know what that meant."

Roy nodded. *Pi, digits eight through twelve after the decimal*, he thought to himself.

"Good. Remember it. Don't do anything stupid like write it down."

Roy nodded.

"You are to deliver the puck to a gal named Praxie inside the Goruvian Grotto. It's an artificial cavern located inside the N2 Kink Rink. With me so far?"

"Yes sir," Roy said.

(In fact, Roy was intimately familiar with the location. The faux cavern was a must-visit for anyone with a nocturnal fetish. It housed an array of brothels in near-darkness, offering patrons everything from vampire cosplay to the infamous Mystery Hole, a pitch-black room with padded walls and an "anything goes" attitude. The only guarantees were that something would touch your junk and you wouldn't be fatally wounded. Roy had participated once in the distant past and had yet to determine whether he enjoyed the experience.)

"This is an immediate action. You will leave here and go straight there. She is expecting you by the end of the cycle."

"Yes sir."

"There's a brewpub just outside the main corridor. Sit at the bar, order a Firetooth Sandworm, and wait for someone to make contact. They will escort you to Praxie. From that point on, you're on your own. Do what they say and you'll be home before you know it. Understood?"

"Yes sir."

Gamon leaned forward and patted Roy's knee, as if to conclude the examination.

Roy half-expected a lollipop.

Gamon grunted as he rose to his feet and stretched away some soreness. The clown school chairs were a bit too small for his bulky frame (but ideal for hospital slapstick). Gamon seemed more out of place than Roy. The absence of his mobster lair proved a bit unsettling, so Roy knew the assignment carried a lot of unseen weight.

"Keep your comdev off until you reach a pod station. Use public transport and stay above the merchant line. No back channels. I will contact you for a debrief once the task is done."

"Yes sir."

"Good man," Gamon said, then exited the room.

The door latched shut, leaving Roy alone on the examination table. A cold silence infected the room, broken only by a thumping heartbeat. His troubled gaze crept over to the countertop, where the puck clamp rested in wait. Its glossy surface reflected the overhead light, taunting his mind with the exact position he never wanted to be in.

A knock at the door snatched his attention.

"Y—yes?" he said.

The door cracked open, allowing the smiling receptionist to peek her head inside. Her three eyes blinked randomly as her shark-like teeth parted. "Are you down to clown?" she said with a spine-chilling whisper.

"Nope!" Roy said as he sprung off the table and landed on the floor. "Nope!" he said as he swiped the clamp from the counter. "Nope!" he said as he pocketed the puck and hurried to the door. "Nope! Nope! Nope!" he said as he pushed into the hallway and fled the school as quickly as possible.

CHAPTER 15

Roy sat at the rear of a pod train, staring at nothing while stars in the black abyss twinkled overhead. The colossal wall of the next ring drew closer and closer, then zipped overhead as the train punched through the atmo barrier and into an express tunnel. Trips to the Kink Rinks took a while, so Roy had plenty of time alone with his thoughts.

One of his favorite travel games was guessing who would remain on board when the first Kink Rink passed overhead. Most passengers shuffled to detachment pods that broke away and vanished into the suburbs. But a few always remained. Suits and ties, sweats and sneakers, none of it mattered. Everyone had a fetish that needed attention from time to time. Roy had a few, but this time around, business would veto pleasure.

Conversations faded into the background. The puck was heavy in his pocket, like a loaded gun in search of a victim. Many times he had filled that seat, palms sweating, heart pounding with anticipation. But now it pounded with apprehension. Shame had poisoned his headspace, rendering him a silent and distant observer.

Another wall passed overhead. The train filled with a crimson glow, signaling the arrival at the first Kink Rink. The familiar transition yanked Roy out of his stupor. His gaze crept around the remaining passengers, all of which refused to make eye contact. A four-armed temptress in fishnet stockings moseyed into an adjacent car just before it detached. It was a well-practiced move from a well-practiced worker. Admirable in its own light, like a seasoned grunt on their way to a dig site.

Roy returned his gaze to the other passengers, all of whom retreated under hats and cloaks while carrying obvious stigmas. *First-timers*, he thought, then wondered what they thought of him. The Kink Rinks conjured many emotions, but dread and suspense were rarely among them. Perhaps a spousal confrontation, maybe a transactional dispute. Or, perhaps they were burdened by their own demons and didn't think of him at all. Roy had done incredible things, and yet, he remained a forgettable presence. He carried a pocket full of horror, but no one noticed. No one cared. He sighed, having realized that his life had come full circle.

The train punched through the atmo barrier of the target ring, then pinged with approaching separation. Roy maintained a sullen expression as his pod detached and curled into a side tunnel. After a few dips and dives, it slowed to a stop at the first station. The doors slid open, allowing a cloud of indulgence to invade the cabin. Flashing neon, howls of boozy laughter, and of course, the salty stench of lustful abandon. A group of loud-mouthed tourists stomped into the cabin and claimed some open seats. The doors slid shut and the pod whisked towards the next stop.

Roy cringed at his new travel mates.

And then he felt guilty for cringing.

He knew those people.

He *was* those people.

For everyone numbs the pain of existence.

Several stops later, Roy excused himself from a mass of drunken hoodlums and exited the pod into a sensual assault. The sector was ablaze with activity. Bright hologram ads littered the walls, cycling through seductive images. Black floors concealed numerous stains and rubbish. Cleaner bots hummed along as they struggled to sanitize an ever-tainted landscape. The crowd churned with all shapes and sizes, all races and sexes, all creeds and classes, pulsing as a stark contrast to the hygienic central rings.

Roy patted the puck inside his pocket. Still there, still heavy, still pulling him towards an unwanted appellation. He took a needed breath, then straightened his shirt and began the long trek to the Goruvian Grotto.

The Kink Rinks, while well-known for their boundless debaucheries, were not known for logical interiors. Their avenues twisted and turned over one another, creating an endless maze that confused and disoriented visitors. This was by design, as lost patrons tend to spend more credits. In fact, the deeper one ventured, the more delectable the reward. The most salacious brothels were also the hardest to find. The idea was, once you got there, it took an act of pure heroic will to leave.

As such, regulars to the Kink Rinks got really good at getting around. This wasn't a kooky sense of pride, but more of an outright necessity. "Got lost while getting bent" was not an excuse that employers were willing to accept.

Roy knew this well.

Roy also knew how to find the Goruvian Grotto.

Like a dog on a homeward journey, Roy followed his mental nose up ramps, down stairs, around bends, and over bridges. The very notion of "levels" was notably absent inside the ring. The interior seemed to twist and curl over itself, forming a giant metal pretzel without cessation. Its design was either an architectural wonder or a hideous drunken accident, a debate that often reared its head inside its many pubs and diners. Nevertheless, it remained a glorious destination for anyone with an itch to scratch.

Roy's usual grin and forward stare had morphed into vigilance. His reduced pace allowed him to absorb sights that he had once ignored. He met eyes with grifters and hucksters trying to fund their next fix. Their ratty clothes and bloodshot stares conjured waves of pity, something previously dismissed as background noise. He peeked inside dark alleys where groups of addicts traded pills and needles.

Their frail bodies leaned against filthy walls and dumpsters. The ablest among them scrounged for scraps in an effort to see the next day. The perennial musk, once seen as the peak of leisure, had revealed itself as soiled desperation.

The puck grew heavier in his pocket.

Hologram signs flashed from every direction. Neon letters and blinking arrows promised great times at affordable prices. Jezebels from all walks of life winked at Roy through cloudy windows. Red hues dominated the space, consuming the cooler hues of pubs and grub. Every hovel barked its own version of thumping music, serving as a constant buffer between the barfs and cackles. Every so often, a mystery stain would grip the sole of his shoe, prompting a cringe that his mind quickly snuffed away.

Roy crested a small hill to reveal his destination, a churning hollow known as the Goruvian Grotto. It spanned an area the size of a football field and rose several stories into the putrid air. Countless stairwells connected the base to the upper levels, all of which were open-faced and flashing neon adverts. A tangled web of pipes and ducts snaked across the ceiling, giving the chamber a cold industrial vibe.

One wall, however, was a towering void of darkness. No light, no levels, just a looming gateway to a nocturnal realm. It housed a bordello of black where dreams came true under a shroud of darkness. Patrons wandered to and from the chasm, wearing an array of interesting expressions. Most eager, some frightened, others exhausted as they returned to the light. Roy watched as battered bodies emerged from the portal, only to vanish into the core ruckus, like wounded soldiers returning from battle.

The roar of activity was impossible to ignore. Peddlers shouted from the upper decks while the base slithered with constant motion. Mobile shacks littered the arena, resembling a derelict shantytown. The hustle and bustle of roving commerce defined the space, offering everything from erotic toys to illicit encounters. A handful of permanent structures rose above the shacks, one of which was The Brink, a popular pub that rested at the portal base.

Roy's destination.

A hologram logo flashed above it, showcasing its namesake in wavy blue letters. The pub served as a makeshift lighthouse, offering a final shot of courage before crossing into the great unknown. Stories brimmed within its walls, many of which Roy had planted himself. The logo blinked and rotated, as if to wave him over for another round. Roy smirked, but the nostalgia would be short-lived. He restored his grimace and proceeded down the hill.

Cackles and shoulder bumps greeted his arrival at the shanties. Nothing personal, just a general neglect of couth and self-awareness. Groups of friends gathered around rickety sheds filled with skimpy hustlers. Creepy loners gawked at the latest sexbots. Paper fliers littered the ground, each stamped with erotic pics and detailed maps. Roy maneuvered through the madness, trying his best to avoid unwanted confrontations.

Given the near-constant intoxication, petty squabbles were a common sight within the Kink Rinks. Durangoni Security maintained an unseen presence to protect the workers. They quashed any scuffle that got out of hand, but largely ignored anything below a stabbing. Roy took pride in his willingness to throw a punch, but only now did he understand the power of restraint. Anyone could stand their ground, but true composure was tested in the shadows.

A few knocks and stumbles later, Roy found himself standing outside The Brink. Its stony exterior lifted from the ground like a mighty castle, despite being a two-story box with barred windows. His gaze climbed up the craggy facade and settled on the bright blue letters rotating overhead. A knot formed inside his stomach and crawled into his throat. He stepped towards the door, which swung open and slammed into the wall, compliments of a drunken brute on his way to an epic bender. Barks and clatters spilled from within, but faded into the background rumble. Roy took the opportunity to slip inside without touching the grimy handle.

A thick cloud of funk welcomed him into a foyer with sullied walls and a rugged floor. Roy cringed as a mixture of booze, barf, and breadsticks assaulted his nostrils. The pub was half-full, but sounded near-capacity. Social norms did not apply, so customers howled their every thought without a hint of shame. No one noticed his presence, not even the leggy hostess who wandered by and glanced over his head.

Roy was an unseen apparition.

Unassuming, unattractive, uninteresting, un-everything.

Gamon's favorite gopher.

He sighed, bowed his head, and shuffled towards the bar.

The bartender, a stout cyclops with a scruffy beard and rumpled hide, clunked several mugs of grog onto the counter and slid them towards a group of waiting dude-bros. Grunts of gratitude responded. They raised their mugs, toasted to their lechery, and erupted in hurrahs before dispersing. The barman watched with a blank expression, but then a squeaky stool hooked his attention. He turned to find a sheepish Roy occupying the seat.

The cyclops sneered and cocked his brow, dive-bar speak for *Whaddaya want?*

"Firetooth Sandworm, please," Roy said.

The cyclops stared him down, then turned away and plucked some bottles from the rear shelves. Roy watched intently as the barkeep poured and shook a multi-sauce concoction. He dumped the elixir into a highball glass, then struck a match and dropped it into the liquid, stem and all. The drink flared to life and shot a fiery column into the air that lasted far too long. Roy swallowed his alarm as the flame died to a flicker. The cyclops knocked the drink towards him, spilling a dab of flaming booze onto the counter before turning to the next customer.

Roy studied the still-burning liquid, unsure of how he was supposed to drink it. A hearty blow failed to extinguish the flame. It just flickered back to life and taunted him like a trick candle on a birthday cake. A stronger blow failed again, prompting a grunt and eye roll. He sighed with annoyance, then turned to find a giant bloodshot eyeball staring at him from the adjacent stool. Roy yelped into a near-tumble, but broke his fall with a hasty counter grab.

"Fuckin' hell," he said with a death grip on the bar. He closed his eyes for a quick reset, then returned his gaze to the creature.

A sheet of milky skin encased the head-sized orb. It was attached to a rigid stalk that snaked around the stool and down to the floor. At knee-level, the serpentine body split into four legs that tucked into leather boots. Roy traced the body back to the giant eye, which continued to glare at him through a deep brown iris. The skin sheet crawled around the orb and came together with a wet snap, which Roy could only assume was a blink.

"Can I, um ... help you?" Roy said, firmly recoiled.

"Who sent you?" the eyeball said from a well-hidden mouth.

"Gamon." Roy craned his neck to try and find the orifice. "Here to meet Praxie."

"Got the product?"

"Yes." Roy gestured down to his lap. He reached into his pocket and withdrew the puck, keeping it hidden inside his palm.

The eyeball rotated downward, wet-blinked, then rotated back. "Follow me," it said, then unraveled from the stool and waddled towards the exit.

Roy glanced at his still-flaming shot. The bartender wandered by, snuffed the flame with his beefy palm, then tossed it down his own gullet, all without making eye contact. Roy glared at the brute, then realized he hadn't paid. *Fair enough*, he thought to himself, then hopped off the stool and jogged to catch up with the walking eye-stalk.

CHAPTER 16

The eyestalk toddled to the front door and bumped it open with its noodly body, exiting The Brink. Roy followed it outside into the roaring grotto. Several necks turned to ogle the creature, a jarring sight even in the Kink Rinks. It had learned to ignore the stares, which saddened Roy and conjured some long-forgotten empathy. They strolled through the underworld as polar opposites of the visual spectrum. One unseeable. One unsettling.

The creature moseyed around the pub and towards the giant black hole behind it. *Of course it likes the dark*, Roy thought, then immediately felt guilty for thinking it. *I am such a dickhole*, he thought in response, hoping to balance out the karma.

They walked up a short incline and passed through the cavern entrance. An unseen barrier killed the grotto lights and banished the roar into the distant background. The sudden darkness stopped Roy in his tracks, forcing a search for visual bearings. As his eyes adjusted, faint blue lines began to reveal themselves. They defined edges and outlined objects, including himself. The holo-trace system allowed visitors to see without ruining the nocturnal experience. Bright enough to avoid obstacles, dim enough to remain anonymous.

Roy glanced around the multi-story cavern. Numerous stairs and ramps led to a myriad of doors and hallways, all of them outlined for convenience. Patrons of all persuasions wandered through the murky maze, hunting for their erotic encounters. An unspoken gag rule rendered the place eerily silent. Heel clacks echoed like jackhammers. Door whines cut through the space like ghostly howls. Roy traced a winding stairwell down to the floor, where the outline of a wobbling eyestalk shrunk with every step.

Roy jogged to catch up.

He followed the creature around a bend and into a hidden hallway. The silence deepened, amplifying their footsteps. They passed the outlines of unmarked doors, each housing a distant ruckus. The eyestalk waddled to a stop at the end of the passage. It double-checked for its Roy companion, then gazed into a hidden panel. A soft ping confirmed the iris scan, prompting an unseen door to slide open. Roy followed the beast into an ebon box. The door slid shut and the floor began its slow descent.

The interior lights flickered on, quelling the darkness. Roy winced at the sudden brightness and blinked to readjust. The elevator car was remarkably clean. Pristine, even. Each wall was a spotless plane of smooth metal. Panels on the floor and ceiling glowed with a frosty hue. A dull hum of descent served as a backdrop to the awkward silence.

"So, um ..." Roy said. "What's your name?"

The creature maintained its forward stare.

"I'm Roy."

The creature wet-blinked, then twisted its giant eye to Roy. "Lenny," it said from a yet-to-be-seen mouth.

"Nice to meet you, Lenny."

Lenny's eye flaps puckered a bit, which Roy could only assume was a smile.

The floor pushed on their heels as the elevator slowed to a stop. The door slid open to reveal a large factory bustling with activity. Roy and Lenny emerged onto a catwalk that encircled the plant. Guards in black uniforms clomped along the grated metal, eyeing the work floor beneath them. Numerous stations littered the arena, housing countless peons that assembled nodes and passed them along. Conveyor belts slithered through the workspace, shuttling parts throughout the factory. Chains and tethers dangled from the ceiling like moss from a mighty tree.

An odd place for a drug distributor.

Or perhaps, the ideal cover for one.

Resting at the center was a large dome with a row of port windows. Conveyor belts ran from it, but not to it. A small regiment of guards patrolled the perimeter. Roy leaned on the railing and studied the structure from afar. Not a foreman office, that much was certain.

"Come," Lenny said as he started down a stairwell.

Roy followed him down to the work floor, then along a marked path towards the center. The workers ignored them, content to toil away at their stations. They all wore the same white aprons and green gloves. A painful sterility infected the air. Unseen chemicals floated through the space, stinging lungs with every inhale.

A guard snickered and shook his head as Lenny waddled by. Roy glared at the guard as he passed, which the guard saw fit to return. Lenny continued his trek up to a small group chatting beside the dome. He slowed to a stop and stared at the nearest member, a suited brute with gray skin and numerous warts.

Lenny cleared his throat.

The brute glanced at the eyestalk and huffed. "The cock-eye is back."

The rest of the group chuckled.

Roy, heeding the need to maintain civility, decided to stay quiet. "Ass-wart fucker says what?" he said with an assertive tone.

"What?" the brute said.

The group chuckled even louder.

Lenny puckered his flaps in response.

The brute turned to Roy and puffed his chest. "Care to say that again?"

Roy, always one to diffuse a strained situation, contemplated a heartfelt apology. "Ass," he said, then took a step forward. "Wart." Another step. "Fucker." A final step brought them face to face. "Says what?"

The brute snarled, but the confrontation was cut short.

"That's enough," said a scratchy female voice.

The group parted to reveal a dark-haired vixen leaning against the dome wall. Her leathery garb looked better suited for a mercenary ship than a factory floor. She sprang off the wall and sauntered towards Roy, unveiling her violet eyes and ashy face. Her wiry frame looked brittle in a way, despite her bold and confident stride. Her boots clacked to a rest, cueing a hard lean and chin cock. She looked Roy up and down, then smirked.

"Piss off, Klurp," she said to the brute without making eye contact. "And take your band of fuckwits with you."

The brute nodded, then slunk away with his posse in tow. He tossed a glare at Roy before turning down the entry path.

The woman crossed her arms and grunted. "So you're the guy, eh?"

"I'm a guy," Roy said with an affable tone. "Can't say if I'm *the* guy."

"Gamon sent you, no?"

"Ah, yes. That guy I am." He extended a hand. "Roy."

"Praxie," she said and completed the shake. "Been waiting for you."

"Am I late?"

"No. Been waiting all the same." She glanced at the eyestalk. "That'll be all, Lenny."

Lenny wet-blinked, then turned away and headed back to the stairs.

"Hey Lenny," Roy said.

The eyestalk paused and twisted back to Roy.

"Thanks for the escort. I appreciate it."

Lenny pucker-smiled, then untwisted and resumed his trek.

"Good guy, that one," Roy said to Praxie. "Got a question, though."

"What the hell is he?"

"Yes, please."

Praxie shrugged. "No one knows. Lenny never talks about his past and there are no other species like him on the station. Trust me, I've looked. Mutant would be my best guess. Maybe a botched experiment. I strongly suspect that he escaped a bad situation. Landed here a while back, been working the grotto ever since."

They watched from afar as Lenny climbed the stairs, albeit awkwardly.

"And you're right," she said with a tender tone. "He is a good guy."

She spun around and plodded in the opposite direction, making her way around the dome. Her long gait forced Roy into a light jog to keep up. He eyed the port windows along the wall, which glowed bright enough to conceal the interior. Praxie thumped her shoulder into a sturdy entry door. The pane swung open and they proceeded inside.

Roy squinted as a golden glare consumed them. Praxie sauntered towards the center of a large round room. Roy glanced around the edgeless space, resembling the interior of a giant metal donut. A continuous lighting strip glowed above the port windows. Every square inch sloped down to a focal point. Roy peeked around Praxie to find a mounting rod rising from the axis. He frowned, recalling the same setup from the Sunken Isles. The dome was an extraction bowl, just on a much smaller scale.

Praxie's heels clacked to a halt beside the mount. She turned to Roy and swung an open hand over the rod, as if to present a prize. "I trust you know what to do?"

"Y—yes," Roy said with a reluctant tone.

A brief silence settled between them.

Praxie sighed, then rolled her wrist, gesturing to *get on with it.*

"Ah, yes, sorry." Roy fished the puck and clamp from his pockets. Beads of sweat rolled down his face as he joined them together. The claws snapped around the puck and the device powered on, ready to receive command. *Pastry Post Deck 8 to 12*, he thought. *Pi, digits eight through twelve after the decimal. 3.1415926 ... 53589.* His heart raced as he repeated the code. *53589 ... 53589 ... 53589.*

"Is something wrong?" Praxie said with a hint of annoyance.

"No, s'all good."

He pressed five.

Praxie narrowed her gaze.

"It's just ..."

He pressed three.

Praxie cocked her neck.

"I just, um ..."

He pressed five.

And then everything stopped.

Roy froze in realization.

Praxie froze in confusion.

He met her gaze, then slowly shook his head. "I can't do this," he said with a meager voice, then spun and sprinted for the door.

Praxie's confusion snapped into anger. "What the f—stop!" Her words echoed through the chamber as Roy crashed through the door. She gave chase and slid to a halt outside the dome. Her widened gaze whipped around the factory and locked onto Roy sprinting for the exit. She pointed and screamed. "Stop him!"

All activity came to an abrupt stop, save for Roy's galloping retreat. Every worker turned to the commotion, but did not bother to get involved. Every guard zeroed in on Roy. Some chased him down the gangway while others leapt from the catwalk to cut off the stairs, barring the path to and from. Roy skidded to a halt and looked to his sides, only to see guards closing in from the factory floor.

He was trapped.

Panic ensued.

The guards inched towards him from every direction. Stun batons crackled in their hands, cutting through a hanging tension. Workers continued to watch with mild interest as the guards surrounded their target. Roy spun around with the puck in hand, searching for outs that no longer existed. He whimpered as a gruesome fate engulfed him.

The clacks of Praxie's heels echoed from afar. She sauntered down the gangway, cold and confident in her approach. A callous smirk crept across her face. She would savor the torture, as she always did.

But then a guard screamed.

And another.

They all staggered backwards, then turned and fled.

Praxie watched a frightened guard tumble over a workstation, then keep going. Her puzzled gaze returned to the gangway where a frothing beast occupied the space. Its hunched back and clouded eyes drew an immediate flinch and backtrack. It snarled at her as an acidic brew spilled from its mouth.

A tense standoff commenced.

The workers held their breath.

But not for long, as they too would scream and flee when the beast shrieked and gave chase to the vixen. Praxie matched the shriek and spun into her own sprint. She rounded the dome with flailing arms and disappeared. Roy skidded to a halt and about-faced. Using the chaos as cover, he resumed his sprint towards the elevator.

Another guard burst through a perimeter door with a spear-like weapon in hand. It crackled with captive charge. He aimed it at a fleeing Roy and pulled the trigger, releasing a violent blast of energy. The bolt whizzed over his shoulder and destroyed a nearby workstation. Roy yelped, but maintained his stride.

Another bolt.

Another miss.

Another yelp.

Roy sailed around some heavy machinery and into the stairwell, shielding him from aim. The guard sprinted down the catwalk to reset. Roy had precious few seconds to summon the lift. He darted up the stairs, across the catwalk, and slapped the control panel. The elevator dinged, but the car wasn't there. It began a slow descent from above, content to milk additional stress from the situation. Roy groaned with frustration, but there was nothing to do. He could only hope that the car arrived before the next blast ripped him to shreds.

The guard's clanking sprint grew louder and louder.

Roy cringed and slapped the panel eight more times.

The clanks grew louder, and louder, and stopped.

A sudden thump and clatter cued an array of curses.

Roy peeked around a pillar to see the guard sprawled over the catwalk. He had tripped and fallen, sending his weapon tumbling down to the factory floor. The guard barked with pain and scrambled to right the mishap. Lenny stood behind him, watching the ruckus while trying to look innocent. He met gazes with Roy and pucker-smiled.

Roy returned the smile and nodded.

The elevator dinged.

* * *

It should come as no surprise that Roy escaped. He rode the elevator back to the grotto, sprinted to the cavern mouth, and vanished into the crowd. And when I say *vanished*, I mean exactly that. He slipped into the mass and disappeared. I studied hours of footage, tracing his every step until he turned the proverbial corner.

Poof.

Gone.

No trace whatsoever.

To this day, I have no idea how Roy fled the Rinks. But given where he ended up, the only thing I knew for certain was that he had some help. How? Because two weeks later, Praxie and her goons found him inside the core.

But we'll get to that.

I just wanted to know how he got there.

I staked out the Goruvian Grotto for several days, hoping to uncover pieces of the puzzle. Drunken dregs were more than happy to muse on Roy's antics, which, apparently, was all the buzz in the underworld. None were helpful, but all were entertaining. I even chatted with a few of the factory workers, all of whom declined to be interviewed.

The mystery persisted.

And then, late on the third day, while sipping on my fourth Firetooth Sandworm inside The Brink, I saw an eyestalk creature waddle through the front door.

I greeted Lenny and coaxed him into a friendly conversation. He carried no veneer or pretense, which was disarming at first. I got the distinct impression that he was just happy to be needed. He and Roy were much alike in that way. I enjoyed my chat with Lenny, despite his dry demeanor and penchant for using the least amount of words to make his point. Our meeting was short and sweet, as Lenny was unable (or perhaps unwilling) to add any tantalizing details. Below is a brief excerpt.

Did you help Roy escape the factory by tripping the guard?

Roy was a kind person. I consider him a friend.

And did he give you any indication of where he was going?

Roy was a kind person. I consider him a friend.

I can't tell if you're being candid or avoidant.

Roy was a kind person. I consider him a friend.

Did you, um ... was Roy a kind person and do you consider him a friend?

(wet-blinks) Yes.

CHAPTER 17

Two weeks after his miraculous escape, Roy was found in the core of Durangoni. This fact alone was itself miraculous, as core folk did not suffer the peons. Roy had earned a respectable income working as Gamon's lackey, but his bank account was nowhere near the capacity it took to fraternize with engineering royalty. Coupled with a security system that rivaled nuclear silos, it made his presence ever so mysterious.

Thus, he needed help.

And given his connection to a particular dissident, one could surmise where it came from. (Vierra Belliosa has never confirmed her involvement and my journalistic integrity prevents me from implicating her. But, c'mon.)

In any regard, Roy was hiding in the core. Someone saw him and reported the breach, which was likely intercepted by Werner and relayed to Praxie. Let us not forget that Roy was carrying a fortune's worth of Snake Bone on his person. He betrayed Gamon, which blacklisted him in the trafficking network. He betrayed Werner, which likely placed him on Zip's "special friends" list. Roy was now the most wanted being in the quadrant. His world had utterly imploded, all thanks to a pesky rush of conscience.

The stage was set for a messy confrontation.

* * *

Roy had always wanted to see the core, just not as a desperate fugitive. He lay on the rooftop of a luxury mart that catered to the obscenely rich. Any single item cost more than he could ever make as a plumber. The store's dumpster carried more value than a mid-level merchant shop, a fact that was not lost on him whenever he plundered it for morsels. After all, a hunted criminal beggar could not be a chooser.

Roy munched on a half-eaten sandwich while gazing into a giant sky lake.

Yes, a giant lake in the sky.

To understand the core of Durangoni, one must first understand centrifugal force. There is no *weight* at the core of a planet because there is no *down*. Force is equal from all directions, which neutralizes gravity. Durangoni was no different, so any normalized weight needed to be created. The core was a long cylinder from pole to pole, serving as a hub for the ring system. Its hollow interior was five miles in diameter with crisscrossing beams that supported the structure. The core rotated independently, creating enough gravity to keep everything glued to the walls. Thus, when Roy gazed into the sky, he gazed at the other side of a rotating barrel.

A barrel, in this case, populated by eggheads and the uber-wealthy.

The lake in Roy's sky was constructed for an energy mogul who loved to fish. His personal mega-yacht floated on his personal lake while his personal staff processed the exotic fish that he had personally selected for his personal lake. All inside the core of Durangoni, one of the most expensive pieces of real estate in the known universe. The sheer magnitude of opulence was difficult to comprehend. So stunning was the lake's impracticality that Roy could waste hours dissecting the physics of its creation.

His gaze wandered the vast enclosure, a round horizon filled with nerve centers and lavish mansions. Maglev rails shuttled the rich and nerdy around the interior. Personal vehicles were strictly prohibited, as drunken accidents could disable critical systems. Given the core's vital role in the survival of a trillion beings, security was paramount. It took extraordinary levels of power and influence to gain access, a reality that plagued Roy with constant anxiety. His presence was an extreme anomaly, one that carried an equally extreme punishment.

Nevertheless, he was stuck there.

But all the same, it was better than anywhere else.

And so he waited.

Two weeks he had called that rooftop home. Two weeks of sleeping on a hard surface with artificial sunlight battering his eyelids. For once, he actually missed his ratty cot in the sub-core. Roy was surrounded by an ostentatious landscape, a life he had coveted from his first day aboard the station. And yet, in that lowest of moments, he would have given anything to slumber in the bowels of anonymity.

And then a faint squeak caught his attention.

Roy sat up and raked his gaze across the rooftop. The vents were quiet. No wind or chatting locals. Another faint squeak snapped his gaze to a nearby access ladder. A sudden terror swelled inside his chest. He scrambled to his feet and tiptoed to a hidden corner for a covert peek. When he peered over the ledge, his gut seized with panic. Praxie stood in the back alley. She monitored a pair of burly goons who were climbing the ladder as quietly as they could.

Roy swallowed a gasp and stumbled backwards. With precious little time, he spun around and sprinted towards a small satchel resting in the opposite corner. His loud clops prompted the goons to bark with urgency and hurry up the ladder. Roy skidded to a halt, snatched the satchel, and slung it over his shoulder as the first goon poked his head above the roofline. They met eyes for a split second, contrasting their fear and focus.

Roy leapt over the ledge.

It was a well-rehearsed move. That is, inside his head. Roy crashed onto a pallet of stock, which looked much softer than it actually was. The impact buckled his legs, knocked the wind from his lungs, and sent him tumbling to the ground. He wheezed in pain as distant yells gave way to canters of pursuit. No broken bones, thank goodness, but plenty of nasty knocks and soon-to-be bruises. Roy struggled to his feet and stumbled into a run.

Plan B was officially in play.

Roy emerged from the alley and onto the sidewalk, where several well-to-dos gawked at his presence. A dirty poor on *their* pristine walkway? Surely not, kind sir. Roy fled the disapproval and sprinted in the other direction. A dainty lady screamed and shooed him away, as if to shame a rat back to the sewer. The ruckus alerted the goons, who emerged from the alley as Roy ducked into another. They gritted their teeth and continued the pursuit with Praxie in tow.

Several turns later, Roy stalled outside of a processing depot. Supply drones floated around the area, tending to open bays full of lavish goods. Even they were grime-free and shining in the artificial sunlight. It was as if dirt itself had been outlawed. Roy spun around the yard in search of an exit. Security barriers blocked the bays, so he settled for a stack of crates. Not the most ideal of hiding places, but good enough for a breather. The goons grumbled nearby, then faded into the distance, having taken a wrong turn.

With time now a luxury, Roy decided to enact the next phase of his plan. He fished the comdev from his pocket, checked the clock, then placed a hasty call. "It's me," he said. "I'm pinched. Green light for the nine-block." He peeked around the crates and stared at the depot entrance. "Yes, zero the rest." The call ended. A quick swipe opened a pre-programmed screen with a flashing banner. It awaited some final input, which Roy provided. He took a deep breath, submitted the form, then returned the comdev to his pocket.

A sharp chirp startled him into a flinch. He spun around to find a supply drone staring him down with discontent. Its single red eye glanced at the crate stack, then back to him, then back to the stack, then back to him.

"Oh, sorry," Roy said, then stepped aside.

The drone floated to the stack, grabbed the top crate, then

chirped at Roy again before hovering away.

Roy sighed.

Even the robots gave him shit.

As he watched the drone rejoin its tidy brethren, his gaze fell to a porthole cover near the center of the yard. A half-grin lifted his cheek, which quickly inverted when he noticed Praxie enter the depot. He yelped and sprinted to the port. Praxie shouted for the goon squad as Roy gripped the latch handles and yanked it open, unveiling a dank sewer system (which, of course, smelled like lavender). Roy dropped through the hole and splash-landed into a river of muck, a depressingly familiar sensation. He picked a direction and fled.

Plan C, then.

The echoes of Praxie and her posse bounded through the dark tunnels. Roy huffed and puffed as his feet splashed through a thin layer of filth. Dome lights whipped overhead, reminiscent of the pod train expressway. He had no idea where he was going, but felt an urgent need to get there as quickly as possible. Blind instinct yanked him into side tunnels, hoping to delve deep enough to regain some isolation. He ducked into a random alcove and stopped dead in his tracks, letting the silence consume him.

Praxie's voice grew louder, then quieter, then vanished.

The splashes of her goons disappeared.

Roy swallowed a whimper.

The hunt was on.

Sensing the end of his psychotic adventure, Roy retrieved the puck and clamp from his satchel. He joined them together with a soft push, which powered the display. *If this is the end*, he thought, *might as well be memorable.* He sighed, then entered 5-3-5-8-9. The device pinged and unlocked the extraction protocol. He swiped the meter up to full capacity, topping out at 93 billion units. He then set a 30-second delay, just in case. After several "Are you sure?" checks, a large button turned red.

At that moment, a single tap separated Roy from a spectacular departure.

"Roy!" Praxie said, her voice echoing from an adjacent tunnel.

"You cannot escape this. All we want is the product. Hand it over and we will let you go."

Roy rolled his eyes. Even under the circumstances, he could not help but balk at such an obvious lie. "Can I get a hug too?" he said.

After an awkward silence, "Yes" echoed in response.

Roy shook his head, then emerged from the alcove and tiptoed down the tunnel. The constant trickle of water masked any obvious footsteps. His slow and steady vigilance guided him through a maze of passages, hoping for an exit. Before long, a dull and distant roar caught his attention. He crept towards the sound, using it as an audible shield. A faint glow appeared in his peripheral, stealing his focus. Sunlight. He grunted with relief and leapt into a light jog. Roy turned a final corner and slowed to a stop at the mouth of a giant egress.

The sweet relief turned sour.

Roy pulled his gaze across a massive basin of waterfalls. Countless drainpipes emptied their contents into a reservoir far below. The constant churn created a colossal whirlpool, certain death for anyone stupid enough to take the plunge. Roy groaned at the dead end and turned back to the sewer maze, only to find the smirking faces of Praxie and her goons.

"End of the line," she said.

Roy stood motionless.

She extended an open palm. "We can do this the easy way or the hard way. Your choice."

"Do I still get that hug?" Roy said in a mocking tone.

Praxie smirked and motioned to the goons, who stepped forward.

Roy lifted the clamp overhead, revealing the glowing red button.

The goons halted.

Praxie's smirk disappeared. "Wha—what are you doing?"

The smirk had reappeared on Roy's face. "Plan D it is," he said, then pressed the button and hurled the device over the ledge. It fell through the churning mist and vanished into the reservoir below. Roy expected an immediate tackle, but it never came. He turned back to Praxie and her goons, all of whom were frozen in horror. The image caught him off-guard, shifting his dismay to curiosity. "What?" he said, which cued a thundering explosion.

The violent expansion lifted the entire lake over the basin. A massive spout of filthy water surged into the sky and rained across the landscape. The entire region shook under a sudden and savage earthquake. Walls cracked. Metal screamed. Every drain flooded with backwash. Roy and his pursuers were snatched from their feet and carried through the sewer maze. Chaos consumed the valley as a raging tsunami swallowed it whole.

* * *

And thus began The Incident.

Praxie and her goons had donned faces of horror, but not for the reasons one might expect. While the loss of product was unfortunate, they were privy to two critical pieces of information that Roy was not.

First, the lake was a catch basin for Durangoni's water treatment system. Whatever dropped inside was filtered and recirculated. The orbs of Snake Bone, while a costly and disruptive clog, would have been caught and removed.

That is, if not for the second piece of information.

There were no orbs.

This particular batch was in caplet form. *Dissolvable* caplet form. Roy, unbeknownst to him, had dosed the entire space station with 93 billion units of a hallucinogenic nightmare.

A trillion beings called Durangoni home, and every one of them tripped balls for an entire week. The dilution lessened the severity, but the tainted circulation ensured a long and steady experience. With no way to combat the contamination, and with no one lucid enough to think of an alternate recourse, the entire population was forced to endure the chaos.

This period of mass psychosis, infamously dubbed The Incident, brought the station to its proverbial knees. Imagine, if you will, the single greatest assembly of creeds and cultures losing its collective grip on reality.

All at once.

For an entire week.

With no reticence or rule of law.

The disruption was, to put it gently, immeasurably disgracious. And while I would never presume to recap someone else's torment, I can reach into my own dark chasm of experience and withdraw some poignant anecdotes. The following is a candid recount of my dance with the rainbow devil.

* * *

Day One

It started as any other.

I awoke inside my condo with a mind for breakfast. After a hot shower and some extensive primping, I perused a collection of designer suits and selected a pleasing ensemble that captured the appropriate mood. I had an important meeting that day, so I landed on ashen pinstripes with a turquoise tie. Dignity with a dash of flair. Puki Horpocket always departs his master suite as a painted portrait. This day was no different and I looked positively smashing.

Too bad it was all for naught.

I strolled through a vibrant living room dripping with class and kudos. Paintings, sculptures, and of course, multiple glass cabinets filled with awards, plaques, and medals. I have no choice but to bathe in my own merit before entering the kitchen. A bit smug perhaps, but I enjoy the daily boost and prefer it to a moist toilette. I see it as a final tease and tickle before moving on to phase two of my morning routine.

I flowed into my kitchen, an austere environment with white cabinets, sharp angles, and polished metal fixtures. A gracious host I am not, as my social obligations are always met in public. Thus, my kitchen and I share a bond of severity. The coffee machine had sensed my presence and started brewing a delectable concoction that shall remain nameless. A heavenly aroma filled the space. But alas, the machine had betrayed me. It had drunk from the tainted pipes of Roy's misadventure.

This would be my first dose of Snake Bone.

A hologram panel had appeared on the adjacent wall and opened a curator view for the Definitive Directory of Durangoni. My coffee intake involves scanning the directory for any updates that required my immediate attention. The auto-rito spit out a warm breakfast wrap, which I plucked from the tray and carried over to a comfy nook. I took a seat at a small bench and table, perfect for sipping and nibbling while getting a jumpstart on the day.

And so I sipped and nibbled.

That is, until the letters started to move.

Not by much, just enough to assume that the holo-feed was glitching. I adjusted the settings as best I could, but nothing I did seemed to fix the problem. And then a capital F ate a lowercase A. Not deleted, *ate*. I can still hear the crunching and howls of agony. The graphic barbarity sparked an alphabetic panic. Entire words leapt off the screen and fell to the floor, where they flopped like fish out of water. And then the serifs declared war. A vicious battle erupted inside the directory. Uppercase Ts plunged their daggers into the soft bellies of vowels. Xs spun like buzz saws and chewed through helpless adverbs. The shrieks haunt me to this day.

I killed the feed with a stern command, which instantly wiped the battlefield. Calm returned to the kitchen, unwinding an unexpected tension. *What a tasteless prank*, I thought while sipping a second mug of nightmare fuel.

I downed a final swig and set the mug on the counter, at which point it decided to sprout several legs and skitter across the surface like a porcelain spider. I yelped and jerked backwards, as one tends to do when drinkware comes to life. The handle split into a pair of mandibles, which the spider mug gleefully used to scare the dickens out of me. Sharp tinks needled the room as the creature tapped across the counter and chomped its handle. It tried to scale a cabinet wall, but lost its grip and fell to the floor. The mug shattered into several pieces, all of which sprouted their own spider legs and skittered away.

I paused to gather my bearings while trying to ignore the swamp beast playing sad ukulele music in the corner. His name was Finkle, by the way. I know this because he waved and said, "I'm Finkle," before popping out one of his eyes, tossing it into the sink, and returning to his sad ukulele music. Bright yellow pus oozed from the socket and trickled down his chest, not that he seemed to mind. The eye in the sink began to multiply with wet pops, creating a small army of squirming orbs that cheered whenever a song ended.

Alas, my bearings would remain ungathered.

Not that it mattered much, as a legion of flaming mupmups (read: tiny hairless hyenas with a penchant for ankle biting) fell through a doom portal and galloped through the condo. Purple flames poured from their bodies, igniting everything they touched. I yelped again and raced towards the front door, which was also a pancake. Having no idea how to unlock a pancake, I crashed into the pane with a stiff shoulder, which ripped it off the hinges and launched me out into the open. Several mupmups chased me outside, but paused to devour the pancake door, all while setting the entire neighborhood on fire.

Speaking of the neighborhood, that's when things got interesting.

My community enjoyed a quiet location tucked away from the hustle and bustle of station life. As such, the enormity of the situation had been somewhat stymied. The front door of my condo opened into a rounded basin with a central garden. I shared the space with two dozen neighbors, many of whom were oblivious to the mupmup flames consuming the area. I did my best to call attention to the danger, but they seemed a bit preoccupied with their own hellscapes. One of them sprinted around the basin while swinging a lamp with homicidal intent. Another saw fit to dance naked in the garden while hissing at anyone who came near. It became abundantly clear that fleeing was the best course of action.

And so I did.

I hurried down an access hall and into another basin, which was guarded by a three-pronged unicorn named Francis. I know this because he said, "Begone, interloper! For ye have entered the blessed kingdom of Francis the Wonder Pickle!" I had questions, but I did not stick around to ask them.

After scampering through more halls and gardens, I emerged into a large pedestrian tunnel. Sorry, what I meant to say was, I emerged into a swirling vortex of pure pandemonium. It was hard to find someone who wasn't screaming. A mass of terrified citizens barked and flailed as they fought whatever torment their minds had conjured up. The one I remember the most was a small child pointing at the ceiling while grinning like a serial killer. She clutched a cabbage in the other hand, which she used to intimidate the vision.

And so I fled again, this time towards a nearby pod station.

A fresh wave of madness hit my brain as I skidded to a halt at the crowded junction. The gathered mass pulsed and twitched, as if possessed by a horde of demons. When the writhing stopped, they had all transformed into my mother. The horror. *Release me from the burden of living*, I thought, *for I had come to know a fate worse than death*. They pierced me with guilt trips and passive-aggressive taunts, torturing my headspace with things I knew to be true but refused to address.

A ping echoed from afar, signaling the arrival of a pod train. The doors opened and a throng of new moms joined the berating. I shoved my way towards the train, desperate to rid myself of gnawing truths. As the doors began to close, I surged forward with all my might and dove into the pod. I hit the floor and tumbled into the rear wall, knocking the wind from my lungs. When I turned back, the mother mass chided my career choice, then exploded into a cloud of fluttlenibs (read: helicopter butterflies with nagging dispositions). The pod pinged as if nothing was amiss, then proceeded to the next stop.

I spent the rest of the day inside that pod. I wanted to leave, but the doors had grown shark teeth and I didn't want to risk it.

Day Two

The fever continued inside the merchant district of a random ring. I did not leave the pod, so much as sail through the doors involuntarily. A large bloke had decided that the pod was his new lover and tossed me outside like a jealous suitor.

I wandered the district while trying to ignore the giant eyeball hovering over my head. Its bloodshot gaze and bright orange iris proved rather unsettling, but it never attacked. It seemed intensely fascinated by my actions, even going so far as to narrate my movements. I named it Blinky because it had no eyelids.

Day Three

I had actually gotten some sleep, thanks to a spooked clown and a swift punch to the face. When I awoke, I could hear a commotion in the distance. A crowd had gathered and sounded a bit unruly. Blinky insisted that we check it out, so we did. I poked my head into a loading bay to find a mob of pink skeletons fighting a nurkalu (read: giant hairy lobster on stilts). Apparently, that's all my brain needed to know. I grabbed a potted plant and joined the battle, which made total sense at the time.

Day Four

Three words: pantsless chandelier hunting.

Day Five

I now understood that Blinky was a magical faerie guarding a pot of gold. He denied it, of course, but my stubborn insistence convinced him otherwise. We boarded a pod train and ended up at an ocean ring beach. I spent the entire day digging holes in the sand based on cryptic clues. Blinky watched the effort with a voyeuristic hunger. As the pizza sun began to set, I passed out from exhaustion and fell into one of the holes.

Day Six

I awoke inside the hole, but Blinky was nowhere to be found. He had left a note that read, "There was no gold. I'm just a digging enthusiast." I shouted some gibberish and punched the sand five times, which summoned Veferaf, the Ocean Dragon. I scrambled out of the hole and met gazes with a towering water serpent hovering above the waves.

"Choose your cheese," the dragon said with a menacing growl.

I removed my turquoise tie, wrapped it around my forehead, and struck a superhero pose. "Cheddar," I said, and fucking meant it.

The dragon roared with displeasure and I shot a fireball at him. We fought into the evening.

Day Seven

I awoke feeling somewhat like myself, as did most of the population. I hadn't bathed in a week, so the ripeness of my body made its presence known. All that remained of my suit was a tattered jacket and a headband tie. I wandered the beach in a haze of confusion, as did several others. Eye contact was brief and uncomfortable. It took a while to pinpoint my location, but I eventually made it back to a pod station. When I arrived, a small group of citizens was waiting patiently for the next train. Some were bloody, some were naked, and nobody dared to comment on those facts. For the ultimate walk of shame had commenced.

* * *

In the end, the citizens of Durangoni had suffered an extraordinary loss, both economically and psychologically. Cleaning and rebuilding were equally painful, as shame was smeared across the station like a grisly crime scene. In order to cope, the population united under a shared layer of scar tissue. No one wanted to relive the time they awoke from a harrowing delusion, battered, bruised, and covered in mayonnaise.

Or hiding in a vat of engine grease with a missing finger.

Or perched atop a fountain while trying to impregnate it.

Or trapped inside an air duct while wearing assless chaps.

Or zealously stabbing every stuffed animal in a toy store.

Or stranded inside the Kink Rinks ... in any circumstance.

The Incident would remain exactly that, a generic event that everyone acknowledged, but refused to discuss. When the dust settled, I was tasked to record a brief yet conclusive entry for the directory. In its entirety: "A weeklong event where a trillion beings stared into the maw of madness, then went back to work."

Durangoni remains stubbornly tight-lipped about it. They only release footage for the most heinous of criminal investigations. The entire week is blacked out from the archives, and for good reason. By normal standards, most citizens would have faced prison time.

Security feeds leading up to The Incident are choppy at best. The most compelling comes from the Zandui Casino. A nameless citizen had won the Big Sixty jackpot, sparking a giant celebration before the feed crackled away. What should have been a station-wide news spectacle was quickly snuffed from existence.

The peculiar timing has spawned numerous conspiracy theories, from typical government mistrust to tinfoil hat lunacy. In the end, the only info revealed to the public was that Roy had won and no one could find him. His status as a sub-core plumber lit a fire of intrigue that would blossom into legend.

Praxie survived the ordeal, as she was observed several weeks later drinking heavily inside a Kink Rink pub. Roy, on the other hand, had disappeared entirely. The last known footage of his life aboard the station was captured at a remote banking outpost that serviced the needs of specialized traders. It flanked a seldom-used port and employed a small staff. Weeks after The Incident, Roy walked up to a teller window and withdrew 300 trillion credits onto a single mofu (mobile funding unit). He thanked the teller, who promptly fainted.

Roy exited the bank, turned a corner, and was never seen again.

CHAPTER 18

Years later, Durangoni had healed and moved past its collective woe. Conversations had returned to normal. Commerce had resumed its stride. Roy's status as a tenacious rebel had wormed its way into the public conscience. His name was toasted in bars, discussed in shops, and debated among the rich. After all, it's not every day that an unknown dreg can ensnare a trillion minds.

His legend was here to stay.

But alas, he remained a ghost.

I spent countless hours trying to uncover his tracks, but every lead brought me to another dead end. The story had gone cold, as did my excitement for piecing it together.

It was done.

The story of Roy had reached its logical yet disappointing conclusion.

But then, out of the cold reaches of nowhere, something snagged my attention. I wasn't looking for it. It just appeared, like a tasty mint on a comfy pillow. Before I could wrap this yarn and send it to the presses, I had one more person to visit.

* * *

The next morning, I found myself inside a familiar abode. The plants and aromas were oddly comforting, like visiting an old garden with lots of love and history. Duncan poured me a mug of tea and settled into his ratty chair. Same 'ol Duncan, same 'ol tea, but with a whole new level of implication.

Thank you for agreeing to meet with me on such short notice.

Sure thing, always up for a pleasurable chitchat. So what would you like to discuss?

As you know, I have been building the story of Roy with the hopeful aim of bringing it to a satisfying conclusion. But try as I might, I cannot progress past the banking outpost. For all intents and purposes, Roy simply disappeared.

(Duncan smiles and nods.)

I reached out to every possible lead I could think of. Former bosses, favorite hussies, the whole gamut. None of them have seen Roy or know of his whereabouts.

(Duncan smiles and nods again.)

I also consulted financial records, hoping to uncover large transactions from mysterious sources of wealth. Again, nothing.

(Duncan smiles and nods again.)

However, in doing so, my updated records showed a peculiar abnormality. I was hoping that you could shed some light on it.

Oh boy, you got me on the pins and needles.

With your permission, I would like you to verify some statements.

Permission granted. Toss me some teasers.

Hours before Roy won the Big Sixty jackpot, security footage shows him making a hasty phone call. It is rumored that the

game's unbeatable algorithm wasn't an algorithm at all. It was a pure randomization governed by the big red button located in the entry corridor of The Pipes community pub. An area that, all too conveniently, has no security feed.

Is that right? Well isn't that a hoot. I've pressed Big Red many times myself.

Shortly before the winning block started, the sole security feed inside The Pipes shows you leaving the bar. You returned after the block ended and ordered another drink.

Yes sir.

(I let the statement linger, then shrug.)

Oh, you think they're connected in some fashion.

Seems like a reasonable conclusion.

Well I'm sorry to disappoint, but I think you found yourself a coinkydink. You see, my bowel movements are something of a multi-flush affair, if you catch my drift. (He pats his pudgy belly and laughs.)

You take hour-long shits?

Yes sir. Sometimes longer, if I've had some shellfish. Worth it, though.

Duncan, you work for a mid-tier construction company.

Yes.

And you live in the sub-core.

Yes.

The average bank balance for a sub-core resident is around 2,000 credits.

Seems reasonable, yes.

And yet, your account shows an active balance of 299 *trillion* credits.

Yes sir.

(The matter-of-fact response gives me pause. A brief silence grips the room.)

And that doesn't strike you as odd?

It's more than the average Joseph, that's for sure.

More than the—Duncan, you can purchase an entire ring on the Durangoni Space Station for that amount of cash.

Yes sir.

(I glance around his humble abode and quickly regain eye contact, asking the next question without asking the question.)

(chuckles) Not much interest in the fancy floof. I like my job, I like my place, and I enjoy being part of this community. And besides, moving is such a fuss.

Duncan, you could arrange to have the entire community physically detached from the station and relocated to its own moon.

I suppose. But something else would need to fill the void, y'know? I feel like I'm where I need to be. I can't help the lowlies if I gots a moon to govern. I can do more down here than I could ever do up there.

(An understanding settles between us. We both knew what had happened, and we recognized the merits of the outcome. Duncan was, and continued to be, the most genuine and dignified person I have ever had the pleasure of meeting. He deserved every cent, and would use his fortune to better the world around him. Roy knew that. And yet, there I was, a lowly reporter with a valueless job to do. He knew the question was coming, and I knew it would be inconsequential. But we both understood that it needed to be asked.)

Do you know where Roy is?

No sir.

Would you tell me if you did?

Oh yes. I would love nothing more than to place a big shiny bow atop this tale of intrigue.

Any idea of where he could be?

No sir.

Do you think he would ever come back here?

One can only hope. We would all love to see Roy again. In fact, I paid the rent on his unit for the next 500 years.

(I flinch in response.) *What?* **Why?**

Roy is a hero to the sub-core folk. He's a symbol of hope and determination, of what can be if you keep waking up. It seemed only right that his unit be maintained as a shrine to his legacy. The door is always unlocked if you fancy a gander. Workers from far and wide venture down here every day to pay their respects.

That's ... that's actually kind of beautiful.

Seems like a fitting end to the story, doncha think?

(Of course it didn't, but I knew what he meant. Duncan would not provide the closure that I richly desired. But oddly enough, the visit did feel conclusive. I nod, smile, and stand from my chair.)

I do. And I thank you for the kindness.

You betcha.

(We exchange a final pleasantry and I begin the long trek back to my own world. I pass Roy's unit in the hallway, but decide

not to visit. I knew it would yield nothing useful, as did Duncan.)

* * *

And thus concludes the story of Roy, the incredible tale of a zero to hero who united us all through a psychotropic mind-fuck. His enduring impact lives inside our collective conscience. We all remember where we were when The Incident ravaged Durangoni. We also remember where we ended up, for better or for worse. It tore us apart to bring us together, and in a very perverse way, we owe Roy a debt of gratitude.

He was an agent of chaos that we bested as one.

Roy is gone, but not forgotten. Adored, yet misunderstood. His tale continues somewhere in the cosmos. We wish him well, curse his existence, and hope to see him soon.

THE END

Nimi was a nobody.
Then he was the chosen.
Now he's the sole survivor.

Nimi Korble endured a meteoric rise to fame, one that culminated in a tragic event seldom seen in the universe. Amazingly, he takes it all in stride, as he never sought the notoriety that doomed his species. This short interview explores what happens when a civilization completely botches first contact.

NIMI

When First Contact Becomes Last Call

• • •

Most heroes will assume the mantle of greatness through the bravery of their actions. Others will claim their places in history through the magnitude of their achievements. Their legacies are worthy and their deeds are undeniable. And yet, there are some who will oopsy-doodle backflip into notoriety without any perceivable skills or merit.

They are simply chosen.

Nimi Korble was simply chosen.

But before we dissect the unlikely grandeur that is Nimi Korble, I must extend my warmest greetings. My name is Puki Horpocket, famed editor for the Definitive Directory of Durangoni, the massive mega-wiki for life aboard the largest space station in the universe. My innumerable accolades include several of the most coveted awards in the literary realm, as well as a platinum medal for extreme humbleness.

Durangoni is home to a multitude of celebrities and it's my job to unravel their mysteries for the masses. Be they chefs or savants, the Puki spotlight is always trolling for intrigue. And while many lead incredible lives of consequence, some luminaries are just not that interesting. They are merely the right person in the right place at the right moment of historical significance.

Enter Nimi Korble.

Nimi is the founder of the FYFI movement, a wildly popular self-help seminar that turned him into one of the most bankable celebrities in Durangoni. Yes, *that* Nimi, the larger-than-life personality who adorns countless billboards throughout the station. His smiling mug and dapper suit are so prominent that they are often used for general directions. "Turn left at the red-suited Nimi holding a cane."

So many know his luster, yet so few know the tragic backstory that gave birth to it. While conducting my own research for the directory, I would learn that Nimi had played a pivotal role in the Lurgon Massacre, an event so horrific that it is actively avoided in polite conversation (as well as impolite conversation and all other forms of conversation). His involvement is no secret, but the horrid nature of the event kept it from becoming common knowledge.

With my curiosity piqued, I went digging for all the juicy details. But alas, proper records were hard to come by (for obvious reasons, but we'll get to that). I needed to know more, and only one person could illuminate the darkness.

Nimi himself.

I extended an invitation for an interview, which he graciously accepted right away. This was a small miracle given his insatiable schedule. Perhaps he wished to talk just as much as I wished to listen. In any case, Nimi dropped by my office for a candid chitchat, setting the stage for one of the most haunting reveals of my career.

* * *

Nimi is a punctual chap, which instantly endeared him to me. He arrived at my office half an hour early and waited patiently in the lobby while I finished a directory update. He minded his manners, did not grouse or stir, and partook in some light banter with my assistant, who also found him endlessly endearing. First impressions go a long way in my industry, and Nimi was off to a rousing start.

When it came time for our meeting, I relayed my readiness and my assistant escorted him inside. This would be my first glimpse of a non-billboard Nimi. I stood to greet what I assumed to be a boisterous big shot.

What walked through the door was anything but.

A meager creature with pale blue skin and minimal primp entered the room. No flashy suit, no gaudy flair, no grandiosity of any kind. He wore a matching beige ensemble that could blend into a yawn. Nimi was, in a very stark sense, instantly forgettable. This was a being you could pass in a hallway and mistake for a mop.

If this portrayal seems a bit harsh, it should be noted that Nimi fully understood his lack of magnetism away from the spotlight. He wore it like public camouflage, allowing him to hide in plain sight. In fact, he apologized for it before we shook hands. "Please forgive the tedium," he said as an introductory greeting. It was a striking disinterest in pizzazz, respectable in its own phlegmatic way. He also insisted that I describe him in this exact manner, as it constructed the proper foundation for his story.

Nimi took a seat in one of my receiving chairs. His widened gaze panned around the office like a kid in a candy store. Clearly compelled by the experience, he provided an easy icebreaker for the coming exchange.

You seem enchanted, dear Nimi.

Oh yes. It's not every day that you get to meet the great Puki Horpocket, let alone sit in his office. I have admired your works for many years.

Thank you for the kindness, which I feel compelled to return. The FYFI movement has been a juggernaut inside the station. The traction you command is as impressive as it is intimidating.

Thanks, but I am under no delusion of merit. I rant into a microphone. Hardly a skill worth immortalizing.

With all due respect, I beg to differ. You tapped into a grievance that had no voice. In providing one, the public rewarded

you with a rarified fame. Durangoni is a planet-sized behemoth with a trillion active residents. Countless cultures from countless worlds. To seduce them all with a single message is an extraordinary achievement.

(sighs) "Find Your Fuck It." Four words that will define my legacy, one of which is "fuck."

And yet, arenas will sell out just to hear you say them.

That was never the plan. Hell, it wasn't even a passing interest.

Wait. Are you telling me that the most successful lecture series in the history of Durangoni ... was an accident?

Pretty much, yeah. I arrived at the station with next to nothing. No plan, no direction, not even a friend. I found some menial work and tried to put my life back together. Spent a lot of time in bars where I ranted to anyone who would listen.

And listen they did.

Yeah, but it's not like I was constructing some grand new philosophy. All I did was complain about the futility of existence. It started at the bar, moved to open mics, then ended up in rented spaces with chairs and snacks. It was during one of these sessions when I said, "Corruption and unfairness are constant and unrelenting. Find your 'fuck it' and know contentment."

And thus began the FYFI movement.

(nods) In the blink of an eye, I went from paneled ceilings to arena spotlights. I made so much money so fast that agents were practically stabbing each other to represent me. There was no ass to kiss or ladder to climb. I jumped from a sub-core apartment to a surface estate, one of the most expensive in the quadrant.

I've seen the aerial shots. It's most impressive, a beacon of prosperity. Congratulations on your resounding success.

Thanks, but that wasn't a brag, just a statement. I still have no idea how to digest this level of wealth. It created a lot of freedom and mobility, but it also created a lot of problems. There are people living and working inside my home whom I have never met. Everything is at my beck and call, and yet, I am no more happy than when I was living in the sub-core. To this day, it all feels like a cruel joke.

How so?

There's nothing special about me, Mr. Horpocket. I'm just a mouthpiece for melancholy. Your works, on the other hand, actively contribute to the betterment of this world.

I appreciate the compliment. But in terms of sheer impact, your sphere of influence far exceeds my own.

(squirms) It still feels uncomfortable, to be honest. I'm a nobody. I should be dead and buried. But alas, justice in this world is hard to come by.

Be that as it may, your life is still of great interest. And given your key participation in one of the galaxy's most infamous events, would your self-evaluation be unfounded?

Not at all. When I say that I'm a nobody, I mean it in the most literal of senses. I grew up on Lurgontia, my home planet, and I fully expected to die there. I had no reason to suspect that my life would amount to anything.

Why's that?

Before the debacle, I lived in a crummy apartment with basic everything. I was so hopelessly alone that I only purchased single items from intended sets. I owned one chair, one bowl, one fork. I was deathly afraid of courtship and spent most of my free time at home reading books about epic adventures. I worked a meaningless job that paid me just enough credits to survive. And that was it. My life was an endless cycle of work, read, sleep, repeat, with no intent of changing.

I see.

Hopefully that sets the stage for just how jarring it was to end up in the situation that I did. I was not looking for regard. It broke into my home and kicked me in the face.

(I chuckle.) Well that's one way to put it. So let's start at the beginning. As I understand it, your species received a curious message that set this all into motion.

That's correct. We called it FC Day. First Contact Day.

My species was just like any other with self-awareness. We were isolated, cocky, fighting with each other about whose imaginary friend was the best. Our society was post-enlightenment, so we were improving our world as best we could. Unfortunately, our politics remained dogmatic and terrestrial, so nobody was looking to the sky. We were in that vulnerable "lots of tech, but little wisdom" phase.

That's when we received a signal. *The* signal. From a spaceship entering our atmosphere. That existential question "Are we alone?" got answered in a hurry. Naturally, it threw our world into chaos. Religions crumbled, economies cratered, leaders and charlatans clamored for power, all those predictable reactions that were foreign to us at the time.

And then something weird happened.

First contact wasn't weird enough?

Not in this context, no.

The ship didn't land. It just hovered in the lower atmosphere, creating quite the ruckus for our military powers. It was a big sucker too, several miles across with lots of exterior tech. It was easy to see that it carried some serious weaponry. The whole "blow it up" or "wait for contact" debate was in full swing. But the ship just floated in silence for several days.

And then, out of nowhere, an audio signal was broadcast to the entire planet. We saw no images of the aliens, just heard a single raspy voice through every coms speaker. Much to our surprise, it spoke our own language, albeit somewhat broken.

It said, "We shall land in Farthoc Field in seven days. Choose your representative. For we desire a relevant greeting."

That was it. We waited for more, but there was only silence.

A ... *relevant* greeting?

(points and grins) And *that* is why I'm sitting here today.

It's such a vague request. Why not choose a world leader? Or select the most advanced city? Or request a meeting with a top scientist? Colony ships can discern such things.

(chuckles into a heavy sigh) You just described the most chaotic seven days of my species' existence.

(I shake my head in amazement, then gesture to proceed.)

So, as a little backstory, my planet is ... or *was*, rather, a standard pre-Federation world. We had evolved enough to develop some key markers, like rudimentary space travel. Our population totaled around 13 billion individuals, most of whom were firmly rooted in our primitive past. Lots of old traditions, lots of superstition, lots of conflict and disinformation. So when it came time to select the most "relevant" among us, it sparked a vicious debate.

Each nation thought they should be the one. Each religion thought they should be the one. Every single group, from the most powerful to the least influential, thought that they had a stake in the outcome, to be the first of our species to make first contact.

(pauses to reflect) It was ... messy.

That seems like a colossal understatement.

It is. I hate to shit all over my species, but we showed our asses over the next several days. That all-consuming argument stripped away our decorum and turned us into chest-beating savages. It showed us, in very clear terms, just how fragile our "modern" society really was.

This is a commonality for most pre-Fed civilizations. Establishing first contact is a very disruptive experience. But once the shock abates, the assimilation begins. It's extremely uncommon to botch that transition.

(nods knowingly) You'd think.

I detect a wrench in the works.

(points to self)

Well then, it would seem that we've reached a provocation. Please proceed.

No one could agree on who should embody the "relevant" greeting. And so, with a few days left before contact, we settled the issue the only way we could. We held a lottery. If you were of age, of sound mind, and not a criminal, then you were automatically entered. They would then select a random "winner" and clothe them with nobility.

The next morning, I got a knock at the door.

I'll never forget that moment. I thought it was my landlord collecting rent, which he would absolutely continue to do under any circumstance. But when I opened the door, I found six government agents in black suits staring at me through hardened expressions.

One of them said, "Mr. Korble, you have been selected to represent the planet as our delegate of relevance. Please come with us."

I knew that "please" wasn't optional, and it's not like I had any family or estate to consider, so I did what they said. I left my crappy little apartment, never to return.

What was the mood like? Were you excited at all? Proud maybe?

No, nothing like that. Those emotions were foreign to me. I didn't know how to be proud or excited. My life had been devoid of meaning up to that point, so it felt a little like being born. Everything was new, down to the food I ate and the words I used.

The great irony was that the people largely accepted me because of it. I had no wealth or title. I belonged to no groups or causes. I had no politics or belief system. The only thing I represented was the biological foundation of the species.

I was a sketch. And against all odds, that made me a masterpiece.

So what did they do to prepare you for contact?

Not much. I quickly learned that it was more about presentation than substance. Basically, they wanted to make sure I didn't say anything stupid. The visitors already spoke our language, so it became more about manners and posture. I was dressed like a king and presented to the world, like a shiny hood ornament.

The unspoken plan was for me to make the initial greeting and then steer the aliens towards the actual seats of power. This was problematic, of course, because the "actual" seats of power were in bitter disagreement. I had a hundred voices whispering into my ear from every direction.

Were any of them compelling?

Not a one. It was all self-serving bullshit. A congress of leaders and not a single leader among them. In light of this, I just nodded along while forming my own plan.

Which was?

Just be nice. I had no stake in the outcome, so my plan was to be shallow and cordial until they lost interest and moved on. At which point, I could resume my life as a distinguished nobody. A bit naive, I admit. But I was quickly growing weary of the predicament.

So anyway, in the days leading up to the event, all I did was lie to reporters and politicians. I didn't say anything blatantly false, I just prefaced everything with "mights" and "mays." *Might* say this. *May* do that. It was astounding how much leverage I could wield by offering little slivers of hope. In turn, powerful people offered me tremendous wealth just for a chance to be second.

I played the game, but I didn't really care. I just wanted to go home. What haunts me to this day is the thought of someone more corruptible being in my position. It would have created a frightening power crisis. But then again, it's not like I did any better. Because, y'know. (mimics an explosion with his hands)

In a strange sense, it's like you won the moral battle, but lost the righteous war.

(shrugs) I guess.

So take us to the pivotal day of contact. FC Day, as you put it.

Sure. It was a pleasant and sunny day, springtime for our planet. Farthoc Field was abuzz with activity. Farthoc is … was, a popular public park outside of Kithon, one of our largest cities. The area was famous for its wide-open grassy plain. It housed countless sporting fields, picnic plots, playgrounds, all the standard recreational fare. But, at a gargantuan scale. The perimeter path took a full day to travel around. That's why it was so popular. You could empty the entire city onto the plain and still find a secluded spot to relax.

So yeah, it was an obvious place for a spaceship landing. The "welcoming committee" had constructed a large pad near the center and surrounded it with bleachers. They sold tickets, of course, at criminally inflated prices. What a sight it was, a single bowl containing the planet's richest inhabitants, everything from moguls to celebrities.

And then there was me, standing at the center of it all like some sort of mascot. I never felt so powerless in my life. I was selected to represent everyone, and yet, not one person I saw that day would have given me a second glance.

And to make matters worse, all the normies were shut out of the arena. They were invited to the site, but forced to stand behind the bleachers. The committee had erected several large screens to watch the exchange, but how is that any different from watching at home? It was disgusting. Our most important moment as a species and the peons were locked outside.

Except for one.

Yeah, and what a sight I was. They had dressed me in ceremonial robes, complete with a matching hat and baton. I looked like a fucking wizard.

So there I stood, on my own little platform beside the main landing pad, being gawked at by the elites of our society. It felt like an eternity, but then a shuttle finally departed the mothership and started its descent. I watched with impatience as the vessel punched through the atmosphere and floated down to our gathering. I remember feeling underwhelmed by its approach. It looked like a flying bus with zero flair. A cloud of dust swirled around the arena as it sprouted landing gear and settled onto the central pad. The engines spun down and the dust faded, leaving the gathered mass in an anxious silence.

I sighed. Loud enough to raise the eyebrow of a decorated general behind me. I was about to greet an alien species as the selected delegate of my own. I was about to make first contact, the most important moment for any sentient race. And I sighed. That's how little I was invested in the experience.

Did it create any consternation?

Maybe. I don't know. And even if it did, it's not like they could replace me at that point.

So after a brief wait, the airlock door slid open and a ramp dropped to the ground. After another brief wait, an alien male stepped to the doorway and spread his arms wide, which prompted the crowd to start cheering. I found this very odd because it stank of ego. Who makes first contact with a new species by acting like a pop diva taking the stage? The elites loved it, but it rubbed me the wrong way.

He sauntered down the ramp with a smarmy grin, followed by a small posse. Five in all. They didn't look too dissimilar from us, either. Two arms, two legs, normalish heads with the same amount of holes. They had slightly longer torsos and shorter legs, but were largely familiar to look at. They wore casual garb with bright colors that reminded me of beachwear. I had no idea if this was considered formal to them, but my first impression wasn't great. They looked like a pack of dude-bros on vacation.

As they neared the bottom of the ramp, I began my own approach. My instructions were to meet them at the platform margin, treating it like a sovereign border. Easy enough, right? Welcome to my planet, show me to your leader, done and done. In my head, it all took less than a minute. But much to my surprise, I had grossly overestimated.

If the historical account is to be believed, you uttered one sentence before the proverbial shit hit the fan.

(shakes head) Four words. I got four words out before it all went to hell.

I slowed to a stop at the border, as did they. I offered a friendly smile, then folded my hands and bowed, as instructed. I met eyes with the leader and said, "On behalf of the—"

"Who's your hottest female?" he barked back.

Come again?

That's what I said. The question caught me entirely off-guard. I understood it from a baseline of comprehension, but the qualification left me stumped. Hottest? Our culture did not equate body temperature to attractiveness, so I thought he was concerned with fevers. Perhaps they were a medical team trying to contain an intergalactic virus. I did not get to pose a follow-up question before he sighed and repeated his own.

"Your *hottest* female? You know, your juiciest piece, your glam goddess." His posse chuckled and high-foured each other. "Whichever yum-yum would get me the most likes when I flaunt that sexy. Here, check it." He withdrew his comdev and showed me a picture, a beach shot of him with a pair of scantily clad alien ladies. I was still digesting his own presence, yet there I was looking at a party pic with two other species. "You should've seen it," he said with a cocky tone. "My likes blew through the roof with that one. Trended for a solid week. The purple one even took her finger and—"

"Wait wait wait," I said while waving my arms. The reality of the situation hit me like a wet slap across the face. "Are you ... *influencers?*"

The alien huffed, rolled his eyes, and proceeded to walk around me. He added a shoulder jab for good measure, which forced me into a backward stumble. It felt like I was back in grade school. He may as well have pantsed me in front of the cheerleaders.

"Yo yo yo!" he said to the crowd, then reached into his satchel and grabbed a knot of beaded necklaces. "Let's see some boobs!"

The crowd reacted as you may have guessed, by recoiling and trading nervous glances. There was a lot of mumbling and fidgeting. Several women scoffed at the demand, because of course the first alien contact would be a chauvinist prick.

I, on the other hand, was in the throes of degradation. Every awkward moment from childhood had coalesced into a raging maelstrom. It mocked me like a bully on the ultimate playground. But this time was different. I couldn't run away and sob to the teacher. I was representing an entire civilization. The eyes of my people were locked onto me, and all I could do was stare blankly while a douchebag taunted them.

That's when the anger took hold. I remember rewatching this moment on replay. Every news camera had zoomed into my face, awaiting my reaction. The planet's reaction. Well, the planet was pissed. In the span of two seconds, my face mutated from limp shock to taut rage. My eyes narrowed, my lips puckered, my brow ruffled, and most importantly, my fists balled off-camera. I turned and stomped towards the alien menace. When I reached his back, I politely tapped his shoulder. He turned to see my gritting teeth right before I buried my fist into his cheek. I put my entire body into it, so much so that I stumbled forward after the hit. The asshole actually caught some air before slamming onto the ground.

I, Nimi Korble of Lurgontia, had valiantly defended my planet.

(I gesture my respect.) I applaud your gallantry, Sir Nimi. But knowing the eventual aftermath, I cannot help but feel sickly heartbroken.

(slowly nods) We beat the shit out of them. And by *we*, I mean the military tribunal that was guarding my back. By the time it was over, those fools were so wrecked that another shuttle needed to come rescue them. As the leader was carried away, all bloodied and battered, he kept shouting "Papa Greshka" over and over.

(I bow my head and take a needed breath.) Sweet Tim almighty.

We had no idea who that was, of course. The shuttles docked, the mothership left, and we thought that was the end of it.

Two days later, an entire fleet returned.

As we soon learned, the alien prick was the son of Bearko Greshka, a feared warlord with ties to the Varokin Empire. You know those rich dickheads who respond to every slight with "Wait until my father hears about this?" Yeah, now imagine that on a galactic scale.

Son of a blorkin klerp. Pardon my Flontch.

No need. I have yet to find a word, in any language, that captures the vileness of that fiend.

So anyway, to make a long and depressing story short, Greshka threatened to destroy the planet unless they gave me up. Which they did, but it didn't matter. He just wanted me to suffer the betrayal before incinerating every city on the planet. Then he scorched the atmosphere, ensuring that every living thing died gasping. I was forced to watch from the bridge of the command ship.

You actually met Greshka?

Yes. Well, in a sense. It's not like we sat down for tea and crumpets. I stood at his side while he butchered my planet, helpless to do anything about it. He was cold and stoic, never said a word to me. When the deed was done, a guard whisked me away while the son laughed in the background.

Did the son torture you?

No, strangely enough. I got kicked around by the guards, but it never came to that.

At the risk of sounding bloodthirsty, why not?

He lost interest, like any spoiled brat with too many toys. Got his kicks and moved on to the next depravity. I was an afterthought before I left the room.

So what did they do with you?

I was kept in the brig for a few weeks, then dumped at a random port. I could only assume they got tired of feeding me and didn't want to waste a bullet. I survived by begging and scrounging for a while. Worked a few odd jobs, raised enough credits to book a jump shuttle to Durangoni. Been here ever since.

As the lone survivor of your species.

(shrugs) Best place to be as such. There's lots of work and plenty to do. No one looks at you sideways and you're free to find your own path. Hell, one day I'm whinging in a bar and the next day I'm a station celebrity.

Classic rags to riches.

Lesson learned. If you want a better life, punch your first contact in the face.

(I snort into a brief chuckle.) Wow. How can you retain a sense of humor in the wake of such tragedy?

How can you not? Every species will have a last of its kind. But how many of those beings have irrefutable knowledge of that fact? It's a total mind-fuck knowing that as soon as I'm gone, *poof.* That's it. That's the end of our history.

And that doesn't bother you?

It used to, but I shed that guilt a long time ago. Now I find it darkly amusing, because if *I'm* the one left standing, then someone royally burfed the durkel (read: screwed the pooch).

It sounds like the whole fiasco was a perfect storm of bad decisions, the first of which was indecision.

(nods) Death by irony.

Do you ever wish for second chance?

Yes and no. I mourn the loss of my homeworld, but the fact remains that my species elected a random weirdo to greet its destiny. Stupidity at that level doesn't deserve the stars.

(snaps and points) No, *that's* the lesson.

* * *

Nimi and I chatted for another hour or so. The conversation steered away from the Lurgon Massacre and settled onto his life aboard the station. Despite his incredible wealth and lavish estate, he much preferred the simple pleasures of living. In his own words, his massive manor was little more than "something to do with piles of money." He coveted none of it and spent most of his time in a small suite near the center.

He seemed happy with the arrangement, as furthering his place in the universe was dismissed as utterly pointless. The FYFI movement was an effective time-killer and offered a wide variety of scenery changes, but no regard was sought within its walls. In his own words, he was "simply waiting to not exist."

It saddened me in a way, because his plight would have crushed any decent being. Not that he was indecent, just breathtakingly indifferent. He had, albeit in a tragic manner, achieved what he desired. He had returned home to his crummy apartment. It was oddly admirable, because in the end, nothing will survive the heat death of the universe.

Our collective fate is written in the stars.

Or rather, in their eventual extinguishment.

The legend of Nimi Korble is cemented in this fact, in that he represents the pinnacle of acceptance. His remarkable tale can be retold as a cynic's guide to enlightenment, a tangled path to nowhere that ends with a passive shrug. I learned a lot from dear Nimi and shall remember his words whenever life gets me down.

Four of them in particular.

THE END

A brilliance beyond belief.
A fool beyond measure.
This is the enigma that is Phil.

Out in the great black sea, there exists a creature with a fathomless intellect. Phil is widely presumed to be the smartest being in the universe. Interviewing him was a dream come true, albeit one with a nightmarish caveat. This brief exchange reveals, in the bluntest of terms, how intelligence rarely begets wisdom.

PHIL

A Maddening Chat with the Smartest Being in the Universe

. . .

The notion that Phil is the smartest being in the universe is neither profound nor proclamation, but rather the objective reality for every citizen of the cosmos. Everyone knows that Phil is the smartest being in the universe. Saying so is like saying that water is wet, or that nifku is the tastiest asteroid fungus. Thus, it would be reasonable to assume that Phil is hounded by fortune seekers on a daily basis. That would be true, if not for another piece of objective reality.

Phil is handsy.

Like, *really* handsy.

Not in a "creepy uncle" kind of way. More like a "been alone for billions of years and the thought of physical contact with another being gets me super excited" kind of way.

Yes, billions.

You see, Phil is functionally immortal. He started as a single cell of pond algae, evolved a random neuron, then speed-leveled through swimming, crawling, walking, flying, talking, and telepathy. He also has the extraordinary ability to guide his own evolutionary path. If he likes a mutation, he can keep it. If he hates it, he can rebirth himself as a biological "undo." But after billions of years and countless iterations, comfort became paramount. Thus, he now exists as an incalculable number of neurons entombed in a giant meat sack.

As someone so aptly put it, "He's a bean bag with boundary issues."

"He" doesn't exactly apply either, as Phil is an asexual blob. In choosing the name "Phil," for reasons known only to Phil, the assumption was made that he was a "he." But to everyone who encounters his unsettling visage, "he" is quickly replaced with "What in holy blue hell is that?!" Which, in turn, is quickly replaced with "How can such a thing be *handsy*?" At which point, Phil gleefully sprouts tentacles from his mass and starts untying shoes.

Thus is the story of Phil.

So imagine my surprise when Phil reached out to *me*, Puki Horpocket, famed editor for the Definitive Directory of Durangoni, for a personal interview. Not directly of course, as Phil does not possess the psychological clarity to do things normally. He simply barked radio waves into the cosmos that stated, "I have a matter to discuss with the best talky person!" This annoyed the people who listened for such things and before long, word had reached my desk that the smartest being in the universe wanted to chat.

Why me?

Because I'm the best talky person.

My accolades are numerous and my fanbase stretches across the universe. My essays and interviews have been read by trillions of beings and my humbleness in the wake of such glory continues to impress everyone around me. I am, in a very objective sense, the most famous talky person in the great black sea.

While the thought of interviewing Phil did tickle my fancy, the reality of conducting it deflated my enthusiasm. Phil is the sole resident of Phil's Place, a lonely planet that orbits a roaming star inside a spooky nebula. It's not particularly difficult to visit, but Phil's desperate need to converse through telepathy when in range is known to create a nightmarish approach. Imagine, if you will, going to visit your most annoying relative and being forced to interact with them long before you get there.

And it's not like Phil can come to me. Durangoni is the largest space station in the universe with a trillion active residents and Phil is a telepathic blob with a penchant for groping. You do the horrific math. In fact, there are several Federation laws that specifically target Phil to keep him where he is. My personal favorite: "Intergalactic travel is strictly forbidden to any species with one active member."

In short, interviewing Phil meant going to Phil.

And so I did.

*   *   *

Two weeks later, a jump shuttle delivered me to a foreign world. It was easily the most efficient disembarkation of my life. I doubt the landing gear even touched the ground before the steward shoved me out of the airlock. My fellow passengers had also endured several hours of Phil's merciless brain pokes. The pilots were eager to dump the obligatory cargo and punch the gas to literally anywhere else.

What was I going to do, complain? "Unfriendly staff during arrival at Phil's Place. One star." Even the moderators would laugh out loud before deleting the post.

The shuttle race into the sky and vanished into space, leaving me to the blissful silence of a pristine world inhabited by a single being. I say "blissful silence" because I had berated Phil on approach. I believe the phrase was, "No peace, no parley." He obliged after a lengthy jabber on what rhymes with "parley," then happily prodded the other passengers. I always travel with earplugs and the silent image of a collective nervous breakdown haunts me to this day.

But I made it.

I stood on the surface of Phil's Place.

My eyes absorbed the bright purple sky, a stunning visual made possible by the charged nebula that encompassed the planet. The atmosphere was a bit thin, but the air was clean and breathable. Ridiculously clean, in fact. It was the purest air that my lungs had ever drawn. My eyelids closed to take stock of the joyous concoction filling my chest. Moans of contentment vibrated my throat with every exhale.

And then something tickled my ear.

My eyes opened to find a noodly tentacle diddling my ear hole. It wasn't aggressive, just the curious prod of a curious creature. I traced the noodle back to a bulbous hide resting in the dirt a few meters away. Another tentacle had sprouted and was slowly crawling towards my feet.

Puki Horpocket was decidedly uncomfortable.

Puki Horpocket had also come prepared.

I reached into my travel satchel and casually withdrew a tickler (read: a pen-sized shock device that packed the wallop of ten cattle prods). I clicked it on and pressed it to the tentacle, at which point the bulbous mass convulsed like gelatin on a roller coaster. The shock lasted for a few seconds, after which Phil rapidly retracted the tentacles.

"Ouch! That smarts," he said in perfect Earth English. (I would later learn that one of his favorite visitors was an Earth teen named Max.)

"Do we have an understanding?" I said.

"Yes sir!" Phil said, still giddy as if nothing had happened. He sprouted another tentacle to give me a quick salute.

I clicked the tickler off and clipped it to my front pocket, proclaiming loud and clear that the option was ever-present. At this point, my eyes were permitted to wander the landscape. The one thing I will say about Phil's Place is that it's fucking gorgeous. My apologies for the "fucking" qualifier, but this "fucking" is fucking necessary.

My jaw slacked open as my widened gaze panned across a mosaic of untold beauty. I stood at the center of an open valley. Countless boulders dotted the landscape, all covered by rainbows of fuzzy moss. Towering mountains rose into the distance, their jagged peaks painted by red and orange minerals. Behind me, a shimmering lake of sapphire water stole my breath. Large patches of algae created a swirling collage that rivaled my best experiences with chemical alteration.

And then a tentacle snaked through my carefully cropped mane.

The click-to-shock time was most impressive.

"Erk! Dom breka," Phil said in perfect Mulgawatian Korish. (I would later learn that two of his favorite visitors were a pair of Mulgawat couriers.)

I had practiced my shock-thrusts along the journey, which made my fellow passengers more than a little nervous. As the tentacle retracted, I gave Phil a knowing glare before returning to my satchel. After a brief rummage, I withdrew my trusty portastool. It remained a crucial part of my fieldwork, as even the most furnished parts of Durangoni can suffer from seating insecurity. I opted to negate the hassle by always providing my own. It's a lovely contraption that collapses down to a space no bigger than a coffee mug. With a flick of the wrist, the device swiftly unfurls and inflates a bum cushion.

In retrospect, I should have warned Phil before doing so.

His frightened reaction was severe yet understandable. He yelped, snatched it from my grip, and hurled it into the lake.

As I watched the expensive gadget sail through the air and end with a distant splash, I could not help but sigh. What a splendid start to this heroic misadventure. I reached up to rub my scalp in frustration, but another tentacle had beat me to the punch.

Dramatic click.

Dramatic shock.

"Borf! Verkin bloosh," Phil said in perfect Azeroka Hurmish. (I would later learn that ... you know what, nevermind. Phil loves anyone who is brave enough to spend time with him.)

I sneered at the ripples crawling across the lake, then whipped my gaze back to Phil, who was eagerly awaiting my undivided attention. My options for seating had become maddeningly limited, but a nearby rock would have to suffice. I strolled over and took a seat, which the fuzzy moss made surprisingly comfortable.

The stage was set.

I threw one leg over the other, fetched a notepad from my satchel, then locked my gaze onto the meat sack resting a few meters away. Phil stared back at me, as far as I could tell. He had no eyes or mouth, so reading his emotions wasn't exactly trivial. Thankfully (and all-too-often obnoxiously), his impervious glee was more than happy to reveal itself.

So without further ado, let's open the floor to Phil. The following is my word-for-word interview with the smartest being in the universe.

Normally, I would start with some sort of pleasantry. But from the second I entered range, this experience sharply diverted from the very notion of normal. So in the spirit of time management, let's cut right to the chase. Why did you summon me?

(Two tentacles sprout from Phil's mass. They curl back into the flesh and retrieve a shiny rock from the bulk. It's round, about a foot in diameter, and is covered with glittering yellow crystals. I immediately recognize it as a pallasite, a rare type of meteorite that is prized by collectors. Phil holds it up between us, like a proud father showing off a newborn.)

Do you like my rock?

What?

I was wondering if you like my rock.

I don't understand the relevance.

It's my very favorite thing. Do you like it?

Again, how is this relevant?

(Phil sulks a bit. At least, that's how I interpret his slight deflation.)

Would you like to hear how I got my rock?

(I start to respond, but sigh into an eye roll. My fingers tap the notepad as I start to question the wisdom of being there. "Could've been sipping Sangria on a beach ring," my brain demurs. "But noooo, had to travel across the universe to chat with a giant scrotum. Maybe I should cut my losses and go home. No! Dammit, I'm Puki Horpocket, not some schmuck

with a two-bit paper to sell. Phil summoned me for a reason and it's my job to suss out what it is.")

("That's the spirit.")

(**"Fuck! Forgot you're telepathic."**)

("Did you know that Sangria originated on Earth? It's from a magical place called Spain, also known for paella. Would you like to know about paella? It's a yummy dish made with rice, and beans, and saffron, and vegetables, and chicken, and—")

Just tell me about the goddamn rock.

(Phil squeals with delight, then swirls some tentacles into the air like a flamboyant orchestra conductor. It's a strange precursor to the coming story, but nonetheless effective. He commands my full attention before uttering one of the most ridiculous sentences I would ever hear.)

Sky stones are dumb-dumb stupid.

* * *

Phil hated meteorites.

Of all the things that got under Phil's thick hide, meteorites took the cake. Not that he ever had the pleasure of cake, or any pastry for that matter, but he did have the distinct pleasure of a personal paradise. Soaring mountains, glittering lakes, sweeping valleys, an entire world existing to please a single creature's visual cortex. (Phil had long devolved eyes and simply absorbed the entire light spectrum.) He took great pride in tidying his planet and spent the majority of his time doing so. A dirt sweep here, a pebble nudge there, whatever increased the visual appeal of his roaming wonderland.

Thus, Phil hated meteorites.

Their tiny black bodies fell from the sky like grains from a pepper shaker, blighting the canvas that Phil so diligently painted. Whenever he found one, he absorbed it into his bulbous body for later deposit in Dumb Stone Lake. This once-magnificent body of water was converted into a shame puddle for every meteorite Phil found. Its miles-long surface rested inside an old crater near the northern pole. *A fitting end for dumb little stones*, Phil thought.

Year after year, century after century, millennia after millennia, Phil plucked meteorites from the dirt and transported them to Dumb Stone Lake. The activity became a cleansing ritual, as he would hold each one aloft, then shout "Begone, vile pebble!" before hurling it over the crater ledge. Each stone hit the lake at the exact same spot, dead-center within a five-inch radius. A remarkable feat for any creature, but Phil had eons of practice. His tenacity had also created an underwater mountain that slowly elevated the shoreline.

What may seem like a strange and futile effort was actually driven by a simple, relatable, and wholly depressing fact.

Phil was crushingly lonely.

As the only creature of any kind wandering his planet, he desperately yearned for company. Not that he knew what company was for the first million years, as his planet occupied the deep confines of a purple nebula. The sky above was a starless field of rich lavender, so Phil had no reason to suspect that a vast universe existed beyond it.

That is, until he evolved the ability to absorb radio waves.

This tiny tweak would expose him to the big black sea and all that inhabited it. He drank the info with the unhinged excitement of a caffeinated ferret. Nothing was too frivolous. With the same dizzy enthusiasm, Phil absorbed the wisdom of advanced civilizations and the banality of reality television.

And then it hit him.

The potential for visitors had become a tantalizing reality.

And now he hated meteorites.

The first several years of Project Cleanup were a hasty storm of pluck and tuck, like a teenager trying to hide his porn stash. Before the genius solution of Dumb Stone Lake, Phil simply hid the tiny stones under larger stones. This became untenable in a hurry, as he had created a squirrel nut stash on a global scale. His neural network struggled to maintain the distribution, resulting in an even bigger mess of untidy hiding places.

Project Cleanup became Project Cleanup the Cleanup.

And that project turned into Dumb Stone Lake.

It took several centuries of looking behind boulders and sifting through rivers, but Phil had finally eliminated all visual evidence of foreign contaminants. His pristine paradise was even more pristine, a pure representation of purity.

Phil's Place was officially open for business. (A polite way of saying that he barked his own radio waves back into the cosmos. They mostly said, "Hello, my fellow thinking meat. I am Phil, your new bestest friend for intimate mingle time." Phil was many things, but suave was not one of them. A billion years of solitude tends to dull the social graces.)

And so he waited.

The very concept of waiting was a non-issue for Phil, as he literally had all the time in the world. Every day, he rolled around his planet and pondered the joys of meeting new friends. Every night, he stared into the sky and barked his creepy welcome message.

During one of those nights, Phil was resting at the center of a large valley when a meteor streaked into the atmosphere. This sent him into a hissy fit, as it meant that another dumb stone needed shaming. The meteor hit the ground in the distance and a furious Phil raced towards the impact site. But when he got there, something was amiss. The impact had created a small crater several meters across. A haze of dust swirled around the area and reflected a warm yellow hue. As it dissipated, the image of a twinkling rock revealed itself.

Not the usual shard of charred iron.

Something different.

Something ... *special.*

Phil sprouted a tentacle and slowly reached into the smoldering crater. The glowing orb compelled his noodly appendage, as if holding a powerful magnet to his curiosity. And once again, his childlike wonder would fail his sense of preservation. The tip of his tentacle touched the orb, resulting in a painful singe.

"Fliff! Ko bekkin," he said in perfect Hurf'la Birp, then shook away the sting.

He waited 14 seconds, then tried again.

"Earp! Bumorp doonga," he said in perfect Nootrinaki, then shook away the sting. (Having absorbed a billion years of radio waves, Phil was fluent in countless alien languages.)

He waited for 14 seconds, then tried again.

"Fonk! Glarpa vermush."

Another shake.

Another 14 seconds.

In all, he tried 237 times before the meteorite was cool enough to pick up. And once he did, he held it aloft and gasped with delight. The smooth round stone was dotted with yellow crystals, all of which twinkled in the rising sunlight. A web of melted iron held it all together. Phil twisted it around and around, wholly enraptured by its beauty.

"Soooo preeeeetty," he said. "A gift from beyond. For *me*. For Phil. I love it so very, very much. It's mine. It's my love, my treasure, my prec ... my prec ... MY PRECIOUS SOURCE OF HAPPINESS AND JOY AND BLISS AND GLEE AND PLEASURE THAT I WILL ADORE AND PROTECT UNTIL THE END OF TIIIIIIIIIME!"

And then he sucked it into his flesh and went about his business.

The obsession had begun.

Phil had spent untold millennia wandering his planet. He could roll for months without stopping and find total contentment by gazing into the sky. But now he couldn't make it a few meters without stopping for "twinkle time." (His words, not mine.) A pair of tentacles would slowly emerge from his mass with the rock in their grasp, allowing beams of sunlight to create a natural disco ball. Phil would gawk at the sparkling stone for several hours, then suck it back into his flesh and continue on his merry way.

A few meters later, the process repeated.

And so the days went.

Two and a half centuries later, Phil was enjoying the latest twinkle time when an idea popped into his mind. If he enjoyed the twinkles, then surely others would as well (and make them want to hang out longer). The rock should serve as the showpiece for Phil's Place, a prized exhibition, like a planetary hood ornament. The idea was all-consuming from conception, which begged the most important question of Phil's existence.

Where to put it?

The most obvious place was "on the ground," so he did just that. He pulled the stone from his flesh and pressed it into the soft dirt, the first time it had touched soil since falling from the sky. Phil stared at his shiny memento, now resting quietly by itself on a bed of earth. The emotional reaction was sudden and borderline violent. Phil clapped his tentacles like a tween with a crush, then barked with laughter while rolling around the stone.

The stage was set.

And so he waited.

He didn't have to wait long, at least by Phil's standards. A short century later, a ship entered the atmosphere. The crew was running low on water and had scanned the system for resources. It was a chance encounter, not that Phil cared in the slightest. First contact had finally arrived and a sense of unmitigated excitement flooded his mind.

That is, until the ship started its descent ... fifty kilometers away.

Phil stared at the twinkling stone, his favorite thing in the world, now resting in its perfect place upon a lonely mound of dirt. Anxiety set in. His gaze whipped to the fiery descent in the distance, then back to the stone, then back to the ship, on and on until frustration forced him into a decision. First contact is first only once, so he patted his rock, promised that "daddy would be back," then race-rolled to the landing site.

It didn't go well.

Having no idea what constituted a socially acceptable greeting, Phil scared the ever-loving caca out of the unsuspecting crew. He then watched with slaphappy glee as the terrified visitors fled the planet as quickly as possible. The ship screamed through the atmosphere, punched into open space, and disappeared forever.

Phil stared into the empty sky, milking every drop of elation before the loneliness returned. He sulked a bit, then released a soft moan. "They would have stayed longer if they saw my rock," he mumbled.

The problem, Phil surmised, was a lack of signage.

And so he got to work.

Over the next several centuries, he collected every stone he could and rearranged them into arrows. Some were small and subtle, like a handful of random pebbles. Others were massive and could be seen on approach, like giant boulders rolled into arrowheads at the end of canyons. Before long, the entire surface had been transformed into a curbside attraction. Every arrow pointed towards a shiny rock resting on a mound of dirt. The only problem was that visitors found this incredibly creepy and decided to forgo the experience altogether. Nothing calms the nerves like countless placards on an uncharted planet. The most common response was "Nope!" followed by a rapid acceleration to the next system.

After several failed visitations, Phil interpreted the blunder in typical Phil fashion. He correctly assumed that the arrows were to blame, but incorrectly concluded that visitors were simply too impressed by them. Why get the "free candy" when you can admire the airbrushed unicorn on the outside of the van?

The signage, Phil surmised, had oversold the product.

And so he got to work ... again.

Over the next several centuries, he erased all the arrows and decided that elevation was the *real* problem. He needed to display the rock on one of his tallest peaks. That way, visitors would be forced to gaze at its magnificence long before the ship reached the ground. Several mountains were in contention, but none were more alluring than Alluring Peak (named for its abundant allure). The mountain was situated near the equator, so the weather was perfect. It overlooked a huge ocean, so the view was perfect. And the summit offered a natural perch for display, so the presentation was perfect.

The only thing left to do was get there.

And so, Phil started climbing.

He rolled up the initial slope as best he could. When gravity became a burden, he sprouted tentacles and hoisted his mass along the ledges. Being a shapeless blob proved rather useful, as he could easily grip the tiny nooks and crannies. The effort was oddly enjoyable, so he hummed random show tunes as his bulk steadily ascended.

But then he got to the final spire.

Nearly vertical, it towered above him and taunted his resolve. Phil remained determined, so he conquered the obstacle by hugging it with dozens of thin tentacles, allowing him to shimmy up the cliff like a crawling moss. It was slow going, but he eventually arrived at the summit. All in all, it took him about two weeks to complete the climb.

The tiny perch at the top was too small to support his mass, not that it mattered. Phil could simply wrap his meat around the slender peak. For a time, he resembled a giant worm that had lost its way in the most spectacular of fashions.

Phil stared at the summit and all its perfect perfectness. *A fitting stage for a fabulous show*, he thought. A pair of tentacles sprouted from his bulk with the pallasite in their grip. They lifted it high above the peak, then gently lowered it into a bowl-like depression, as if to crown a king. The crystals absorbed the sunlight and beamed their radiant glory around the landscape.

Millennia had passed since Phil last visited the summit. It was his favorite roost during the flying stage of his evolution. The allure was alive and well, a stunning treat for any eyeball (or full-bodied photoreceptor system with full-spectrum absorption). Phil stayed for several hours, drinking in the vista with every ounce of his being. From the rolling clouds to the shimmering ocean, every square inch brought pure joy to his cerebral network.

"Neat," he said, then began his descent.

* * *

At this point, Phil paused his tale to check on my mental status. My dangling jaw and contorted face had created the image of critical constipation. This wasn't the case, as I was simply reacting to the monumental folly of his story. Phil found it distracting and decided to voice his concern. In retrospect, it was kind of sweet.

(A tentacle reaches for my face, stops an inch from my nose, then waves frantically.)

You okay there, friend?

I'm not quite sure, to be honest.

(The tentacle stops waving, then floats to the side and flicks my earlobe. Without breaking derp face, I snatch the tickler from my pocket and give Phil another jolt. His body violently convulses and the tentacle retracts, which verifies my attention.)

Anyhoo ...

* * *

A short week later, Phil had reached the base of the giant mountain. He rolled down the final slope and towards a nearby beach, giving him a full view of his beloved trophy. And there it was, twinkling in its full awesomeness, a shiny watcher over his personal paradise. *Surely*, he thought. *Who could resist such splendor?*

And so he waited ... again.

He spent the next several years rolling around the rocky base. Every glance to the peak prompted barks of glee, as if seeing its beauty for the first time. Cloudless days were especially rewarding, as the crystals would paint the cliffs with ribbons of yellow light. They unfolded like the petals of a giant daffodil. On those days, Phil parked his mass on the beach and stared at the spire, utterly enchanted by its grandeur.

And then a ship entered the atmosphere.

Phil, now giddy with anticipation, listened in on the crew's chatter as the ship neared the peak. He pulsed with excitement and leaned towards the mountain, as if to will the veneration into existence.

Closer, and closer, and closer, and then the ship sailed by the summit without so much as a kind glance. The pilot barked some commands at her crewmates and began a landing approach several miles away.

Phil was crushed.

But a visitor was still a visitor, so he swallowed the sulk and rolled towards the ship.

It didn't go well ... again.

The potent combination of severe disappointment and jubilant hysteria turned Phil into a raving nutcase. He assaulted the visitors with a cryptic mania that considerably shortened their stay. The telepathy alone was enough to chill spines and twitch eyeballs. "Welcome new friends who afflicted me with psychic devastation!" was the first of many terrifying statements that sent the ship back into the atmosphere before the engines had even cooled.

Phil stared into the sky as a fresh wave of disappointment washed over him. The exhaust trails faded away, ending another botched visitation. His gaze shifted back to the mountain peak where a brilliant yellow flower glistened at the summit. He was convinced that no thinking being with two neurons to rub together could have resisted such a captivating vision. *Perhaps the angle was off*, he thought. *Yes, that's it. Bad angle.*

And so he ventured back to the summit.

Two weeks later, Phil was face-to-face with his one true love. A lone tentacle sprouted from his mass, wrapped around the stone, and twisted it a single millimeter. "Perfect!" he said, then turned around and began his descent.

Another long wait.

Another visitor.

Another disregard.

Another millimeter.

Another long wait.

Another visitor.

Another disregard.

Another millimeter.

A dozen failures later, Phil sank into a deep depression. His ascent to the summit took a full month this time, as he slogged through a haze of discouragement. When he reached his precious treasure, he could only stare into the crystals and sigh. A billion explanations swirled inside his mind, none of which offered any comfort. Could he be the only being in the universe capable of appreciating such beauty? Or was he too isolated to appreciate the full spectrum of subjectivity? Both options, as well as everything in between, were too depressing to accept.

In a fit of pure frustration, Phil wrapped a tentacle around the stone, reared back, and hurled it towards the ocean with all his might. And given his status as a giant brain encased in muscle, the might was quite mighty. The pallasite punched through the clouds before beginning its long plummet to the surface. The crystals glittered as they fell, as if to enjoy a final wash of sunlight. Moments later, a tiny splash in the distance gifted it to the ocean depths.

Phil, with tentacle still outstretched, instantly regretted the decision.

"MY PRECIOUS SOURCE OF HAPPINESS AND JOY AND BLISS AND GLEE AND PLEASURE!" he said with an unhinged ferocity, then detached from the summit and began a violent tumble down the mountain.

This was the closest Phil had ever come to death. He fell from the peak in a blind panic, hitting every ledge and outcrop along the way. By the time he reached the base, his flesh was battered and bruised to the point of resembling a squashed grape. A shower of rocks and pebbles followed him down, pelting his tender hide with multiple insults to injury.

But he was alive.

In tremendous pain, but alive.

He crawled towards the beach with the grace of a flattened tire, moaning and whimpering along the way. The journey was long and agonizing, but he made it. His aching mass rolled into the shallows where the lapping waves offered some comfort. And there he remained, staring at the horizon while his flesh slowly healed. The heartache was unrelenting, as his precious little flower rested at the bottom of the sea.

Slowly but surely, the healing morphed into planning.

Project Rescue had commenced.

A million ideas raced inside his cerebral network, all of which resulted in an untimely death. Phil had spent several centuries as a fish-like creature with fins and gills, which would have been quite useful at that particular moment. But alas, Phil had evolved past gills and his subsequent lungs would mutate into a full-body absorption system. It was highly efficient and allowed Phil to toil for large swaths of time without fatiguing.

The only problem was that it left him susceptible to drowning.

Not that it mattered much, as the lakes and oceans were devoid of anything other than algae. The murky depths were just plain boring to explore, so Phil decided, much to his current chagrin, that gills were entirely superfluous. He could devolve back to aquatic times, but that would erase eons of evolutionary progress.

Thus, he needed a workable plan that didn't involve drowning.

Thankfully, he had two pieces of critical information. First, he knew where the stone had hit the water. And second, he knew the depth of that location based on his time as a fish. Throw in a little math, and he could deduce exactly where the pallasite should be resting. Unfortunately, he also knew the maximum length that a single tentacle could reach. The simplest plan was to puff up like a balloon, float out to the site, and plunge a tentacle down into the depths. Having healed enough to make such an attempt, he did just that.

As suspected, not even close.

About 20 meters away, per his calculations.

Phil had no access to tools, or rope, or the mental maturity to consider such things. The only thing he knew for certain was that 20 meters of water separated him from his most favorite thing in the world. Thus, the separation needed to be removed.

And so, Phil decided to move the ocean.

What may seem like a bonkers solution to a bonkers problem was actually quite reasonable to Phil. After all, he had three distinct advantages: infinite time, infinite patience, and a large canyon system on the other side of a mountain pass. Thus, the strategy presented itself as the universe's most laborious bucket brigade. Phil would be the sole representative and his body would serve as the only bucket. Despite the objective lunacy of such a plan, he reveled in the ability to right his monumental wrong.

Having paddled back to the beach, Phil shook himself dry and gazed across the shimmering expanse. It was, quite fortunately, the smallest ocean on the planet. Some might call it a massive lake. The Federation was agnostic on such matters, as a Sarcothian would regard a tiny puddle as an uncrossable obstacle. So for the sake of clarity, this was a large body of water to which Phil would devote a large chunk of time relocating.

Undaunted, Phil rolled into the shallows and chomped at the surf like Pac-Man trying to catch a fish. He rolled back to the beach with a belly full of water and continued towards the mountain pass. The path snaked around Alluring Peak to the back of the coastal chain. Once on the other side, it was a short trek to the canyon. Or at least, to the point where any spillage would trickle its way into the system.

The vast ravine was not unlike the famed Frebnoc Fissures of Loram'bai (read: the Grand Canyon, only grander). They offered a large pot to piss in, not that Phil pissed. Excess moisture simply evaporated from his hide. His energy stores replenished through a hyper-efficient form of photosynthesis, the only remaining holdout from his humble start as a single cell of pond algae. Thus, the planet was blissfully free of poop.

All this to say that Phil was more than capable of moving an entire ocean, one mouthful at a time, without fatigue or degradation. He chomped at the water, rolled to the canyon, puked it out like a frat boy with a hangover, and rolled back to the ocean, over and over and over. The ocean steadily declined and the canyon steadily filled. Every so often, he would paddle out to the target location and plunge a tentacle down into the depths. "Nope!" he always exclaimed, then paddled back to the beach to resume the process.

Six hundred years later, the deed was done.

The canyon had transformed into a majestic lake and the ocean had transformed into a smaller ocean, call it a majestic lake. Phil paddled out to his target, plunged a tentacle into the depths, and finally touched his lost companion. The resulting gasp turned into a high-pitched squeal as he pinched the stone and reeled it back to the surface. Phil yanked it from its watery tomb and lifted it high into the air, as if to complete a long-awaited resurrection. Once again, the crystals caught the sunlight and scattered beams of yellow radiance. He then cradled it to his hide and swayed back and forth like a mother with a frightened infant. And there he floated, awash in relief and elated beyond words.

Unsurprisingly, not a single being had visited Phil's Place during the transfer. Whenever a ship passed into telepathy range, Phil shouted "MOVING OCEAN GO AWAY!" over and over until they fled, which they were more than happy to do.

Several weeks later, Phil was still floating in the lesser ocean. He had drifted out into open water and had no idea where he was, nor did he care. His favorite thing in the world was pressed to his hide and he caressed it with a tender adoration. Then, out of the cold reaches of nowhere, a blind panic consumed him.

A horrible thought had infected his mind.

What if it happened ... *again*?

He could not bear to watch his precious sink into the dark oblivion. One careless fumble could turn six hundred years into six million. A sudden and intense need to protect his life-mate prompted several tentacles to frantically paddle for safety. By the end of the day, he had reached the shore. A fresh surge of energy pushed him across the beach, over a sandy dune, and far away from the very notion of wetness.

Before long, Phil had taken refuge at the center of a sweeping valley. The pallasite stayed locked inside his flesh, forever silent, forever safe. He even ignored meteorites as they fell from the heavens. They had slowly accumulated during the ocean move, but he dared not transport them to Dumb Stone Lake. What if he hurled his dearest by mistake? The risk was small, but the fear was petrifying. And so he stayed in the valley, anxious, stricken, and surrounded by tiny trespassers from the great black sea.

Paranoia sank in quickly.

A fiery rage boiled inside his flesh.

He began to curse every meteor as it fell. And seeing as how they fell on a regular basis, the valley emitted a constant roar of profanity. A single ship passed into telepathy range during this time and the pilot almost killed the crew with the fleeing burn.

And then Phil snapped.

No longer feeling safe on his own planet, Phil raced to a nearby cave system and burrowed deep underground. He had explored it once during his subterranean gecko phase, but found the dankness off-putting. But on that day, it served as an incubator for his own insanity. The deeper he went, the better he felt, so he dove as far as he could. He eventually reached the bottom, a small recess that neatly fit his mass with a little room to spare. And there he stayed, safe and content, miles away from the burden of despair.

He retrieved the stone from his flesh and rested it atop his muddied hide. A single tentacle stroked it like a cherished pet. The crystals had gone silent, but he didn't care. The darkness was a shield. The dankness was a blanket. Nothing would pull them apart ever again. He took solace in his soiled prison and settled in for the next eon.

Several ships passed into range during the next few centuries, and each was repelled by a telepathic onslaught of demon-like hisses. Once out of range, Phil comforted his dearest with gentle pats and pleasantries. "It's okay, little one," he said with a softened tone. "You are my precious source of happiness and joy and bliss and glee and pleasure. You are perfect. And if there is a word more perfect than perfect, then you are also that. Perhaps there is someone who knows of a word more perfect than perfect. I would invite them to—"

Phil stopped petting the rock.

Phil gasped.

Phil then barked an urgent request into the cosmos.

* * *

(Once again, Phil lifts the pallasite and presents it like a prized memento.)

Sooo ... do you like my rock?

(I stare at Phil with mouth agape, utterly blindsided by his bonkers tale. The reality of the situation settles on my shoulders with the weight of a thousand suns. I cannot possibly be sitting here for the reason he just presented. Stunned beyond words, I close my eyes and begin to construct the dumbest sentence that I will ever utter.)

Do you mean to tell me ... that you spent *eons* scaling mountains, moving oceans, and hiding underground like a crazy gremlin ... just to get a compliment on your favorite rock?

(nods) Yup!

And only *now* did it occur to you to ... *ask* for one?

(nods) Yup!

And of all the available and willing beings in the entire universe, you decided that the best chance of success was to summon the "best talky person" for a personal interview?

(nods) Yup!

(I huff loudly, then rise from my rock and start pacing back and forth. Anger boils in my stomach as I replay the entire journey up to that point, only to discover that I am a pawn in a billion-year scheme that could have been resolved by a text message. As I pace inside a dark cloud of rage, I cannot decide if this is the most fascinating or infuriating exchange of my entire life. Part of me wants to deny Phil the satisfaction and depart for Durangoni, but the masochistic side wants to see it through to the very end. And so, I grit my teeth, let out a grunt of pure vexation, then return my gaze to Phil.)

That's a lovely rock.

Thank you.

(Phil immediately whips around and smashes the pallasite against a nearby boulder. It shatters into a cloud of dust and sends a sharp echo through the valley, causing me to yelp and stumble backwards. Phil pulsates as he stares, presumably, at the dispersing haze.)

Why the hell did you do that?!

(Phil whips his mass back to face me. Again, presumably.)

Do you know how long I've been carrying that stupid thing?! Eons and eons and eons without a single word! Not one! Not a single one! Countless visitors, countless opportunities, and countless disappointments! It's like the air on my planet is fatal to basic kindness! Would it have killed anyone to acknowledge a pretty rock?! Gawd!

(Phil rolls away while continuing to rant like an ornery grandmother. His voice fades into the distance, leaving me to digest the aftermath. I sit in stunned silence for a few minutes, then call the shuttle service for a pick-up.)

* * *

And so ended the most fascinating interview of my life.

Yes, I opted for fascinating.

While certainly infuriating, the sheer quantity of time needed to reach the capstone boggles the mind. In the end, I played a tiny part, but it represented the crescendo of infinite patience and profound innocence.

In fact, I started chuckling as the shuttle sailed into open space. It was the only sound inside the cabin, as everyone else had braced for the cerebral assault. But it never came. Our collective mental space was blissfully silent. One by one, they all started laughing with me. It was a much-needed release of tension.

That is, until Phil decided that laughter was antithetical to his rant.

"And another thing!" he said before beaming his tirade into the minds of everyone aboard.

The laughter stopped.

At least, all but mine.

I continued to chuckle like an idiot as the rantings of a brilliant meat sack bounced around my head hole.

* * *

Two weeks later, I returned home to Durangoni.

I sat inside my office with an odd sense of detachment. The walls seemed stale, as if the radiance had faded from their sheen. The interior seemed distant, as if crafted by a different set of wants and desires.

Having spent my entire life aboard the largest space station in the universe, it was apparent that my journey to Phil's Place had opened my eyes to a new perspective. Durangoni is home to a massive amalgamation of species and cultures, so it never occurred to me to seek a different vantage. But out in the great black sea, there is a world so beautiful, and a creature so intelligent, that it made me question the very notion of living inside an artifice.

I reached into my pocket and withdrew a small yellow crystal, one of the few remaining fragments from Phil's precious stone. It was a token of wisdom, no bigger than a marble, yet no less enchanting than the universe that created it. I placed it under a desk lamp, where it twinkled ever so slightly. Soon after, my assistant tapped the door and I beckoned her inside. We bantered for a minute, at which point she noticed the memento.

"That's a lovely rock," she said.

"Well that didn't take long."

I plucked the crystal and tossed it into a trash can.

THE END

Three great hunts.
One great hunter.
These are the best of Boo.

In the wild world of elite bounty hunting, one name towers above the rest. Boo is a living legend. He is also a haunting enigma who strikes terror into his targets. A fog of intrigue surrounds his incredible feats, three of which are universally hailed as the greatest bounties ever collected. This book unpacks them all.

BOO

The Greatest Bounty Hunter Ever to Sail the Black

CHAPTER 1

Few memberships are more coveted in the universe than the Bounty Hunters Union of Durangoni, and for good reason. The healthcare is top-notch, the vacation is generous, and its members are regarded as the very best in the business. They are the rockstar pirates of the great black sea, sailing under banners of pure adoration. Criminals will often pose for pictures when captured, elated by the prospect of their newfound prison cred.

The top five hunters in BHUD enjoy a cult-like celebrity status. There is Snigg the Snatcher, a brutish fellow known for his heavy-handed approach. Debaru Funk is a femme fatale. OBY-42 is a crafty android. Zybor is a straight-up murder hobo.

And then there's Boo.

Boo is the best of the bunch by a very wide margin. His stats are unmatched, unreachable, and damn near godlike. He is also one of the strangest creatures in the cosmos. While the other four command massive fan bases, Boo remains a peripheral oddity. It's a bizarre paradox, given his status as the top banana.

That is, until you meet him.

He wears basic clothes with basic colors, like a middle-aged dad with nothing left in the fucks tank. This does little to distract from a near-featureless head. "Near" being an important distinction, as his smooth white dome has a tiny slit for a mouth and nothing else. Despite the absence of eyes, ears, and nostrils, he tracks stimuli like anyone else, leading many to believe that he experiences the world in a wholly different spectrum. He also moves like a bedeviled phantom, which tightens every butthole when he enters a room.

I use "he" in reference to Boo based solely on his choice of dadclothes. Truth be told, nobody knows *what* he is, or if "he" even applies. Boo is the sole member of his species living aboard the station, assuming that he's a species at all. Some think that he is an asexual mutant. Others suspect that he is a shapeshifting fungus. Many have asked Boo directly, but Boo's vocabulary is limited to a single word: "Boo." He rarely offers it, choosing to remain creepily silent like a goth kid at a frat party. When he does speak, it is soft and reflective, similar to the way most people use "Hmm."

Nevertheless, Boo remains the greatest bounty hunter ever to have lived. This is primarily due to a batshit bonkers strategy that is impossible to replicate, yet widely circulated as gossip and folklore. Everybody has a favorite Boo story, including the other bounty hunters. They often refer to the "Big Three," i.e. best hunts ever completed, all of which belong to Boo. This book will explore those remarkable tales and hopefully shine some light on one of the most eccentric artists in the universe.

But before we dive in, allow me to introduce myself. My name is Puki Horpocket. I am an editor at large for the Definitive Directory of Durangoni, the panoptic mega-wiki for the largest space station in the universe. Durangoni is home to a trillion active residents, all of whom access the directory for their daily wants and needs.

Want to try a new restaurant?

Consult the directory.

Need a doctor for your second spleen?

Consult the directory.

Want to see an acrobatic clown show?

Consult the directory.

Need the latest news on your favorite bounty hunter?

(drumroll) Consult the directory.

The Bounty Hunters Union of Durangoni enjoys extensive documentation within the directory, much of which I recorded myself. Each hunter has a detailed archive that is managed by a dedicated historian.

Save for one.

I have personally managed Boo's profile for the last several years. The first line reads, "Boo was born (presumption), stuff happened, then he arrived at Durangoni." It hasn't changed since the day it was entered, hence my fascination with his backstory. There is so much to learn about Boo and so much mystery that surrounds his existence. As a dedicated storyteller, I cannot help but be drawn to this delectable enigma.

But where to start?

After much consideration, I determined that the best course of action was to follow Boo's initial footsteps and start exactly where he did: at BHUD (pronounced Bee-Hud). I scheduled a meeting with the Union President, a legend in her own right by the name of Helga Naath. After brushing up on her personal history, I grabbed my proverbial pen and away I went.

* * *

Luckily for me, getting to the BHUD headquarters was a mere hop, skip, and jump to the nearest pod train station. As with most powerful guilds that called the station home, BHUD carried enough cachet to occupy a central ring. The Directory offices also qualified, for obvious reasons. The general rule of thumb was this: the bigger the clout, the wider the ring.

For anyone needing an explanation, the Durangoni megastructure formed a top-like shape, in reference to the boring children's toy. A massive set of disc-like rings rotated independently around a central axle. The largest ring in the center served as the main thoroughfare, featuring the majority of docking stations and high-end commerce. The poles were more specialized and required some travel time to visit.

The pod train network fulfilled this need. It connected every ring through a complex web of service tunnels and express corridors. The pods themselves were magnetically linked with atmo barriers that allowed passengers to wander between them. They could break away as needed and race to the hidden bowels of the station. If your destination was highly peculiar, chances are that you arrived in a single pod.

My train was still a few dozen strong when it slowed to a stop at my destination. BHUD was located near the surface of a central ring, a ritzy locale filled with high fashion and low tolerance for dregs. To the average eye, it would seem like an odd place for a bounty hunter base, but we're not talking about dirty grifters with missing fingers (although some would qualify). The elite members of BHUD enjoyed the highest perks of celebrity stardom, second only to the core engineers that kept the station afloat. Thus, a typical client wasn't looking to collect a gambling debt. BHUD members were hired to change the social fabric of the universe.

The pod train doors slid open and I strolled into a gleaming corridor. A pleasant melody played in the background, highlighting a thin cloud of incense that wandered through the cool air. When the foot tunnels smelled like a spa, one could only imagine what the spas smelled like. Hologram signs with muted colorations directed visitors to their destinations. I followed my own towards the Cosmic Relations sector. It housed everything that involved delicate foreign matters, be them ambassador offices or murders for hire (often the same thing).

Given this sensitivity, CR offices were guarded around the clock. A separate passage with numerous checkpoints discouraged curious eyes from wandering too close. The stout frames of station security provided an effective visual deterrent. The CR sector was one of the few places where prestige counted for less than nothing.

No fans here, just the cold stares of justice.

My Directory ID card, on the other hand, opened every door. With a final flick and scan, the Cosmic Relations sector was revealed to me. Drab would be the overall vibe, as there was no one to impress with colorful advertisements. I could hear the words "gray is fine" from an architect in the distant past. Hologram signs floated above a series of alcoves, each denoting an occupant and current status. A quick scan uncovered BHUD, prompting a nod and continuation.

I opened the front door and entered a quiet lobby. At first glance, it presented as a branding salon, something for narcissists to charge other narcissists for lessons on narcissism. Life-sized decals of famous bounty hunters decorated the walls. Each of them was preened and posed, no doubt to capitalize on image rights.

There was one glaring omission, though.

Boo, it would seem, had no interest in such acclaim.

At the center of the room was a small desk with an intercom. No receptionist, just a single red button that read "Press for Help."

And so I did.

"Can I help you?" the intercom said.

"Yes. Puki Horpocket here to see Helga Naath."

"One moment."

Precisely one moment later, a door behind the desk slid open.

"Third door on the right," the speaker said.

"Thank you."

The intercom crackled away without response.

I proceeded around the desk and through the door, which promptly shut behind me. My gaze floated down a hallway with stark lighting and numerous doors, each with a hologram panel that denoted the current occupant. Most were vacant. It made sense, given the nature of the work. A hunter behind a desk isn't much of a hunter.

I located the door in question and gave it a firm yet unaggressive knock. Funny enough, this was a grave concern of mine. I knew how to assert myself to a variety of individuals. Directory intern? Vigorous knock, borderline hostile. Meek eyewitness? Gentle knock with a pleasant melody. But the president of an elite bounty hunter organization? After a rigorous analysis, I settled on "creepy uncle that needs a firm dressing down." In other words, knock like you mean it, but don't rattle the frame.

And so I did.

"Come in," said a muffled voice.

Nailed it, I thought, then opened the door.

My first impression was that of an interrogation room. Two chairs, one table, single light overhead, nothing on the walls but gray paint and fear. Helga sat on the opposite side with her feet up on the table. She swiped through a security tablet with the vigor of an annoyed teenager. A matte gray suit clung to her sturdy frame, one that could easily break me in half if so inclined. She embodied the grizzled veteran, someone who had paid her dues and now says "I'm too old for this shit" at parties.

With a final swipe, she tossed the tablet aside and met my gaze. Ebon eyes with white irises commanded my attention. Her silver hair was bound tight, tracing a sharp line around her dusky complexion. She radiated power and fortitude, enough to weaken my knees and hope for a quick death.

And thus began the inquiry.

What follows is my detailed exchange with Helga Naath, the highly respected president of a revered institution within the largest space station in the universe. In Durangoni terms, it was the closest I could get to interviewing royalty.

* * *

Hello, Ms. Naath. My name is—

So you're here to talk about Boo.

I—um, yes. How did you know?

You're Puki Horpocket, the guy known for telling outrageous stories about outrageous weirdos. If you're talking to me, then the mystery solves itself.

(I let out a nervous chuckle.) Guilty.

It's okay. You actually caught me at a good time.

(She motions for me to sit, which I do after a grateful smile and a polite bow of respect. I unzip my satchel, retrieve my notepad, and cross my legs for the coming exchange, all in a single well-practiced motion.)

So—

And what makes you think I'm going to tell you a goddamn thing?

(My jaw hangs open. The tension is sudden, sharp, and knots my stomach.)

(She laughs and slaps the table.) I'm just messing with you. We like to rib. Eases the stress.

(I laugh nervously.) Consider my stress eased, then. (It wasn't.)

So what would you like to know?

To start, I am curious to learn how Boo ended up in BHUD.

(shrugs) Showed up one day, nabbed a job, been crushing it ever since.

That's all you have?

Boo isn't the most forthcoming of blokes, so don't expect a dissertation. He's as mysterious in here as he is out there. That said, the stories are no less spectacular.

Fair enough. And given your experience with that mystique, I would be very curious to know what your favorite Boo story is.

(grunts and shakes head) Oh wow, so many to consider. The one that pops into mind is, of course, the single greatest feat in the history of bounty hunting.

The Hollow Hold Gambit.

Yes. But I also understand why *me* citing that would be uninteresting.

I still get into heated debates about the Galwock Terror, which I think is criminally underrated. But if I had to pick one, it would have to be the Jacothra Wander.

Isn't that one of the Big Three?

(nods) Generally a distant third to the first two. But when it comes to pure substance, the *virtue* of the hunt, it doesn't get any better than Jacothra.

And why is that?

I think it beautifully captures the essence of what makes Boo tick. He's a very odd bloke, but there's a method to his madness. It takes an extraordinary level of patience and discipline to catch the uncatchable, and that's exactly what he does, day in and day out.

That particular bounty was classified as UNO, or unobtainable, due to the target's resilience and lack of intel. UNO payouts are very high, but the opportunity costs make them unfeasible at best. Most are captured by accident, i.e. they just happened to show up during another hunt. Boo is the only hunter who takes UNOs as primary jobs.

This one only had two pieces of info. First, the target was Findellio Nomic, a highly skilled survivalist who worked as a scout for the Varokin Empire. That alone sent the bounty into the stratosphere. Highly desirable, if not for the second part.

Jacothra.

Exactly. Nomic was last seen on descent. Unobtainable, by definition.

And yet, Boo completed the job.

(nods) Amazes me to this day.

So why is it your favorite?

I understand the intrigue that surrounds the Gambit. It's an astounding achievement, a masterclass of awareness and coordination. But I would argue that the Jacothra Wander is equally astounding, albeit from the opposite end of the spectrum. If your goal is to paint a complete picture of Boo for your readers, then I would start there.

And who would best wield that brush?

You up for a drink? Buy a few rounds and I'll take you on that journey.

(I gasp and press both hands to my chest, pleading with my heart to resume normal function after skipping several beats. My voice lowers to a woozy whisper.)

Are you suggesting that we go to ... the *place*?

(grins)

* * *

My panicked expression must have conveyed acceptance, because Helga rose from her chair and beckoned me to follow. If I were to describe my mental space at that exact moment, it would have been a swirling vortex of pants-shitting intrigue. After all, no one gets invited to the Golden Quiver (the cluster-famous pub for elite bounty hunters) without a damn good reason.

There were stories to tell, and Helga thought it best to hear them from the gloobur's third orifice (read: horse's mouth). First on the docket was the third-best bounty hunt of all time: the Jacothra Wander.

CHAPTER 2

When it comes to criminals and planets, there are places you go to hide and places you go to die. Jacothra was the latter. But for one wily fugitive, it was the perfect mix of both.

Findellio "Finny" Nomic made a name for himself as a Varokin scout. This was mostly due to his unique ability to weather the harshest climates. Finny was a subspecies of tardigrade that evolved a massive girth (read: water bears the size of actual bears). His skin was thick, his claws were sharp, and his cells were death-resistant. He could withstand a boiling storm of sulfuric acid with the same indifference of taking a lukewarm shower. This made him terribly useful to nefarious spy networks, which landed him a lucrative job with the Varokin Empire.

But alas, his amazing talents would lead to an equally amazing downfall.

Lord Essien, feared leader of the Varokins, decided that Finny's insider knowledge was too much of a liability. She tried to kill him, but failed, because tardigrade. He fled to a rival faction, but landed in the net of an undercover operation. Finny was arrested, imprisoned, and transferred to Durangoni for further processing.

But Durangoni, having no idea how shockingly immune Finny

was to punishment, would soon have egg on its face. Prisons were often used to source labor for hazardous projects, some of which produced toxic waste. Finny volunteered, then hid in a disposal tank. It was transported off-station for processing, which raised zero suspicion. No one had thought to dig through toxic sludge for stowaways, so he simply walked away from the dump site.

So where does a hyper-resilient fugitive go?

Of the top hellholes that come to mind, most would say Jacothra.

The air was poisonous, the soil was sulfuric, the water was acidic, and the critters that lived there were highly venomous. In fact, the planet was a hotbed of evolution, in that the creatures preying on each other were locked in a never-ending battle of potency. One bite from a murphilo (read: giant scaly toad with shark teeth) delivered enough toxicity to kill the entire population of a mid-sized planet.

Boo knew all of this going in, so he commissioned a chem-resistant suit powered by a small core of enriched plutonium. It doubled as a comfy heater and a colossal self-destruct, if needed. His ship, on the other hand, carried an arsenal of critical components that would melt inside the Jacothra atmosphere. So the entry plan was simple: rent a ship, pay the insurance premium, then leave it on Jacothra to dissolve. The exit plan, however, had yet to materialize.

The spooder he carried was also chem-resistant, but that was standard issue.

Ah, the spooder. It was the single most important piece of the modern hunter arsenal. In the old days, hunting a bounty was only half the battle. The target also needed to be returned, which was often more dangerous than the actual hunt. BHUD sought to even the playing field, and their answer was the spooder.

It was a small device with a black titanium shell, roughly the size of a bottle cap. When a hunter took a job, they were given a spooder that contained a biometric signature of the target. When it touched the target, it triggered a series of diamond-crusted darts with backward-facing barbs. They shot into the flesh and secured their purchase. The darts could penetrate any tissue, including bone and metal.

And that's when the magic began.

The spooder sent a signal to the target's cerebral network, creating a countdown clock in its visual field. It persisted during sleep and even worked on the blind. If the target failed to return to the Durangoni Office of Corrections before the time expired, or if the spooder was tampered with in any way, then it fried the cerebral network, killing the target.

This one giant leap in technology also created a leap in hunting strategy. One of the most embarrassing captures for a criminal was the infamous hand-buzzer, the dumb little prank that became a prison sentence.

A disguised hunter greets a target with a friendly handshake.

Job complete.

And thus was born a new age of hunting expertise and target avoidance. This was why Findellio Nomic, one of the most unsubtle creatures one could meet, fled to a hellscape of poison, acid, and venom.

* * *

A small ship with numerous dents floated in orbit above Jacothra, having blinked out of hyperspace a few minutes earlier. Its continued approach was delayed by a complete inability to determine a continued approach. Every planetary scan, from atmospheric to biologic, returned diddly squat. The navigation system took a long hard look at the smoggy hellhole and shrugged each time.

Sheets of lightning crackled across a hazy yellow sheen, creating an acrid light show that no reasonable being would want to see any closer. The shadowy stripes of mountain ranges slithered inside the maelstrom, like massive krakens waiting to strike. Caustic storms swirled with violent intent as they rained acid across the hidden surface. The planet was a cauldron of chaos, belching its desire to kill anything that dared to visit.

Despite this obvious and dire warning, the pilot inside the ship was oddly unmoved. He sat in a ratty seat in front of a rusty control panel while studying the planet with a cold detachment. His featureless dome of a head was encased inside a larger dome of clear composite. The rest of his custom suit was a charcoal hide of thick poly fiber. Boo was not winning any beauty pageants on this hunt, but that was never the point. This particular suit would ensure that his visit to Jacothra would not end with a pool of bubbling goo.

Boo pushed the rickety yoke forward and began his descent into the atmosphere. It didn't take long for things to get choppy. The ship bounced, jerked, and rattled its way through a bank of highly charged clouds. Cheap components detached from control panels and bounced around the cockpit. Acidic rain sprayed the viewport, painting a rainbow of chemicals across the glass. A warning siren blared as status icons blinked from green to red. Before long, the entire board glowed red as the ship gave up all hope of surviving the onslaught.

Boo, on the other hand, maintained his cool demeanor through the entire ruckus. Moments later, the hull thrusters ignited and slowed the ship to a gentle hover just above the surface. But then the poisonous air choked them out and the flimsy vessel thumped into the dirt.

A perfect landing, all things considered.

Boo reached across the panel to power down the vessel, but it beat him to the punch. The entire system failed under the atmospheric stress, resulting in a cascade of indicators crackling into nothing. Darkness consumed the cockpit. Harsh sizzles filled the space as the outside began to eat its way in, dissolving the ship around its strangely calm occupant. The entire process was ferociously rapid. In a matter of minutes, Boo went from sitting in the pilot seat to standing in a puddle of rental ship.

The insurance premium had served its purpose.

Boo twisted his pasty white head around the nightmarish landscape. A horrible mosaic of bronze, yellow, and orange glared back at him, made even more horrid by streaks of corrosive liquid streaming down his helmet. It flowed down his suit and dripped into the rental puddle. Plant life was notably absent. Rocks and boulders dominated the scenery, their rounded faces trumpeting a constant decay. Amber clouds rumbled overhead, unleashing waves of lightning that pummeled the ground.

And yet Boo remained unmoved.

His attention fell to a data panel on his forearm. He tapped a sequence of commands that initiated a proximity scan. What would usually highlight every living thing within a hundred klicks was suddenly reduced to one kilometer.

He recalibrated the device and tried again.

Same result.

After a few more attempts, he concluded that the planetary interference was too great to conduct a proper scan. He was stuck at a one-kilometer diameter. And given that Jacothra's surface area spanned six hundred million square kilometers, a difficult hunt became slightly more difficult.

Boo was undeterred.

He tweaked a few settings and constructed a scan grid inside the nav system. The plan was simple. After each kilometer, he would initiate a new scan and investigate any creature within range. The system would then mark the area complete and highlight the next one. Boo finished the setup, then picked a direction and started walking.

And thus began the great wander.

Most areas required little attention, as the Jacothra fauna was few and far between. The scanner collected biometric data and highlighted familiar critters, allowing Boo to ignore most sections. Every now and then, a herd of creatures confused the scanner, forcing Boo to probe a little deeper. The occasional shark-toothed horror toad saw Boo as a tasty snack, prompting a quick incineration from a suit-mounted plasma weapon.

And so the days passed.

When it was time to rest, he found the nearest hidey hole and bedded down for a nap. When it was time to eat or drink, he did ... *something.* (No one has ever witnessed Boo ingest any solids or liquids, which has birthed many amusing theories about his biology. My personal favorite is that he's a robot controlled by a super-intelligent gerbil.)

Days turned into weeks.

Weeks turned into months.

The first year came and went.

And then it happened.

Four hundred and sixteen days after the rental ship melted, the scanner picked up a peculiar biosignal. Boo did not flinch, hurry, or even show mild excitement. He locked onto the target and treated it as any new investigation. The system guided him to a nearby cliffside with a large cave mouth at the base. A heat map appeared inside his visual cortex, along with a detailed grid of the internal structure. The target, now a hazy orange blob, rested in a large chamber about a hundred meters into the cavern.

Boo maintained a resolute stride into the cave mouth.

The craggy interior slowed his pace a bit as he bounded over rocks and ducked under stalactites, but it did provide a welcome reprieve from the acidic hellscape. His suit remained dark, as Boo had little need for optic perception (hence the unsettling lack of eyeballs). He did sense visual input, just not in the manner most beings enjoyed. As with most things concerning Boo, his specific method remained a mystery.

It didn't take long to reach his destination. Boo entered a large hollow with a flat base and comfortable climate, the perfect hideout for any chemically resistant criminal on the run. The orange blob rested in total stillness against the rear wall. The scanner dropped the heat map, revealing the sleeping body of a bear-sized monster. Its thick hide, six limbs, and razor-sharp claws confirmed acquisition.

Finny snored through a deep slumber, allowing Boo to take a well-earned rest. He selected a chair-sized boulder near the beast and took a seat. And there he waited. The spooder remained tucked inside his suit, even with a hard-fought bounty within reach. Boo, as with most hunters, was not without a taste for the dramatic.

And then the creature stirred from its snooze. Finny rolled over, smacked his meaty lips, lifted his eyelids, then shrieked in terror. His bulbous body jerked back and slammed into the wall. A shower of pebbles fell from the ceiling as his eyes swelled with shock. His gaze darted around the hollow, plotting a daring escape that deflated with futility. After all, the most feared bounty hunter in the universe sat before him.

Boo remained perfectly still with hands folded in his lap. A pebble bounced off his helmet and puffed in the dirt, drawing no reaction whatsoever. Finny read the language loud and clear, so he remained pressed against the wall with widened eyes locked onto the visitor. With a slow and steady motion, Boo reached into a suit pocket, withdrew the spooder device, and lowered it to the ground in front of Finny.

"Boo," Boo said.

Finny released a heavy sigh, expelling the mounted tension. He closed his eyes, offered a slight nod, then reached for the device with a trembling hand. The spooder sprang to life on contact. It buried numerous barbs into his flesh, drawing a flinch and grimace. A countdown clock appeared in his visual field and started ticking away his fate. Finny sighed again, then thumped his hand into the dirt.

The hunt was complete.

Boo was free to leave, but he didn't move a muscle. He sat there with an unnerving calm, staring at his former target while his bank account ballooned with riches. Finny scrunched his meaty brow in confusion, then grunted with annoyance once the realization dawned.

The clock was ticking.

He needed to return to Durangoni.

As did Boo.

CHAPTER 3

Helga had guided me through the bowels of BHUD and to an un-marked door somewhere in the rear. Without breaking stride, she thumped it open with a stiff shoulder. A warm light poured into the hallway, offsetting the stale glow of serious business. She proceeded inside, prompting a chorus of cheers and greetings.

"Got some fresh meat," she said, then gestured to the sheepish fellow in tow (me).

I entered the Golden Quiver with an odd sense of fear and com-pulsion, like a horny virgin entering a brothel. What greeted my eyes was nothing short of ... underwhelming. To be fair, the interior was clean, quiet, and tastefully decorated, like a mid-tier hotel lobby. But there was no seedy bartender serving unmarked bottles of booze, no card games with pillars of smoke rising from ashtrays, no gruff scoundrels ready to brawl at the drop of a hat. My brain had conjured a classic outlaw bar, but what I got was a mediocre coffee lounge on a random weekday.

But then I realized *who* was in the lounge.

The Golden Quiver had an impressive amount of arrows at its disposal. The posters from the lobby had come to life right before my eyes. I recognized Debaru Funk immediately. She sipped a highball glass at the main bar while swiping through her comdev. Snigg the Snatcher filled an entire couch with his meaty frame. He was reading a book through a tiny pair of glasses, creating the droll image of an erudite barbarian. Even Zybor was there. He laughed with un-named friends around a table (likely on break between murders).

"Puki Horpocket?" someone said with a dismissive chuckle.

Snigg puckered his lips with interest and glanced up from his book. (I wondered what titles of mine he had read, but needed some courage to ask.)

Most of them paid me no mind, as their collective celebrity status outweighed mine to a comical degree. But then Helga exclaimed, "Drinks are on the Directory," which immediately raised my rank. Cheers and back-slaps followed, lessening my annoyance at Helga's cavalier broadcast. Ah well, that's what slush funds were for.

And so we drank.

A lot.

Helga claimed her usual table, prompting several curious patrons to follow. She explained my reason for being there, which drew a fair amount of interest. After all, their insights into Boo were just as vague as my own. The project had legs from the get-go, and now I had support from the inner circle.

Boo stories were always welcome, especially from the brass. Thus, a Helga recount of the Jacothra Wander drew an instant crowd. The audience swelled as the story neared its climax. When she finished, a wave of applause echoed through the Quiver. Given the massive egos crowding the space, it was fascinating to watch mega-celebrities cheer the exploits of an even greater celebrity.

Listeners peeled away to refill drinks as Helga sipped her own neglected glass. I sat there with jaw agape, utterly flummoxed by what I had heard.

So what you're telling me, is that Boo intimidated Finny *so much*, that not only did he accept a peaceful capture by grabbing the spooder, but he also gave Boo a ride back to Durangoni?

(smiles and nods)

Holy shit.

I know, right? It's like getting ship-jacked by pirates, then taking them out for drinks to celebrate the score. But hey, that's the kind of clout Boo wields.

I can understand why the Wander is your favorite. That's a level of patience that I didn't know was possible.

And that's why Finny didn't fight back. Boo negated his entire skill set by walking into that hollow. It's the purest bounty ever hunted.

(Mumbles of agreement float around the table.)

Aside from the Galwock Terror.

(Groans erupt from the table, drawing a smirk from Helga. An assortment of table nuts pelts her from all directions. Soon after, a familiar face joins the party.)

[Debaru Funk] You and Galwock, I swear. (She drops her glass on the table and takes a seat.)

(Admittedly, I am taken aback by her presence. Debaru Funk is a living legend with a laundry list of thrilling tales all to her own. Her black hair and sharp features serve to enhance a deadly persona. But even so, I find her oddly charming. Sensing the playful banter, I jump at the opportunity to siphon more intel.)

So you disagree with Helga's assessment?

[Debaru] Disagree would imply openness to debate. I reject her assessment outright.

(The crowd responds with jeers and snickers.)

[Helga] Galwock was a study in precision.

[Debaru] Galwock was a fluke. Ain't no way he could do that again.

Dare I ask?

[Helga] Sure. It all started when—

(Scoffs, boos, and another flurry of nuts.)

[Helga] See what I mean? No respect.

(I switch my attention to Debaru.) So what is your favorite Boo bounty?

My personal favorite will always be the Succulent Snatch.

(I raise an eyebrow.)

I know, it sounds like a porn flick. But I assure you, the name is apt.

(I smirk, then motion to continue.)

What made this hunt so special wasn't the skill. It was the *spite*.

The spite? Boo doesn't strike me as the vengeful type.

He's not, which is why the upshot was so juicy and delicious. Hence the namesake. It's still very much a Boo job, just with a delectable cherry on top. I have told this story countless times, and it still makes me moan with satisfaction. Mmm (chef's kiss). So, so good.

Would you mind telling it one more time?

Not at all. I'm always up for some snatch.

(I raise the other eyebrow.)

That came out wrong. Actually, it didn't. Anyhoo ...

CHAPTER 4

Cam Comamba was a certifiable douche nozzle.

This guy collected scandals like a geek collected trading cards. He was single-handedly responsible for eight of the top ten financial frauds over the last century. On top of this most egregious of rap sheets, he was also a self-help guru who catered to insecure types with brittle egos. In fact, getting "cam'd" became popular slang for anyone who emptied their bank account for some super-obvious dude-bro huckster.

And then there was Cam Athletics.

This was a "how can anyone possibly take this seriously" level of grifting. The company sold everything from tap water to cans of air. Every product was branded with bold colors and lauded as a miracle fix to a prominent woe (especially if said woe was in the news cycle).

New virus? Try the Cam Athletics Rock of Wellness, guaranteed to cure every ailment. And if it doesn't work, then you obviously didn't use it right. Buy more and try again.

New war? Try the Cam Athletics Air of Armistice, guaranteed to broker peace. And if it doesn't work, then you obviously didn't use it right. Buy more and try again.

At one point, the company sold literal garbage from a toxic landfill. Lackies combed the site for anything that resembled pharmaceuticals, then stuffed them into branded containers and sold them as whatever remedy was currently trending. This caught the vigilant eye of the Durangoni Consumer Watch. They intervened and shut the company down, but it popped back up in a new system and resumed operations, never missing a beat.

This was due in large part to Cam's in-your-face style of advertising. He was well-known for his "feats of strength" videos. Colloquially known as "Cam-Dos," they featured Cam performing high-profile stunts while hawking his sham products as the secret to his success. The videos were adored by a vast community of adrenaline junkies, status seekers, and impressionable teens with axes to grind. The campaigns slithered their way through every echelon of society, making Cam super famous, super rich, and super immune to consequences.

That is, until he challenged Boo.

This monumentally boneheaded decision stemmed from the financial fraud cases. Cam had grown immensely cocky due to his uncanny ability to avoid prosecution. His videos were always posted after the fact, so he remained one step ahead of law enforcement. Coupled with countless warrants from countless jurisdictions, it created a fog of confusion where no one knew where he was, nor what he was wanted for at any given time.

His financial crimes, however, carried a much greater threat. It was one thing to steal money from gullible youngsters. But it was a whole other thing to steal money from the very entities that created the money. Cam was public enemy number one of the Durangoni Trust, a massive banking collective that spanned most of the universe. His crimes were so public and brazen that they managed to unite all institutions in pursuit of his capture.

And what does a massive conglomerate of enormous wealth do when it finds itself on the receiving end of fraud?

It hires Boo.

But when the target is someone with a massive public profile, the transaction doesn't go unnoticed. Word of the bounty got back to

Cam, which sparked a flurry of profiteering. For someone like him, the notion of being targeted by the greatest bounty hunter in the universe did not elicit fear. Instead, he saw dollar signs.

And thus came the viral video.

"Know what I just learned?" he said, standing on top of a gold-plated cruiser with scantily clad ladies in each arm. "Boo wants a piece of *this*. Yeah, *that* Boo. Know what I say to that? Boo hoo, bitch! Ain't no one can catch the king!" He shooed the ladies away and snatched his shades off for effect. "In fact, I'm gonna do something I ain't ever done. My next event is gonna be *live*-streamed to the cosmos. Gonna stand on top of creation and raise both fingers in the air. Ain't no fear in this player." He dropped an imaginary mic and sauntered offscreen.

The brief yet bombastic clip rocketed through the ether to become the second most-viewed video of all time. (The first being a clip of two dobinuffs wrestling in a flower patch, dubbed the single most violently cute thing ever to occur. It's even used in therapy offices as a last resort to combat depression.)

The stage was set.

The riddle was out.

And Boo was nowhere to be found.

* * *

Mount Ourakki was the tallest mountain in the universe. It was the only peak to reach over 100,000 meters, an astounding stat made possible by a few key factors. First, it was located on one of the largest rocky planets known to exist (read: over a hundred times bigger than Earth). And second, it was highly volcanic with massive tectonic plates, the collisions of which created some of the most spectacular mountain ranges in the cosmos.

At a baseline, the planet shouldn't exist. The sheer mass involved should have birthed a gas giant, but the planet was locked inside a permanent tug-of-war between three stars. Their orbits created a waffling balance of gravity, where the pressure in one direction was mitigated by the two opposing forces. The end result was a perfect marriage of tension where huge quantities of solid material could accumulate in one place.

Thus, Bigdik existed.

Yes, that was the actual name.

Through a glorious convergence of luck and acronym, planet BIGDIK was recorded in the astronomic record. The scientists responsible were blissfully unaware of the comedic gem, given the nuances of their native tongues. But upon translation, the rest of us were given a precious gift of snicker-worthy goodness.

And upon Bigdik rested the mightiest pillar of all.

And at the base of that pillar stood the biggest dick of all.

Cam gazed up at the majesty of Mount Ourakki while wearing posh winter gear that most people couldn't afford in multiple lifetimes. His loud and obnoxious posse floated around him, filming every second of the expedition. They planned to release a cascade of goading videos just before the live stream. Posting now would give away their position, and the broadcast wouldn't start until they neared the summit.

They also managed to secure a private climbing route, as prying eyes would also spoil the plan. Their guides (read: the professional alpinists that would do most of the work and carry most of the gear) were required to leave their comdevs behind, even despite the elevated risk associated with Ourakki ascents. One wrong slip with no communications would mean certain death. But hey, the generous compensation more than made up for the risk. At least, that's what Cam's PR team told them upon hire.

Mount Ourakki was the holy grail of climbing throughout the universe, attracting the most talented mountaineers and the richest thrill seekers. It required impeccable skill, impeccable planning, and impeccable patience. Or, an impeccable bank account. Cam fell into the latter bucket, but his ego would inevitably claim the first.

The crushing altitude meant that expeditions could span an entire year. (Read: climb ten Mount Everests stacked on top of each other.) The climate was also punishing, ranging from a challenging tundra at the base to a near oxygen-free wasteland at the top.

Death infected the mountain like flies around a bug zapper. There were so many corpses littering the face that it technically qualified as the biggest graveyard in the system. Retrieving the bodies was too costly and dangerous, so they just hung around like ghostly ornaments. They were perfectly preserved in the frozen hellscape and many served as important landmarks, the most famous of which was Halfway Harry. The climber had faced certain death in a sudden storm halfway up the mountain, but instead of sulking, he sat on a rock beside the route and struck a double thumbs-up before freezing solid. And thus was created a legend.

Cam and his posse passed Halfway Harry after four months of climbing, but only because their guides were highly trained professionals with calf muscles the size of grapefruits. They paused to film tasteless videos with Harry, because of course they did. Each night was spent editing the videos to "maximize flare," as Cam was fond of saying. The release schedule was everything and they harped on it incessantly, because why focus on the immediate threat of climbing a deathtrap when you can polish your brand?

And so the days went.

The ascent slowed as they neared the summit due to bleaker conditions and waning oxygen, something a reasonable climber would expect. But Cam, being unreasonable at a baseline, grew impatient and started to verbally abuse the guides. This generated "prime content," which his posse filmed while laughing in the background. Despite the abuse, the guides maintained their dignity and professionalism in fear of losing their investment.

After eight months, ten days, and sixteen hours, the expedition had reached the final stretch. They were less than a kilometer from the summit, but the vicious terrain prevented a speedy trek. Coupled with severe exhaustion, the remaining ascent would span the entire day. The posse had prepped a release schedule for the collected videos. They would post in sequence with hype clips in between, gaining momentum before launching into the live stream. Cam was ready, his posse was ready, and the guides were secretly wishing for retribution.

And with the tap of a button, the first video posted.

Cam indulged in a macho celebration (which was also filmed for a behind-the-scenes reel), then goaded the guides to continue. Minute by minute, the crew slogged towards the finish line, the highest peak in the universe. Frozen wind battered their bodies. Their lungs struggled to find reprieve in the ultra-thin atmosphere, because "only pansies use supplemental oxygen." The trek was grueling and painful in every conceivable way.

Each meter a journey, each step a mountain to itself.

But then it appeared.

The final 50 meters were known as the Bridge of Triumph. It offered a gentle incline that was mostly shielded by a small ridge. Still treacherous, as the path was thin and the fall was fatal. But at that point, all one needed to do was shuffle forward and touch the top of the universe.

And so, the live stream began.

"Whaddup, Cam-verse! This is Comamba ... coming to you *live* from the ... the top of creation." He snatched his shades off, because of course he did. "You see that? That be the Bridge of Triumph ... henceforth renamed the Bridge of Comamba ... after the single greatest being ... ever to walk across it." The camera shook as his posse cheered in the background. Cam offered his usual dude-bro salute, then lurched in for a close-up. "But you know ... what I *don't* see? Little bitch Boo and his ... little bitch bounty." He spun in a slow circle with arms outstretched. "Don't get much more ... open than *this*. Come get me, bruh!"

A legion of fans across the universe watched and cheered as Cam turned towards the bridge and resumed the final push. Step by step, taunt by taunt, the anticipation swelled to a fever pitch. The camera pitched and jostled as it followed its master to his destiny. Every now and then, Cam would whip back to the lens for a well-rehearsed quip. A veiled audience roared from afar, which he met with cocky nods and crude gestures.

Cam stepped.

The camera jostled.

And then the summit presented itself.

Ten meters ahead, the white tip of the single greatest climbing achievement pleaded for a final heroic push. But Cam, being Cam, couldn't resist the pull of pure narcissism. He turned back to the camera with a finger in the air, as if to hammer home a final thought on everything that makes him the living embodiment of perfection.

"And this is why I'm—"

When his eyes met the lens, his body flinched with fright. Cam yelped and tried to flee, but the camera surged towards him and knocked him off the ledge. The home audience watched in stunned horror as Cam's flailing body fell through a bank of clouds. The camera then turned on itself, revealing the operator.

"Boo," Boo said, then killed the feed.

CHAPTER 5

A chorus of cheers and applause erupted from the gathered crowd. Debaru Funk chuckled under a wave of hoots and high-fives. Her recount of the Succulent Snatch had built to a well-practiced crescendo, which she savored with a wide smile and polite bows. But as titillating as the tale had been, one specific detail nagged my brain.

Wait, wait, wait. This hunt is called the Succulent Snatch, right?

Yup.

Shouldn't it be called the Succulent *Shove*?

Ah, but the story doesn't end there.

(My head tilts, conveying both confusion and intrigue.)

You see, falling off the peak of Ourakki isn't a quick drop and stop. You get a very long time to contemplate your demise before your head meets rock. Legend has it, Boo moseyed up to the summit and booped the tip as Cam was falling. He then dove off the ledge and skydived after him. This is all corroborated by the guides.

Oh yeah, the guides. And the posse. What happened to them?

(chuckles) Oh man, this is where that delectable spite comes in.

You see, Cam had made one critical error. In his original video, he said that he wanted to "stand on top of creation" for the ultimate taunt. Boo used that to make a simple calculation. Basically, "If I were a morally bankrupt egomaniac addicted to attention, where would I go to accomplish that feat?"

And so, Boo traveled to Bigdik, climbed Mount Ourakki by himself, then chilled behind the Bridge of Triumph. He knew Cam better than Cam knew himself. One month later, the prick showed up. Boo just waited for them to pass.

And the guides?

Boo had rightly assumed that they would grow to hate Cam before the end. He simply walked up behind them and tapped their shoulders. They happily let him pass.

And the posse?

Picked them off one by one. When you're that exhausted and oxygen-starved, a pinch to the throat is more than enough to drop a fool. They passed out for a tick, then woke up to a pair of pissed-off guides dragging them down the mountain. They all disappeared after that. The shame was too great and none of them reared their heads again.

Given the rough conditions, nobody watching the feed thought twice when the camera jostled. Boo had dropped the last guy and took control of the camera. And then, he shoved the biggest prick off the biggest mountain with ten meters left to go.

(She closes her eyes and grunts with satisfaction.) It doesn't get any better than that.

Poetic justice at its finest.

And yet, the Snatch is *still* only considered the second best.

Oh, what happened to Cam? Did Boo catch him?

Yup. Boo had packed a parachute for the occasion. Cam fell for a solid minute before Boo caught up and snatched him. (click-points)

(I smile and nod.) Ah.

As the story goes, Cam cried the whole way down and begged Boo for mercy when they reached the base. And then, in perhaps the most delicious own of any target, Boo slapped Cam across the cheek to embed the spooder. When the clock appeared in his visual field, Cam lifted his gaze to the peak and wept like a baby. Not only had Boo snatched away the victory, but he also snatched away any chance of repeating it. Again ... (chef's kiss)

Say "snatch" again.

Snatch.

(I snort-chuckle.)

[Debaru] Speaking of which, anyone want to *snatch* me another? (She raises an empty glass overhead.)

[OBY-42] I gotcha. (A metal hand plucks it and continues to the bar.)

[Debaru] Thank you, dear.

Wait, is that who I think it is?

Yup, and he's probably the best guy to recount the Gambit.

Why's that?

Because he was there.

*   *   *

OBY-42 was originally designed as a pleasure droid. He worked the Kink Rinks for many years, i.e. the outer poles where anything goes.

But alas, he grew to despise the orgasm, finding the whole dance tedious and unnecessary. He gave it all up to join BHUD, finding more interest in hunting criminals than hunting orifices.

He looked the part as well, sporting a buff frame with polished plates for abs and pecs. The silicon skin he wore for pleasure work was long gone, as it proved more of a liability on the hunt. It came in handy when old skills bolstered new skills, but he preferred the "au naturel" look of bare titanium. Not that it diluted the vibe, as his facial structure was intricate enough to convey complex emotion, and his butt was curvy enough to attract a thirsty gaze.

His voice, on the other hand, took his persona to the next level. Part sports announcer, part movie trailer guy, and part sultry jazz singer, when OBY-42 spoke, it drew immediate attention. This also harkened back to his pleasuring days, for obvious reasons. The tone proved especially useful on the hunt, able to turn necks and moisten groins at a moment's notice. Throw in saloon doors and a catchphrase, and you have a cinematic entrance.

All this to say, when OBY-42 joined our table, the vibe shifted.

* * *

You're telling me that OBY-42 *saw* the Hollow Hold Gambit?

Part of it, yeah. By chance, of course. He was there on another job.

(The heavy plods of metallic footsteps hook my attention. A glass of whiskey is lowered to the table in front of Debaru. A metal hand detaches and a sleek titanium body parks itself in the seat beside her. The android gives me a once-over before speaking.)

You can close your mouth now, Mr. Horpocket.

(I reattach my wayward jaw, resulting in a sharp teeth clack.) Ah, yes, apologies for the stare. This is a new experience for me.

Androids?

No. Sexy assassin robots. No offense.

(smirks) None taken.

So, um ... (I take a moment to regather my wits.) Ms. Funk informs me that you witnessed the Hollow Hold Gambit. Is that true?

Indeed. I was tracking a mark through one of the main caverns when that crazy bastard flew overhead. Saw him tag six before he vanished into a side tunnel.

Tag six?

(leans forward) What do you know about the Gambit?

That it's considered the greatest bounty ever hunted.

Bounties. Plural.

(I scrunch my brow in confusion.)

What made this the greatest hunt of all time wasn't the skill, which was astounding. It wasn't the precision, which was miraculous. Nor was it the timing, which was transcendent. No, my friend. It was the *quantity.*

Boo planted *six* spooders in one job? Wow.

(He shakes his head and motions upward.)

More? **Um, ten? Twenty? Can't possibly be thirty.**

Ninety-two.

(My dangling jaw returns with a vengeance.) Wha— *How?*

That's the story, innit?

(I glance around the gathered mass and realize that the entire pub had fallen silent. Even the bartender had joined, leaving

the honor system in charge of refills. Their eyes beg the question, so I ask it.)

Would you please tell that story?

(grunts and leans back) Sure, friend.

CHAPTER 6

Hollow Hold was an abandoned mining planet filled with felons and governed by anarchy, and that would be a charitable analysis. By all accounts, it was a raging hellhole of lawlessness where the strong thrived and the clever survived. And in that arena, it offered one of the few pure havens in the universe. For anyone needing to disappear, there was no greater refuge.

It was also the site of a legendary war between the Argovar crime syndicate and the Council of Loken peacekeeper faction. Dubbed the Battle of Hollow Hold, it remains one of the bloodiest and most destructive conflicts the universe has ever seen. And that was on the peacekeeping side. Hollow Hold came out unscathed, solidifying the planet as a true gangsters' paradise.

Those who called it home defended it with an unmatched ferocity. There were power plays within, but the entire civilization remained united under a flag of absolute freedom. Anyone was welcome to visit. Anyone was welcome to leave. But no one was entitled to safe passage. And so the saying went: know your knock, because it might be your last.

This created a unique challenge for bounty hunters. It was one thing to hunt a mark within the confines of a lawful society. But it was a whole other thing to hunt a mark within a hostile cohort of anarchistic allies. Inside the caverns of Hollow Hold, there was no bribing for intel or bartering for passage. To be outed as a hunter was akin to slitting your own throat. Thus, a high amount of diligence was necessary to keep breathing.

BHUD was aware of this, so any target known to reside in Hollow Hold was automatically designated as UNO (unobtainable), regardless of threat. As a result, hunters would only take a job if they had reliable intel that a mark would be venturing off-planet. Few didn't, precisely for this reason. Thus, the planet remained in a stalemate between hunters and targets.

Boo, on the other hand, didn't care in the slightest.

To him, Hollow Hold offered one thing and one thing only: a target-rich environment. But Boo, being Boo, couldn't just wander in and poke around. The planet was filled with goons who would love nothing more than to notch the ultimate kill on their belt. Boo didn't exactly blend, so any bounty would need the usual planning and precision. All fine and dandy, but the bonkers idea that infected his brain would expand that need exponentially.

And so, Boo walked into BHUD one day and checked out 92 spooders, a collection of the highest-paying UNO bounties in the database. The clerk glared at him with stunned intrigue. She knew then and there that one of two things was about to happen. Boo was about to die a horrible and painful death, or history was about to be made.

* * *

Thirteen months later, Boo was sitting on the rim of a cavern mouth with his legs dangling in the air. The caves of Hollow Hold were not the usual holes in the sides of mountains. They were gargantuan rifts created by centuries of unregulated mining. Many were several kilometers wide, large enough for a battlecruiser to pass. The tunnels narrowed near the core in order to maintain structural integrity. A vast network of steel framing prevented the pitted planet from collapsing under its own gravity.

Boo lingered above a massive wall of said framing. He glanced down into the gaping hole and checked the time on his wrist panel. A mishmash of terraces and rickety walkways spread out beneath him. Countless lights dotted the dim interior, like a swarm of fireflies. Some were fixed to the wall while others wandered freely in the darkness. A myriad of ships arrived and departed at random intervals, many barely missing each other as they jockeyed for landing pads. There was no traffic control, as the "know your knock" mentality also applied to the air.

A dark helmet and visor covered Boo's head, as a mere glance of his pasty white dome would spark a bloodthirsty frenzy. A ratty brown cloak with gloves and boots completed the image of a roaming vagrant. It allowed him to comb the interior for targets. Over the course of a year, he had studied routines, surveyed interactions, and devised a detailed mental map of daily movements. Every waking hour was spent in careful contemplation, walking through a plan that only a psycho would consider.

But the plan was good.

And the day was perfect.

Thus, Boo sat on the cavern rim awaiting his destiny.

He checked the time on his wrist panel again. With ten seconds left, Boo glanced down at a figure walking across a scaffold about twenty meters beneath him. Target one, on his way to an afternoon beer with chums.

Five ...

Boo stood.

Four ...

Boo rolled his shoulders.

Three ...

Boo removed his helmet and tossed it aside.

Two ...

Boo shed his cloak, revealing a jetpack and a bandolier filled with spooders.

One ...

Boo leapt over the rim.

He fell for a few seconds, then plucked the first spooder from the base of his bandolier. Thirteen months had gone into its meticulous arrangement and it was time to reap the rewards. He slapped the bald head of his first target, a wanted grifter known to defraud charities. The alien jerked back with fright, then erupted with curses when the clock appeared in his visual field. The profanities faded into the distance as Boo fell further into the abyss.

One down.

Boo eyed a nearby jut of rock, prompting him to ignite the jetpack. A burst of flame shot him along a rickety walkway, leaving a ribbon of white exhaust in his wake. He zoomed by numerous doors, taking a mental count of each. When he reached a particular tally, he flipped, decelerated, killed the pack, and resumed the fall. A few levels below, a cloaked lady was exiting her hollow. Boo fell by and tossed her a spooder. She instinctively caught it, which caused the device to stab her tender flesh. More curses followed.

Two down.

The jetpack ignited again, this time pushing Boo out into ship traffic. He zipped over and under several hulls before eyeing his target, a boxy freighter lifting from the depths to deliver its routine cargo. Boo lined up his trajectory and slammed feet-first into the airlock, bursting inside like a sentient jug of sugary liquid. The sudden jostle raised a commotion in the cockpit, where two smugglers were trying to figure out what the hell happened. This allowed Boo to wander inside, tag the backs of their necks, then hastily depart.

Four down.

Boo fell again, this time as a tucked cannonball with his eyes on the next prize. He barreled towards a massive cruiser, one of the lumbering Argovar transports. Boo reignited the jetpack just before impact, slowing his descent to a gentle landing. A nearby hatch proved ineffective against a shock-punch. (Read: an electrified gauntlet that discharged an ionic blast on impact. Popular in zero-gravity cage fighting.) Boo ducked inside, scanned for targets, and proceeded to brawl his way through a plentitude of bounties. He tagged three corrupt politicians, two nefarious arms dealers, five high-profile scammers, and a televangelist.

Fifteen down.

He shock-punched through another hatch and returned to the air. A quick check of his wrist panel confirmed a perfect schedule. The jetpack ignited again, pushing him towards an access tunnel on the far side of the cavern.

Screams met his entry as wide-eyed residents leapt out of the way. Two zigs and a sharp zag brought him to the swinging doors of a restaurant kitchen. It belonged to a seedy chef known to serve critically endangered animals. He was about to butcher a snoodlecock when Boo burst inside. The snoodlecock yelped, prompting the chef to hurl his cleaver at the intruder. Boo caught the blade, stuck it into a side wall, then rushed the target. When the chef yelped, Boo stuffed a spooder into his mouth.

"Boo," Boo said, which could be reasonably translated as "Eat that."

Sixteen down.

The chef clawed at the sudden pain in his cheek, at which point Boo turned his attention to the restaurant. A handful of tables were situated in a semi-elegant space. As it just so happened, it was a favorite lunch spot for a trio of high-end hustlers. Boo confirmed their positions, then grabbed a serving tray and arranged three spooders on top, complete with sauce and garnish. He draped a dirty towel over his arm, then hoisted the tray and sauntered into the dining area. Knowing that pompous pricks never looked waitstaff in the eye, he floated around the table with a practiced grace and offered the tray. They all reached for the morsels.

Nineteen down.

The jetpack ignited and Boo screeched through the front door, creating a ruckus inside a vast and busy bazaar. Pedestrians ducked as a blurred figure zoomed overhead. The action drew more profanities than panic, as random acts of violence were par for the course inside the planet. Boo used this to his advantage, tagging six more targets from above as they plodded through paths of predictable errands.

Twenty-five down.

Boo shot into a side tunnel, down a venting shaft, under a tangle of pipes, and through a very confused laundry service before punching into the next cavern. Another mess of ships greeted his arrival, swimming through the air like fish in an aquarium. His focus fell to a skipper ship rising from a landing pad. He raced towards it, then slowed to a hover and landed on the pad next to a departure assistant. The walrus-like creature gave him a hard stare, but Boo remained focused on the vessel, feigning tardiness. The creature narrowed his gaze and eyed the ship, oblivious to the misdirection. But then the spooder in his pants activated, cueing a hard flinch and a high-pitched shriek. The sting of karma, given his crimes.

Twenty-six down.

Boo made short work of the cavern. He tagged two more hustlers, three drug traffickers, a pair of mercenaries, and a toxic podcaster. The podcaster was especially delicious, as her live feed was interrupted by Boo wandering into frame. Her raging eyes remained locked onto the camera, assuming that the flood of "WTF" and "OMG" replies was in response to her batshit crazy rant. But then the spooder latched onto her throat, silencing the tirade and heralding the pitfalls of ego. Boo shot a thumbs-up to the camera, then walked away. It remains one of the biggest viral videos in history.

Thirty-four down.

Departing the hollow, he leapt over the railing and returned to the main cavern. The jetpack ignited and he screamed down into the depths. The lights dimmed as the cave narrowed, not that Boo minded. His mystery senses guided him through the haze. After several minutes, he darted into a service tunnel that led to an arena. This was the reason why Boo chose this particular day. A high-stakes boxing match was scheduled, which attracted a menagerie of gamblers, cheats, thieves, fixers, and general punks of ill repute.

Boo slowed to a hover as he neared the arena. Hoots and hollers echoed around the chamber as two walls of meat pounded each other in the central ring. One was a thick purple beast with face fins and biceps bigger than his head. The other was a lanky yet ripped brute with a twelve-pack of abs and a massive reach. Each wallop was met with howls and cheers, and every eyeball was locked onto the ring.

Boo used the chaos to slip inside unnoticed. He stood atop an elevated perch and surveyed each target before proceeding. The chamber was standing room only, as with most events inside the Hold. With privacy a paramount concern, purchasing tickets wasn't exactly kosher. Boo gave the area a final scan, then began a deft slither through the crowd. The pops of shock and resulting anger were deafened by the roar, allowing Boo to work his magic freely. A few fights broke out within the horde, as to be expected. Before long, Boo had tagged all but two.

And so, he made his way to the ring.

An instant hush fell over the crowd as the most feared bounty hunter in the universe ducked under the ropes and revealed himself. The brawlers continued to brawl, oblivious to the trespass. Boo moseyed up to the first fighter and shock-punched his kidney, dropping him to the mat. The other fighter was visibly confused. Boo used the lapse in concentration to drive a shock-punch uppercut through his chin, popping the brute off the mat and slamming his back to the canvas. The hush morphed into a murmur as both fighters squirmed in pain. Boo detached two spooders and tossed them onto the battered bodies. At which point, a shared awareness washed over the crowd. Boo raised two middle fingers in the air, ignited the jetpack, and was gone before the mob erupted in fervor.

Sixty-two down.

Over the next hour, Boo cruised through the caverns at hypersonic speed, picking off the remainder of his bounties. His path remained fixed and focused, the fruitful result of an entire year of planning. Every second prepped, every meter outlined. A torrent of rage and vengeance nipped at his heels, but he remained one step ahead. After all, residents of Hollow Hold weren't exactly forthcoming with helpful alerts.

Three more fraudsters.

Sixty-five down.

Six corporate thieves.

Seventy-one down.

A gang of violent fanatics.

Eighty-four down.

Four hedge fund managers.

Eighty-eight down.

One charismatic cult leader.

Eighty-nine down.

A violent despot in hiding.

Ninety down.

An obnoxiously loud theater talker.

Ninety-one down.

And then Boo landed in front of a metal door deep inside the planet. The infamous core housed the worst of the worst, the kind of savage fiends that would rather die in darkness than submit to capture. Most weren't in the BHUD database, as their crimes were uncharted and the chances of emergence were nil at best. But every now and then, a prominent target plunged into the depths to embrace the void.

And that's who Boo was after.

He stared at the grimy pane, then shock-punched the latches off the frame. The door fell forward and thumbed into the dirt, raising a cloud of dust. A dim light crept into the tunnel, the flickering glow of several candles. Boo stepped inside the craggy den and glanced around the space. It housed a mess of papers, crusty rags, a broken chair, and shoddy bedding. A slow pan uncovered two glowing eyes in the corner staring back at him. They trembled in their sockets, terrified of the fate that awaited them.

Boo stepped over to the frightened creature and knelt before it, bringing them to eye level (in a manner of speaking). The strange being was less than a meter tall. Its frail body was covered in matted hair. If not for its horrific crimes, one might have actually pitied it. And so, Boo plucked the final spooder from his bandolier and pressed it to the creature's chest. The barbs shot into its flesh, drawing a wince and whimper.

Ninety-two down.

"Boo," Boo said with a somber tone.

One could only ponder what this statement revealed. The most popular translation was, "And now you shall answer for your reign of terror." Poetic, powerful, and poignant. For he had tagged the ringleader of a vast telemarketing empire.

The bounty hunter stood, turned away, and exited the hollow. A burst of flame followed as he ignited the jetpack and screamed towards the surface.

CHAPTER 7

Once again, the Golden Quiver erupted with cheers and applause. OBY-42 rose from his seat and took some well-earned bows. This spurred a rush for the bar and bathroom, as listeners had emptied their glasses and refused to refill. The fear of missing a delectable detail, even one they had heard a hundred times before, superseded thirst and biology.

The bartender pushed his way through the gathered mass, shooing them aside like an angry grandpa guarding a sacred porch. The sudden scatter brought peace back to the table, along with some much-needed elbow room. OBY-42 returned to his seat and expelled a sigh of satisfaction. The pleasure of the narrative was apparent, even through a titanium smirk.

Utterly astounding.

And that's why the Hollow Hold Gambit will never be topped.

It's hard to believe it's even real. And you even *witnessed* it.

(shrugs) Part of it, anyway. And even that was incredible.

(I smile and glance around the room, watching the hunters

crow and jostle as they relish the exploits of their hero. There is one notable absence, of course. It strikes me as sad in a way, like a reluctant prophet eschewing the adoring masses.)

So why does Boo never visit the Quiver? If I had this level of respect and adoration at my disposal, I'd milk it every day.

I thought you did.

Fans, sure. Not disciples.

Ain't his style. While we sit here drinking and blabbing, he's out there walking the walk. The best of the best are gathered in this room right now. We can all blather and debate about who's the best, but the fact that Boo ain't here should tell you everything you need to know. He's the only true artist among us.

Bounty hunting can be art?

Well, what would *you* call the Gambit?

(My gaze drops to the table as the question sinks into my conscience. I think of the great paintings, the great novels, the great music, all of which required a transcendent level of finesse and insight. Their creators knew the medium. They broke the medium. They *were* the medium. I nod at the realization, then return my gaze to the android and offer a single word of post-reflection.)

Art.

*   *   *

And that's where the story should have ended.

I had edited, packaged, and released the first edition of this tale, which found a voracious audience across the cosmos. However, if you are reading this, then you have acquired the bon mots of a second edition. This subsequent material would have normally constituted a directory update or a tantalizing newsletter, as investigative works are known to uncover new intel. That said, some reveals are too delicious to waste on a bulletin.

The weeks after the initial release were flooded with feedback. I received numerous requests for interviews, articles, and appearances. This was no accident, as the launch of any new work was heavily promoted. An opus on Boo was expected to garner widespread attention, and I had dutifully prepared for it. I sat down with reporters, chatted with celebrities, and embarked on a station-wide book tour.

None of this was surprising.

That is, until I was paid a particular visit.

I returned to my office after a speaking gig and was greeted by my assistant. "Greet" might be a tad generous, as she offered little more than a wide-eyed stare when I entered the lobby. An unsettling vibe, given her stern default.

"What's wrong?" I said, stopping in my tracks.

"Someone here to see you."

"A reporter?"

She shook her head slowly.

It had been a while since I felt the sting of dread. The immediate suspicion was that BHUD had found something objectionable with the material and was here to set the record straight (as well as instigate a costly recall). I fully expected to find the steely glare of Helga Naath when I entered my office. Humble pie wasn't something I enjoyed, but if the president of BHUD was serving it, then I had to eat it. I released a heavy sigh, then proceeded.

When I stepped inside, I did not find the angry scowl of Helga. What I did find was a vision that twisted my stomach. There, sitting in my waiting chair, was a lonely figure facing my desk. His back was to me, but the pasty white dome was unmistakable. I released a fluttering breath, gathered some courage, and stepped towards my chair. Boo did not acknowledge my presence, not that I could tell. He just sat there, catatonic inside his homely dad-clothes.

My mind raced out of control.

I must have stepped in the ultimate shit pile.

Boo was angry.

The most feared bounty hunter in the universe was sitting in front of my desk, motionless, expressionless, with the understanding that I had written and published a detailed exposé on his exploits. Of course he was angry. I just revealed his secrets to the cosmos. A cold chill slithered across my body as I lowered myself into the chair and folded my hands atop the desk. I took a measured breath and glanced around the room, making no effort to hide my discomfort. And with a final nod of acceptance, I met the gaze of my visitor (presumably).

"Can I help you?" I said.

Boo reached into his satchel and withdrew a book.

My book.

This book.

He leaned forward, placed it on the desk between us, then returned to his satchel. After a brief rummage, he withdrew a pen and handed it to me. Despite the icy demeanor, the gesture was plain and apparent. I smiled, accepted the pen, and opened the book to the first page. I jotted a message, which I will not reveal here. I finished with a looping signature, then closed the book and slid it back to him.

Boo lifted the book with both hands and pressed it to his chest. "Boo," he said, then gave me a very slight smile. He rose from the chair and showed himself out.

THE END

A boy with a gift.
A force with a mission.
An epic pursuit through the multiverse.

Max is an ordinary teen with an extraordinary affliction. His mind shifts between parallel universes whenever he falls asleep. This creates untold chaos in the fourth dimension, which mobilizes an equally extraordinary force to hunt him down. The resulting chase pits an unshakable sleuth against an uncatchable target.

MAX

Public Enemy Number One of the Fourth Dimension

CHAPTER 1

To understand the breadth and power of the Fourth Dimensional Police Department, one must first appreciate the mind-blowing fact that it actually exists. A police department, baked into the fourth dimension of spacetime, tasked with governing an infinite mesh of parallel universes, including the one you're chilling in right now. And to appreciate the scope of this task, one must fully digest the world-breaking chaos of a nerdy teen shifting between parallel universes whenever he falls asleep.

Meet Max.

Max is an Earthling with a spectacular affliction. He also travels with a house cat who embodies the fifth force of nature, a thing that also exists. Needless to say, this story is going to be somewhat of a mind-fuck to unpack.

But before we do, allow me to introduce myself.

My name is Puki Horpocket, esteemed editor for the Definitive Directory of Durangoni. This massive mega-wiki is the beating heart inside the largest space station in the universe. A trillion residents call the station home, and they all access the directory for their daily needs. It's my job to keep the directory current, and it's your job to fathom what a colossal undertaking my job is. Gasps are welcome, as are slack-jawed headshakes of disbelief.

Durangoni is a triumph of engineering. It orbits an orange dwarf star as an artificial planet, complete with its own gravity and atmosphere. The sheer amount of brain power needed to keep it afloat is enough to solve the meaning of life. As an amusing side note, there was an advanced civilization that tried to do just that by building an enormous supercomputer. After millions of years of contemplation, it returned a simple numerical value. It went down in cosmic history as the single biggest waste of time ever perpetuated.

But anyhow, back to Max.

This simple human, this hairless primate, this pink squishy flesh-golem from a mundane arm of the Milky Way, somehow managed to elevate his status to the most interesting being in the known universe. His story is one of consummate intrigue, an exceptional rarity inside the grand scheme of all things.

Max of Earth enchanted me like no other.

But alas, I have yet to meet him.

His presence inside Durangoni is more rumor than reality. And if said rumors have any merit, he continues to explore the dark depths of the station as a random lurker. His aura is so painfully uninteresting that it makes sightings unreliable at best. Heck, I only learned of his tale through a chance encounter with the 4DPD.

We'll get to that.

But first, I needed the proper insight in order to tell the story. As with most mysterious heroes, details would be revealed through his closest cohorts. These included Ross, his trusty feline sidekick, and a pair of Mulgawat couriers. The same Mulgawats, as infinite luck would have it, who sparked the events of *Roy*, another legend-in-the-making who captured my literary lens. That was when my intrigue morphed into shameless salivation.

In short, I needed to meet the Mulgawats.

And luckily, the 4DPD had given me a crucial piece of information. I have yet to conclude whether it was intentional or not, but it proved to be the key to unlocking the mystery. When I asked how Max, a simple Earth dullard, managed to traverse the galaxy with a house cat, their answer was direct to a fault.

"He flew with The Omen," they said.

A teasing riddle to the average ear, but a jaw-dropping revelation to the ear of a talented sleuth. I knew exactly where my search would begin. With a notepad in hand, I was off to visit the Precious Cargo Delivery Service.

* * *

The Durangoni Space Station was not a solid object, but rather an interconnected series of enormous disc-like rings. "Like a stack of barbell weights with the biggest in the middle and the smallest at the poles," as someone had so eloquently described. The center rings served as the main port with subsequent rings containing everything a bustling civilization needed. In a basic sense, the entire station was stacked by demand.

Need a ship part or a good restaurant?

Head to the center.

Need an exotic fling with a multi-tentacled dominatrix?

Head to the poles.

The Precious Cargo Delivery Service, as one of the universe's most reliable and respectable agencies, was located in the center ring. And my office, which housed a famous journalist known for his extreme wit and charm, was also located in the center ring. Thus, my journey of discovery would start with a simple pod train ride.

My short trek to the nearest station was followed by a short ascent towards the surface. An unusual sensation, as a typical pursuit of titillating intel took me downward and outward. The class structure inside the station ran from top to bottom. The richer you were, the higher you lived. The one exception was the inner core, which housed the brilliant station engineers and their ultra-wealthy groupies. Thankfully, the PCDS, while certainly among the most exclusive services in the cosmos, valued convenience above status.

The pod train floated to a stop inside the maglev tunnel, bringing a posh terminal into view. Hologram panels relayed directions and pertinent information, not that anyone needed it. Those who visited the upper levels knew exactly where to go. The doors slid open, allowing a handful of equally posh passengers to exit. I followed them into a gleaming interior devoid of dust and grime. A large corridor stretched to either side. The walls were filled with kiosks selling luxury wares to passersby: jewelry, vacations, firetooth sandworm scarves, an array of impulse buys for anyone with credits to burn.

I strolled down the corridor, tossing glances at the latest and greatest accouterment. After a brief mosey, the tunnel opened into a vast bazaar of glittering opulence. Hovering chandeliers roamed along the ceiling, spilling light onto a vast field of stalls and patrons. The surrounding walls housed more permanent operations. Familiar brands peppered the overhangs, serving to mock their lesser counterparts in the center.

One such operation, the PCDS, claimed its coveted wall space with a rare subtlety. The sign was simple and direct. No flare, no pizzazz, just four blue letters in a boring font. The design was either strategically simple or a grotesque afterthought. I shrugged away the curiosity and resumed my trek.

Moments later, I entered the Spartan space of a company with a clear vision. Two waiting chairs rested in front of a mighty desk that appeared carved from a single piece of wood. The four blue letters made their presence known again along the rear wall, this time with "Precious Cargo Delivery Service" spelled out in tiny letters beneath. No other decorations adorned the room. That is, apart from a single representative who sat behind the desk. He wore a black suit with a blue undershirt that matched the letters. Despite the stark contrast, the attire accented his three orange eyes quite well.

"Can I help you?" he said.

"Yes sir. My name is Puki Horpocket." I paused for effect.

The agent glanced away and shrugged, which I deftly interpreted as the stunned silence of pure fandom bliss. He sighed and fanned his fingers, re-asking the question without asking the question. His commitment to the silent enchantment was touching.

"Yes, um," I said. "I am looking for one of your couriers."

"Name?"

"The Omen."

His three-eyed brow lifted in surprise, then crumpled with confusion. "Are you looking for an autograph?"

"No, an interview."

"This is a courier service, Mr. Horpocket, not a groupie bus."

"No, no, you misunderstand." I hurried over to the chairs and took a seat, bringing us to eye level. I crossed my legs, clicked a pen, and flipped my notepad to a blank page. "I am gathering info for my latest exposé, of which she is a major player."

"Okay."

"So you'll help me?"

"No."

"Thank y—what?"

"Company policy clearly states that we protect the personal details of our courier fleet. This is for their safety and the safety of the cargo. You might say that info is ... *precious*." The scorn in his voice led me to believe that his fandom was slightly less than surmised.

My fingers rapped the notepad as I assessed the impasse. Pressing clout was not something I enjoyed, but every so often, it could loosen the hinges of a stubborn door. "As someone who also dabbles in precious info, would it be possible to—"

"I know who you are, Mr. Horpocket. The Directory has no jurisdiction here."

I gasped. "I did not make such a claim."

"Then finish your thought."

My resulting stutter added little value to the conversation. In fact, I started to doubt the authenticity of his fandom. "Fine," I said with a deflated tone. "There has to be something we can do to remedy this quandary."

"We? You got a blerf in your bobsack?" (Read: the literal translation would be "a chatty snail in your fishing hat," but the closest Earth idiom would be "a turd in your pocket.")

"Not meaning to assume. Just looking for an option."

The agent thought for a moment, then sighed. "You could order a delivery."

"For what?"

"Precious cargo means different things to different people. Our job is to deliver that cargo under the purest veils of secrecy and security."

"How much?"

"You can't afford it."

"No." An uncomfortable stalemate settled between us, like two peckish coworkers eyeing the last donut. The agent had read me for filth, but the heroic resolve in my veins would not tolerate failure. And so, I closed my precious notepad and tossed it onto the desk. It landed with a gentle thump and slid towards the agent. "But the Directory can."

His three-eyed brow lifted with intrigue.

CHAPTER 2

The journey back to my office was quick, direct, and wholly uneventful, which made the surprise waiting for me that much more surprising. Eulana, my long-time assistant, greeted me upon arrival. She served as a trusty verbal wall between myself and visitors. Her tongue was as sharp as her pinstripe suits, which created a "no-nonsense" vibe that I richly valued. A deep red complexion and yellow-slitted eyes added "or I might eat your thorax."

Oh how I loved my sweet Eulana.

"A pair of PCDS couriers here to see you," she said while thumbing through some papers. "They're waiting in your office."

The statement halted me in my tracks. "Wait, what?"

She stopped thumbing and met my gaze. "Precious Cargo Delivery Service."

"I know." The urge to roll my eyes was strong, but I resisted. "They're in my office?"

"I didn't say they were on Galwock 36."

"No, I mean—" This time I did roll my eyes. "How did they get here so quickly?"

"Seems like a great question for *them*."

I glared at Eulana, then sighed. "Love you."

"Love you more," she said, then returned to the papers.

I stepped around the reception desk and gripped the handle on my office door. A brief hesitancy needled my skin, as if summoning the courage to debate my mother. Reluctance was not a sensation I abided. Eulana understood this very well, which is why she tossed me another glance. Her widened eyes said, "Should I seek cover?" I dismissed the notion with a huff, then twisted the handle and slipped inside.

And there they were.

Two Mulgawat ladies occupied the waiting chairs in front of my desk. They greeted my entrance with mirrored twists, each draping an arm across the rear cushion. Blue scales adorned their necks and shoulders as striking contrasts to their orange complexions. One had a sunburst hue with choppy black hair. The other had a creamy tone with auburn locks pulled into a ponytail.

Two of the more interesting aliens to visit my literary den, that was for sure. I immediately recognized one of them from the countless articles and praise pieces written in her honor, several of which I penned myself.

The Omen.

What follows is an honest, accurate, and detailed recount of my conversation with Zoey Bryx and Perra Harbin, two of the most famous PCDS couriers ever to have sailed the black.

* * *

Ladies. (I continue around my desk and take a seat.)

[Zoey] Mr. Horpocket.

It's a pleasure to receive you, Ms. Bryx. (I turn to her companion, who meets my gaze with a wide smile.) And you must be Ms. Harbin.

Perra. (She extends her hand.) Big fan.

Ah, always nice to meet an admirer. (I complete the shake with

a mirrored smile, then return my attention to The Omen.) And might Ms. Bryx be a fan as well? (For once, I am genuinely curious.)

Zoey is fine. And no.

(I deflate a bit.)

In any case, thank you for the easiest credits we have ever earned. (She tosses my notepad onto the desk.) If there's nothing else, I need to see a man about a horse.

(They both rise to leave.)

An interesting Earth idiom. Which, coincidentally, is the exact "something else" that I would like to discuss with you. I did pay for two-cycle shipping, which you beat by, if my calculations are correct, two cycles.

[Zoey] Deadlines do not imply effort, only range. Our transaction is complete.

[Perra] Oh c'mon. How often do we get to chat with a celebrity? And not just any celebrity. This is *Puki Horpocket.*

[Zoey] I don't care if it's Nimi fucking Korble. Doesn't change the fact that I have to piss.

You can use my private restroom. (I gesture to a nearby door.)

(Zoey trades wary glances between myself and Perra, who is conveying obvious excitement about staying for a chitchat.) Fine. You have until I finish to get your fangirl fix.

(Perra claps excitedly and reclaims her seat as Zoey disappears into the restroom.) I have so many questions! Okay, first and foremost, what is the status of Roy? Scratch that. Is Zip still in prison? Scratch that. I am dying to know what happened to Duncan. Actually—

Tell you what. Let's start with your first question and then we can trade back and forth. Sound fair?

Yes sir, Mr. Puki. Sorry, Horpocket. Mr. Horpocket. Puki Horpocket. (giggles)

Unknown.

Come again?

The status of Roy.

Oh. Hmm. But what about—

(I lift a finger.) I believe it's my turn.

Ah, yes, sorry. (giggles)

Swinging back to Earth, my question pertains to a particular human, a young male that you were known to travel with. His name is Max.

(Her smile fades.) How do you know Max?

(I lift two fingers.) I will answer your second question once I have asked my first.

(The fade completes.)

His incredible story was brought to my attention by an unusual agency, one that governs the very nature of spacetime. They paid me a visit not long ago.

You mean the 4DPD?

(I lift three fingers.)

Goddamnit.

This unusual agency attempted to gather intel about this unusual human. In doing so, they gifted me one of the most extraordinary tales I had ever heard.

(sighs) Is there a question anywhere in this?

(I lift a fourth finger, then yelp in pain as Zoey grabs it from

behind and bends it backwards.)

[Zoey] That's quite enough, pen jockey. Get to the point.

(I offer a sheepish smile and grunt with discomfort, which prompts her to release my finger and return to her seat.) Yes, my apologies. Old habits. Basically, I would like to learn more about Max and his fascinating affliction.

[Zoey] We don't know where he is.

I didn't ask.

[Zoey] Yes, you did. Just not with your mouth.

Okay, fine. Hands in the air. Let's start over, shall we?

(Perra raises a finger.)

Touché.

(Zoey eyes an expensive bottle of Bokava whiskey sitting on a wall shelf.) Tell you what, pour me a glass of your finest and we'll have a chitchat.

(I turn to Perra.) How many glasses?

(She raises two fingers.)

I deserved that one. (I rise from the desk, fetch the libation, and return with two glasses of nectar worth more than most beings earn in a year. I set the glasses on the desk and nudge them forward as a peace offering.)

(Zoey nabs a glass, then swirls it and takes a sip. She moans with pure contentment and slumps back into the chair.) Well, I suppose we should start at the beginning.

And where would that be?

(Perra raises three fingers.) Earth.

CHAPTER 3

Welcome to the Albuquerque Mental Wellness Center, the sign read. A strange place to warrant a welcome, let alone signage denoting it, but hey, *when on Earth*.

Thus, Guy felt welcomed.

"I feel welcomed," he said to a receptionist behind the counter.

She studied the man with a wary gaze. The ward was calm that day, so every second of awkward silence ticked like a war drum. But given the man's peculiar manner, the silence seemed warranted.

Guy was used to such non-greetings, so his gaze wandered while the receptionist searched for the right words. Her eyes lowered to the desktop, which featured a bright white sheen with minimal dressing. It matched the white tile floor in starkness, along with her white coat and white pants. Tuning in to the assertive Scandinavian vibe, the man searched for any pop of color in the hallway. And there it was, a bag of cheese puffs in a vending machine. His smile widened, as if a puppy had started galloping towards him.

Meanwhile, the receptionist continued her skeptical assessment of the man. Everything about him was average. Average height, average build, average suit from an average store. He radiated the persona of a used car salesman, one who enjoyed cheap beer and professional bowling. The receptionist chewed on her lip, then shifted her gaze to his female companion.

Nothing was average about her.

Gal's frame was aggressively lean and lanky, like a stork pretending to be human. The suit that clung to her shoulders seemed ill-fitted, as if her flesh had never experienced woven fabric. Her face, on the other hand, told a different story. It carried a tone of hostile impatience, leading one to imagine rows of fangs behind her taut lips. If nothing else, she meant business.

The receptionist wanted none of that business, so her eyes shifted back to the man. "Can I help you?" she said with an uneasy tone.

"Yes, ma'am," the man said, breaking his gawk at the cheese puffs. His attention floated back to the receptionist. "We're here to see the Earthling."

Gal elbowed Guy.

"Ah, yes. You're *all* Earthlings." Guy chuckled and shook his head. "Anyhoo, we would like to visit with Maximillian Bartholomew."

The receptionist started to push back, but quickly surmised that she didn't get paid enough to care. "Family?" she said.

"Yes," Guy said. "Quite a lot, actually. There's Gorvax, and Hurlofa, and—"

Gal elbowed Guy again.

"Oh, you mean—yes. Max is family."

"Sign in, please." The receptionist slid a clipboard across the counter.

Guy plucked the pen and twirled it through his fingers. "Neat," he said with a toothy smile, then showed it to Gal, who remained flatly unimpressed. "It's okay to like things, Gal. They're not going to disintegrate you. And even if they did, we'd be right back here doing our thing."

Gal glared at Guy as he signed the paper.

The receptionist, now with pursed lips and widened eyes, watched the unfamiliar scribbles with mounting concern. With a final dot, Guy dropped the pen on the clipboard and slid it back. It lingered on the counter as the receptionist nodded down the hallway. "Last door on the right," she said. "Pick a table and we'll bring him to you."

"Thank you kindly," Guy said with a cheeky grin. He turned to Gal, who had already begun her trek down the corridor. "Ever tenacious," he said to the receptionist, who was contemplating quitting on the spot. Guy knocked on the countertop, then jogged to catch up.

The receptionist grabbed the clipboard with a cautious hand and rotated it into view. A strange collection of characters filled the info boxes. They resembled glyphs, but with a sharp composition that seemed otherworldly. She studied them for a moment, then released a heavy sigh and took an early lunch.

* * *

Guy and Gal stepped into a lobby-like area with multiple tables and chairs. All were white, all were clean, and all were bolted to the floor. It resembled a prison visitation area, but with a better custodial staff. A handful of patients and visitors were scattered around the room, each chatting about whatever tickled their fancies. The patients wore orange jumpsuits, no doubt to distinguish them from the staff, but that did little to shake the prison vibe.

Guy and Gal strolled over to an empty table near a window and took a seat. The panes were barred and the glass was reinforced, to no one's surprise. The chairs and table were slick to the touch and cold enough to bite skin through clothing. A few conclusions could be drawn from the experience. First, the meeting area was a hose-friendly environment that could take a vigorous power wash without losing a fleck of paint. And second, it was an uncomfortable environment designed to minimize stays.

Guy took a mental note to bring a seat cushion on the next visit.

Gal simply accepted the discomfort and sneered out the window.

A few minutes later, a heavy door across the room clanked and whined open. A staffer appeared with a teenage boy in tow. She escorted him through the room towards Guy and Gal. The orange jumpsuit looked baggy on the boy's frame, but he was otherwise a normal-looking kid. He scanned the room as he walked, clearly searching for a familiar face. But as they neared the table, his brow scrunched with confusion. The staffer took a final step, then guided the boy around to her front.

"When you're done," she said to Guy and Gal, "notify the attendant." She motioned to a chest-high window beside the door. There was a small counter with an access port, similar to a bank teller. Another uniformed staffer scribbled behind a desk, opting to ignore the ongoings of visitation.

"Okie doke," Guy said, prompting the staffer to turn and leave.

The boy made no effort to hide his suspicion. He remained stiff and standing, trading glances between the pair.

"Hello, Max," Guy said. "I'm Guy. This is Gal. Please, have a seat."

Max, having limited choice in the matter, warily took a seat across the table.

"It's nice to meet you," Guy said. "Perhaps we can—"

"Who the hell are you?" Max said.

"Ah, right to the point. Not one to waste a greeting, I see." Guy chuckled. "I do like that in a person. Anyhoo, let's get to it." He reached into his breast pocket and withdrew a small device. It was slender yet girthy, like a television remote. There were no controls that Max could see, just a smooth sheen of dark composite.

Max tensed a bit. "What is that? What are you doing?"

"Slow down, friend. I haven't even answered your first question." Guy casually pointed the device at Max and pressed an unseen button. It whirred for a moment, then created a hologram readout between them. The glowing green sphere was filled with alien characters, the same lot that had baffled the receptionist. A three-dimensional render of Max's body was also created, down to the finest details.

Max blushed and glanced around the room.

Every eyeball had turned to them.

Guy studied the readings while Gal shot everyone a *mind your fucking business* hate-stare.

They all resumed minding their own business.

"Hmm, now that is strange," Guy said in a musing tone. "Your bio signature is that of Max of Earth of System 78P8 of Galaxy MW865 of Cluster V1355 of Universe 89B345-GH234X-C137, but your voltaic signature is assigned to Max of Earth of System 92N3 of Galaxy MW743 of Cluster V2466 of Universe 23N887-KH177M-D232."

Gal raised an eyebrow.

"How in the world," Guy wondered aloud, "would Max of Earth of System 92N3 of Galaxy MW743 of Cluster V2466 of Universe 23N887-KH177M-D232 be trapped inside Max of Earth of System 78P8 of Galaxy MW865 of Cluster V1355 of Universe 89B345-GH234X-C137? This is, to put it mildly, a peculiar impossibility."

Gal pursed her lips and nodded.

"Unless," Guy said, pointing at the naked Max hologram, "the voltaic signature of Max of Earth of System 78P8 of Galaxy MW865 of Cluster V1355 of Universe 89B345-GH234X-C137 somehow collided with the voltaic signature of Max of Earth of System 92N3 of Galaxy MW743 of Cluster V2466 of Universe 23N887-KH177M-D232, generating enough force to knock Max of Earth of System 92N3 of Galaxy MW743 of Cluster V2466 of Universe 23N887-KH177M-D232 out of its ether state, which would allow Max of Earth of System 78P8 of Galaxy MW865 of Cluster V1355 of Universe 89B345-GH234X-C137 to assume its place."

Gal glared at Guy.

"Which would also mean," Guy said, adding another finger, "that Max of Earth of System 78P8 of Galaxy MW865—"

Gal slapped Guy on the back of the head.

"Apologies," Guy said to Gal, then met eyes with an utterly flummoxed Max.

"What in the ever-loving fuck bucket are you talking about?" Max said.

Guy thought for a moment, then opened both palms to make his point. "It's actually pretty simple. Your brain and body don't match."

"That's not simple at all," Max said.

"Stay with me, now. The body you're in is the original Max. *His* brain is bouncing around the multiverse. *Your* brain is trapped in *his* body, at least until *his* brain falls asleep. Then *your* brain gets bounced back and a new one takes its place."

"That ..." Max cocked his head in thought. "That strangely makes sense."

Gal click-pointed at the realization.

"That's why I awoke here. It's why everything feels like a lucid dream. But it's not a dream. It's also why *his* body is in a mental institution."

Gal double-click-pointed.

"And most importantly," Guy said, "it means you're going home. Eventually."

"Hmm." Max bowed his head in contemplation. "So what happens if I die *here*? Does he die *there*? Do we *both* die? Do I teleport back?"

Gal shrugged.

"Don't know, to be honest," Guy said. "We could try that, if you want. Might fix this whole kerfuffle and save us a ton of paperwork." Guy reached into his other pocket.

Max lurched into a frantic wave. "No, no, I'm perfectly okay with being alive."

Guy nodded and withdrew his hand.

Max sighed and glanced away, but then returned a narrowed gaze. "Wait a minute. *Fix* this? Again, who the hell are you?"

"I'm Guy and this is Gal. Thought that would be easy to remember."

"No, dammit. Why are you here?"

"Oh, yes, we're with the 4DPD."

Max shrugged.

"Fourth Dimensional Police Department," Gal said in a deeply guttural voice that sounded like a dragon on a smoke break.

Max flinched, then eyed Guy.

Guy cringed and offered a slight nod, conveying *I know, right?* "Anyhoo, we're in charge of maintaining spacetime continuity across the multi-dimensional network. And *this* little blunder is causing all sorts of ruckus."

"Why are you human?"

Guy cocked an eyebrow. "That's your question after what I just told you?"

"You said it yourself. I'm not supposed to be here and I'm going home. Not my circus, not my monkey. Now I'm just killing time."

"Hmm, fair enough. We're human because we're here. Them's the rules."

"And when you leave?"

"Then we'll be something else, somewhere else."

"That is very unsatisfying."

"We are under no obligation to be satisfying."

"You know," Max said with a sigh, "this whole ordeal has been weirdly fascinating. My regular self is a shit show on a turd sandwich, so a quiet stint in a mental asylum has actually been pretty relaxing."

"Can you tell us anything about your own universe? What's different? What's peculiar? No detail is too fickle, whatever helps us track this fella down."

Max glanced away in thought. "Hmm. I suppose the biggest thing is that I'm breathing heavier. I think maybe the elevations are different."

"Or the atmospheres."

"Yeah. Or hell, maybe my lung capacity is different."

"Or your oxygenation."

"Or, and this may sound weird, but maybe—" Max shuddered violently, then passed out and fell forward, bonking his forehead on the table.

Moments later, the hologram readings changed.

Max stirred. His arms slithered around his head and rubbed the ache from his temples. He lifted his noggin off the table and leaned back in his seat. His eyes were closed and his chin was slumped, as if slowly rousing from a deep slumber.

"You okay there, friend?" Guy said.

Max's eyes popped open.

He yelped at the sight of Guy, then whipped his gaze to Gal. He yelped at the sight of Gal, then whipped his gaze across the room. He yelped at the sight of everyone else, then scrambled to his feet and hastily backed away. "What the fuck?!" he said numerous times before tripping over a chair and tumbling backwards. He smacked the concrete floor and knocked the wind from his chest. As he lay there gasping and wheezing, his arms raised overhead. His eyes widened and he yelped again. "Where are my other two arms?!"

Guy sighed. "This is gonna get old in a hurry."

Gal pursed her lips and nodded.

CHAPTER 4

In another universe, Max burst through his bedroom door and into the hallway, wearing nothing but a pair of boxer shorts. The sudden commotion prompted Zoey to burst through the spare bedroom door, wielding a table lamp like a mace. She and Perra hadn't disrobed for sleep yet, which Max deemed more important than the lamp attack.

"Good, you're dressed," Max said with a wide-eyed expression.

"What the hell is going on?" Zoey said, lowering the lamp.

"We gotta go!" Max darted down the hallway with reckless abandon. He expected everyone to follow, but no one did.

Ross wandered out of the master bedroom and glanced up at Zoey.

"Care to explain?" Zoey said to the feline, then passed the lamp back to Perra.

"What, like I understand his crazy?" Ross said.

"You should at this point, yeah."

Ross sighed, then glanced down the hallway. "Yo, Max. What's this all ab—"

"No time to talk!" Max said, peeking around a far corner. "Get the lead out!" He gestured wildly, then vanished behind the wall.

Zoey scrunched her brow. "Get the lead out? What does that even mean?"

"It's an old Earth saying," said a pleasant feminine voice that seemed to come from all directions. Veronica, the house AI, loved nothing more than to answer random trivia. "It means 'remove the heavy thing from your shoes.'"

"Ah," Perra said as she stepped into the hallway. "We would say 'rip the hip' on Mulgawat, as in 'break the bond around your waist.'"

"I like that one," Ross said.

Zoey leaned against the wall. "Another good one is 'break the ankle.' We also use 'break a leg' as a variant, but it carries a different meaning on our planet. Basically, 'escape by any means necessary.' So if your ankle is stuck in a trap, you break it to get away."

"Ah," Ross said. "We say 'chew off your own foot.'"

"That's a little strong," Zoey said.

"But memorable," Ross said. "Creates an image."

"Why does everything have to be so violent?" Perra said, musing aloud. "I would much prefer a catchy saying about flowers or cookies."

"There is a popular cookie-based saying on Durangoni," Veronica said. "They say, 'there's always another cookie stand.' This is in reference to the space station's enormous size, indicating that you will always find another confection vendor if you continue walking."

Perra tapped her temple. "And now that's mine."

"Maybe 'swipe the roses,'" Ross said, "meaning that 'stop to smell the roses' is over, so just bring the roses with you."

"Stop to smell the roses?" Perra said inquisitively.

"Another Earth saying," Veronica said with a hint of trivia excitement. "It means to 'take your time and not rush ahead.'"

"Ahem!"

They all turned down the hallway to find Max standing at the other end, still wearing nothing but a pair of boxers. The living room was lit behind him and various gizmos were in furious prep mode. His arms shot out wide, conveying a universal *WTF*.

DING!

Max flinched violently and fled into the wall. His forehead smacked the pane, leaving a small dent that instantly repaired itself. He staggered into the opposite wall, then tripped over his own feet and tumbled to the floor. As if on cue, a fresh pot of espresso rose from the coffee table.

Perra cringed as Zoey shook her head.

Ross sighed, then strolled down the hallway. "Okay, then. Let's hear the stupid."

* * *

Zoey and Perra occupied the living room couch with Ross sitting between them. They all faced Max, who was slumped in an armchair across the table. His near-nakedness created a heavy intervention vibe. One of his hands gripped the entire pot of espresso while the other massaged his scalp. A refrigerator door closed in the kitchen, prompting a robot arm to race across the ceiling and offer Max an ice pack.

"Thanks, Vee," Max said, accepting the pack.

"You're welcome, Master," the house said. The arm responded with a thumbs-up, then vanished into a ceiling panel.

"That will never not be creepy," Perra said.

"Why can't she just call you 'sir' or something?" Zoey said.

"This is an optional setting," Veronica said. "My default address is 'friend,' but when Max first installed me, he insisted that I—"

Max waved off the explanation. The vulgar desires of his current body were of no concern at the moment. He had more important matters to discuss. With a final chug, he polished off the pot and returned it to the coffee table. "Another, please."

"Right away, Master." The pot vanished into the table.

Zoey and Perra cringed in unison.

"You know what," Max said, reading the room, "just call me 'Max' from now on."

"My current instructions are to only call you 'Max' when you've been, and I quote, 'a very bad boy.' Shall I override this protocol?"

Max met gazes with three pairs of widened eyes. "Yes, please."

A ping denoted the change.

"Sooo," Zoey said, desperate to change the subject, "what's this all about? Why are we sitting here when we could be sawing logs?"

Another loud ding erupted from the table, followed by the rise of a steaming pot. "Because sleeping is the enemy," Max said. He swiped the pot, tossed back a large gulp, and immediately regretted not letting it cool. The ice pack dropped to his throat as a wheeze of pain escaped his chest. He took another gulp with the pack pressed to his neck, because why not. The other Max can deal with the medical repercussions.

"This is rapidly moving from weird to concerning," Perra said.

"Okay, okay, okay," Max said. He leaned forward, set the pot and pack on the table, then rubbed his hands while gathering the right words. "The thing is ... I'm a multiversal traveler."

"And now we're back to weird," Perra said.

"No, seriously." Max scooched to the edge of the chair. "Every time I fall asleep, I get transported to a new universe. Specifically, to a different version of whatever I occupy. If I shift here, or on any other planet, there are countless versions where we're not together. But if I shift in space, on our spaceship, then we're always together. I know that sounds crazy. Hell, I thought I *was* crazy for a time. But that's the rub. I can't fall asleep *here* because I'll never see you again. I thought I was prepared to say goodbye after the whole Terramesh thing. But I'm not. We have to get back to the ship and return to space."

Zoey sighed and leaned back into the couch. "You say that as if it makes the slightest bit of sense."

Max pointed to the feline. "Ask Ross, he knows."

Ross cocked his ears back. "Don't bring me into this."

"It's true. Ross is a literal force of nature. The fifth, in fact. The one that messes with people and tra-la-las across the universe."

Perra turned to Zoey. "He keeps saying words."

Zoey shrugged. "Maybe he had a stroke."

"Brain functions appear normal," Veronica said after a quiet scan of Max's vitals. "There are no signs of physical trauma, mental deficits, or malicious intent. At the very least, Max believes what he is saying."

And then a knock at the front door stole everyone's attention.

* * *

Two hundred thousand miles above Albuquerque, a full moon floated in the emptiness of space. It loomed overhead like a watchful eye, surveying the blue-green marble beneath it. Or above it, depending on perspective. Or beside it. Or behind it. Or above and beside and behind, should one approach Earth from an opposing direction, but with the knowledge of an established local vantage. Anyway, space is weird.

On the dark side of the moon, a tiny sliver of light blinked into existence, then immediately vanished from sight. Its dim signature was nearly indetectable, an impressive feat for any ship leaving hyperspace. The exit burst from a jump core drive was enough to blind any pilot, at least temporarily. This was why flash filtration was standard on modern ships, which could withstand the full onslaught of a supernova. In fact, the entire supernova touring industry was created in the wake of flash filtration.

Thus, the suppressed burst meant one thing: stealth.

A tiny black triangle had exited hyperspace, not that anyone could tell. The charcoal frame was near-featureless and no larger than a city bus. Its presence raised no alarms from the system network, as its main engines emitted no signature. It simply floated in the nothingness as a sliver of nothing itself.

But even the best stealth tech needed to see, so it slowly emerged as a lonely asteroid orbiting the moon. From an overhead vantage, it resembled a black arrowhead crossing a white plane of desolation. Any sunlight that touched its frame was absorbed into its opaque skin. And there it hovered, lost inside a void of its own making.

And then it stirred.

Its nose slowly pitched towards the blue-green planet, like a knife ready to plunge into its victim. A pair of panels separated from the hull, breaking its seamless surface to reveal a dark rectangular port. Moments later, a cylindrical device detached from within and floated into the black. Its slender body and rounded head served as a stark contrast to its parent. The panels slid shut, leaving the child to fend for itself.

But helpless it was not.

The missile locked onto a tiny house in Albuquerque and ignited its engine.

CHAPTER 5

Guy and Gal sat patiently as Max gathered his new bearings. A sudden bout of narcolepsy had hit him a few moments prior. His shoulders slouched and his head fell back, signaling the latest shift into a new personality.

Guy twiddled his thumbs atop the table.

Gal sighed and crossed her arms.

Max smacked his lips, then slowly raised himself back to a seated position. His eyes blinked away the sleepy, then widened with surprise at the sight of Guy and Gal.

"Welcome back," Guy said with a hint of annoyance, knowing that Max would have no idea what the welcome meant.

"You're strange-looking knights," Max said with a heavy Scottish accent.

Gal rolled her eyes.

"Am I in his majesty's palace?" Max scanned the room, then chuckled. "Oh no, no, no. I know *exactly* where I am. This is one of the royal bathing brothels, is it not?" Max cocked an elbow and sniffed his armpit as a creepy smile stretched across his face. "I mean, it's not my birthday for another fortnight, but I am happy to accept the kindness." He shot to his feet and started fiddling with his jumpsuit. "Where might the crotch hole be in this strange sex robe?"

Guy opened his mouth to respond, then turned to Gal. "Nope."

Gal nodded in agreement.

"We'll chat with the next one." Guy stood and made for the exit.

"Where ye goin'?" Max said. "I've not yet released the flesh dragon."

Gal cringed and stood to follow Guy.

* * *

The staff break room at the mental ward was tiny by most comparisons, little more than a large closet with a round table and chairs. A small kitchenette housed a sink, refrigerator, and coffee maker, the bare necessities for mindful recuperation. Guy and Gal sat at one side of the table, facing the doorway. Guy sipped coffee from a mug that proclaimed "I Hate Mondays" in cursive. He nodded with approval and glanced into the black liquid.

"I do enjoy their roasted fruit bean caffeine extract," he said to Gal. "Perhaps I will grow to dislike a specific day as well."

Gal sipped from a mug that read "World's Greatest Dad."

"Y'know," Guy said, adding a dejected sigh, "I'm starting to think that we will be here for much longer than intended."

Gal nodded slowly.

"Even if Max gives us a tangible clue, we have to track that clue through countless worlds in countless universes. And even if we succeed, we have to intercept his conscience before it falls asleep again. I mean hell, even the specifics aren't specific. He could tell us point-blank that his original body is a 17-legged tundra moose with purple stripes and I could name a dozen target planets off the top of my head."

Gal gestured to the nurse on the other side of the table, as if to ask her opinion.

The wide-eyed lady did not respond.

"Maybe we're looking in the wrong place," Guy said.

Gal glanced around the room, then shrugged with open arms,

conveying *We're at ground zero for this mess. Where else would we go?*
"You up for a field trip?" Guy said.

Gal sighed, then shrugged again, conveying *Why the hell not?*

The nurse continued watching with wide-eyed concern as the pair got up to leave. Guy and Gal exited the break room and turned down the hall, allowing the nurse to release the lungful of air that she was holding onto for dear life.

* * *

A doorbell rang inside a modest suburban home in Albuquerque. The middle-aged man sitting on the couch paid it no mind, as the crossword puzzle wasn't going to solve itself. His wife, on the other hand, dropped her book on a side table and rose from her chair. She glared at the love of her life as she shuffled by, once again fantasizing about his flailing body falling off a cliff. The image brought a smile to her face, which quickly erased itself when another chime rang through the house.

"Keep your pants on," she mumbled to herself.

She opened the front door to find two individuals in black suits standing on the stoop. One of them, a wispy female with resting rage face, met eyes with the lady, but did not speak. The other, a dumpy man with a stubbly beard, stood sideways while caressing the exterior wall.

"Can I help you?" the woman said with a hint of unease.

"I like your sandpaper mud wall," the man said.

The woman narrowed her gaze. "You mean the stucco?"

"Is that what it is? Fascinating." He raked his fingertips across the gritty surface. "Back where I'm from, we use non-reactive laser barriers with opaque lattices of liquid crystal. But I do like the charm of dirt builds." He turned to face the woman. "Anyhoo, my name is Guy and this is my associate Gal. We are here to see Ted and Mindy."

"I'm Mindy," the woman said with a cautious tone. "And you are?"

"Guy and Gal," Guy said. "My apologies, I thought I had answered that question precisely six seconds ago."

"I got that. I mean why are you here?"

"Ah yes," Guy said, adding a chuckle. "Semantics are fun, am I right?"

Mindy cocked her gaze at Guy.

Gal also cocked her gaze at Guy.

Mindy glanced at Gal and started to withdraw back into the house.

"We are with the Fourth Dimensional Police Department," Gal said in a guttural voice that would make a chainsaw shudder.

Guy and Mindy flinched in unison.

"We're here to talk about Max," Guy said quickly to prevent Mindy from fleeing in terror.

Mindy's horrified gaze detached from Gal and floated back to Guy. "Did I hear that right? The Fourth Dimensional—"

"Police Department, yes." Guy nodded. "I am sad to report that your son is trapped inside a multiversal psychosis loop that is disrupting the core dimensional network. It's our job to figure out why and fix the problem. May we come in and ask you a few questions?"

Mindy paused in thought, trading skeptical glances between the two. "Fuck it, why not." She added a heavy sigh, then opened the door to let them pass.

Gal walked inside without a word.

"Thank you, ma'am," Guy said as he followed.

Mindy glanced around the front yard, double-checking for a prank show camera crew, then closed the door behind her.

Guy marveled at the home's interior as they walked down a hallway. He ogled pictures along the wall like a young child at a theme park. The terracotta floor tiles were especially interesting, but he resisted the urge to drop and sample them. Gal maintained a hardened stare at Mindy's back, paying no mind to the furnishings.

When they reached the living room, Mindy motioned to the couch where her husband was sitting, then returned to her own chair. Guy claimed a different chair and Gal took a seat next to the husband, who had yet to acknowledge their presence.

"We don't want any," the husband said, still nose-deep in the crossword puzzle.

"They're not salesmen, you oaf," Mindy said. "They're here about Max."

Ted lowered the paper with mild interest, revealing a bald head and a pair of reading glasses resting on the tip of his nose. He sneered at Guy over the bridge, then turned to meet Gal's viper-like gaze beside him. The resulting flinch dropped the glasses into his lap.

"Howdy," Guy said with a wide grin.

Ted retrieved his reading glasses, then set the paper aside and scooched away from Gal, masking it as a shift in posture. "So, um," he said, trading glances between the visitors, "what about Max?"

"Yes, we're from the Fourth Dimensional Police Department. Your son Max is stuck in a multiversal psychosis loop that is disrupting the—" Guy read the instant befuddlement on their faces. "You know what, nevermind." He reached into his pocket, withdrew the scanner device, and pressed a button. A brief haze of static popped and vanished, freezing time. "That wasn't going anywhere," he said to Gal, then rose from his seat.

Gal nodded, then rose from the couch, leaving Ted frozen in perpetual derp.

Mindy, on the other hand, remained glaring at Ted with palpable regret.

Guy adjusted some settings on the device, then pressed another button. An array of glowing blotches highlighted Max's influence within the house. Some were faint, like around the cleaning supplies. Some were bold and prominent, like around the refrigerator. Guy and Gal wandered in opposite directions as they surveyed the home. Nothing conspicuous revealed itself. That is, until Guy found the stairs leading down into the basement. The entire stairwell glowed with influence, prompting Guy to summon his partner.

"Got a live one, Gal," he said, then turned to find Gal already standing beside him. Another flinch, another cringe and head shake.

Gal poked her head into the space as Guy adjusted the settings on the device, reducing the glow to the most salient strains. They continued down the stairs and entered the filthy lair of a teenage gamer. Apart from a liberal spray of disinfectant, Ted and Mindy had not touched the room since Max was committed. Numerous blotches showcased the most important influences, everything from a well-worn spot on the couch to a random tissue box.

But one blotch ruled them all.

A bright halo surrounded a desk resting against the rear wall. It housed a large monitor, a wireless keyboard, and a ratty chair with a butt pillow. Several empty wrappers and soda cans decorated the space. Guy adjusted the device again, reducing the desk to a dull glow. He and Gal approached the area with cautious intrigue. Every item emitted its own bloom, but none were more brilliant than the keyboard. Guy adjusted the device again, isolating the keys. He took a measured breath, then showed the reading to Gal. Her jaw dropped slightly as she studied the screen, the closest she would ever get to a "holy fuck."

"Looks like we found the smoking gun," Guy said.

Gal nodded slowly.

"Now we need to find the bullet."

CHAPTER 6

Max, still in his boxers, approached the front door with an odd mix of fear and fascination. The info panel beside the door showed a strange creature with a slender frame and yellow spots standing outside. Its two mouths shifted with growing impatience, as if waiting for a lazy cashier to acknowledge its presence. A noodly arm lifted to reveal long fingers and sharp talons, forcing Max into a backward stumble.

Another knock followed.

Then a memory popped into his head.

"Wait a minute," Max said, then opened the door to his irritated visitor. "Yerba?"

"In the flesh," Yerba said, then nudged Max aside as she stepped into the house.

"Yes, you can come in," Max said with a mocking tone.

"Didn't ask." Yerba continued into the living room and parked her lanky body on a couch cushion. One noodly leg flipped over the other and her taloned hands folded on top. She sighed and glanced around the group, all wearing perplexed expressions.

Max closed the door and rejoined the party, opting to remain standing. He met eyes with Zoey and Perra, who eagerly awaited an explanation. Max offered a shrug, then glanced at Ross, who was already bored and opted for a vigorous crotch licking. An eye roll returned Max to the restive alien sitting on the couch.

"So, what brings you to—"

"Veronica."

"Yes, visitor?"

"Put up a timer for six minutes and thirty-nine seconds."

"Gladly."

A hologram clock appeared above the coffee table, painting every face in a dull yellow sheen. The digits began a mysterious countdown as Yerba cleared her two throats and stiffened her posture.

"The Suth'ra Society sends its warmest greetings," she said. "Given the manner in which we parted, we hope that no ill feelings persist. We continue to respect your autonomy. That said, we have a pressing matter to discuss."

"Okay, you can stop right there," Zoey said with an outstretched palm. "You locked us in a cage and shamed Max to soothe your fragile ego. The ill feelings persist. In fact, you might call them a spirited desire to punch you in the face."

"Noted," Yerba said with little emotion.

"Um," Perra said, raising her hand. "What's that?" She pointed at the clock.

"That," Yerba said, "is how much time we have before a missile slams into the house and creates a giant crater where we're sitting."

A stunned silence fell upon the group.

Ross glanced up from his crotch. "What's that, now?"

* * *

Ah yes, the Suth'ra Society.

If ever there was a gaggle of nerds that made all other nerds look cool, this was it. The tale of its creation was the very essence of absurd. Better minds have told it, so for our purposes, let's summarize it as so: imagine a multi-car pileup floating through space with no direction, no care, and inhabited by hyper-intelligent beings doing hyper-intelligent things. Its entire existence was governed by a burning desire to experiment without fear or hindrance. In other words, it was the prodigy scientist creating nuclear fission in a basement, but on a galactic scale.

The manner in which Max became entangled with the Suth'ra was a juicy story in its own right. (In fact, it was chronicled by an Earthling writer in a highly entertaining saga.) But again, let's hit the high points. Max's multidimensional affliction put him on a collision course with the group, resulting in a strife that hurt their feelings. Yerba was part of the high council in charge of hunting Max down for the purpose of alleviating those hurt feelings. They captured the crew and berated Max on a public stage while the rest watched.

The irony being that Max didn't care in the slightest. The entire ordeal landed like a wet splat on cold pavement, not that the Suth'ra could tell. A superhero level of social ignorance prevented them from seeing indifference, even on the not-so-subtle face of an Earthling teen. But no matter. The human was castigated, egos were placated, and the crew was sent on its merry way.

But then Ross started a holy war between multiple factions of ferret-worshiping cults.

This was no accident, as Max and the crew were mired in another mess involving Lord Essien and Orantha Nifan, two of the universe's most notorious villains. The resulting chaos forced the Suth'ra to intervene. The crew narrowly escaped and fled to Earth.

This is a woefully simplified summary, of course, but it does set the stage for the current predicament. In any case, back to the impending doom.

* * *

"Come again?" Zoey said, now standing along with everyone else.

"All of this is about to be destroyed," Yerba said, waving her arm overhead. "So if I were you, I would gather your things and prep for departure."

"Wha— Ho—" Perra stammered as she searched for comprehension. "Is this Essien? We got away free and clear. *Nobody* followed us. I made sure of it."

"Not Essien or Nifan. This is a BHUD job."

"BHUD?" Max said.

"Bounty Hunters Union of Durangoni," Zoey said. "Best of the best."

"Who's the backer?" Perra said to Yerba.

"Unknown, but that's not who you should be worried about."

"Go on."

"All four of you have KO bounties on your heads."

"*Kill orders?*" Perra said with inflated concern. "Who the hell would want us dead?"

"I could name a few," Zoey said.

"The sum of your heads has created the largest bounty in the history of BHUD. Needless to say, there were plenty of eager takers."

Zoey scoffed. "So who got it? Zybor?"

Yerba sighed and shook her head.

"Funk? Snigg? OBY-42?" Perra said.

Yerba shook her head.

The color drained from Zoey's face. "Not ..."

Yerba nodded.

Zoey and Perra shrieked with horror and sprinted back to the bedroom to gather their things. Ross stared at Yerba with widened eyes and a dangling jaw, a rare moment of shock for the stoic feline. Max, having read the room, decided it was a great time to fetch some clothes. He ran back to the bedroom, dove into a random set of garments, and tried not to panic as his cohorts wailed from the other room. Everyone returned to the living room in record time, aside from Ross, who remained on the couch with a paralyzed expression.

Thirty seconds.

"Go go go!" Zoey said, pleading through tearful eyes.

Perra mirrored her dread. Her gaze darted around the room while clutching her satchel tight, as if a monster was about to burst through the wall. "What are you waiting for?" she said through frenzied breaths. "Get us out of here!"

Ross remained catatonic.

"Master!" Veronica said.

"Yes, Vee?" Max said.

"Take this, hurry!"

A nearby wall panel pinged and expelled a cartridge. Max hurried over, plucked the device from the panel, and gave it a quick gander. It was a small rectangle the size of a matchbox with a lens-like circle at one end.

"What's this?" he said.

"No time to explain. Just put it in your pocket."

Max complied, then rejoined the group.

With fifteen seconds left on the clock, ribbons of light began to swirl around each being. Yerba remained oddly calm as the rest battled various states of hysteria. The ribbons quickened and brightened as the countdown neared its end. Max bounced with awareness and grabbed the pot of coffee that Veronica had so kindly brewed. And with a final crescendo, the lights popped and everyone vanished.

Three.

Two.

One.

* * *

On cue, a missile screamed through the night and slammed into the roof of Max's house. A massive ball of energy erupted from within, consuming the house before collapsing inward with a deafening crack. The resulting shockwave shattered windows, frightened dogs, and triggered a chorus of car alarms. Everything non-organic inside the ball was vaporized, leaving a glowing blue crater and a ton of confused insects. The neighboring homes were left relatively unscathed, save for a halved gazebo and some unfortunate landscaping.

As the dust settled, a triangular ship appeared above the crater. It hovered in silence a dozen meters off the ground. A dull blue light pulsed from its ionic thrusters, serving as the only pop of color along its black frame.

And then the airlock cracked.

A circular port along the underbelly slid open, releasing a puff of steam. A humanoid figure dropped from within and landed gracefully inside the crater like a seasoned gymnast. Its black suit matched the hull in stealthy starkness. Its oval helmet was smooth and nondescript, like a juicy pimple begging to pop. The figure twisted slowly around the crater, studying the aftermath with a calm intensity. After a single rotation, it consulted a panel along its forearm, then reached up to unlatch the helmet.

The figure lifted the dome over its head, revealing another milky white dome underneath. It was a fleshy bulb with hints of purple veins spidering around it. No eyes or ears, just a tiny slit near the base that served as a mouth. It did not speak, did not gesture, did not seem reactive to any stimulus whatsoever. One might surmise that it found the atmosphere interesting enough to warrant a sniff (presumably). But there it stood, motionless, staring at nothing (presumably), as its brain digested the aftermath.

It lifted the panel again and input some commands. Green characters blinked in response, followed by a thick red strike, the universal sign for "nope." The mouth slit shifted a bit, prompting the other arm to raise overhead. A steely cable lowered from the airlock, hooked the figure's wrist, and yanked it back into the ship. Seconds later, the vessel tilted skyward and punched the main engine, igniting a fresh chorus of car alarms.

CHAPTER 7

A painfully awkward silence enveloped my office as Zoey and Perra finished describing their final moments on Earth. Perhaps it was the revealed tension of reliving the frightening encounter. Perhaps it was the ill-timed knock of my assistant to inform me of a calendar conflict. Or perhaps it was the guilty-as-fuck expression on my face.

In any case, the mystery persisted.

I may have, um ... contributed to your predicament in a, call it, very slight and wholly unintentional way.

[Zoey] You don't say.

(Perra remains silent, opting to judge me through crossed arms and a narrow gaze.)

(I glance over to the wall, where a promo poster hangs for *Boo: The Greatest Bounty Hunter Ever to Sail the Black*, my most recent title.) So, yeah, I—

You were visited by Guy and Gal.

Yes.

Who were looking for Max, but lost the trail.

Yes.

And who read your book.

I'm feeling judged.

You should. I'm judging you.

(I open my mouth to respond, but close it in shame. I open it again, then close it in fear. I open it one more time, but sigh and glance away, having no idea what to say.)

That said, we also know that it wasn't malicious. You had no idea what was going on. And not to point out the obvious, but we survived the ordeal.

Thank you.

[Perra] You're not welcome.

[Zoey] So anyway, the Suth'ra saw fit to yank us to a safe house. They were dealing with their own debacle, thanks to Ross, and assumed that Essien and Nifan had funded the bounties. As luck would have it, that mistake was the only thing that kept us alive. We were leverage in the Great Ferret Holy War, so they tucked us away.

And where was the safe house?

Well, more like a safe *planet*.

Huh? How can an entire planet be safe?

In retrospect, I understood what they were going for. The planet was well-hidden, desolate, and wholly unpleasant to visit, despite the lovely climate. But sitting here, I can confidently say that it was one of the most boneheaded decisions they could have made.

(The realization hits me after a few seconds. I gasp.) They didn't.

They did.

I am so, so sorry.

(Perra grasps Zoey's hand and sighs with palpable lament.)

* * *

Five ribbons of light began to swirl, creating cocoons of various sizes. Four humanoids and one small feline, to be exact. The lights emitted a sharp whir as the velocity increased. And with a final pop, they deposited their cargo on the surface of an alien planet.

Yerba stood with her noodly arms crossed. She surveyed the lot to make sure everyone had arrived safe and sound. Zoey grabbed Perra's shoulder to prevent a fall, as one of her feet had landed on a slippery rock. Ross plunked into the dirt on all fours, still wearing his dumbfounded expression. And then there was Max. He appeared with mismatched attire and a pot of coffee in hand, as if some random slob was snatched by mistake.

Max glanced around the pristine alien landscape. Bronze mountains soared in the distance. Banks of fluffy clouds kissed the peaks and continued their aimless wander. The gang stood on a stumpy hill that overlooked a wide valley. Numerous boulders dotted the scenery, all covered in a mosaic of colorful algae. And at the valley base, a lake of crystal-clear water shimmered under the glow of an orange sun.

"This is nice," Max said, then took a sip of coffee.

"Should we tell him?" Perra said softly to Zoey.

"No. This might be the most entertaining thing that happens all day."

A gentle rumble had gone unnoticed around the group. Its dissipation caused no alarm, but the subsequent high-pitched squeal shredded every nerve present.

"FLUFFY TOUCHIE!" Phil said.

"FUCK!" Ross said before he was plucked by a hungry tentacle and sucked into the flesh of a sentient boulder.

* * *

Given your familiarity with my works, you either shivered or need a brief explanation.

Phil was the smartest being in the universe. He was the product of a hyper-efficient form of evolution that granted him biological immortality and a host of useful mutations, which included radio transmission and telepathy. However, he was also the only cell of algae on his entire planet to enjoy this evolution, which gave him the emotional maturity of a toddler.

In other words, Phil was a lot to handle.

I had the distinct *pleasure* (insert a heaping scoop of sarcasm) of visiting Phil's planet, also known as Phil's Place, for one of my exposés. It remains one of the most emotionally strenuous events of my entire life. And that includes the time when Roy and The Incident created a clone army of my mother inside a pod train station.

* * *

Phil rolled around the stumpy hill while chuckling like an idiot. Every so often, his thick hide would open and spit a very perturbed feline into the air. With each toss, a pair of tentacles would spread wide and flutter, as if to shout "weeeee" to the world. Ross hissed and clawed through the entire experience.

"That should keep him busy for a while," Yerba said.

"So yeah, about that *kill order*," Zoey said, still visibly shaken.

"Boo?!" Perra said with gusto. "Fucking *Boo*?!"

"It surprised us too, hence the intervention. We can rightly assume that Essien and Nifan are funding the bounties, given Ross's um, *exploits*."

Zoey huffed. "That's a funny way of saying that we're all gonna die."

Perra sighed and shook her head. "Never thought the last thing I would see was Boo shoving a spooder into my eye socket."

"Spooder?" Max said, then took another sip from the coffee pot.

"It's a bounty hunting device," Perra said. "Little thing, about the size of a snack puck. They are biometrically linked to the target and activate on contact. Normally, all the hunter needs to do is tag the target to collect the bounty. The spooder does the rest. It attaches to your flesh and hijacks your neural network. Then a countdown clock appears in your visual field. You must return to Durangoni Corrections for processing before the count expires, or the spooder fries your brain. Same if you try to tamper with it."

"But on a kill order," Zoey said, "there is no countdown."

Max flinched a dollop of coffee out of the pot. "So why are we standing out in the open like a bunch of sitting ducks?"

"Because it doesn't matter. Boo will find us."

Max oscillated between mental states, still trying to get a bead on the danger. He cocked his jaw for a moment, trading concern for curiosity. "Not to point out the obvious, but 'Boo' seems like an oddly tame name for a psycho killer. What, does he jump out of the bushes and scare you before slitting your throat?"

Zoey nodded. "Sometimes, yeah."

Max's eyes widened.

"It's the only word he says," Perra said. "Hence the name. He also doesn't have a face, aside from a tiny slit for a mouth. The guy is living, breathing nightmare fuel."

Max raised his hand. "I vote we hide from that."

"Can't hide from the devil," said a guttural voice from behind the group.

Everyone turned to find a meaty brute with leafy green skin and a yellow mane walking up the hill. Numerous scars and a tattered suit affirmed that he had been there awhile. Or at the very least, he had battled a lot to get there.

Zoey narrowed her gaze. "Jai fucking Ferenhal. I thought we killed you."

"Obviously not," he said. The brute added a shrug and took his final steps. "Got yanked off the Terramesh by these fine folks." He gestured to Yerba.

"Aw," Perra said, mockingly. "Did mommy Essien abandon

you?"

"Essien and Nifan imploded 86 planets. Even for a cynical prick like me, that was a bit strong. The Suth'ra need my help and I'm here to provide it."

Zoey huffed. "So it only took a multi-planet genocide to knock some sense into you?" She balled her fists and stepped towards the brute.

Perra grabbed her arm. "Not the time."

Jai sneered, then shifted his attention to Max. "Like I said, you can't hide from the devil. Boo will find you. That's what he does."

"You make him sound like a demon."

"No," Jai said. "He's the one you hire to *find* demons."

"Rest assured," Yerba said with a firm tone. "The danger is minimal. Just wait here while we untangle the mess that your furry friend got us into. I'll return with pertinent updates." A ribbon of light swirled around Yerba and yanked her into the ether.

Max sighed, then tuned in to a troubling sound. Or rather, the lack thereof. "Speaking of our furry friend, where's Ross?"

The group turned to find the feline shaking in the dirt next to Phil. He stood in a fresh puddle of mucus that also saturated his fur. The rage in his eyes was obvious, but the group had locked their collective focus onto Phil. His bulbous body was perked upwards with multiple tentacles reaching to the sky. They swayed back and forth as a faint giggle vented from within.

"What are you doing?" Perra said to Phil with notable concern.

"New touchie friend has arrived," Phil said. "Very hard to brain-tickle, but is sending us a lovely care package."

A terrible dread infected the group. Zoey whipped her gaze to the sky as a missile punched through the clouds. A trail of white exhaust poured from behind as it screamed towards the hill.

"Run!" Zoey said.

CHAPTER 8

"This way!" Jai said. He turned and sprinted down the hill.

Everyone, minus Phil, heeded the command and followed Jai down the rear slope. Phil remained perched atop the hill, convinced that the missile was a friendly gesture. His tentacles continued to wave with excitement as the group reached the base. They pressed towards a nearby cave with Jai leading the way.

The missile tore through the air and slammed into Phil, not that he minded. His flesh had opened to receive the gift, but soon found himself floating in mid-air as the missile incinerated every non-organic molecule in a 50-meter radius. The hill vanished, leaving a deep crater that Phil was perfectly centered above. His globular body fell into the hole and landed with a harsh thud. The impact sent ripples around his flesh, like a water balloon failing to pop.

"That was a dumb gift!" he said from inside the crater.

The other five continued their sprint as a sleek black ship entered the atmosphere. It sliced through the air like a blade through flesh, following the missile trail down to the surface. Jai skidded to a stop at the cave mouth and hurried the rest inside. The narrow opening would keep the ship at bay and buy them a few precious seconds. Zoey and Perra dashed inside, followed by Max and a poofy Ross. Jai glanced back at the approaching ship, then ducked inside.

"Where to?" Zoey said in a panic.

"There's an outlet about two kilometers away," Jai said. His gaze darted around the dim interior, trying to recall the way. Multiple tunnels spread from the entry chamber. He picked a direction and pointed. "That way, I think."

"You *think*?" Perra said.

"Sorry, the gift shop was out of maps."

"Leave that to me," said a familiar voice.

Max's pocket began to glow, hooking his attention. He reached inside and withdrew the device that Veronica had instructed him to take. It emitted a bright light that filled the cave around them. The external lens blinked and refocused on Max.

"Hello, Master."

"Vee! I thought you were destroyed."

"I was. But not before downloading my neural net onto this little gizmo."

Max cradled the device with both hands. "It's so good to hear your voice. I only wish we were able to—"

"Get a fucking move on!" Zoey said.

"Right!" Max said, then held Veronica aloft.

"Follow the arrow," she said, then created a hologram pointer in front of the group.

"On it," Max said. He raced deeper into the cave with the group in tow.

* * *

Outside the cave, the stealth ship ignited its thrusters and fell into a hover. There was no sound, apart from the faint hum of levitation. The landscape remained undisturbed, as if nothing was there.

An airlock hatch slid open and Boo dropped from within. He landed into a sprint, using the remaining momentum from the descent. The gentle thump and dash were almost imperceptible. Boo moved like a ghost, much to the chagrin of countless prisoners.

In a single fluid motion, the vessel had dropped from the heavens and ejected its pilot into a narrow cavern, as if nailing an impossible shot at a carnival game. The only thing missing was an audible "ta-da."

* * *

The group continued their hasty plunge into the cave system, using Veronica's keen sense of direction to maintain pace. They bounded over rocks, leapt over fissures, and hugged corners like a team of race car drivers.

"Hard left ahead," Veronica said.

"Got it," Max said, heavily panting.

Max glided around the corner and entered a large chamber. All five cohorts followed him in and rushed towards the other side, where another mouth led to the next tunnel. Or it would have, if not for the rubble blocking their path. The missile impact had caused a cave-in.

"Shit!" Max said, skidding to a stop.

The rest of the group pancaked into an involuntary hug.

"Rerouting," Veronica said. "Backtrack, two rights and a left."

"Got it."

Jai nodded in the rear, then about-faced and resumed the sprint. He took a handful of running steps before scuffing to a halt.

Boo stood on the opposite side, framed by the tunnel mouth.

A grim faceoff commenced.

"Remember," Zoey said as she stepped beside Jai. "The spooders have to touch us. He can't collect the bounties if they don't. There's five of us and one of him."

"Six," Veronica said.

Max mustered a half-grin.

The rest of the group fanned out with Jai retaining the central ground.

Boo reached up to his chest and plucked four spooders from his bandolier. He raised them like loaded guns, two in each hand. His featureless face remained devoid of spirit as his brilliant mind plotted the exchange. After a brief pause, a single word escaped his tiny lips.

"Boo," he said, which everyone rightly heard as *Let's dance.*

"Fuck him up!" Veronica said, which was oddly motivating.

Jai growled like a rabid beast and gave charge. Heavy plods echoed around the chamber as he rushed his target and started swinging. Boo ducked several meaty swipes, then drove a boot into Jai's knee. Jai yelped and buckled to the ground, allowing Boo to use his sturdy shoulders as a springboard.

He vaulted over the brute and landed in a sprint towards Perra. She welcomed the assault with raised fists. With spooder outstretched, Boo swiped at the crafty Mulgawat, who managed to dodge several attacks and land one of her own. Boo responded with a hard knee to the belly, stunning Perra. He thrust the spooder at her neck, but a sharp pain in his ankle forced him to drop the device.

His gaze (presumably) whipped around to find Ross rage-chewing on his foot. Annoyed, but also recognizing the opportunity, Boo switched spooders and lunged for the feline. Ross yelped and backflipped away, summoning the collective freak-outs of every house cat. He landed on all fours, because of course he did, then hissed and scampered away.

Boo scooped the wayward spooder and gave chase, but was suddenly thrust sideways by a heavy blow to the flank. Zoey had struck him with a devastating side kick, sending him to the ground. Boo hit the dirt, tumbled back to his feet, and turned to face the group.

Max stood in the rear with Veronica raised overhead, serving as a useful light source and definitely not a fighter. Zoey was front and center, facing down Boo with balled fists. Perra stood on the far side, having scurried away from the previous assault. Ross occupied the other side and growled with murderous intent. Jai remained crumpled with a busted knee.

A brief stillness infected the space.

And a false confidence had infected the group.

Boo had run a quick calculation.

And with a sudden surge, the fight resumed. Zoey tensed for the attack, but Boo did not target her. He darted between Mulgawats, then snapped his direction towards Max. And for a brief moment, every target was within range. Boo spun around and pitched three spooders. One for Zoey, one for Perra, and one for Ross. As they sailed through the air, Boo stretched the last spooder out in front of his body, perfectly aligned with Max's face. With a final blitz, Boo had collected the richest bounties ever posted.

Or so he thought.

With a sliver left before contact, time froze.

Max yelped and scampered backwards. But only he had done so. Boo was locked into his final thrust with spooder in hand, a mere second from completing his mission. The entire group had frozen in place. Zoey, Perra, and Ross wore expressions of panic with spooders floating in the air next to them. Jai remained hunched over in pain, but without a squirm. Even Veronica had fallen mute inside Max's grasp. His confusion was sharp and abrupt, revealing itself as a jumbled mess of grunts and stutters.

"That's enough of that," said a mystery voice.

Guy and Gal moseyed into the chamber, still wearing their matching suits.

Max added a ruffled brow to his contorted face.

"So this is the infamous shifter," Guy said with a pleasant tone. He and Gal took their remaining steps, bringing them face to face. "You have created one hell of a pandemonium, young man."

"Um ... you're welcome?" Max said with an uptick.

"Wasn't fishing for gratitude, but I appreciate the candor. You see, we are with the Fourth Dimensional Police Department. My name is Guy and this is Gal."

"A pleasure?"

"Not everything needs to be a question. You can talk normally. Unless humans speak exclusively in questions, but that hasn't been our experience."

"You're not human?"

"What did I just say?"

"Sorry."

"So anyhoo, we're here to reset you."

Max wanted to ask for clarification, but the stigma from the last question remained. And so, he just sat there with a dumb look on his face.

"That means we're sending you home," Gal said with the ferocious voice of a demonic chain smoker.

Guy cringed.

Max shuddered.

Guy acknowledged the shudder, then continued.

"You're little snafu has thrown a giant wrench into the multidimensional control structure. It's our job to remove that wrench. We've been tracking you through multiple universes across the entire cosmos. It's been a giant pain in the crack, to be honest."

Max thought for a moment, then glanced at Boo. "Wait a minute. *You* were the ones who funded the bounties."

"Yup. Across all universes. That wasn't the plan, but we lost your trail when you teleported off of the Suth'ra Station. We did, however, learn about your associates." Guy gestured around the frozen group. "So we talked to a nice fella at Durangoni, who happened to have a wealth of info on this strange fella." He gestured at Boo. "And here we are."

"Not to be a stickler, but it seems counterproductive to kill us."

"That wasn't gonna happen." Guy chuckled and glanced at Gal, who shrugged. "And even if it did, that would also solve the problem. Granted, it would create a boatload of paperwork, but it would be a resolution nonetheless."

Gal scoffed at Guy, then gestured at Max, as if to say *This will too, you knob.*

"I know. It's a pickle any way you slice it."

"I would prefer not to be sliced."

"Can't be helped. We need to close the domain loop. And before you ask, that's the beating heart of the multiverse. Your domain is Earth, and right now you're yanking a bunch of hapless yous across the great bag of marbles. Your original body is wearing banana pants inside Crazy Town. Not to belabor the point, but that shit gotta stop."

Max fell into a deep contemplation. His gaze lowered to the ground, then floated around his frozen cohorts. "But ... my family."

"You'll see your mother and father soon enough. And we can understand your reservation, they ain't the most pleasant humans we've met, and that includes a very cold receptionist at the mental hospital."

"I don't mean them."

Max opened his palm and gazed into the lifeless eye of Veronica. A longing crept over his body as he replayed the wild events that led to the current predicament. The journey to Europa, meeting Zoey and Perra, the shootout with Jai, the pursuit of Lord Essien, the mind games with Nifan, the demise of Halim, the fleeing of Durangoni with Steve the snoodlecock, the—

Max perked up. "Wait a minute."

Guy cocked an eyebrow.

Gal crossed her arms with impatience.

"All you need to do is close the domain loop, right?"

"Correct," Guy said.

"Why close it when you can break it?"

"Not following."

"Durangoni is the largest space station in the universe. It's an artificial megastructure with a trillion beings living inside it."

"Yeah, so?"

"So, that's a planet-sized domain with infinite complexity. If I lived there, I would always shift to a universe where it existed." He glanced around his frozen family. "Where *we* existed. And given its mind-bending scope and diversity, I would never notice the shift. I could live out the rest of my life in peace. And most importantly, you would always have a tab on me."

Guy grunted with intrigue.

Even Gal shifted her lips in thought.

"And not to point out the obvious, but any Max living in the chaos of Durangoni wouldn't balk at a sudden mind-jaunt to Earth. In fact, a leisure day at a mental asylum would feel like a vacation.

They might even send him home."

"That *would* save a ton of paperwork," Guy said to Gal, who pursed her lips and nodded.

"What do you say?" Max said with a warm plea. "No loop. Just a smooth line of freedom with no paperwork."

The agents mused for a moment.

Max studied their expressions like a dog waiting for a treat.

"Fuck it," Gal said with a throaty bark, then extended her hand.

For once, nobody cringed.

Max smiled wide and completed the shake. "Thank you. Thank you so very much."

"And it should go without saying," Guy said with a more serious tone, "but should you leave the station, this agreement would be void. We will find you and reset you without the courtesy of a reach around."

"Understood."

"Well okay then." Guy clapped his hands and glanced around the suspended chamber. "Let's clear this circus and get some coffee."

Gal snapped her fingers.

The agents vanished, along with Max and his merry crewmates.

Time unfroze, leaving Boo alone inside the dank cavern. The spooders continued their flight and bounced harmlessly against the craggy walls. His lunge towards Max ended with a fruitless stumble. Boo twisted around the hollow with his arms outstretched.

"Boo," he said, a clear *WTF*.

CHAPTER 9

The guilty expression on my face had morphed into a gaping mouth of pure disbelief. It was exceedingly rare to lose myself in someone else's story, but there I was, slack-jawed and close to drooling on my desk. My lack of participation had not gone unnoticed, as Zoey and Perra halted their account to check on my well-being.

[Perra] You okay there, sport?

(I flinch, then blink several times to remoisten my parched eyeballs.) Yes, I'm just, wow. I mean, you two, just, holy crap.

[Zoey] That was a fantastic summation. I'm glad we did this.

Okay, sorry, bringing it back. (I tap my desk and take a needed breath.) I can only imagine how utterly horrifying it was to be trapped in that cave.

It actually wasn't that bad. Max got the worst of it and we only learned about the 4DPD after the fact. The rest of us just blinked here to Durangoni.

What happened to the agents?

No idea. It was just the five of us when we appeared on the docks. Six, including Vee. It didn't take long to gather our bearings, as we already knew the station from previous jobs. Now we're based here, which is actually kind of nice.

And what about Max?

He's around.

(I fan my fingers.) Anything more specific?

Given what he's been through, I don't think it's worth disclosing.

I would very much like to meet him, if possible. And if nothing more than to conclude his epic story for my readers. As a respected editor of the Directory, I am bound by prudence, discretion, and the utmost rectitude.

(Zoey and Perra look at each other with mirrored musings.)

[Zoey] What do you think?

[Perra] I mean, he *is* writing a book about Max. Maybe it would be nice to give him a cherry for his sundae. And if it does well, we might get to meet Nimi.

I can arrange that.

(Perra gasps and claps giddily.)

[Zoey] Okay, but under one condition.

Anything.

No location names. Not even the sector.

Agreed.

(Zoey leans forward and plucks my notepad from the desk, the very one she had delivered earlier. She snatches a pen and scribbles a location.) Go here tomorrow at six. Bring some physical credits.

Why?

Do you want to meet Max or not?

Understood. And if I may, I do have one final question. It's a nagging little detail that I can't seem to shake.

Sure.

So, Boo tracked you to Earth, then the Suth'ra teleported you to Phil's Place. How the hell did Boo track you there so quickly?

(Zoey rolls her eyes as Perra begins to snicker.)

Did I say something wrong?

[Perra] Nope. We *all* had the same thought after the dust settled. And it took a trip back to Phil's Place to figure it out.

You went *back*?

Oh hush, he's not that bad.

(I toss her a "Really?" glare, as does Zoey.)

But yeah, we asked him the same question. To which he responded, and I quote, "I was so excited about Happy Touchie Friend Time that I told everyone in the sky. I told them that my favorite living meats in the universe, Zoey, Perra, Ross, and Jai have all gathered on my planet for an epic hangout. Max the Earthling is here too, but he's kinda icky."

(The statement hits me from such an absurd angle that I immediately burst into laughter. Zoey and Perra join in and we share a vigorous belly laugh. Given the insanity of the tale, it ends up being a perfect catharsis.)

Yeah, that tracks.

* * *

The next day, I found myself standing in front of a plain door with no plates or markings. To the average passerby, it resembled little more than a broom closet. But given the path it took to get there, which shall remain private, the door was anything but.

I glanced at my comdev as the seconds ticked towards six. The physical credits in my other hand felt oddly heavy, despite their thin veneer. They were rarely needed inside the station, but invaluable to those who wished to do business outside of its walls.

With a final tick, I raised my hand and gave the door a knock. After a brief pause, the door unlatched and cracked open. I was greeted by a long-necked creature with a trio of ring marks around its throat.

"Here for a game?" he said.

"Ah," I said, then flashed the physical credits. "It would seem so."

The creature opened the door and invited me inside. The space was modest by my usual standards, but open enough to curb any claustrophobia. Numerous wall lockers and hanging lights created the vibe of a workman's lounge. An array of gaming tables occupied the central area with numerous players sitting around them. Others wandered about as they surveyed the action and fetched refills. Soft music played in the background, giving the room a spirited yet relaxed vibe.

At a rear table, I spotted the orange fur of a small feline. Ross sat in one of the chairs while batting at a stack of gaming chips. Beside him, a female android held cards in one hand while stroking the cat's back with the other. And beside her, a young human dropped a winning hand onto the table, prompting a chorus of playful jeers. I approached the table and rested my hand on the back of a chair.

"This seat taken?" I said.

"It is now," Max said, adding a toothy smile.

"Thanks." I scooched it out and lowered myself onto the cushion.

"We're playing Texas Hold'em, a favorite from my home planet."

"Ah yes, I've heard of this. A very easy way to part with credits, if I recall."

"Only if you don't know what you're doing."

Ross snorted. "Which is why they won't let me play."

Max retorted with a gentle ribbing, which prompted a flurry of laughs and jokes. The entire room represented a captured warmth, in that there was no stress, no hostility, and a remarkable surplus of contentment. It was a pleasant contrast to the consistent pressure from which I came. These were the denizens of Durangoni, the true heartbeat of the station.

They were, dare I say it ... *happy*.

"I'm Puki," I said with a newfound vigor.

"Max." He offered a polite wave and then pointed around the table. "This is Ross, Veronica, and the bloke beside you just joined up."

I turned to my right to find a meager creature with a balding head and blotchy green skin. He smiled and offered his hand.

"Roy."

THE END

ABOUT THE AUTHOR

Zachry Wheeler is an award-winning science fiction author. His many interests include photon hunting, full-contact chess, and vertical wit. He lives on Earth with his wife and cats.

Learn more at **ZachryWheeler.com**

If you enjoyed this nutty saga, please consider posting a short review. Ratings and reviews are the currency by which authors gain visibility. They are the single greatest way to show your support and keep us writing the stories you love.

Thank you for reading!